BLOW ME DOWN

BLOW ME DOWN

Katie MacAlister

A SIGNET ECLIPSE BOOK

SIGNET ECLIPSE
Published by New American Library, a division of
Penguin Group (USA) Inc., 375 Hudson Street,
New York, New York 10014, USA
Penguin Group (Canada), 90 Eglinton Avenue East, Suite 700, Toronto,
Ontario M4P 2Y3, Canada (a division of Pearson Penguin Canada Inc.)
Penguin Books Ltd., 80 Strand, London WC2R 0RL, England
Penguin Ireland, 25 St. Stephen's Green, Dublin 2,
Ireland (a division of Penguin Books Ltd.)
Penguin Group (Australia), 250 Camberwell Road, Camberwell, Victoria 3124,
Australia (a division of Pearson Australia Group Pty. Ltd.)
Penguin Books India Pvt. Ltd., 11 Community Centre, Panchsheel Park,
New Delhi - 110 017, India
Penguin Group (NZ), cnr Airborne and Rosedale Roads, Albany,
Auckland 1310, New Zealand (a division of Pearson New Zealand Ltd.)
Penguin Books (South Africa) (Pty.) Ltd., 24 Sturdee Avenue,
Rosebank, Johannesburg 2196, South Africa

Penguin Books Ltd., Registered Offices:
80 Strand, London WC2R 0RL, England

First published by Signet Eclipse, an imprint of New American Library,
a division of Penguin Group (USA) Inc.

ISBN 0-7394-5969-4

There are always many people who I feel deserve a public thank-you whenever I finish a book, but seldom am I as grateful as I am to four people who turned me into a die-hard pirate fan. For that reason, I offer my appreciation and sincerest gratitude to Tobias Barlind (the coldest shark around), Vance Briceland (for telling me about YPP), Daniel James (who can resist a man with a cleaver?), and Brian Murphy (the best captain a girl could have). Yarr, maties!

And a quick explanation for those of you who may wonder about the source for the quotations at the beginning of each chapter: They are all from the Gilbert and Sullivan opera *The Pirates of Penzance*. Although *Penzance* itself wasn't the source of inspiration for this book (see the note at the end of the book for those details), I found so many quotations that seemed to fit perfectly with the action of the story that I couldn't resist using them.

Chapter 1

A pirate.
A very contemptible line of life,
with a premium at a high rate.

—Gilbert and Sullivan,
The Pirates of Penzance, Act I

"You know what your problem is?"

I waited for the rumble from a distant clap of thunder to fade away into nothing before answering. "Yes. We can't get the legislature to understand why their repeal of the roadless act is going to devastate this country's wild forests to the point where they will never recover."

Tara sighed. "No, that's not it."

"Ah, then it must be the blatant disregard of the Clean Water Act by the cement industry, and the subsequent poisoning of several hundred streams and the countless generations of salmon who spawn there."

Another sigh followed, drawn out and martyred as only a sixteen-year-old could make it. "No, not that either."

I frowned at the computer screen, giving Tara only part of my attention as I typed up a press release that would be sent out the following day. It sounded like a storm was coming, and I wanted to finish before I had to turn off the electronic equipment. "No? Hmm. Well, you must be talking about the fact that our state legislature took a step into the Dark Ages when it caved to the pesticide industry's pressure by removing hazardous pesticides from the program to eliminate toxic chemicals from the environment."

"No! I'm not talking about that! And you're not even listening to me."

Another rumble of thunder stopped conversation for the count of five. "You wouldn't by any chance be referring to the fact that I have a daughter who doesn't understand the concept of not disturbing her mother while she's working?"

"N-O spells no. Besides, you're *always* working."

"Pays the bills, pays the mortgage, and pays for you to hang out at the mall rather than working at a local McDonald's. Hand me that paper, honey. No, the 'Indigenous Streams of the Pacific Northwest' one. Are the stereo and TV off? It sounds like that storm is heading right for us."

"Yes, and you didn't answer my question," the spawn of my loins answered after she passed me a bound collection of environmental position papers, hands on her hips, thick straight brown brow, so much like my own, furrowed as she glared at me.

"I did. Four times, in fact."

"Mom!"

"Hmm?" I double-checked a couple of statistics in the fact sheet, adding them to the press release in hopes they would be quoted verbatim.

"I asked you a question."

"And I answered it." The silence that followed, pregnant and pointed, chafed at me enough to disrupt my train of thought. I took my hands off the keyboard and swiveled in my chair to face Tara. "All right. You have my undivided attention. For . . . er . . ." I glanced at the clock. "Forty-five seconds."

The blue flash of lightning and a subsequent loud crack of thunder were perfectly timed with Tara's "*Mom!*"

I heaved a martyred sigh that rivaled hers, fighting to keep the smile from my lips at her look of righteous indignation. She might have my eyebrows, but her flair for dramatics came straight from her actor father. "Very well. I'm prepared to be generous. You have two minutes. Use them as you will."

"*Your* problem," she said, following me into the kitchen as I refilled my jumbo coffee mug with Espresso Roast, "is that you don't know how to play."

I gave in to the urge for a little eye roll and made sure everything that safely could be was unplugged. Another blue-white flash illuminating our tiny backyard heralded the onslaught of the storm.

"I'm serious, Mom. Free Spirit says that people like you use the excuse of work to compensate for the things that are lacking in their lives."

"Free Spirit?" I leaned my hip against the counter and sipped my coffee, watching my daughter as she stood in front of me. She was looking more and more like me, her thick strawberry blond hair just as unruly as my own, defying all attempts by hair spray, styling mousse, and industrial-strength hair gel to form it into something other than a wild tangle of curls. Her blue eyes were a shade darker than my own, but those straight brows that refused to arch no matter how many trips to the beauty salon she made were all mine.

"Free Spirit Blue. Hello, she's just my counselor! The one you talked to last month?"

"Oh, right; the one who wants to start her own commune and thinks I should encourage you to express yourself in artistic media rather than apply yourself to your schoolwork. Rather an interesting attitude to find in a school counselor."

"Everyone loves her," Tara protested, her hands gesticulating at she talked. That was another trait she got from her emotional father; generations of phlegmatic Scandinavian ancestors who preferred to keep their emotions tightly reined did much to give me control over mine. "She's all that, *and* she knows the coolest people. She got me an interview with PC Monroe. *The* PC Monroe—I'm going to meet him next week. Sarah promised she'd give me the front page of the school paper for the interview."

"Ah. Good. Er . . . who's *the* PC Monroe? Singer? Actor? One of those guys on the reality shows who eat insects for insane amounts of money?"

She gave me a look that wouldn't have been out of place had I been a five-headed alien that popped suddenly out of a potato. "He's only the hottest thing online in the whole world!"

"Internet boy toy?" I asked, sidling toward the door. Although writing press releases for the conservancy organization I worked for wasn't part of my job description as a financial analyst, I had volunteered to do it, and it irked me to leave any task undone.

"Try millionaire software genius," she answered, swiftly moving to block my retreat from the kitchen. "He lives here, right here in Merida. He's *only* created an inexpensive virtual reality unit that will revolutionize the Internet world by making fantasy real, and bring the unbelievable to the grasp of everyone with a computer and an Internet connection."

I cocked an eyebrow at her. "Get that from a press release, did you?"

"Yeah." She had the grace to look a little embarrassed but quickly covered it up with antagonism. "PC Monroe and his VR game are the hottest thing on the whole planet! He sent me a beta version of his new VR simulation. Everyone is talking about it. It's due to be released in two months, and it's going to totally blow every other online game out of the water. Don't you pay attention to *anything*?"

"I've been busy trying to set up our lives." By dint of a slight feint to the left, I managed to squeeze around her and out the door. She followed me down the hallway.

"You're always busy; that's my point!"

"Yes, I know; you think I need to play. I heard you the first time. Hold on a sec." We paused to count between the flash of lightning and the sound of thunder. "Five miles. It's getting closer. Now, if you don't mind, I'm going to get this press release done before the storm hits, then I think I'll do a little research for Robert. He's never as prepared as he should be for staff meetings."

"Free Spirit says people who work all the time and don't give their inner child time to play die of heart attacks before they're forty."

"Ah?" I asked, sitting down at the computer.

"You're almost forty," she pointed out.

I shot her a narrow-eyed look. "I'm thirty-six, missy. That's not even close to forty."

The little rat smirked. "Four years, Mom. Four years, then ziiiiiiip!" She made a gesture symbolic of imminent death. "Dead as road kill."

The press release nagged at me, but behind Tara's flip tone, I sensed real concern. I was well aware that I hadn't been spending as much time with her as I wanted to, but starting a new life and a new job in a new town took a lot of work. "Point taken—you believe I need a few more leisure activities in my life."

"*Any* leisure activities. You don't do anything but work."

I let that slide. "What would you suggest?

She took a deep breath. "Buckling Swashes."

"I beg your pardon?"

"Buckling Swashes. It's the online game PC Monroe created, the one he's converting over to a VR world. I told you that he sent me a beta VR unit. It's part of the next-generation release, and I got to see it months before it'll be made public."

I frowned, absently counting the time between lightning and thunder, a horrible suspicion coming to my mind. "You wouldn't be referring to that RPH that you were so addicted to during the summer?"

"RPG, not RPH. It stands for role-playing game and technically it's MMORPG—massive multiplayer online role-playing game."

The way she avoided my eye said a lot. "I see. That would be the same online game that I forbade you to continue playing because you did nothing else but pretend you were a pirate for three solid months?"

Belligerent blue eyes suddenly met mine. "You didn't forbid me to play. You just stopped paying for it."

I thought for a moment, mentally reviewing the latest credit card statement. "Ah. That would explain the rash of phone calls to your father when we moved here last month. You talked him into paying for that game."

"It's not just a game," she said, her hands on her hips. "It has *layers*. And it's about to become virtual reality."

"Uh-huh." I turned back to my desk. "As I recall from what you showed me, it was simply a simulation of some vaguely Caribbean pirate setting with a lot of murder and mayhem."

"That's only one part of it. Most players think that the goal of the game is to go pillaging—that's attacking other ships to take their money and goods—but really the game is a complex social infrastructure of colonization and world building. Right now my crew is about to go into defense mode to protect our island from the evil Black Corbin, who wants to take it from us."

"Your crew?" I asked, making a mental note to talk to Bill about feeding Tara's unhealthy addiction to online games.

"Yeah, I'm the crew wench."

My eyebrows rose as I envisioned the letter I'd send to the game's creator about putting a minor in an adult situation.

"You can just stop with the Mom Brows. It's nothing like that," Tara said, the disgusted tone in her voice doing much to reassure me. She hadn't yet expressed an interest in the opposite sex, something I was all too happy about. "Our crew is led by Bartholomew Portuguese. He's based on a real pirate, by the way. PC Monroe said he did tons and tons of research on him to make the character believable."

"I see. Still, I told you two months ago that schoolwork took precedence over world building. Playing a pirate won't get you into college—"

"PC Monroe says the economical model that the game uses is a real one, and that to understand and be successful at it means I have a good head for business. I have a weaving shop. I sell cloth. I make money at it, Mom."

Her calculated dig hit pay dirt, despite my better intentions. "What sort of economic model? How much profit do you make?"

"A lot." The smile that blazed across her face was rife with pure satisfaction. "Enough to buy me three sloops. I even have a spreadsheet that I use to keep track of costs and profits."

I narrowed my eyes at her again. "That was a low blow. You are an evil child to use my love of spreadsheets against me like that."

Her grin turned up a notch. "You always say you have to be ruthless in business, and this is all economics. Buying and selling and profit margins and supply and demand. Only it's set in a pirate world rather than this one."

"Hmm." I wondered for a moment what pirate finances would look like. How much would monthly grog expenditures run, and could you depreciate the costs of storing it?

"*You'd* make a killing there," my little rat-in-child-form added in a persuasive tone of voice. "With your business degree and stuff, you'd be rich in no time. I bet you could even have your own crew."

For a moment an image flashed on my mind's eye of myself standing at the helm of a tall ship, the sails fully rigged, the bow of the ship cutting through the azure waters, salty sea air brushing my face as I ordered the cannons to fire on some helpless ship. A little voice deep inside of me let out a cheer, but it was quickly squelched as another rumble brought me back to the present and reality. I turned back to my computer. "Good try, Tara, but not quite good enough."

The teasing light in her eyes died. "Dad would do it."

I flipped a couple of pages of the symposium paper to find a quote I needed. "I'm sure he would. He has little else to do with his time while he is between acting jobs."

"At least he spends time with me! At least he's interested in the things I'm interested in! All you want to do is work, work, work. You don't care about me or anything I want to do. I wish I was living with Dad instead of you!"

"I refuse to get into a comparison argument of my parenting skills versus your father's," I answered, quickly typing up a couple more sentences. "And I hardly see how my lack of participation in a silly game can be thrown in my face as depriving you of attention."

"Because! If you were playing it, too, we could be on the same crew. And you could help me with my weaving shop, and I could teach you how to sail a ship."

"I don't have time to learn how to sail a ship, and besides, I get seasick easily."

"You won't even try! You won't even look at it!" she wailed, throwing her hands in the air in a gesture of sheer frustration.

I'm not a monster. I might admit to being a bit more caught up in my job than was normal, but I took pride in the fact that I had a solid work ethic, and took responsibility for making sure that my job, and the jobs of those I could help around me, were done to the best of my ability. Despite all that, the underlying plea in Tara's voice generated an unpleasant ripple of guilt within me. I had no intention of wasting my time playing a nerdy online game, but if it would make her feel I was more involved in her life, it wouldn't hurt me to at least see what it was about.

"All right," I said, forestalling the emotional eruption I knew that was soon to follow. "If it will make you happier, I'll take a look at the game."

She was silent for a moment. "You will? You'll sign on? The whole thing, the VR unit version? It's majorly cool."

I frowned. "How much does it cost?"

Her stormy brow cleared like magic. "You can use my account. We get four characters per account, and I've only made one. You can make one, just to see if you like it. It won't cost you anything. Here, I'll write down my password and user name." She snatched up a sticky notepad and scribbled out the name *Terrible Tara* and the name of our deceased dog. "Later on you can get your own account so we can play together at the same time. Maybe I can get a second VR unit."

"Whoa, I just said I'd take a look. I have no intention of doing anything more—"

She stopped in the doorway, her eyes dark with mutiny.

"I knew it! You won't go into it with an open mind! You'll just look and say it's a silly time waster!"

"Hey, now. I am just as capable as the next person of keeping an open mind," I said, giving her my best quelling look. It didn't do any good. It seldom did.

"You will not. Your mind is already made up to think it's silly."

I held up my hand to stop her. "I admit to being a bit biased, but I will promise to give the game every chance. Happy now?"

"No," she answered, her face still stormy.

"Are you questioning my word of honor?" I asked, frowning.

"Yes. No. Maybe. It's just that you are so . . . so . . ."

"Dedicated to my job?"

"Dead," she answered, throwing her hands up in a frustrated gesture. "Honestly, Mom, you don't do anything fun! This VR game has all sorts of things that you'll like, if you just give it a chance. There's tons of economy stuff."

"I do have interests beyond those of a fiduciary nature," I pointed out, vaguely insulted.

"Name one," she countered.

I glared at her and ignored the challenge. "I have said I would give the game a fair chance. That's the best I can do."

Her eyes narrowed as she chewed on her lower lip for a moment. "I know! You have to make officer."

"I what?" My gaze strayed back toward the computer screen and my work.

"You have to make officer. It's a goal. You like goals; you're always telling me to have them." She hurried on before I could point out that the two things weren't the same. "If you advance in the game to officer status, I'll know you really kept an open mind."

"How hard is achieving officerhood?" I asked, flipping to a spreadsheet of the current year's budget.

"Piece of cake. I was an officer in, like . . . well . . . really quickly."

I knew how those computer games worked—to advance you had to open a secret passageway or collect some object or run over a magic spot or something silly like that. It shouldn't be much of a challenge, and if it kept the peace, it would be worth the sacrifice of my time. "Hmm. All right, since it means so much to you, I will give the game an hour or so and become an officer."

"Woohoo! You can use my laptop—it has the game client on it already. I'll bring it and the VR parts down here right now. You can play on the battery so you don't have to be plugged into the wall in case the power goes out. Thanks, Mom!" She gave me a quick hug before running out of the room. "I'm going to go tell my captain really quickly that you're logging on later, so if he sees you he'll be nice to you and stuff."

"Wait. Tara, I didn't mean this second—oy." The door to her bedroom upstairs slammed. I started to roll my eyes again but switched to a flinch when another loud peal of thunder and gust of wind made the windows rattle. As quickly as I could I finished typing up the press release, e-mailed copies of it to the organization's director, the media contacts, and my work e-mail address, then made a quick backup of all my recent work.

"You are so anal it's not even funny," Tara said fifteen minutes later as she deposited her laptop on my desk, plugging the power cord into the wall. On top of it sat a pair of thick black wraparound glasses.

I filed the CDs I'd burned with the week's work away with the other backups, one in the collection organized by date, the other in the one organized by subject. "If it's worth doing, it's worth having backed up. Why are you plugging that in? The storm is almost on top of us."

We both were silent while another *flash-boom!* shook the house.

"I don't get a good connection to log on to the system on the battery. It's just to log on. Once you're into the game, you can unplug it. Here is the VR unit. Cool, huh? Looks just like a pair of shades. There're speakers built into the part of the glasses that sits behind your ears, so you hear everything, and here"—she flipped down a fiber-optic-sized black extension from the sides of the glasses—"here is your microphone. The software has speech recognition capabilities, so you can talk to other characters just like you normally would. It's so totally cool."

"Uh-huh," I said, trying to avoid her as she shoved the glasses toward my face, but it was useless. A few seconds later I was wearing the VR glasses. "I can't see anything."

"They're not turned on. Here, let me do it. Okay, you're set. Gotta go do the rest of my homework before we lose the lights," Tara called over her shoulder as she hurried out of the room. "It's all set up for you to log on with a new name, and I told Bart to watch out for you. Oh, and I put you on the list of workers at my weavery, so you can look around there. Have fun!"

"Hey! Don't think I don't see through your hit-and-run tactics! I know full well what you're doing!" I sighed as her laughter spilled down the stairs after her. "Manipulative little so-and-so," I muttered as I turned my attention to the colorful screen that seemed to float in the air before me.

A game client screen that read "Welcome to Buckling Swashes. Please log in or create a new pirate to enter the game" blinked slowly at me.

"Right. Let's get this over with." I reached out somewhat blindly for the keyboard, able to see only dark, vague shapes of the computer and desk behind the virtual images that danced before my eyes. "Name . . . Amy Stewart."

"That's supposed to be your pirate name, not your real name," came a slightly tinny, ethereal voice drifting from the heating duct in the wall.

"Do your homework and stop listening at the heater," I yelled, backspacing over my name. "Pirate name. I don't have a pirate name. Um . . ." I tipped the glasses down my nose and looked around the room for inspiration, my eyes lighting on a Van Gogh print. "Earless . . . er . . . Erika. That sounds very piratical."

I typed in the pirate name, picked a few character traits (female, blond, with a short bob, and a Rubenesque, curvy body type that most closely matched my own). As I was about to click the CREATE PIRATE button, a tremendous crash of thunder hit simultaneously with a blinding flash of lightning. Upstairs, Tara shrieked as a second crash rocked the house. The lights flickered into a brownout. Mindful of the cost of her laptop, I leaned across the computer and grabbed the power cord at the same time another flash of lightning struck. As I pulled the plug free, a blue arc of electricity shot from the outlet, connecting with me at the same time another deafening roar of thunder shook the house.

I must have hit the RETURN button as I jerked with the flow of electricity through my body, because the last thing I remember seeing before I sank into an abyss of darkness was a little spinning sign on the game screen saying "Entering Buckling Swashes. . . ."

Chapter 2

Here we live and reign alone
In a world that's all our own.

—Ibid, Act I

It was the sheep snuffling my face that woke me up. I didn't realize it was a sheep at first, not being in the habit of keeping sheep in my house, where my last conscious moment was, but when something moistly warm blew on my face, followed by a horrible stinky scent of wet wool, my eyes popped open and I beheld the unlovely face of a sheep staring down at me.

"T'hell?" I said groggily, pushing the sheep face out of mine as I sat up, immediately regretting the latter action when the world spun around dizzily for a few seconds. As it settled into place I blinked at the hand I'd used to shove away the sheep—it tingled faintly, as if I had whacked my funny bone. I shook it a couple of times, the pins-and-needles feeling quickly fading . . . but that's when my wits returned.

"What the hell?" I said again, a growing sense of disbelief and horror welling within me until I thought my head was going to explode.

I used the rough wood wall behind me to help me get to my feet, my head still spinning a little as I looked around. I was in a short alley between two buildings, half-hidden behind a stack of what looked like whiskey barrels, the sheep who'd been snuffling me now engaged in rooting around through some garbage that slopped over from a wooden box. Sunlight filtered down through the overhang of the two buildings, spilling onto a lumpy cobblestone street behind the alley. Vague blurs resolved themselves into the images of people passing back and forth past the opening of the alley.

The game . . . the virtual reality game. I was seeing images from the game. I put my hand up to my face to pull off the VR glasses, but all my fingers found were my glasses-less face. Had they gotten knocked off when I got the shock from the computer? If so, why was I still seeing the virtual world? I lurched my way forward down the alley, stumbling once or twice as my legs seemed to relearn how to walk.

"What the . . . *hell*?" As I burst out into the open, I staggered to a stop.

Two men in what I though of as typical pirate outfits — breeches, jerkins, swords strapped to their hips, and bandanas on their heads — walked by, one giving me a leer as I clutched the corner of the nearest building.

Beyond them, a wooden well served as a gathering place for several women in long skirts and leather bodices, each armed with a wooden bucket or two. Pigs, sheep, chickens, dogs . . . they all wandered around the square, adding to the general sense of confusion and (at least on my part) disbelief.

A couple of children clad in what could only be described as rags ran past me, each clutching an armful of apples. A shout at the far end of the square pierced the general babble, what appeared to be a greengrocer in breeches and a long apron evidently just noticing the theft of some apples.

It was like something out of a movie. A period movie.

One of those big MGM costume movies of the 1950s where everything was brightly colored and quasi-authentic. I expected Gene Kelly to burst singing from a building at any minute.

Instead of Gene, two men emerged from a one-story building across the square, both staggering and yelling slurred curses. One man shoved the other one. The second man shoved the first one back. Both pulled out swords and commenced fighting. The first man lunged. The second screamed, clutched his chest, and fell over backward into a stack of grain sacks. The first man yanked his sword out, spit on his downed opponent, and staggered away around the back of the building, wiping his bloody sword on the hem of his filthy open-necked shirt. A wooden sign hanging over the door he passed waved gently in the wind—a sign depicting a couple of mugs being knocked together beneath the words INN COGNITO printed in blocky letters.

No one bustling around the square gave the dead man so much as a second look.

"What the hell?" I shouted, goose bumps of sheer, unadulterated horror rippling along my arms and legs as I ran toward the body lying sprawled on the dirty grain sacks. I was about to go into serious freak-out mode when I remembered that none of this was real—it might look real and sound real, but it was just a game. No one had actually been murdered in front of me. It was just a bunch of computer sprites and sprockets and all those other techno-geeky things that I didn't understand. "Okay, stay calm, Amy. This is not a real emergency. However, I'm not willing to lose points or bonus power chips or whatever this game hands out for acts above and beyond the norm. Let's approach this as a non-life-threatening emergency, and go for the next power level. Yeargh. How on earth did they manage that?"

As I squatted next to the dead man, the stench from his

unwashed body hit me. I pushed away the skitter of repug-
nance as it rippled down my back, and rummaged around
the dusty recesses of my brain for any knowledge of first-aid
techniques. "Thank God for all of those first-aid classes I
arranged when Tara was in middle school. Let me think—a
sword wound. CPR?"

A glance at the sluggishly seeping hole in his chest had
me eliminating that option. There was no way putting pressure on that would help matters. "Mouth-to-mouth?"

The man's smell took care of that as a choice. "Hmm.
Maybe I should apply a splint?"

I looked around for something to act as a splint but didn't
see any handy splintlike boards, not to mention I wasn't absolutely certain that a splint was a suitable treatment for a
sword wound. "Okay. What's left? Er . . . raise his feet
higher than his head? Yeah, that sounds good. That should
stop the flow of blood or something. Inhibits shock, I think."

I scooted down to grab the man's mud-encrusted tattered
boots, intending to swing them around to a stack of grain
bags, but was more than a little disconcerted when one of his
legs separated from the rest of his body.

"Aieeeeeeeee," I screamed, staring in horror at the limb
that hung stiffly from my hands.

Just as it was dawning on me that the leg was a crudely
fashioned wooden prosthetic and not the ghoulish severed
limb I had first imagined, a whoosh of air behind me accompanied the loud slam of a wooden door being thrown
open. Before I could do so much as flail the false leg, a steel-
like arm wrapped around my waist and hauled me backward
into the inn.

Air, warm and thick and scented heavily with beer and
unwashed male bodies, folded me in its embrace as I was
dragged into a murky open-beamed room.

"Found me a wench, Cap'n," a voice rumbled behind me.

"Toothsome one, too, ain't she? Don't look like she's been used overly much. Can I keep her?"

Now, this was taking virtual realism a bit too far. I pushed aside the issue of how a game could make me smell things and feel the touch of another person, and beat the hand that clutched me with the booted end of my fake leg. "Hey! I am not a wench, and I am not a puppy to be kept, and how dare you invade my personal space in such a manner! Do it again, and I'll have you up on charges of sexual harassment and physical assault so fast, your . . . er . . . hook will spin."

The man whom I'd surprised into releasing me stood frowning at me for a second before glancing to the right, where tables—some broken into kindling, others rickety but mostly whole—lurked in a shadowed corner. The dull rumble of masculine voices broke off as the man asked loudly, "I don't have no hook, do I, Cap'n?"

"Nay, lad, ye don't," a deep voice answered. One of the darker shadows separated itself from the others and stepped into the faint sunlight that bullied its way through two tiny, begrimed windows. The man who swaggered forward was an arrogant-looking devil, with thick shoulder-length blond hair, a short-cropped goatee and mustache, and dark eyes that even across the dimly lit room I could see were cast with a roguish light.

He was a charmer through and through—I knew his kind. I'd married one.

"I believe the lass was being facetious, Barn. As for yer request—we've no need for a female on the *Squirrel*. Grab yer things and we'll be off, mates. We've pillagin' to do."

The man who'd grabbed me—a blocky giant with black hair and a huge beard—frowned even harder. "What be facetious, then?"

"Later, Barn."

The behemoth named Barn looked back at me, disappointment written all over his unlovely face. "But the wench—she's mine. I found her. Ye've said we could keep what we pillaged."

"She's probably got the French pox," the arrogant blond said as he started for the door, giving me nothing more than a disinterested glance. "We'll find ye a woman a little less tartish at Mongoose."

"Oh!" I gasped, outraged at the slur. I wasn't going to stand around and let some cyber-gigolo insult me. "I will repeat myself for those of you with hearing problems or general mental incapacity—I am not a wench, nor am I a tart. I do not have the pox, French or any other sort. And I would rather go without my PDA for an entire year than be with *that* man."

The blond captain paused in the act of following Barn out the door, slowly turning to face me. "What did you say?"

"I said that I am not a wench nor do I have any sexually transmitted diseases. And I'm not, in case you're interested, and I know you are because I know your sort, looking to acquire any. Now, if you don't mind, I have a leg to reattach to a dead man. If you will please stand aside, I will go and take care of that."

"PDA?" the pirate asked, an odd look of speculation on his face. "You said PDA?"

"Yes, I did. And that's a very big sacrifice, considering."

"You're a player," he said, starting toward me in a long-legged stride that I refused to notice on the grounds that I would not allow myself to respond to another love-'em-and-leave-'em charmer.

"I most certainly am not! I'm a woman, in case it escaped your attention, and even if I was a man, I'm not at all the sort to cruise the meat market for a little companionship. I enjoy meaningful relationships with men, not one-night stands."

"Are you?" he asked, a slight smile quirking one side of his mouth.

"Am I what?"

"Are you enjoying a meaningful relationship with a man right now?"

"No, not that it's any of your business. And don't you come any nearer," I answered, backing up a couple of paces and leveling my wooden leg at him. "I have a leg, and I'm not afraid to use it!"

"My sort?" he drawled, interest dawning in those dark eyes as he continued to stroll toward me. "You know *my sort*? I am a sort?"

I backed up a couple of steps more until I bumped into the rough wall of the inn. I could have kicked myself with the fake leg. Everyone knew the thing a charmer loved most was a challenge, and I'd just presented myself as one. Still, he was a virtual lothario, not a real one, so I could handle him. I'd just do a little defusing and be on my way.

"Yes, you are a sort. You're a charmer, a man who thinks he can sweet-talk the pants off a nun. Well, I'm immune to your brand of charm, buster. So you can just take your sexy walk and those tight leather pants and the really cool pirate boots of yours—wow, is that a rapier? Very nice. I used to fence in college—and trot off to harass some other un-poxed, tartless non-wench, because I'm not buying any of it."

"Unless you belong to the Sisters of Harlotry, you're not a nun," he said, stopping just beyond reach of my fake leg. "And you're not wearing pants."

I looked down to protest that I was so wearing pants, but the gauzy wisps of cloth that clung to my body in a very revealing fashion could be termed anything but sensible clothing. They were literally rags, exposing far more of me than I was comfortable with—although, really, what did it matter? These were computer people, not living, breathing human beings. Tara had said no one but the developers and occasional press representatives had access to the beta virtual version.

"If you've got it, flaunt it," I answered, deciding to go with the flow.

"You certainly do it well," the pirate said, giving me a leer that I could swear was almost human. The lascivious way his gaze caressed my scantily clad breasts clearly indicated the origins of a male, rather than female, software developer.

"Just because I'm flaunting doesn't mean you can stare for hours on end. A polite ogle is appreciated and suitable for a flaunt. Slobbering is not. Eyes up here," I said, using the leg's foot to indicate my face. "Look, Mr. Pirate—"

"Corbin," he said, interrupting me before I could get into a really quality lecture.

"I beg your pardon?"

"My name is Corbin. Captain Corbin, at your service, ma'am."

"Hello," I said politely, wondering whether the program gave out bonus points for adroit handling of a lecher. "I'm . . . er . . . drat, I've forgotten. Earless someone. Um . . . Erika! That's it."

Corbin the pirate considered me. "You don't look like an Erika."

"Well, I am."

"Is that your real name?"

"My real name?"

"Yes, your real name as opposed to your user name. Is Erika your real name?"

I frowned. Were computer-generated people supposed to be so nosy? "Maybe. Is Corbin *your* real name?"

"Yes, it is. What are you doing here?"

"What is this, twenty questions?" I gave him a quelling glare, but he totally disregarded it.

"No, just a simple question. Answer it. What are you doing here?"

He stood just beyond reach of the leg, his hands on his hips, the loose white pirate shirt open to his waist, exposing almost the whole of his six-pack abs and manly chest dusted with golden hair. For some reason it irritated me that his character was nicer to look at than mine. Clearly the game designer had issues.

"That, sir, is none of your business. Now, kindly take your seductive self off and let me go achieve whatever goal I'm supposed to do to get to the next level. I think it has something to do with collecting prosthetic legs, but I'm not quite sure. Are yours real?"

He laughed. I gritted my teeth. He even laughed nicer than me. "Yes, they are. I'd be happy to show them to you if you want to verify that."

"Think I'll pass. Now, if you don't mind . . ."

He didn't move despite my "please get out of the way" shooing gesture. "You think I'm seductive?"

"Of course I do," I answered before I realized what I was saying. I clamped down for a moment on the rest of my thoughts, then figured, what the hell. It was just a game. Maybe chitchatty interaction with the natives was part of the scoring process.

That didn't mean my chitchat couldn't be of the speak-your-mind variety, however. "You're clearly the fulfillment of the game designer's most fervent fantasy—the dashing pirate lord handsome enough to sweep any woman off her feet."

He smirked. "Shall I sweep you, then?"

"No, thank you. I've never been one for men who are prettier than me."

I tried to brush past him, but he stopped me, his hand on

my arm keeping me from leaving. "I'm confused—you think I'm handsome and seductive and sweepish, but you don't want me?"

"Surprised?" I smiled. "This game has a logging function, doesn't it? Something so the programming types can look at the beta tests and see what's happening?"

He looked startled for a moment before nodding. "It does."

"Good. Then let me clue you and the issue-laden programmers in on a few things, Corbin the Arrogant—when it comes to men, women don't want lotharios. Handsome looks are fleeting; women like me prefer substance over appearance. A romantic nature is good—a tomcat personality isn't."

"We've only just met. How can you make any judgments about my personality?"

I waved the leg at him. "Just look at you! Tom Jones shirt, tight leather pants, that long gorgeous hair, not to mention the hip action in your swagger . . . you just reek studly sex machine."

"So it's my appearance you object to?" he asked, frowning. Behind him a couple of men emerged from the shadows. Both of them were dressed in blue and white striped pants that ended just below the knee, striped shirts, and leather jerkins over which swords and pistols had been strapped to their waists.

"Look, I don't object to anything. I'm just saying that, no, I don't care for a little virtual nookie with a man ten times prettier than me."

"How about if I looked like this?"

Corbin's image flickered for a moment, then melted into that of a man only slightly taller than me, a man with short, dark curly hair. He was clean-shaven and bore little resemblance to his previous self. His face was rounder, his eyes were warmer, and he wasn't built along the lines of a male underwear model. He looked . . . *nice*.

"What do you think? Would you consider virtual nookie with someone who looked like this?"

I opened my mouth to tell him I wasn't looking for nookie with anyone, but a brief flash of insecurity in this Corbin's dark gray eyes had me blurting out, "Yeah, I would."

"Cap'n? We leavin' now?" one of the two men asked, giving me a less than curious glance. The man didn't seem to notice the change in Corbin's appearance. Assumedly the other computer players knew who he was regardless of his appearance.

"You would?" Corbin ignored his men, his brow furrowed as he watched me. I got the impression he was searching my face for signs I was lying to him. I wondered whether this form—which I honestly did prefer—was based on a programmer's real self rather than his fantasies.

"Well . . . yes. I mean, I don't want to wrestle you to the ground and have my wicked way with you, but if I was looking to have a virtual . . . er . . . boyfriend, then, yes, I'd prefer someone who looks like you do now to the previous incarnation. You look real. He looked fake."

"Hmm."

"Cap'n? Bart and his men'll be sure to be returnin' any time now. Be we leavin' or be we stayin' to fight?"

"Bart?" Hadn't Tara mentioned something about a Bart?

"Bartholomew Portuguese," Corbin answered, moving a step closer. "He and his motley crew are currently running this island into the ocean."

"Har-har," the pirate behind Corbin laughed, nudging his boss with his elbow. "We be takin' care of that problem soon, eh, Cap'n?"

"Aye, we will. These are two of my crew—Bald Bob," Corbin answered by way of an introduction, gesturing toward a man with waist-length black hair, "and Leeward Tom. Loo is my bosun."

"Looward?" I asked, wondering why that word sounded familiar.

"Aye. It's spelled *leeward*. It means the side of the ship protected from the weather," Corbin answered.

Leeward Tom pulled a ragged kerchief off and ducked his head at me before turning back to Corbin. "Be we leavin' or stayin'?"

The new and (to my mind) improved Corbin waved a dismissive hand. "We'll leave in a moment. I want to talk to this charming lady another minute or two."

"Flattered as I am to be promoted from tartish, pox-riddled wench to charming lady, I must insist that you let me pass. I promised my daughter I'd try out this game and advance a level or two. I'll start by hunting down some extra legs."

Tom looked confused. "What be the wench talkin' about?" he asked Corbin in a loud whisper. "What game? Think ye she has the fever?"

"No," Corbin answered, a smile curling his lips as Tom unobtrusively crossed himself. "So you'd like to advance beyond newbie level, would you, Erika? There's one sure-fire way to do that."

"Really? Something beyond collecting wooden limbs?"

His smile turned into an outright grin, a grin that had me responding with a smile of my own despite my better intentions. The blond Corbin was a devilishly handsome rogue, but this one was a hundred times more dangerous with his playful smile and warm, humor-filled eyes. "Swordplay advances your skills. You said you fenced?"

"Yes, for three years. I was on my college's fencing team. Er . . . you want me to fight you?"

"Afraid?" he asked, offering me his rapier with a fancy scrollwork hilt.

"Me?" I wondered whether I remembered anything from my fencing days. I set down my spare leg and took the rapier, trying my best to summon up a sneer. "Never Letting Them See You're Insecure Is the Key to Staying in Control" had always been my motto. "Ha. I am Earless Erika! I laugh in the face of danger. Or . . . er . . . in the face of deranged pirates."

His grin got even bigger as he accepted a rapier handed to him by Leeward Tom. "So I've moved down from seductive to deranged, eh?"

"That's actually an upward move," I pointed out, testing the weight of the rapier. It was nicely balanced. Although I was more proficient with a foil, I had used a rapier once or twice. "Shall we go with the first one who makes a fatal touch the winner? Jugular or heart?"

"Oh, jugular, don't you think?" he said. "No blood, just a touch."

"Good enough. Prepare to be humiliated. *En garde.*"

Both of his men snickered to themselves at my false bravado.

"Eh . . ." Corbin dropped the point of his sword, his eyes speculative as they swept my rag-clad self. "Why don't we make this a bit more interesting?"

"Interesting? Interesting how? That's the same lascivious look the blond you was making. I objected to it then, too."

His teeth flashed in a grin that made something in my stomach flutter. "Interesting as in a wager. If I beat you, you have to give me something."

"Like what?" I asked, waggling the tip of my sword in a meaningful way at him.

"Yourself," he answered, his eyebrows bobbing up and

down. I raised the rapier so it was pointed at his throat. "Er . . . all right; how about dinner, then?"

"Dinner?" My sword point fell as I gawked at him. Was he asking me out on a date? A computer character? He wanted to date me? How pathetic was that? And worse, why was I even considering it?

"Yes, dinner. It's the meal that comes just after lunch." I gave him a look. He smiled. "If I beat you, you agree to have dinner with me."

"Just dinner?" I asked suspiciously.

"Just dinner . . . unless there is something else you'd like to do."

"Not likely, computer boy."

"We will see. Shall we get on with the duel? I have dinner to order and a ship full of mates to clean up."

He raised his sword in the traditional starting position, but it was my turn to stop him. "Not so fast—what do I get if I beat you?"

His two crewmates laughed, unnecessarily long and hard, to my mind. I wasn't a *total* idiot with a sword.

"That won't be likely, lass," Leeward Tom said. "Our captain, here, he be the best swordsman in all of the Seventh Sea."

"Be he?" I said, entering into the whole pirate-spirit thing. "Then he shouldn't mind at all putting his money where his mouth is. What will you give me if I win?"

Corbin looked thoughtful, but I could see a wicked twinkle in his eyes. "Dinner with me?"

I raised my eyebrows. He heaved an exaggerated sigh. "What would you like?"

"Well . . . I don't know. What do you have? No, wait, let me rephrase that—what tangible things other than yourself do you have to offer?"

"Ships, money, fine jewels, rare cloths—"

"Ships, that sounds good," I said, picking the biggest-sounding item from his list. "If I win, you give me ships."

"Ship," he countered, his eyes narrowing speculatively. "A ship. A sloop."

I had no idea what a sloop was, but so long as it wasn't a rowboat, it sounded like a good bet. "You're on. *En garde* again, Captain Corbin."

He was surprisingly good, light on his feet, his ripostes following lightning fast after his parries. Although I hadn't fenced in years, the muscles in my quadriceps complainingly obliged when I assumed the correct fencing stance—elbows in, knees bent, wrist straight, toes slightly turned out, back straight. The rhythm of advance, retreat, advance, retreat—with occasional lunges thrown in to try to score a point—quickly returned, as did the reason I quit fencing.

I really, really disliked it.

"Tiring already?" Corbin asked as I sluggishly parried a particularly quick lunge.

"Not even," I answered, rallying a riposte that had him stumbling backwards. His men sat on nearby tables, yelling encouragement as we danced the peculiar advance, retreat fencing dance. After about five minutes of traditional fencing, he suddenly went Errol Flynn on me, leaping onto a nearby table and yelling a war cry as he flung himself off it. I, having had a fencing instructor who was also an expert in self-defense, stuck my foot out and tripped him. Yes, it was a move clearly against the rules of classical fencing, but so were wild leaps off tavern tables.

Stunned silence filled the room as his two henchman sat in disbelieving horror.

"I'd like my ship delivered now, please," I said as Corbin rolled himself over onto his back. His entire front side was coated with dirt from the unfinished floor, a tiny trickle of blood from his nose indicating that he'd hit the ground harder than I'd anticipated. The tip of my rapier pressed against the flesh of his neck, right next to where his pulse beat strong in his jugular vein.

He spoke very carefully, without moving a single muscle. "If you reach into the leather pouch hanging from my belt, you'll find a deed to a ship named the *Saucy Wench.*"

"The *Saucy Wench,*" I said happily, pulling a battered bit of parchment from the pouch strapped to his hip. The hand-writing was difficult to make out, but the name of the ship and a pen-and-ink sketch of her were legible. "I like it."

"It suits you," he answered, still not moving. "You cheated."

"So did you, Errol."

He started to protest but I added the tiniest bit of pressure to the tip of the blade. His eyes opened wide. I enjoyed the moment for as long as I thought prudent, then swept the blade from his neck with a grand gesture.

"Well, this has been fun. Am I an officer now?" I asked the two still silent crewmen. They stared from the sword I held to their captain, who had risen from his prone position and was dusting himself off.

"Eh . . . ye beat the cap'n," the one who was grossly mis-named Bald Bob said, blinking in surprise. "None has ever done that afore."

A rush of air swished around me as someone flung open the door. "Hoy, Corb, scrape the barnacles off yer ass and let's get crackin'. Bart and his crew will be back . . . Well, hello, there, m'lady."

The man in the doorway had shoulder-length curly brown hair and an eye patch and wore long brown monk's robes. He bowed to me, sweeping his hand in an elegant gesture that wasn't at all matched by the lascivious grin on his face. "First mate Holder McReady at yer delectable service, ye toothsome beauty. I did particularly well with the rags, yes, yes, I did. Don't you think I did well, Corb?"

"No. Go away, Holder."

"Your first mate is a priest?" I asked Corbin.

"No, he's not. He's mad. Ignore him."

"Oy!" the monkish mate protested. "Don't be mockin' the monk's robes. I'm thinkin' this is the best outfit yet. Ye wouldn't believe the sense of freedom it gives ye to have yer block and tackle right out in the open—"

"Holder!"

"Yarr. Me apologies. Now, then, what's been goin' on here while I've been out stockin' the ship?"

"An omen as black as the inside of the devil's belly is what's been happenin'," Leeward Tom said. His eyes narrowed on Corbin. "The cap'n has been beaten in a duel. Never has a wench done such a thing. It fair boggles the mind. Ye be soft on the lass, Cap'n? Ye be *lettin'* her win?"

Holder's dark eyes widened as he looked from me to Corbin. "What? Someone beat the cap?"

"Aye, Mr. Holder, the wench there," Tom said, turning his gaze on me. "Be she a witch, do ye think?"

"You know, I really dislike being talked about like I'm not here," I said. "And for the record, I am perfectly capable of winning on my own. I was the alternate for the college fencing team three years in a row, and you don't get that unless you're a pretty darn . . . sufficient . . . fencer. So let's have none of that 'be lettin' her win' crap, and more telling Erika if she's now an officer."

"Nay, ye're not," Tom said, back to watching Corbin.

Holder blew a low whistle, his eyes also on Corbin. The two seemed to be exchanging some sort of meaningful glances, the translation of which I wasn't privy to. Fine. Let them gaze at each other all they wanted. I had things to do, people to see, legs to hoard. "Oh. Pooh. I suppose I have to do the leg collecting before I reach that level?" I asked, setting the sword on the table before retrieving my wooden leg. "Well, then, I'd best get to it. Later, gentlemen."

As I strolled to the door, Holder said, "Ye just goin' to let her go?"

"Holder, keep out of this," Corbin snapped.

"No one is letting me do anything," I tossed over my shoulder. "I make my own destiny, thank you."

Holder gave his captain a not very subordinate shove. "Go on, ye great lug, say somethin' before ye blow it."

"Will you stop it? I do not need your help—"

"Hoy, lass? Erika, was it?" I paused at the door and looked back to where Holder was standing. "Ye wouldn't happen to fancy our cappy here, now, would ye?"

I rolled my eyes. "What I fancy is a couple more legs."

"Eh," he said, glancing at the leg in my hands. "Kind of an odd hobby, but we can work with it."

"It's not a hobby," I said at the same time Corbin snarled to his mate, "No, we can't. Now, go away, ye rat-infested bilge bucket."

"Whatever," I said and opened the door, intending to go find myself some more legs, but Corbin's voice stopped me.

"Don't make yourself too comfortable on my ship, lass. I'll be wantin' her back . . . as well as a few other things."

Holder slapped a hand to his forehead and shook his head in mock sorrow. "No style. I've tried to teach him, but he remains utterly clueless."

"Pricked your pride, did I?" I grinned, ignoring Holder to salute Corbin with the leg, a tiny bit surprised at how much I'd enjoyed the encounter with the computer pirate. "I think you'll survive the blow to your ego, Corbin. It's a game, after all. None of this really matters. It's all just pretend."

"Perhaps. Then again, perhaps not," he said mysteriously as I marched out the door into the bright tropical sunshine.

Chapter 3

Hold, monsters!

—Ibid, Act I

Corbin's comment rang in my ears despite its soft delivery. What did he mean by it? Was it some sort of a virtual reality reference?

I paused in the middle of the busy square and looked around, admitting to myself that the game designers really had outdone themselves with the creation of a virtual world. The noise of a couple of dozen people talking, laughing, shouting, and generally just getting on with the business of living filled the air, as did the accompanying sounds of donkeys, dogs, geese, sheep, and pigs. I closed my eyes for a minute to block out the computer visions, and drank in the environment.

The sun beat down hot on me, so hot it made a line of sweat prick to life on my forehead. The air was rich with the heavy scent of tropical flowers, counterparted pleasantly— and not so pleasantly—by the heady odor of spices that came from a market stall, and the more earthy smell left by a passing donkey.

Even the salty breeze that swept up a slight hill from the

a small wooden chest that sat next to a rickety-looking bed. "Ye make rugs, then?"

"Not that kind of hooker," I said, kneeling next to her. "I meant the business-girl kind."

She blinked at me.

I dredged up a couple of piratey-sounding synonyms. "Tarts. Trollops. Ladies of the evening."

"Ah?" Renata looked away, gesturing at the trunk. "There be some things in here that ye can use. Belonged to one of me girls who ran off with a captain. Ye look to be about her size. Tch. Looks as if the other girls have been goin' through it. All that's left is a pair of stripy breeches, a bodice, and a wee nothin' of a skirt."

I looked at the garments she was offering me. The green and white striped breeches—nothing more than a pair of clamdigger pants—didn't look too bad, but as I held up the green cloth skirt and brown leather bodice, I could see the latter was cut to act as a push-up bra. "Thanks. They're a bit . . . but anything is better than these atrocious rags. I appreciate them. I . . . er . . . I don't think I have any money."

She waved an airy hand. "Not many folks hereabouts have reales, despite the mine. We mostly barter for the things we be needin'."

"Ray-all?" I asked, confused by the word she used.

"Aye. 'Tis a Spanish word for the piece of silver that be used for coin hereabouts."

"Ah. Gotcha. Well, I'm realless at the moment, and I can't give up my leg because I need it to get to the officer level, but I'm sure if we think hard, I can find something to barter for these things. Er . . . I have a masters in financial management. I don't suppose you run a business of any sort?"

She made a faintly distressed sound. I turned my back and shucked the revealing rags, slipping into the skirt, matching linen shirt, and leather bodice. The skirt definitely covered more than the rags, reaching almost to my knees, but the bodice . . . well, it definitely lifted, separated, and presented my breasts in a way that faintly alarmed me. Not having been overly endowed in the breast area, I found it a bit of a novelty to suddenly have apparently abundant cleavage. I tried a trial bend to make sure I wouldn't pop out, and when I was satisfied that I wouldn't, glanced back to the silent Renata. "Sorry; just wanted to make sure I wouldn't be shocking anyone. Did you say you had a business?"

"Aye, I do. I've this house," she answered after a minute, her eyes troubled. "Ye'll be wantin' somethin' to put in yer belly, no doubt."

"Well . . . I suppose I could spend a few more minutes here," I said, strangely unwilling to leave. "At least until we work out a trade for these clothes. But then I really do have to get cracking and collect my officer legs. I made this deal with my daughter, and somehow I keep getting sidetracked."

Renata gave me an odd look as we walked back to the room with the fireplace. Despite the warmth of the day, there was a fire in the fireplace—and a haunch of something roasting away on an antique-looking spit. "Full marks for the game maker for going into such details," I said, sniffing the air. The scent of the roasting meat mingled with something salty and tangy that reminded me of my childhood summers spent on the northern Oregon coast. "This really is amazing. My mouth is actually watering."

"Eh, lass, there be somethin' ye be needin' to know," Renata said as she plucked a battered wooden plate from a stack on an equally battered sideboard. She turned the haunch on the spit, pulling a knife from her belt to hack off a few strips of meat. I stared in growing horror at the plate she shoved toward me. "This no longer be a game ye're in."

"Um . . . is this . . . uh . . . what exactly is it?" I asked, glancing between the plate of meat slices and the oozing, still bloody slab of meat roasting over the fire.

"'Tis a perfectly good bit of mutton," Renata answered.

I looked at her. "I don't want to sound rude or ungrateful or anything, because I appreciate you giving me the clothes when I don't have any money or anything but my financial skills to barter, but man alive, the California Health Department would have kittens over your idea of safe food handling and cooking. That's still bloody!"

She looked to where I was pointing at the cooking meat. "Aye, but the bit ye've got isn't. Ye be needed somethin' to wash it down, I'm willin' to wager."

"No, thank you, that's not necessary—" Renata ignored me as she bustled over to where a small keg rested on the sideboard. She wiped out a couple of metal tankards with the hem of her skirt, filling both with a dark, thick-looking ale. "I'm alcohol-intolerant, I'm afraid. It's the sulfites. They trigger migraines."

"Ye not hungry?" she asked, shoving one of the two tankards into my hand despite my objections. "Sit down and eat, lass. Ye're about to have a bit of a shock, and ye'll be needin' a bit of food in yer belly to get ye past it."

"Shock? What kind of a shock can a computer game give me? Other than the kind from a faulty laptop plug, that is," I asked, obediently sitting down at the small table she'd indicated. The smell of the cooking meat had my stomach rumbling uncomfortably, reminding me that I'd missed dinner in my haste to get the press release ready. I poked at the long strips of meat, looking them over carefully. "Oh, what the hell. If I pick up a computer version of E. coli, so be it. Do you have a fork?"

Renata looked at me as if I had three heads. "Nay, lass. We use our eatin' knives here. Ah, ye've not got one? Lucky then I've a spare." She hoisted up her skirt and pulled a short-bladed knife from the garter holding up a ratty pair of stockings, shoving it into my hand.

"No, that's okay, I don't need to take your spare . . . er . . . leg knife . . ." I held the knife by the very tips of two fingers, wondering whether she really expected me to eat with a utensil that had been strapped to her leg. "I'll just use my fingers, if you don't mind my ill manners. Now, about the skills I have to offer—I'm a bit fuzzy about just what sort of business it is you're running here . . ."

The door leading to the hall burst open as my words faded on my lips. A redheaded woman clad in an almost translucent blouse and similar lace-bedecked petticoat raced into the room, giggling as she cast provocative glances over her shoulder. On her heels was a middle-aged man with a short salt-and-pepper beard, wearing a pair of boots . . . and nothing else.

"Lay up, ye blighted minx! I'm not as fast on me pins as ye are!"

The woman raced around the table and headed back out the door, scattering giggles and come-hither looks behind her. The naked man, a pirate if the earrings and weathered look were anything to go by, followed without giving Renata or me a second glance.

"Oh," I said, as the door slammed behind the couple. "That sort of business. You're a . . . er . . . this is a . . . uh . . ."

"Sportin' house, aye," Renata said, taking a healthy swig from her mug of ale. "That be Red Beth, another of me girls. Ye not be one of them lasses with yer nose stuck high up in the air who look down on us, be ye?"

"Me? Oh, absolutely not. My nose is right here, perfectly level. I'm known for being very open-minded. Ask anyone. I'm all for . . . er . . . sportin'. Big fan of it."

"Are ye, now," she asked, her eyebrows doing a surprised little waggle. "Ye don't have the look about ye."

"Oh, I'm not a . . . that is, I don't do it for money."

"Ah? That's mighty charitable of ye, dearie, but ye're due somethin' for yer troubles."

"No, no, you're misunderstanding. I don't have sex professionally. It's more a hobby . . . oh, that doesn't sound right. I meant that I'm an amateur at it . . . er . . . that is, I know what I'm doing and what goes where and the approximate time and actions needed to achieve . . . oh, hell, I'm just making this worse, aren't I?"

Renata laughed as I stuffed a piece of undercooked mutton into my mouth more to shut myself up than to satisfy the gnawing hunger. "That ye are, dearie; that ye are. If'n ye've had enough to eat, p'raps now would be a good time to have that talk I've been hintin' at."

"Absolutely," I said, pushing the now-empty plate away. With no other beverage offered, I took a few cautious sips of ale to wash down the last of the meat, figuring that unless the game's creators spent way too much time ensuring that the game duplicated every last aspect of real life, I should be safe from the threat of an alcohol-induced migraine. "As to that, I believe I can be of some use to you. After all, a business of this sort is no different from any other that provides a service. I will simply use the standard small business model and adapt it for your specific needs. If you could bring out your financial records, receipts, bank statements, and a list of expenses that I can itemize, I'll get started and work you up a business plan that will allow you to run with a tightly controlled budget, and yet save sufficient funds for your retirement."

Renata looked at me like three naked customers were dancing on my head. "Financial records? I've this house, dearie."

"No receipts? No tax statements from years past?"

She shook her head, still giving me a wary look.

"Okay. We start from scratch. That's doable, too. Do you

have paper and a pencil?" I asked, looking around the room. "I could work up a model for you now, just something basic so you know where you stand, financially."

"I've no parchment, no," Renata answered, a frown pulling her brows together as she watched me over the rim of her tankard. "'Tis dear, parchment."

"Dear? Oh, expensive. Gotcha. Hmm." I tapped my fingers on the table and considered my situation. Clearly there was going to be more to achieving the officer level of the game than just collecting wooden limbs. No doubt the game's creator felt some sort of a teamwork challenge was necessary. "What I really need is a spreadsheet. I'd be able to adapt one for you with just a couple of keystrokes, but I don't suppose there's any way to get one in the game environment?"

Renata just stared at me.

"Right; I thought not." I tapped my lower lip, thinking hard. "Tell you what—I'll quit the game and load up a spreadsheet, give it a quick modification and plug in some basic numbers, then print out the data and pop back into the game so I can read it to you. Does that work for you?"

She was shaking her head even before I finished speaking.

"Don't like spreadsheets?" I asked.

"Aye, I like my sheets spread, but that be not what I'm shakin' me head over, dearie. It's this idea ye have about leavin' us and returnin' to yer previous life."

"Don't let it worry you," I said, waving an airy hand. "I promised my daughter I'd make it to the officer level of the game, and I thoroughly intend to fulfill that promise. To be honest," I said, leaning forward across the table, "just between you and me—I'm getting a kick out of this whole thing. It's going to cost me to admit to Tara that she was right about a little playtime, but the truth is, this pirate stuff is a bit of a long-suppressed fantasy of mine. I'm not so sold on the game as she is, naturally, but I can see the attraction of such a virtual diversion."

Renata's rheumy-eyed gaze held mine. "'Tis not just virtual, dearie."

"What isn't?" I said on a laugh, my smile fading when her face remained watchful. "Oh, I get it. You're not programmed to acknowledge that this world isn't real. Sorry. Didn't mean to—"

"Nay. I ken well enough the origins of this world. But ye don't be understandin' that for ye, it's more than just a game."

A faint prick of unease skittered down my back. "What do you mean by that? Of course it isn't real. It's pretend, a virtual world, nothing more."

Silence filled the room for a moment while she worked through what she wanted to say. "For others, that may be; I cannot say. But for ye, dearie . . . ye're a part of our world just as much as Red Beth and her Jack Tar are."

"No, no, no, no," I said, mentally asking myself why I bothered trying to argue with a computer character. "I'm real. You aren't. Neither is Red Beth and her boyfriend, or that dead man outside the inn, or that handsome Corbin, or the sheep that woke me up, or anything else here."

She just stared at me with a bit of a pitying touch to her eyes.

"Fine. You want me to prove it? Watch." I reached up to my face, intending to pull off the virtual reality glasses, but there was nothing there. "Um . . . okay. There's got to be a trigger or something somewhere to generate the computer interface."

I looked around the room for inspiration, examining everything from my hands (you never knew) to the surroundings for something that would bring up the computer interface. A sense of claustrophobic panic welled up within me as my searching grew more and more frantic.

"Maybe it's where I woke up," I said, dashing out of the

building to the nearby alley. As I searched the alley for a magic door, or computer keyboard, or even just a big button that said PUSH HERE FOR REAL LIFE, the panic was joined by a horrible sense of life spiraling out of my control.

"No," I said after a fruitless twenty-minute search. I kicked at a wooden water bucket and spun around, desperate for something that would take me out of what had turned into a nightmare. "No, this can't be happening to me. It's a game, a computer game. There were virtual reality glasses. I put them on and, whammo, I was in the game. So, therefore, I must be able to take them off to return to life."

My face was just as barren of glasses as it had been the thirty-odd other times I'd checked it.

"No," I whimpered, remembering the storm and the zap of electricity that had knocked me out when I was in the process of logging in to the game. What if it had done something to me? What if it had somehow rearranged reality and sucked me into a world where the unreal became real?

"Aye, dearie, now ye understand," Renata said, watching me from the mouth of the alley. I slumped dazedly against the wall, my knees threatening to give out under me. "Welcome to Turtle's Back. I hope ye'll be happy with us, since ye'll be spendin' the rest of yer life here."

A black maelstrom swept up out of nowhere and claimed me, sucking me down into its inky depths, but before it wholly consumed me, my mind managed one last coherent thought.

I wasn't going down without a fight.

Chapter 4

A paradox, a paradox,
A most ingenious paradox!

—Ibid, Act II

I have always maintained that tears serve little purpose. They are a waste of energy, they are purposeless, they seldom serve to make you feel better as you might think they would, and they can leave you with red eyes and blotchy skin. Many has been the time I've counseled my emotional daughter that it would be better to channel the energy expended upon emotional outbursts into more proactive, positive actions.

The thought came to me, as I sat sobbing my eyes out in Renata's house of ill repute, that there were times when I was extremely full of it.

"Ye feelin' better now, dearie?" Renata asked as the sobs trickled to heavy sniffling, nose blowing, and the odd hiccup or two thrown in just to make things interesting.

"Yes, thank you; I think I'm past the worst of it. I'm mostly worried about my daughter. How is she going to cope with a vegetable for a mother?"

"Ye're not still thinkin' of throwin' yerself off the dock?" the concerned woman asked.

I shook my head and made another swipe at my nose with the handkerchief she had provided. "No, I'm not suicidal anymore, although I think there's merit in the idea of a near-death experience to bring my mind back. Because, you know, either I've gone insane, or the world has, and somehow I just think I could handle the insanity better if I knew it was something that psychotherapy and a really big dose of Prozac could fix. Finding myself a prisoner in something that doesn't exist is—"

"There she goes again," said the dark-haired Suky, hoisting the baby she had been nursing a bit higher on her hip. "Ye've set her off again, Reggie. Now we'll have her waterin' the rug afore all our Jacks."

"She's a blight, she is," Mags, another of Renata's women, complained as she primped before a tarnished bit of mirror set on the sideboard. "Can't ye do somethin' with her, then? Sittin' there blubberin' like a scalded cat like that, she'll run off all our business."

"Hush, ye heartless tart. Can't ye see the poor thing is upset?" Sly Jez patted my shoulder sympathetically. I sniffled appreciatively at her. "She's had a bad bit of news, she has. What is it, Amy—is yer trouble that yer man's run off with another lass?"

"No, it's not that," I said, giving in to the few more tears of self-pity that welled up.

"Maybe she's lost her mum, like Suky did last week?" Red Beth suggested. The ladies were all lounging around the main room in the house in various states of undress, waiting, so Renata had told me after I had regained consciousness and she had helped me back to the house, for the brisk evening trade.

Suky tossed her head. "'Twas a blessing, that was. Sour old cow."

"No, it's not my mother," I answered, still trying to come to grips with the horrible twist my life had suddenly taken.

"I know!" Mags piped up, doing a little twirl that spun her sheer petticoat out. "The stiffenin's gone out of her man's mizzenmast. That'd make anyone bawl their eyes out."

"That's not what's troubling me. I don't have a man—"

The ladies, as a group, gasped in horror.

"Ye don't have a man?" Mags asked, one hand surreptitiously making the sign of the cross.

"No. I'm entanglement-free at the moment."

"None?" Sly Jez prodded. "Not even a Jack Tar what comes to shore every six months?"

"No, no men, Jacks or otherwise. I had a husband. . . ."

"Ah," the ladies sighed, relieved.

"Died, did he?" Red Beth asked.

"No, actually, I divorced him several years ago. He was not at all husband material, but I was young and didn't see that at first."

"Divorce?" Sly Jez looked to Renata, who was squinting into a rum barrel and muttering to herself.

"It be somethin' out of yer ken, lass," Renata answered.

"So you be havin' no man now," Sly Jez said slowly, her brow furrowed as she puzzled out the sad tangle of my life.

"That'll be hard, what with men in short supply. What the emerald mine don't take, the sea does," Suky said. The ladies nodded.

"But what happened to the man ye had?" Jez asked.

"Amicable divorce. Mostly amicable." I gave one last sniff and told myself to get a grip. Self-pity was like tears— simply not productive.

"Sounds painful," Jez said. "Are ye lookin' for a man, then?"

"Well, not really looking . . ."

"Of course she is," Mags said, rolling her eyes. "But she'll not be findin' one here."

"Actually, I did meet a man here earlier."

"Oooooh," said the chorus of women.

"Fast worker," Suky said, nodding her grudging approval.

"Well, ye have to be, what with the few lads around here," Mags said. The ladies—Renata excepted; she was still muttering at the rum barrel—sighed sadly.

"So, who be the one who's caught yer eye?" Sly Jez asked, taking a seat and adjusting her breasts. She was the only one who was still fully clothed, if you could call breasts straining to overflow her leather bodice clothed.

"What are you doing?" I asked, momentarily distracted by her actions of plumping her breasts so the bodice was almost made moot. "Shouldn't you be . . . you know . . . tucking them back in rather than bringing them out?"

"I'm fluffin' me cleavage," she answered, looking down at her breasts in surprise. "Why would I want to hide 'em? 'Tis me best feature."

I looked at my breasts. Even lifted and separated as they'd never been before, they weren't overflowing the confines of the bodice. I debated fluffing but passed on the idea since there was only so much madness I could stand in any one given moment. "Er . . . Corbin was the man I met."

The sound of a metal tankard hitting the wooden floor was the only sound in the room.

"He seemed nice enough, once he got rid of his blond persona," I added, still eyeing my modest bosomage. Maybe fluffing wasn't such a bad idea after all. Every other woman here seemed to have desirable cleavage. I didn't want to be left behind—good God, what was I thinking!

"Corbin?" Sly Jez asked in a squeak.

"Mmm?" I tried squeezing my arms together against my sides to see whether that gave me bonus bosom power.

"Captain Corbin?"

"Yes, he was a captain. I kind of liked him, after he got through doing the charmer bit." I glanced speculatively at Jez's cleavage. It couldn't all be natural. Maybe she was lacing her bodice tighter than I was.

"Black Corbin?" Red Beth asked.

"I think so, although he was blond at first. But I like him better with the darker hair. He looked more real, you know? More . . . trustworthy."

"Black Corbin, the scourge of the Seventh Sea . . . trustworthy?" Suky choked.

I looked up, finally becoming aware of the strained silence in the room. The ladies all wore looks of stunned disbelief. "Oh, he's not as bad as all that. I'm sure most of that is just PR. He was actually quite nice when I won a ship off him. That bit about revenge was just his wounded male ego talking, I'm sure."

"Ye won a ship off . . . Reggie, did ye hear?" Red Beth turned to the madam. "She won a ship from Black Corbin!"

Renata shot me a long look. "Aye, I heard."

"How'd ye be doin' that, then?" Sly Jez asked.

I gave up trying to have the sort of breasts that overflowed anything and quickly told the women of my meeting with Corbin, including the duel and its outcome. "He said he'd get revenge, but you know how men are—they get all wounded pride and have to talk big in front of their friends," I concluded.

"Black Corbin has no friends," Mags said slowly, giving me a wide berth as she sashayed over to where the hunk of meat was still cooking over the fire.

"Well, I'm in no position to judge that. I haven't been here long enough—" The realization that I'd be stuck here unless I found a way out hit me again, and a few drops of moisture attempted to squeeze out of my tear ducts.

"Oh, Lord, there she goes again," Suky said, taking her baby off for her postdinner nap. "Someone stop her before we are a-drownin' in tears."

"No need to stop me," I said, raising a hand. "I'm done crying. I'm not the crying sort; really I'm not. I think I'm a bit PMS-y is all."

"Eh?" Jez asked, her brow wrinkled.

I glanced at Renata. She seemed to be the only one in the game who actually knew it was a game. Maybe she was the equivalent of a Help file? I set the soggy handkerchief down and paced the length of the room. "PMS is unimportant. What is important is the fact that I'm through with tears. Nothing was ever accomplished through crying. No, what's needed here is a plan of action. Organization, that's the key! My old accounting business admin professor used to tell me that given the proper organization, any situation could be overcome. I'm an intelligent, resourceful woman—I'll simply gather the data available, organize it in an easily understandable fashion, and then use it to solve my problems. Oh, for my laptop! Or even a whiteboard! I could work up a killer PowerPoint demonstration if I just had the necessary equipment, and what I could do with a high-speed Internet connection, maybe a dedicated T3 line . . ."

The three ladies gaped a little bit at me. I decided they weren't up to hearing about modern technology and moved on to a topic that would have a more productive outcome. "This may take a bit of time, unfortunately. Renata, I . . . er . . . could I stay here? I can't pay you in money," I hurried on before she could demand that I become one of her girls, "but as I mentioned before, I can trade my financial skills for room and board. I'd be happy to not only create a business plan for you, but set up retirement plans for all your ladies."

"Aye, ye're welcome to stay, dearie," Renata said, gathering up a basket. "I'd best be doin' me shoppin'. Ye lasses take care of our guest, now."

The ladies murmured unenthusiastic agreements as Renata left the house.

"What be that retirement ye mentioned, Amy?" Mags asked suspiciously, turning the spit the meat was on. "This retirement—is it good?"

"Oh, absolutely. A good 401(k) plan is vital to your financial well-being and security in your old age. Don't worry, I'll explain it all once I have a fund set up. Now, to begin, perhaps I could start with a simple profit-and-loss prediction based on past—"

The front door of the house was thrown open with a shout of greeting. "Ahoy, the house! First Mate Pangloss is here! Come out, ye comely wenches."

"Panny!" Sly Jez squealed, jumping up to open the door leading to the entry hall. A big, burly redheaded man swept into the room, not even staggering when Jez flung herself on him, cascading kisses all over his beard-roughened face as she wrapped her legs around his waist.

"Hoy, there, me beauty. 'Tis missin' ye I've been, as well," the man named Pangloss answered in between kisses of his own.

Behind him another man lurked in the doorway, finally resorting to a shove to get Pangloss and Jez out of the way. "Gangway, ye scurvy bilge rat. Let yer captain through. Hoy, Suky. How be yer charmin' self today? And all ye lovely ladies . . . sink me, ye've a new recruit? Welcome, lass." The man paused in front of me, jerking a maroon captain's hat from his head as he swept low in an exaggerated bow. "And a lovely addition to the house ye are."

"Oh, I'm not with them," I said quickly, then realized how rude that sounded. "Not that there's anything wrong with being a . . . er . . . that is, I'm just staying here. I was, for lack of a better word, stranded here, and until I can find my way home again, Renata has kindly offered to let me stay here. But I'm not a . . ." I glanced over to the corner, where the man named Pangloss stood, still lip-locked with Jez.

"This be Amy, Bart," Suky said, offering the man a tankard of grog. He was a tall, wiry man with shoulder-length golden brown hair, a hard jaw, and eyes that didn't seem to miss much. "She's a newcomer hereabouts. Amy, so ye're knowing . . . Captain Bart is by way of bein' the governor of Turtle's Back."

"A governor? How fascinating. It's a pleasure, Captain," I said, offering my hand. Bart stared at it for a moment, then took it, turning it over and placing a kiss on the back.

"The pleasure, lass, is all mine. A newcomer to our fair parts, are ye? Well, then, ye'll be lookin' for some help to be gettin' what ye want in life."

"Well," I said, pulling my hand from his, pleasure mingling with a faint sense of discomfort at the look of admiration in his eyes, "actually, I originally wanted to become an officer, but my goals have shifted since I discovered I was stuck here."

"Ye're lookin' to be an officer, eh?" he asked, his gaze turned speculative. "What sort of experience do ye have?"

"Oh. Well, I have . . . er . . . I have a ship."

"And she beat Black Corbin at swords," Red Beth said, spreading the skirt of her petticoat and batting her lashes at the captain.

"Did ye, now?" Bart said, his look changing to one more calculating.

"It's nothing, really," I said modestly. "But I was alternate on my college fencing team for three years in a row."

"Eh . . . nice. Well, there may be somethin' I can do to help ye, lass," he said. "I'm always lookin' for good officers to help defend this lovely isle."

"Oh, thank you, but officer isn't really my primary goal now—"

"'Tis the way off this island," Bart said smoothly, the blondish beard stubble on his cheeks catching the afternoon sunlight as it slanted in through the window.

Hope rose within me at his words. Maybe that was the way to bring up the virtual reality interface? Maybe I had to achieve the next level in order to quit the game? "Oh, well, then, consider me an officer!"

Bart laughed. Red Beth and Mags and Suky laughed. Sly Jez and Pangloss sucked each other's tongues. "'Tis not quite so easy as all that," Bart said. "But if ye meet our qualifications to join the crew, ye can go on the account."

"Er . . ."

"It means become a pirate," Suky explained, topping off Bart's grog.

"Oh, become an officer in your crew? Okay. Sounds good to me. Only . . . what are the qualifications? I haven't done too much sailing, although I did go to Catalina once. That was on a ship. Boat. Whichever."

Bart smiled. "'Tis more of an indoctrination than qualifications, really . . ."

"Ah?" I asked, starting to get worried as his smile grew larger and amusement danced in his pale blue eyes.

"Aye, lass, and a simple one for someone as fierce as yerself. All we ask is that ye take care of a pest that's been plaguin' our fair paradise."

"A pest?" I asked suspiciously. "It's not a rodent, is it? Because I have a thing about rats—"

"That's as good a name as any." Bart laughed. "The rat's name be Black Corbin, and all ye have to do to join me crew is to kill him."

Chapter 5

You may go, for you're at liberty, our pirate rules
protect you,
And honorary members of our band we do elect you!
—Ibid, Act I

"It's not happening," I told Bart as I stumbled behind him up the patchily cobblestoned main street that led from the town up to where the governor's house sat on a bluff overlooking the harbor.

"It wouldn't be hard for ye, lass. Not if ye've beaten Corbin already. The next time, ye just slide yer blade into his neck rather than lightenin' him of a sloop."

"It is not happening," I repeated, glancing a bit nervously at the four men following us. The big guy named Pangloss had remained at Renata's house, having disappeared into a back room with Jez, but the rest of Bart's men, so hastily introduced that I didn't catch any of their names, were a tough-looking lot. They *looked* like pirates, all sneers and scars and unshaved beards and patched clothing, and a virtual arsenal of swords and firearms strapped to their persons.

"'Twould be a simple act," Bart argued, pausing a moment to grab my arm as I stumbled over a loose cobblestone.
"No."

"Just a wee slip of yer sword—"

"No! I am not killing anyone!" Bart and the men all stopped and stared at me. I realized that I had made a major gaffe in a game whose entire social structure was built upon bloodthirsty pirates. Not only that, but I may well have blown my chance to join their crew and advance to the point where I could get the hell out of Dodge. So to speak. "That is, I'm not killing anyone *tonight*. Arr!"

"Yarr!" Bart's men answered in a snarling cheer.

I grinned at them and tried to look murderous before hurrying to catch up to Bart, where I could speak to him without his men overhearing. "Look, Bart, it's not that I don't want to be part of your crew, but murder is wrong. Morally and ethically wrong. Even in a game it's wrong. I was never one for shoot-'em-up-type games."

"This be not murder, lass. It be eradication of a pest. Black Corbin and his scurvy lot of lubbers want to destroy Turtle's Back. They swore to fire the town and run out every last soul as resides here. He's like a plague, wantin' to wipe out every livin' thing so he can take over as governor."

My mouth opened and closed a couple of times as I tried to think of something to say. "Are you sure?" was what finally emerged. "That doesn't sound like the guy I met. He was a bit arrogant, sure, but all the men here are arrogant. I think the programmer wrote them that way on purpose."

Bart paused before the main entrance to a big house that loomed up in the darkness. The flames from torches on either side of the doors flickered and danced wildly in the steady breeze that swept up the cliff from the ocean. "I'm not mistaken about Black Corbin, lass. He's as murderous a rogue as ever ye've clapped eyes on. Someday I'll tell ye the full list of our grievances against him, but until then ye'll just have to trust that he's the devil's own son."

"Hmm." I entered the house when he waved me in, mulling over the conflicting opinions about Corbin. Granted I had only just met the man, but was my judgment of people really so off that I could be fooled that easily?

"Go into me library and we'll get ye into the crew," Bart said, gesturing toward a room that led off a large, dark hall. "In a probationary capacity only, ye ken," he added when I looked hopeful.

"Ah. Yes." I went into a small, cozy room lit by a dozen beeswax candles and a small fire in the fireplace, and spent a moment in admiration of the game's artistic qualities. Everything from the polished mahogany desk that lurked in the corner to the brightly shining brass candelabrum on the mantelpiece, the long, linen curtains that gently swayed in the breeze from the open windows, right down to the coal scuttle and twisted spills used to light the fire were authentic. As ran my hand along the spines of books in a floor-to-ceiling bookcase, I realized with a start just how comfortable I was in this world.

"Oh, no, you don't," I told myself, glancing out the opened door to where Bart stood in the hall giving orders to his men. "You are not getting used to this place! It's not real. You have a daughter and a home and a real life. Think, Amy, think—there's got to be a way out of here other than killing someone."

I was still desperately trying to come up with another solution when Bart entered the room, followed by one of his men. He thrust a foil and scabbard at me.

"Oh, thank you. I like foils." I strapped the leather belt around my waist, adjusting the scabbard until I could withdraw the foil easily.

"Wear this. It'll mark ye as one of me crew," he said,

shoving a green and white striped bandana in my hands. "As I've told ye, to be a full member of me crew, blood must be spilled. Yers in addition to Corbin's."

"What?" I shrieked, jumping back when his cohort moved toward me, a wicked-looking curved-blade knife glinting in his hand. I pulled my foil and took a self-defensive stance.

Bart cocked an eyebrow at me, but his eyes laughed at my outraged indignation. "'Tis just a little nick Maggot is wantin' to make. Just a little bloodlettin' to act as yer bond."

"Well, my word is going to have to suffice as a bond, because there's no way I'm letting him stab me with that thing. It looks positively riddled with tetanus."

"Aye, well . . . I suppose we can hold off with this part of the crew initiation until ye've completed yer appointed task," Bart said graciously, waving his crewmate out.

I waited until the door closed behind him before turning to Bart and saying, "There's not going to be any completion of my appointed task, Bart. As I've said at least a half dozen times before, I'm not going to kill Corbin."

"He's a murderin' thief," Bart answered, leaning his hip against the desk, his arms crossed over his chest. Bart was clad in a dark blue captain's jacket, thigh-high boots, black pants, and a shiny gold earring. He looked like a pirate off the top of a Disney float, perfect in every way. I had the worst urge to muss him up a bit. I wasn't a big history expert, but I knew enough about the seventeenth and eighteenth centuries to know this sanitized version of pirateness wasn't strictly kosher. To be honest, I much preferred Corbin's scruffiness to this dandified version.

"Look, I'm not going to do it, okay? So let's talk compromise. I want to be an officer in your crew. Aside from killing a man who may or may not be innocent, what else can I do to achieve that?"

"Nothin'. Ye kill him, or ye don't join the crew."

"What is it about 'I'm not killing anyone' that you don't understand?" I asked, annoyed with the shrill tone my voice had taken, but losing my patience. Honestly, were death and mayhem *all* these people thought about?

"What is it about 'ye must' that ye don't ken?" Bart countered.

"I'm not doing it," I said abruptly, crossing my own arms over my chest.

"Ye won't be joinin' me crew, then."

"I'm crying in my beer over that," I said, admittedly flip, but I wasn't in the mood to censor myself.

"Ye won't be makin' officer, either," Bart said, picking up a dagger and fingering the tip of it.

"Big deal. I'm not one hundred percent sure that will help me, anyway."

"And ye won't be goin' home," he said, completely ignoring my comments.

That stopped me just as I was about to tell him where he could stick the dagger. "Er . . . just how dead do you need Corbin?"

He tossed the dagger up and snatched it out of the air while it was still a spinning blur. "I want him removed from the Seventh Sea. Does that answer your question?"

"Yes, it does," I answered, my mind chewing over the loophole I'd been hoping to find. Maybe there was a way I could contact the game's creator and ask to have the character of Corbin deleted from the game. What I needed was a piratey version of e-mail, some way I could get a message out to the real world.

"There's no other way, lass," he said, giving me a surprisingly knowing look.

"So you say," I said slowly, racking my brain for any tidbits of knowledge about how computer games worked. Didn't people always write something in called a back door, a secret way for the programmers to get in and access things? Maybe if I could find it, I could get out of the game . . . or at least contact the programmer. "But how do I know you're telling the truth?"

"How do ye know I'm not?"

"Good point." Dammit.

"If it's out of Turtle's Back ye want, ye're going to have to play the game."

Was he speaking of the game itself, or metaphorically? Hmm.

He set the dagger down and went to a mahogany glass-fronted hutch to pour himself what looked like brandy. "I'll have one of the men show ye the way about a ship tomorrow. Ye'll be needin' to sail to Mongoose to find Corbin."

"Mongoose?"

"'Tis the island where he puts into port. Ye'll either find him there, or skulking around its shores. Until ye've got yer sea legs, ye're welcome to stay here with me."

"Eh." I accepted the small tumbler of brandy he gave me without comment, absently sipping at it, enjoying the burn it made going down my throat. What was I going to do? I couldn't kill anyone, not even in a game, but on the other hand, if doing so was the only way I'd get back to reality and my own life, how awful could it be? It wasn't like Corbin was a real person, after all.

My stomach turned over a couple of times at the thought. Quickly I set down the brandy and squared my shoulders. The situation couldn't be as bleak as it appeared. I just needed to examine the circumstances fully, and another solution would be sure to come to me. "Thank you, but I'm staying at Renata's. I would appreciate your help with the ship thing, though. As I said, I'm not much of a sailor."

Bart's eyes smiled at me over the rim of the tumbler. "Ye will be, lass. Ye will be. To get ye started, I'll loan ye a few men to help ye sail yer ship. Ye should be fine with three able-bodied seamen and a cabin boy, I think. Maggot!"

I jumped at Bart's sudden bellow, taking the chair he absently gestured to while he talked to his man. "Round up three seamen for the lass. And be that half-witted little mongrel still clamorin' to be a cabin boy?"

"Aye. Maltwise Sam threw him in the drink yester eve, but the bilge rat didn't drown. He's hangin' around the gates, beggin'."

"Fetch him in. He'll do for the lass, as well."

"Er . . . thank you. I think."

"Ye'll note that I be bendin' the rules for ye, m'dear," Bart said as he poured himself another drink. "Maggot'll be thinkin' I've gone soft in the head, but I've an idea that ye're worth the trouble."

"Oh. Thank you. I'm sure I am. That is, I appreciate everything you're doing for me. Almost everything. That death order I could do without, but we've been over that—"

The door opened to admit a small boy of about seven or eight, dark-haired, dark-skinned, covered from head to toe in filthy rags, mud, dirt, what smelled like manure, and no doubt a host of other things that I really didn't want to identify. His right arm ended in a crudely fashioned metal hook. Perched on his scrawny shoulder was an equally dirty ratty black bird, wearing the same air of abandonment and squalor as was settled around the boy.

"Scupper me," Bart said, a look of profound distaste flickering across his face. "He be even worse than I remember. What's yer name, lad?"

The boy stood impassive, his face a dirt-encrusted mask of indifference. "Don't got one," he finally squawked when Maggot gave him a none-too-gentle shove of encouragement. The bird squawked as well, fluffing out his feathers enough for me to see that, like the boy, he was missing part of a limb—in the bird's case, one of his wings was stunted, no doubt unusable.

"No name, eh?" Bart glanced at me. "Seems a bit light in the wits, but if ye use the strap on him often enough, he'll train up right smartly, I'm thinkin'."

I glanced at the boy, about to refuse the offer—the last thing I needed was a child to watch over while trying to get out of the game—but the look in the dirty little urchin's eyes stopped me. They weren't full of horror or pity; they weren't even pleading with me to help him. They were flat, cold, and empty. No child's eyes should look like that.

"Thank you. I'm sure we'll work out well together. Do you live anywhere in particular?" I asked the boy. He stared at me as if he couldn't understand what I was saying. Poor little disabled mite. Obviously he'd had a cruel upbringing so far, not to mention having the handicap of just one arm. He would be toast if I didn't do something to help. "No? Well, I'm sure Renata will be able to find a bed for you, too. We'll have to find a nice name for you. Does no one call you anything?"

The boy thought for a moment, then said simply, "Bastard."

"I beg your pardon?"

"They call me bastard. They're always sayin', 'Get outta me way, ye scurvy little bastard.'"

"Yes, well, I don't think they mean it as a name—"

"Suits ye right well, it does," Bart said, clapping his hand on the boy's uninhabited shoulder, quickly withdrawing it to wipe it on his pants. "Bastard be yer name, lad."

"No, it's not," I said firmly.

Bart shrugged. "Bas, then. Good enough. Off with the two of ye. The rest of the men'll join ye in the mornin', lass."

"No, wait; I can pick a more fitting name—"

"Me bird's got a name," the boy announced as Bart made shooing motions toward the door.

"I wouldn't rightly be callin' that mangy collection of feathers and lice a bird," Bart said, picking up the fire tongs and using them to prod the boy toward the door.

"His name is Bran. Me ma said it means raven in Welch."

"Welsh," I corrected, giving in and following Bart and the filthy boy out to the hallway.

"Me ma said a raven on yer doorstep meant death to everyone who lived there. Me ma saw a raven and she died the next day," the boy added with grim relish.

Bart stopped for a moment to have a few words with one of his men.

"How horrible. You poor thing; when did she die?"

Bas's shoulders twitched in what I assumed was a shrug of ignorance. Bran the raven fluttered his scraggly feathers in mute protest of the action. "Don't remember. She drowned, though."

"I'm so sorry. Was she out sailing?" I asked, aware of the morbid tint to the conversation, but unable to stop myself from encouraging the lad to talk.

"Nay. She drowned in a vat of ale." Bas scratched his ear with the tip of his crude hook, examined the results closely, then wiped the hook on the ragged remains of a pair of woolen breeches. "Fell in trying to skim a bit off, and stayed there to drink her fill. The night watchman found her dead, floatin' on the top, all bloaty and puffed up and swollen."

"Good God!" I stared at the boy in horror. He didn't look the least bit disturbed by the retelling of his mother's appalling death. "How very tragic."

He made the odd half-shrugging motion again. "Don't know about that. The watchman said she was smilin'."

I opened my mouth to respond with some sort of sympathetic platitude but couldn't think of a damn thing to say to that. So I allowed Bart to give me details about meeting up with his first mate for sailing instructions and guidance, thanked him for his help, and finally headed down the hill with a new provisional crew, a foil strapped to my hip, and a cabin boy who would make Eeyore seem like the life of the party.

"Have ye ever seen a corpse what's been in the water for a few days?" Bas asked in a conversational tone of voice.

I flinched. "No, nor do I want to discuss it."

"They be all pasty white and green and sometimes fishes eats bits of them—"

"Right, I think it's time for a few house rules, Bas."

The boy looked around as we trod the path from the governor's house down to the town proper. "We be outside now."

"Yes, I know; it's just a figure of speech."

"Look, a death's head. He who sees that with an unclean soul will be dead afore dawn," the boy said, pointing to a cloud that passed over the newly risen moon.

"Er . . . yes. Now, as to our rules. I don't know what the going rate for cabin boys is, but I will find out and give that to you, as well as making sure you have food, regular baths, and some decent clothes. How does that sound?"

Bas stopped next to a small house, his head tipped as he listened intently, interest lighting his dark eyes. "Hear that tappin'? Deathwatch beetle. Someone be dyin' in that house."

"Oh, for God's sake," I muttered under my breath. "Rule number one: No discussions of what bodies look like when they've been drowned."

"I saw a man what had been partially eaten by a shark," Bas said as I hurried him down the irregular cobblestones. "Both his legs was gone, and half of his head—"

"That includes bodies that have been partially eaten. In fact, I think we need a moratorium on bodies altogether."

Bas didn't look too happy about that, but I didn't care. Obviously his early years had tainted him with an unusually morbid obsession with death and dying. He just needed someone to turn his mind to more healthy subjects. "You'll like Renata and the ladies. They are very . . . uh . . . popular women, so don't pay any attention to the gentlemen you see visiting them at night. And . . . er . . . during the day, too. Probably a few in the morning, if I know Suky."

"Be they tarts?" Bas asked.

"No, certainly not! They are businesswomen who have made their own choices, and taken charge of their lives, which is always a good thing. Just remember that we are not here to judge. And besides, if I get an investment scheme going, they might just be able to retire early." I got a whiff of the boy's foul odor as the breeze whipped through the narrow alleyway between Tara's weavery (which I'd stopped in briefly earlier) and a blacksmith's shop. "Phew. You need a bath. I'll see that you get one when we get to Renata's."

"Tarts get the pox," he said blithely, walking right through a pile of donkey manure. "Me ma said they do. The pox eats away at ye until ye're nothin' but bloody pustules and scabby sores and boils that erupt all over yer—"

"Rule number two: You are to make no references to tarts, the pox, or pustules, oozing or otherwise. Sores and boils are also verboten."

Bas fell silent as we marched along. I began to mentally compose a plan of action for the boy, so that when I did find my way out of this world, he'd be in a better place than where I found him.

"Old lady Jenkins, she had a bath last year," Bas said suddenly, distracting me from my thoughts.

Warm yellow light from oil lamps spilled out the open windows of Renata's house, creating dappled pools on the cobblestones outside. Laughter, the sounds of a fiddle, and several delighted shrieks of the female variety accompanied the light, giving proof to Renata's claim that the house did very good business. I debated taking the boy around the back way, so he would be spared the sight of the ladies flirting with their prospective customers, but trusted that he wouldn't see anything he hadn't seen a hundred times before. "Did she? Good for her."

"Aye." Bas waited for the count of five, then added with morose glee, "She died a se'ennight later."

Chapter 6

Although we live by strife,
We're always sorry to begin it....
                                                    —Ibid, Act I

The next two days were hell. If I thought I'd gone through bad patches in my life before, I was mistaken—nothing could compare to the nightmare I found myself in.

"This be a yar ship," Pangloss, Bart's first mate, told me as he emerged from a tiny captain's quarters in the aft— back—part of the ship. "She'll do well in beatin' to windward and close-hauled sailin'."

"Well, of course she will," I said, wondering whether I could possibly pull off pretending I knew what the hell he was talking about.

"I've always had an eye for a good ship design, and this one be the best," Pangloss told me. "She's got a bluff bow and a fine run aft, and the mast is set forward in the hull. See those oak leeboards? They be hung well forward amidships for balance, ye see."

Then again, it never hurt to learn something new. "Er . . .

actually, I don't see. I'm afraid this is my first time on a ship like this."

"Yer first time in a sloop?" Pangloss asked, running a hand down the polished side rail. "Never say it is! Well, then, ye'll be wantin' a bit of explanation about her so ye can appreciate just how fine a beauty she is. Ye see the mast?"

"Yes," I said, looking up at the tall mast, which was about a third of the way from the front of the ship. "It's big."

"Aye. Sloops have only a single mast, and fore-and-aft rig."

"You've lost me," I said, frowning up at the mast. The sails, kind of a yellowy white in color, were bound tightly around the poked-out bits, which Pangloss said were called spars.

"Ye have a boom-and-gaff mainsail there," Pangloss said, pointing up to the mast. "Then ye have a forward triangular staysail which we call a jib. And aft ye have a mainsail that be controlled by yer boom. Do ye see that?"

"Yeah," I said, wishing I had a nautical dictionary. "What's that pointy bit on the front of the ship?"

"That be the bowsprit, lass. It's what makes yer ship one of the fastest vessels to sail. If the wind be favorable, ye can make eleven knots."

"Ah."

"Ye've got fourteen cannons aboard, as well. That with yer speed will let ye hunt all but the biggest of prizes."

"Fourteen, eh? Cool." I looked around the deck of the ship, a warm glow of ownership filling me. It may not be real, and heaven knew I didn't want to stay here, but for the moment, at least, I had a fast, deadly ship, and the sudden desire to pillage and plunder and fire off all fourteen cannons in a dashing display of might and power.

My exultation was short-lived. The rest of the day was spent learning how to sail my fast, deadly ship. Or rather, *trying* to sail her. Pangloss rounded up three motley-looking crewmates to help me sail her, introducing them as the bosun's boys. One was a wrinkled, hunchbacked man who'd evidently come in far too close contact with a sword, while the other two were spotty teens with greasy hair, unkempt, ragged, and filthy clothes, and feet almost black with things I didn't want to think about.

"That's Tar—he be the one without the nose—and the twins there go by the name of Prudence and Impulsive."

"Prudence?" I asked, smiling at the three men clustered around the front part of the ship. Forward, I corrected myself. The front was the fore, the rear the aft, and I was going to go mad trying to learn everything in the day I'd allotted to getting up to speed. "Isn't that a girl's name?"

The twin named Prudence snarled something inaudible as Pangloss laughed. "Aye, it is, but in this instance it refers to the fact that Pru always be jumpin' into things afore he looks."

"Ah. And Impulsive?"

"He be the opposite of his brother."

"Excellent. Nice to meet you all. This is Bas, my cabin boy, and Bran, his raven. Ignore their respective pouts. They had a bit of an issue with the baths I made them both take last night."

"We almost drowned, she were that mean," Bas muttered. "I'm thinkin' I have the consumption from it."

I glared him into silence.

"This lot be good lads," Pangloss said in an undertone to me, "although they may need the taste of the captain's daughter now and again."

"I don't care who they date on their own time, but I intend on running a tight ship," I said, giving the twins a quelling look.

Pangloss laughed. "Nay, lass, the captain's daughter be another name for the cat."

"There's a ship cat?" I asked, looking around the main deck.

"Cat-o'-nine-tails," Pangloss corrected me.

"Ergh. You expect me to beat them?" I asked in a whisper through my teeth, sending my new crew of three plus Bas what I hoped was a reassuring "I wouldn't dream of physically assaulting you" smile. "I couldn't do that!"

"Sure, ye could," he responded with a humorous twinkle in his eye. "Ye'll be changin' yer mind quick enough when ye're becalmed because the lads are three sheets to the wind. Smartly, ye sprogs! Put yer weight onto the halyards! Hoist the sails!"

The actual training part of the trip wasn't too awful, although I got horribly mixed up with all the nautical terms Pangloss was throwing at me. After getting rigging confused with the spars (spars are the poles used to support sails and rigging), mistakenly referring to the main deck as the poop deck (I just liked saying poop deck), and repeatedly confusing starboard (right) with port (left), I thought things couldn't get much worse, but then we left the calm waters of the harbor and hit the open sea.

"Ye all right now that ye've chucked yer breakfast?" Pangloss asked as I lay crumpled over the railing of the deck, my head hanging over the blue-green water that slid past us with insidious ease.

"No. Dramamine. Please, if you have any mercy in your soul, get me some Dramamine," I croaked, my voice hoarse from my seemingly endless bouts with seasickness.

"I'm thinkin' we're not havin' that aboard ship," Pangloss said, looking around like he expected a giant box of Dramamine to tap-dance its way toward him. "What ye need is a wee bit of grog until ye've got yer pins under ye."

I turned my head enough to eye the metal tankard of grog he offered me. "I'll die if I drink that."

"Nay, ye won't. It'll settle yer gut, see if it don't."

For one moment I contemplated just throwing myself overboard and ending my misery, but my pride got the better of me. I was a strong woman, capable, respected, and in control of every situation. Was I going to let a little thing like seasickness get the best of me?"

"Hell, no," I snarled, snatching the mug of grog from Pangloss and drinking the whole thing down in one gulp. Maybe Pangloss was right. Maybe a touch of rum would settle my stomach and allow me to survive the hell into which I'd found myself thrust.

"Ye be a right pretty shade of green," Tar the sailor said as five hours later we pulled back into port. "I had me a hat just such a shade when I was a lad."

I slumped to the deck and wondered whether I could pay someone to scoop me up and cart me to Renata's house.

"Eh . . . lass?" Pangloss, that evil personification of everything sailorish, loomed overhead giving me a meaningful look. I stifled the urge to vomit on his feet and tried to get my still spinning mind to focus on what he wanted.

"Oh. Right. Sorry. I forgot you put me in charge of the trip. Uh, guys? Can you do the belaying thing? With the running lines? Make them fast and all that stuff."

Grudgingly my pitiful crew, who evidently didn't much like a woman being in charge of them, secured the ship to the rickety dock.

"Thanks, guys."

"Mates," Pangloss hissed.

"Er . . . thanks, mates. Yarr 'n' stuff. Could one of you get a wheelbarrow and pour me into it? I don't think I'm going to be able to stand up."

Pangloss rolled his eyes and dismissed the men, hauling

me to my feet with assurances that by tomorrow, I'd have my sea legs.

"Oh, I have sea legs already," I told him the following day. "My legs feel like they're made up of seawater, thank you very much."

"I once knew a man what chucked so much, he started spewin' up blood," Bas said helpfully as I lunged for the railing. "He died two days later, covered in cankers. *Oozin'* cankers."

Pangloss shooed Bas off to a maintenance task within the boy's one-handed abilities, and waited until I was done heaving over the side of the ship before answering. "Some takes a bit longer to get their legs. Here ye be—have a wee sip of grog to settle yer belly."

I knew from experience that the grog wouldn't do anything of the kind, but I took it nonetheless, swishing a mouthful of it around to rid myself of the unpleasant taste my seasickness had left.

Pangloss flinched as I spat it out.

I eyed him malevolently as I handed him back the tankard of grog. "Don't give me another lecture about the sins of wasting rum. Do something to distract me from this horrible up-and-down thing the ship is doing."

"It's called sailin', lass."

"Whatever. It's evil. Distract me."

He stood in front of me, hands on his hips as he frowned down at me. "What would ye be likin' me to do, then?"

I waved a vague hand around. "I don't know. Talk to me. Tell me about Turtle's Back. Tell me what it is that Corbin has done that has put a price on his head."

His frown deepened as he settled on the deck, pausing to call out an order to the twins, who were engaged in whittling obscene shapes in wood. "Now, that be a good idea. 'Tis only right ye know about the man ye'll be goin' up against."

I lurched off the railing and slid down the curved side of the ship until I was slumped next to him.

"Ye know that he be the most feared pirate in the Seventh Sea," Pangloss said by way of an opening. I nodded, trying to ignore the roiling of my stomach that seemed oddly out of synch with the ship's movements on the swells. "No one knows where he came from—one day he just appeared on the horizon, sailin' into the harbor as bold as brass and twice as shiny, just as if he owned the island. Naturally, the captain had a thing or two to say about that."

"Naturally," I agreed, so far not finding anything that disagreed with my impression of Corbin. Arrogance he had in abundance. But it was the other claims that didn't mesh.

Pangloss scratched his bristly chin. "From what I've been told, the cap'n went down to meet Corbin at the docks and welcome him to Turtle's Back."

"From what you've been told? You weren't there?"

"Nay," he shook his head. "I was off with a crew foragin' the Box for game."

After three days on the island I'd learned that game was pretty much nonexistent here, so Bart's men made frequent runs to the rocky shores of Pandora's Box, a nearby island uninhabitable by all but the heartiest breeds of goats, deer, and boar.

"The cap'n, he be a pirate from long ago, and he knows how to talk to our kind. So he was all friendly-like, offerin' Black Corbin his finest rum and wenches, but that blackhearted devil turned up his nose at 'em, sayin' without so much as a by-yer-leave that he'd be havin' the island instead."

"That seems rather pushy of him."

"Aye. Cap'n Bart, he just laughed and told Black Corbin he was welcome to try, but he had a strong crew who'd be givin' him no quarter if Corbin attacked the town."

"Hmm. So what did Corbin do then?"

Pangloss shrugged. "He left."

I gawked at him for a moment or two. "He left?"

"Aye."

"He didn't sack the town or burn the buildings or any of those piratey-type activities?"

"Nay."

I closed my eyes and leaned back against the side of the ship. "Then why is Bart so riled up about Corbin? Clearly the man is all bark and no bite."

"Ye'd call murderin' sixty-five men in cold blood no bite?"

"What?" My eyelids snapped open as I turned to stare.

"Aye," Pangloss nodded, his face hard. "When the cap'n told Black Corbin that he be havin' a strong crew, Corbin called down a curse on 'em. Less than a day later, the black flags of Corbin's crew were sighted off the leeward side of the island. Fearin' a sneak attack, the cap'n sent the entire crew off to meet him and send Corbin's scurvy bones to the salty depths. But Corbin, he be as black as the devil's heart, and he had men and cannons hidden onshore. Our crew was caught between their fire, and every last blessed soul— sixty-five there were—all of them perished. Ye'll be noticin' there're not a lot of men on Turtle's Back. Black Corbin killed 'em, all but what were foragin' with me, that's why."

"Oh, my God," I said, my throat suddenly tight. "That's awful."

"Aye," he said, his eyes dark with pain. "I lost a brother that fateful day, and swore an oath of me own to see Black Corbin dance with Jack Ketch."

"Er . . ." I said, confused.

"I'll see him hanged," Pangloss explained.

"I don't blame you for feeling so strongly, although I'm not a believer in capital punishment. So what happened after the crew was so brutally murdered? Why didn't Corbin take the town then?"

"A storm came up as if summoned by the good Lord himself. It drove Corbin's men back off the island, and by the time it blew itself out, they were nowhere to be seen. Bart himself met with every grievin' widow and mother and promised retribution. He used his own gold to hire a few men to start rebuildin' the crew, bringin' 'em to Turtle's Back to defend her shores against the murderous devil who swore he'd be back to take what doesn't belong to him."

"How horrible," I murmured, my mind full of the image of all those dead men and their grieving families. How could anyone act in such an inhuman manner over a piece of rock in the ocean? How could a man live with himself knowing what he had done? How could he appear so damned *nice* when he was really a monster?

Telling myself it wasn't a real world didn't help wipe out the sense of horror I felt. Within the context of the game, it was real—the people here thought it was real. I'd been here long enough to realize that they were remarkably well fleshed-out. The people here *were* people, in every sense but one. In this world, they existed; joys, sorrows, warts, and all.

"He might have fooled me once, but he won't do so again," I told Pangloss a short while later as we ported. I had recovered enough from my usual bout of seasickness to snap out an order or two. "Belay those lines, Prudence. Impulsive, mainsail, please. Tar, please fix the break in the fiddle block; then you're through for the night. Bas, stop picking your ear with your hook—there's nothing there you haven't seen before."

The twins, less intelligent and thus quicker to follow my orders, jumped to it, but Tar spat over the side of the ship a few times, picked something out of his teeth with the point of his dagger, examined the tip of the blade for a moment or two, then nodded his head and shambled off to where the jammed fiddle block (pulley) sat.

"Ye did that right smartly," Pangloss said with a satisfied nod. "And as for that devil Black Corbin—ye'll not be likely to see him around these waters again. Captain Bart has pressed men from other islands to serve on the watch and crew. Corbin won't be skulkin' around Turtle's Back again; that I can promise ye."

That thought made me strangely sad. I tried to give the emotion a good long look while I went through the checklist of tasks related to putting a ship in port, sending my three crewmates off with a few copper coins that Pangloss had given me for that purpose, as well as my profound thanks. The first mate toddled off after he corrected a couple of my mangled knots, telling me the first tankard of ale would be on him when I joined the crew at the Inn Cognito.

"I'm just tired, that's all," I told Bas as I tucked away the captain's logbook that I used to write down sailing notes and details about the booty we'd plundered. Thus far the sum total of my plunderage consisted of a piece of tattered sail-cloth I'd found on the remains of a wrecked sloop, and a pretty ruby necklace that I'd won sword fighting a fat merchant. I jumped off the *Saucy Wench* and hurried down the dark dock toward the soft glow of light coming out of the inn's windows. Although I had the foil Bart had given me to protect myself, I preferred not having to use it against any of the unsavory pirate-types who hung around the dark edges of town.

"Aye, Bran and I are, too. It's all them baths ye keep makin' us take—they're wearing our skin out."

"Do we remember rule number eighteen?"

Bas's lips thinned. "No complainin' about the baths, washin' me hands after I've used the privy, or discussin' what I find when I blow me nose?"

"Very good."

"If it's not the baths makin' ye tired, what is?" he asked as we headed for the inn.

"Hmm? Oh, that was merely a figure of speech. I was talking to myself about the fact that I can't stop thinking about someone."

"Madness?" he asked hopefully.

I laughed. "Not quite, no. The thing is, I'm a very down-to-earth person. I am not at all the type to be swayed by one meeting with a man. Especially not when the man in question is a psychopathic killer. Corbin is nothing special. He's not even real, for Pete's sake."

A shadow parted from the side of a building I knew housed a small rum distillery.

"Now, what makes you think I'm not real?" Black Corbin asked, his teeth gleaming whitely in the dim light from the distillery.

I had only enough time to gawk at him for a second before something heavy and black descended over my head, binding me so tightly I couldn't even think of moving, much less actually do it.

Chapter 7

For I am a Pirate King!
And it is, it is a glorious thing
To be a Pirate King!

—Ibid, Act I

"I object to this sort of treatment."

"I had a feeling you would. I'm not too proud to say that I'm taking immense pleasure in it, however."

"You're a rotten computer character! I'm reporting you to the program's creator!" The soft linen cloth used to tie my hands behind me, around the back of the chair upon which I was sitting, didn't give an inch as I struggled to free myself.

The man leaning against the desk in front of me tipped his head to the side as he watched me. "You can try, but it won't have any effect. Would you mind doing that little squirm you did just a second ago? I really enjoyed it."

I stopped struggling and packed everything I had into a glare. "You're incorrigible, too. I'm adding that to my list of complaints, which, I might add, now includes items like kidnapping, torture, and abuse of fundamental human rights.

You're totally beyond the Geneva Convention, and I am *so* going to make you sorry just as soon as I get my hands free."

"Was that a threat?" Corbin the Tormentor's eyebrows rose. "Did you just threaten me with retribution?"

"You bet your barnacle I did, and if you recall the day I whipped your butt at swordplay, you know I can back up anything I say. What do you mean it won't have any effect to complain about you? You're just a bit of software code, buster. You can be replaced. Erased, even. So put that in your megabyte and smoke it."

"Actually," Corbin said, tapping a finger on his chin, "I'm not, and I can't. At least, not in the sense you mean. I'm just as real as you are, Amy."

The use of my real name had me pausing a moment in my contemplation of how satisfying it would be to fulfill Bart's requirement for permanent inclusion in his crew. I narrowed my eyes at Corbin as he smiled at me. Despite the fact that he'd kidnapped me in the best pirate romance style, I was finding myself reacting to him in a way I hadn't reacted in a very long time. "How do you know my name?"

"I have ears. Everyone calls you Amy."

I relaxed a little, giving the bonds holding me down another pull. He'd heard my name mentioned by someone in town, that's all. His claim to be real was just the cyber-delusion of a bunch of computer code.

"But I plan on looking up the account information for your daughter—name, address, phone number, and billing history—as soon as I log out of the game. I'm sure I'll find an Amy Stewart somewhere on the credit card records. I take it you're enjoying the VR unit?"

Or not. My jaw dropped. "What . . . what . . ." I was so stunned I couldn't do much beyond sputtering. "You're not real."

"I am."

"You can't be."

"Sure, I can. I was born. It was easy. My mother did all the hard work."

I shook my head, refusing to believe him. "You're a program. Someone programmed you to believe you're real. But you're not."

"Aye, lass, I am."

"Nope. Real people don't change their appearance. You went from gorgeous blond to . . ." I waved my hand at him.

He glanced down at himself, a frown between his brows as he looked back up to me. "I thought you said you preferred me looking like this."

"I do. But people who are real can't change their appearance like you did," I said slowly, as if I was explaining something to a child.

His lips twitched in a wry smile. "Ah. That. Er. You are right about that being a computer-generated character. But this one is me, the real-life me. I was a bit surprised that you preferred me this way rather than the other since my research had shown that women reacted best to men like him, but my data was based on a skewed survey."

I looked my question at him.

"My ex-wife's comments as she ran away with a long-haired, blond bodybuilder," he answered, a bit sheepishly.

An almost overwhelming urge nearly had me blurting out how much I liked this form over the other, but I bit it back, reminding myself that I had more important things to discuss. "Then she was a fool," was all I said.

"You are not alone in that opinion," he said, his mobile face unusually expressionless. "I take it you believe me now?"

"Not at all. I think you are programmed to believe you exist outside the game in order to fool the people who play it."

"I repeat: I am as real as you are," he said, pulling a wicked-looking knife from his boot. My eyes widened at the sight of it, the sudden memory of everything I'd heard about the murdering Black Corbin returning with a vengeance. "Which is one of the two reasons why reporting me to the creator of Buckling Swashes isn't going to do you any good."

"What do you think you're going to do with that?" I asked, my voice rising in panic as Corbin strolled nonchalantly toward me. He might not be *real* real, but in the game, he was a murderer, and it was always a good rule of thumb not to taunt murderers.

He paused in front of me, a truly evil glint to his gray eyes as he dangled the knife in front of me. "Afraid? The brave Amy? The woman whose praises the whole of Turtle's Back is singing? The defeater of the dread pirate Black Corbin?"

"I'm brave, not stupid," I said, watching the sharp point of the knife as it swung back and forth in an arc. "And I'm not above pleading, if it will have any influence on you, not that I suspect it will. As for the praise singing . . . eh . . . you know how people exaggerate."

"But they must have heard the story from someone, and since my men and I didn't tell anyone, it's logical to assume that you have been spreading tales."

"It was the truth!" I protested, then gulped when the knife spun in his hand so the flat side of the blade rested just beneath my chin. He tilted my head up, examining me closely as I bit back all the things I wanted to say. "Never Chastise a Man Who Has a Knife to Your Throat" was the motto I quickly adopted.

"So it was," he answered, and before I could do so much as gasp in surprise he was behind me, the coolness of the blade sliding between my wrists, slicing the material binding them. "I trust you've calmed down enough to listen to what I have to say without disabling any more of my men?"

I leaped from the chair, rubbing my wrists as I glared at him. "I never! I defended myself from attackers, that's all. And if you hadn't kidnapped Bas and me to begin with, they'd never have gotten hurt." I paused for a moment, remembering the knock-down, drag-out fight I'd given Corbin's men after they unrolled me from the hemp sack in which they'd captured me. It hadn't been pretty, and I was strangely ashamed of the fact that I'd taken advantage of Corbin's decree that none of the men harm me in any way. Still, if he hadn't started it all by having us plucked off the street, Leeward Tom wouldn't be limping, and the behemoth named Barn wouldn't be wondering if he'd ever be able to sire children. "How is Barn? He's not . . . er . . . permanently . . . you know . . . damaged?"

I made a vague gesture that made Corbin's left eyebrow twitch. "No, he's not, although you're not in his best graces at the moment. Loo has forgiven you for kicking him in the knee, though, claiming you're a saucy wench who just needs a firm hand to tame your wild spirit."

"I suppose you think you're that firm hand?" I asked.

He grinned. "The thought did go through my mind. Right now Loo is talking to that black storm cloud you insisted on bringing, comparing amputations."

"I told you, his name is Bas, he's my cabin boy so I'm responsible for him, and what amputations? That is, what amputations does Leeward Tom have? He looked fine to me."

"Toes," Corbin said succinctly. "Four of them altogether. Drink?"

He moved behind the captain's desk, rustling around in a drawer before he pulled out a silver flask.

"Please." I all but licked my lips as he flipped open the flask and handed it to me. The rum in it burned a fiery path down my throat, ending up in a warm pool in my stomach. "What's the second thing?"

"Hmm?" Corbin took a swig from the flask.

"The second reason why reporting you wouldn't do any good."

He looked momentarily surprised, an oddly pleased look quickly replacing the expression. "You aren't a lawyer, are you? You have a wonderfully persistent mind."

"I'm a financial analyst, as a matter of fact. We are just as persistent. What is the second reason?"

"There's no one to report me to," he said simply. "I own Buckling Swashes."

"Corbin, you're just a computer character—"

"My name is Peter Corbin Monroe. I was born in 1965 in a small town in Idaho. I am divorced, and I have two children whom I see far too seldom and no known diseases or ailments beyond fallen arches. I went to school at the University of Wisconsin, where I got a master's in information science. My likes include Thai food, women who can beat me in a duel, and pirates. My pet peeves are people who act without regard for anyone else, commercial television, and the color pink."

I stared at him, starting to wonder which one of us was real, and which wasn't. Could he be what he said he was? If so . . . hope sprang to life in me as I stared at what could well be my way out of this virtual world.

"You own this? All of this?" I asked, waving my hand around to encompass everything in the captain's cabin. "You created this?"

"Well, I didn't do it single-handedly. I programmed the first version of the game in an office in my garage, but later I had a partner, and now I have two teams of programmers— one that works on the Internet version, and the new crew working on the VR side. You met the art director, Holder McReady."

"Holder is real, too? The guy with the monk delusions?"

"Yes. He is in charge of all the artwork you see around you. Everything from the clothing on down to the pattern of the rug. My partner was in charge of the VR technology, but he left me a few months ago to form his own company. Still," Corbin said, looking around the cabin with satisfaction, "I'm happy with how it turned out. I think people are going to enjoy it, don't you? We've worked hard to make it as realistic as possible."

"Oh, you've done that all right," I said, relief mingling with the irritation that he'd written a program that would trap unwary players. "If you don't mind, though, I'd like to get the hell out of here."

"Why? Aren't you having fun?"

"No. I want out."

He frowned. "I can't believe anyone wouldn't have a blast here, but if you aren't enjoying it, why don't leave?"

"I'm stuck, that's why," I said in a half snarl. "Your game is a trap! It won't let go of me!"

"No, no, that's impossible," he said, setting down the knife to take another swig of rum. "I had the programmers write in all sorts of safeguards against the program locking. It's impossible."

"Look deep into my eyes," I said through gritted teeth. "Do I look like I'm having so much fun I never want to leave the game?"

He took me at my word, setting down the flask before striding over to where I stood next to a tiny window. He took both my arms in his hands, leaning forward until our noses were almost touching. "You look . . ."

"What?" I asked on a breath, all the air suddenly having been stripped from my lungs. Standing so close to him was making me a little dizzy, the scent of leather and man teasing my nose in a way that had dark, secret parts of me coming to life and starting to take interest in the proceedings. "What do I look?"

"Sexy," he answered, his voice a rumble deep in his chest, his fingers hard on my arms as he pulled me toward him.

My hands unfisted, but rather than pushing him away from me as I thought they would, they slid up the front of his leather jerkin in a caress that gave me as much pleasure as it gave him, if not more. Beneath the warm leather I could feel the contours of his chest, my fingers skimming lightly over the jerkin as if they were mapping out terrain.

"Really? I don't think anyone has ever called me that," I finally managed to say. Croak might be another description—my voice was suddenly very hoarse.

"Then you have not met the right man," he answered, his breath fanning across my mouth as he spoke. "Because I think you have all the qualifications. Would you mind if I kissed you now?"

"Mind? Well . . ." I said slowly, pretending to think about it. My body knew better. It was all but throwing itself on him. I let my fingers wander up to his neck, tangling them in the short curls of his hair. "I have this policy against kissing murderers and kidnappers, and you're both."

"Says who?" he asked, his hands sliding up my arms to my shoulders, then down my ribcage. Even through the barrier of my clothing, little rivulets of molten pleasure followed his touch.

His mouth was hot. Hot and spicy and tasting of rum, his tongue flicking across my lips in a polite request for admission. I tried to tell my lips to stand firm, reminding them of my rules of sexual engagement (*caution* had hitherto been my byword), informing them that I wasn't about to suck the tongue out of a man I'd just met a few days before, but my lips were traitors. They parted without the slightest display of modesty, allowing the kiss to deepen and change from an act that seemed pleasing to something much more profound.

I shivered a shiver of blatant excitement as his lips parted from mine, my thoughts so muddled I couldn't seem to hold on to one for longer than a second or two. "Um? What were we talking—oh, the crew. They aren't real people, are they? I mean, you know they're not real. Before, when I thought you were one of them, that bothered me because from your point of view, that poor crew was real, but you're not, and you know they're not, and now that I know that you know they're not, it's all different."

"Amy, I haven't the slightest idea what you're talking about."

He didn't want to discuss it. That was fine with me—I'd much rather pursue more entertaining avenues. "It doesn't matter. I don't despise you now, although I'm going to have to knock off a couple of points for the kidnapping."

"It was the only way I thought you would listen to me," he answered, his lips brushing against mine. The hands that had been counting my ribs slid around to meet on my belly, then started an upward climb. My breasts, not normally given to thinking for themselves, suddenly came to life and decided that more than anything in the world, they wanted out of the thin blouse and leather bodice, and into Corbin's hands. "I knew you'd joined Bart's crew, and with the bounty on my head, I half thought you might be after my blood."

"I'm sorry," I said, too distracted by the sudden throbbing in my breasts to do more than mentally flinch from his words about the bounty on his head. "I seem to be having some difficulty with my breasts."

His brows pulled together as we both looked down to

where my cleavage was front and center. His hands were just below them, poised to scale the linen-clad impudent mounds. "Difficulty? What sort of difficulty? They look perfectly fine to me. Positively tasty, in fact."

"They're unruly," I admitted, then gasped when Corbin's thumbs swept across my straining nipples. "Hoocheewawa! Don't do that again, you'll make them revolt or something!"

"No? They look like they need mouth-to- . . . er . . . breast resuscitation. Would it help if I did this?"

Before I could try to force air back into my lungs, Corbin's head dipped to my cleavage, his tongue snaking out to caress the valley between my breasts.

My knees buckled.

"It's not really helping, no," I said, clutching his shoulders for support.

"Maybe I'm not resuscitating them well enough," he murmured into my chest, tugging down the linen blouse until one (extremely happy) breast was exposed to his attention. "Maybe I should . . ."

A wave of undiluted pleasure rippled from my breast to all points on my body as his mouth closed over my aching nipple, setting my skin tingling, my bones melting, and my brain into shutdown mode. I couldn't even form words; I just whimpered encouragement at him. Oh, the random thought popped into my head that I was not behaving in a discreet manner at all, that I had never been one for throwing myself into intimate acts with men I hardly knew, and that I really should be focused on getting out of the game rather than enjoying myself with the man who was currently making me mindless with the tongue swirlies that were laving my breast, but I pushed that thought down just as easily as I pushed the others.

Tara told me I needed to play more. Well, Corbin was here, I was here, and we were playing. End of story.

Only it wasn't, of course. I knew that as Corbin raised his head, his eyes liquid silver with arousal. "I think it's going to make it."

"It might, but I may just die if you don't do the other one."

His lip, which I deemed from firsthand experience delectable, curved in a smile. "We wouldn't want that, now, would we? Shall we continue this discussion somewhere more comfortable? Say . . . my bed over there?"

I looked from the dark cherry captain's bed snuggled up against a wall in the cabin to Corbin. His words acted like a bucketful of seawater splashed in my face. "Whoa, now. You wouldn't be hinting not so subtly that you'd like to have sex, would you?"

His eyes went even more molten. "You didn't seem to me like the sort of woman who likes playing verbal games about natural desires, but yes, as a matter of fact, I would very much like to make love to you. I'm not ashamed to admit that I wanted you the minute I realized you weren't a computer-generated player."

"It was the fact that I don't play—verbal games or anything else—that got me stuck here in the first place," I said, tucking myself back into my blouse. "I like you, Corbin, I really do. I enjoyed kissing you, and while I admit that allowing you to . . . er . . . resuscitate my breast might be considered leading you on, sex, actual sex, is out of the question." I paused for a moment, something he said striking a chord. "You wanted me the minute you knew I was real?"

"Yes." His frown was back. He let go of me and crossed his arms over his chest.

I took a step closer to him. I couldn't help myself, I seemed to be drawn to him by some strange, magnetic force.

That's my story and I'm sticking to it.

"When was that?"

"When you mentioned being willing to trade away your PDA. The computer characters lack contemporary references in their dialogue array. Only other players, real people, would know what a PDA was, let alone mention it. As soon as I heard you say it, I knew you were a real person."

"Wow. I figured you, as the game master or whatever you call yourself, would be able to see that I was a real player."

He shook his head. "The in-game admin panel was too buggy, so we removed it while it's being recoded. The only way I can tell which players are real and which aren't is to access the admin panel, and I can't do that while I'm in the game."

"Hmm. Back to the other thing . . . are you always instantly attracted to women?"

"No." His frown deepened, the lovely melty look in his eyes turning cold.

"I see." I didn't really, but I wasn't about to admit that he had me confused as well as bemused. "Always Be the One to Remain in Control": that was my motto (I'm a firm believer in a motto for every situation), and it had served me well for many a year.

"Are you trying to say that you don't feel an instant attraction?"

"No, of course not. I might have a physical response, but there's much more I look for in a relationship than someone who chimes my bells," I said, my eyebrows pulling a little frown of their own.

"As do I," he answered, his hands on his hips now.

"Well, then, I guess we're in agreement." My eyes strayed to the bed as my brain decided to indulge in a little fantasizing about what it would be like to romp with him in it.

"If we were in agreement, you would be naked at this moment, and I would be resuscitating your other breast."

Another shiver of excitement zipped through me at the

image his words drew. I squelched it down, reminding myself that there was more at stake here than a fling with a handsome computer genius. "Look, Corbin, I appreciate the offer, and I'm sorry if I gave you the wrong idea about me, but I prefer some sort of emotional commitment before I jump into bed with someone. That said, I'd like to see you. In person, I mean. In real life. Maybe you could come over for dinner one night?"

His frown cleared as if by magic. "I would like that."

I smiled, happy that I had taken charge of the situation and turned it around to one that was more reasonable. "Good. Now, if you'll just tell me how to get out of this game, I will give my calendar a look-see, and we can pick a night."

The look he gave me was an odd one. "Amy, all you have to do to log out of the game is to turn the glasses off. There's a button near the hinge. Just press that, and the game will be saved, and you'll be logged out."

A horrible chill ran through me. "I don't have the glasses anymore. There's got to be another way out!"

He shook his head, holding his hand up to stop me. "No, I mean the real-life glasses, not ones you might be wearing in game."

"That's what I'm talking about!" I said, the chill growing.

"If you didn't have the glasses, you wouldn't be here," he pointed out.

"Well, I am! Look, no glasses!" I ran my fingers around the eye region of my face. "Feel for yourself—there's nothing there."

"I wouldn't be able to feel them," he said, his eyes puzzled. "Reach up to your temple. You should feel the arm of the glasses, and follow it back to the hinge."

"All I have here are temples," I said, panic joining the

chill as I felt the sides of my head. "Don't tell me there's no other way out?"

He frowned. *Again.* "This is impossible. You can't be here without having the glasses on. Look, I'll show you. I'll log out and log back on, so you can see. Now watch my hand. I follow the line of the arm to the hinge of the glasses . . ." He put his hand to his head, an odd, confused expression flitting across his face. He tried the other side, the expression turning to one of deep concern.

"Oh, my God! You don't have them, either, do you? We're stuck here! Forever! Aaaack!"

Chapter 8

The midnight hour is past,
And the chilly night-air is damp. . . .

—Ibid, Act II

"Amy, you're being irrational."

"*I'm* being irrational? *I* am? I'm not the one who failed to write a back door into the program. I'm not the one who wrote software so devious it traps innocent players in some sort of mental limbo. I'm not the one who created a world of murderous pirates so real that it was almost impossible to tell them from the real thing."

Corbin glanced down to where I was holding his knife to his crotch. "No, but you are the one threatening to emasculate me if I don't get you out. I'm doing my best, I assure you. And what do you mean *almost* impossible? Holder and I spent six months researching the history of piracy just so everything was accurate."

"I don't believe it," I said straightening up from where I had been bent over Corbin in order to threaten him with the knife. "You trap us in a form of cyber-hell, and the only emotion you feel is to be insulted by the fact that I could tell reality from a virtual world?"

"If you didn't know this was a VR game, you'd believe you were back in pirate days; it's just that realistic," Corbin argued.

"I'd also probably be insane."

"Granted, but you'd still think it was real. You can't imagine the countless man-hours that went into designing the environment and artistic renderings in this game."

"It's very nice, but—"

"We digitized videos of hundreds of actors and actresses," he said. "We used the same technology movie studios use."

"The people look very real—"

He stood up and spun the chair he'd been pinned to around so I could see it. "Every object in the game, every item of furniture, every building is authentic to the period."

"Yes—"

"Everything right down to the smell of lime in the privies is realistic," he all but shouted at me.

"Stop yelling at me," I yelled. "I saw the privies! They're disgusting!"

He stopped for a moment, glaring at me before speaking. "Aha! You wouldn't find them disgusting unless they struck a realistic chord with you. I rest my case."

I rolled my eyes, setting the knife down on the desk. I didn't really need it, nor had I meant to threaten his noogies with it; I was just upset on finding my sole hope of getting out of the game turn into a pipe dream. "I'm not going to argue about this. Whether or not the game is realistic—"

"It is," he said.

"—is of no matter. What does concern me is how you're going to get us out of here."

Corbin stopped looking annoyed at me and looked

thoughtful instead, half sitting on the edge of the desk. I slumped into the chair upon which I'd formerly been held prisoner, and tried very, very hard not to cry. "What I want to know is how it happened in the first place."

"Who cares how it happened. I just want out!" I wailed. "Wait—there was a storm when I logged on. Could lightning have something to do with it? I think it hit a power line near me. Maybe that zapped us into the game?"

"Lightning? Oh, the storm." He looked slightly amused. I wanted to kick him. "I'm afraid you've been watching too many sci-fi movies. The lightning couldn't have done anything to drag us into the game. It was just a coincidence."

"Then what does it matter how the game trapped us? We're stuck here. That's the important thing."

"If I knew *how* the fail-safes were corrupted, then I could get us back to reality," he pointed out.

I sniffled pathetically.

"Aw, Amy, don't cry." Corbin dropped to his knees before me, resting his hands on my legs, his pretty gray eyes all clouded with concern. "Big pirates don't cry."

"I'm not crying. I already went through that. Crying is a waste of time. Corbin, what are we going to do? What's going to happen to us? And what is happening to our bodies? Oh, dear God, I've been away from home for five days now. What happens when I have to go to the bathroom?" With each sentence my voice rose higher and higher. I hate being out of control, and the thought of my body sitting in a chair, brainless, alive but not cognizant, soaked in bodily effluences, filled me with a sharp, cutting sense of panic. "What about my daughter, Tara? She's never been left alone longer than a weekend—oh, my God, she could be in any God-knows-what sort of trouble, not to mention probably panic-stricken over my catatonic body! You've got to get me out of here!"

"First of all, calm down," he said, his hands warm on my legs.

"But I've been here for five days—"

"So have I. But it hasn't really been five days," he said in a soothing voice, his face filled with compassion. A rogue thought flitted through my mind that any other man would have told me to get a grip, but Corbin was a nice guy, and nice guys don't like to see people in pain.

"I've slept four nights," I pointed out, ignoring the rogue thought. I could think sweet, romantic things about him later, after I was out of the game.

"You only *think* you've slept," he said in that same reassuring voice. I opened my mouth to tell him I knew the difference between sleeping and not sleeping, but he continued before I could get the words out. "The human mind is remarkably easy to trick, which is why virtual reality works so well."

I forbore to point out that this program wasn't what I would call "working well."

"The VR glasses do more than just flash images at you. A transmitter is built into them that plays on sympathetic brain waves. That's how you can taste and touch and smell things here—the transmitter sends the data to your brain, interrupts the signals that tell you what your current environment is, and instead tells you that right at this moment, you're sitting on a ship docked at a tropical island."

"You're messing with my brain?" I asked, horrified. "Am I a vegetable now?"

"No, no, nothing like that. The program only interrupts signals that tell you things about your environment. Nothing more. As soon as you take the VR unit off, your brain will recognize the return to reality."

"All right," I said. It didn't sound like it made much sense, but I couldn't dispute the fact that the world I was in seemed remarkably real. "But what has that got to do with the fact that even now, my daughter is probably calling paramedics to come and revive my catatonic body?"

"The game would be unplayable if it were run in real time. People would lose interest. Ships would take weeks to sail from island to island. No one would have fun. So the software is written to give the appearance of taking place in real time, but in actuality, a day in Buckling Swashes takes about a quarter of an hour in real time, give or take a few minutes, depending on your activity level."

"A day takes fifteen minutes?" I asked, astounded.

"Yes. It's like when you dream, and you swear you've been dreaming for hours but it's really just been a few minutes or less—your brain can actually function much faster than you know. We use that fact to condense a day's activities down to a reasonable amount of time."

"But . . . I slept," I said, trying to understand how a day could be compressed down to fifteen minutes and still seem like a full day.

"You *think* you slept. The program plays on the fact that your brain learns certain truisms and expects them to apply until informed otherwise. You see nighttime fall, and your brain tells you that you feel sleepy, so you go to bed and sleep seven or eight hours. But in this world you don't really—the program tells your brain that you've slept, and you wake up feeling refreshed and ready to tackle another adventurous day sailing the Seventh Sea."

I thought about what he was saying. "You're absolutely sure?"

"Absolutely. Let's see, if you have been here for five days, that means you probably logged on around nine p.m.?"

I nodded.

"If your daughter sees you, she'll just think you're involved in the game, nothing more. Your body isn't doing

anything odd, just sitting at the computer, pretty much relaxed, as a matter of fact. We coded in some subliminal re-
laxation commands so people wouldn't get stiff sitting too
long."

I allowed myself to be mollified. "All right. I won't
worry anymore that my body is doing odd things without
me. But as for the rest—you're saying that even though I
know that I'm not here, my brain has been fooled into thinking I am?"

"Yup. Your mind is given a set of circumstances, and
based on past experience, it makes judgment calls. All the
VR unit does is take advantage of that, and gives you positive feedback that your brain is making the right choices."

"But if that's true," I said slowly, trying to think my way
through the strange new world of virtual brain napping,
"then I should be able to tell myself that none of this is real,
and get out of the game."

He smiled. "Go ahead and try it."

I did. I told myself that none of this was real, and that I
wasn't really sitting in a chair on a gently swaying boat,
teased by a fragrant salty breeze that slipped in through an
open window, adrift in a reproduction of historic Caribbean;
no, I was sitting at home in my comfy leather office chair,
hooked into a laptop, and probably starting to get stiff from
sitting still for an hour.

"Hmm," I said, looking around the cabin.

Corbin stood up. "Doesn't work, does it? That's because
of the positive reinforcement the VR unit feeds your brain."

"I just wasn't trying hard enough," I said, annoyed. No
one controlled my brain but me! "Now I'll really focus."

I marched over to the captain's bed and made myself
comfortable, or as comfortable as I could be in a lotus position. I closed my eyes. I took several deep breaths, allowing
my mind to clear itself of all the detritus that it normally

stored. I thought of blizzards and snowflakes on white sheets, and gallons and gallons of white paint. Then, when my mind was reasonably focused, I instructed it to ignore the signals coming from the VR unit, and recognize reality.

When I opened my eyes, instead of my beautiful hunter green and cream den, I was staring into the eyes of a deranged pirate.

The pirate smiled. "I'm good, huh?"

"No comment. We're stuck?"

He sat down on the bed next to me, wrapped one arm around me, and pulled me up close. "You're not going to cry, are you?"

"No. You're poking me." I squirmed uncomfortably.

"I'm nowhere near poking you, sweetheart, although you only have to say the word and I'll be happy to fulfill your every wanton desire. Unless it includes another man, a ferret, or grape jelly."

"I meant, your sword is poking me," I said, squirming to the side.

"Baby, my sword is all yours . . . oh, that sword. Sorry." He unbuckled his rapier and laid it on the bed next to him, pulling me back into his side. I thought briefly of objecting to such forward treatment, but decided, upon consideration, that I was due a little comforting. "Now, let me think about how this could have happened, and I'll see if I can't find a way to return us to normal life."

I sent him a quick glare before allowing myself to relax into his side. "You're awfully cheerful about being stuck in a virtual world."

He shrugged. "Not much sense in ranting and raving. Besides, what better world is there to be stuck in than this one?"

I let that go without comment. "What about your friend Holder?"

"He's not logged in right now."

"How did he get out if we can't?" I asked.

"I can't answer that until I know what happened," he answered, reasonably enough, I had to admit. "But I suspect that he managed to get logged off before whatever it is happened to trap us."

"Oh. Well, can't he do something to get us out? Shut down the program or something?"

"Not from within the game. It's a fail-safe to keep the VR units from overloading. The game can't shut down until all players are out. Normally we just do a manual log-off and boot people out of the game when we want to shut it down, but with us in here, there's nothing we can do."

"Crap. So how do we get a message to Holder?"

"We can't. Messaging isn't implemented in this version. It's on the list for future ones."

My shoulders slumped. "Maybe if he comes into the game, we can tell him to boot us out and shut down the game?"

Corbin shook his head. "In all probability, when Hold logs on, he'll be caught in the game just as we are. Thank God the rest of the VR crew is off at a training seminar, so they won't be trapped here as well."

"That's good, but does it help us in any way?"

"No. We can't look for help from outside the game. The answer is something here, in this world."

I closed my eyes, figuring I'd give my poor overstimulated brain a little break. Corbin could deal with the situation for a few minutes. I would just sit there and . . . man, he was warm. And he smelled good. I turned my head slightly, searching for the elusive scent that was his. I caught it again—leather and a faint lemon essence, and something vaguely musky that appealed to me despite the fact that I disliked musk.

"Hey!" I said, a couple of minutes later, the sound of my voice disturbing the rhythmic sound of waves slapping against the hull of the ship, and the oddly pleasing creak of wood as the ship gently rolled with the current. I opened my eyes and frowned at Corbin. "Does this brain thing mean that when you and I were . . . er . . ."

"Necking?" he asked with a grin.

"Breasting is more apropos," I said with a warm feeling of pleasure in my belly. "Does this mean that it was all in my mind?"

"Well . . . it was in my mind, too," he said, a touch of leer hitting his grin. "But I know what you mean, and yes, it didn't really happen. Your brain reacted to a stimulus that it knew, making you feel as if you and I had physically been together."

"I hardly know you at all," I said, a bit outraged. Did he think I was cheap to allow things to go so far so fast?

"You reacted to what I represent, not what I actually did," he said, his grin slipping a couple of notches. "Sexual stimulation is a learned experience, like all others. Your mind responded the way it had learned."

"Oh." Somehow, I felt cheated. "It sure felt real. Although I wasn't sexually stimulated. It was just . . . pleasant."

"You weren't?" he asked. "So if I do this, it doesn't turn you on?"

Without any warning whatsoever his hand slipped into my bodice, his thumb gently flicking over my nipple.

"Holy cats!" I screeched, stiffing up at the amazing feeling of his fingers on my breast. I tried to remind myself that it wasn't real but had absolutely no luck. So far as my brain was concerned, my breast was about to go up in flames of pure desire.

I'd die before I told him that, though. "No, I mean, it's

nice and all, but it takes more than a little groping to get my motor running."

"Really? How about if I . . ." His free hand slid under my skirt, up my bare thigh.

"No!" I yelled, slapping my hand down on his. "All right, I admit it, you're doing something to me, but just a little. Stop that! And take your hand out of my bodice. My boob is not bread to be kneaded."

He chuckled as he withdrew both hands. I pushed my skirt down and rearranged my breasts in my bodice (fluffing them up a bit when he wasn't looking—this might not be real, but I wasn't a fool). I couldn't help but sneak what I hoped was a covert glance at his groin.

"Yes, I'm as aroused as you are," he said, causing me to blush a little. Damn. I'd have to work on my covert glancing.

"I was just checking to make sure that you're playing fair."

"Women are such contrary creatures when it comes to sex. You parade around like scantily clad vixens but blush when you're caught staring at the erections you cause."

"I didn't stare; I glanced! There's a big difference. Besides, you're the one who created the clothes here, Mr. Pirate Expert."

"Actually, Holder did, but your point is taken. Now, if you're done trying to make me explode out of my breeches"— he ignored my outraged squawk of protest—"let me tell you what I think happened."

I pinched his leg but told him to go on.

"I told you I had a partner in the company, right?" he asked, absently rubbing his leg.

"Yeah. You said he left."

"His name was Paul Samuels. He was in charge of the VR unit and did most of the work on programming the glasses. In other words, I provided the data and program that the Internet version had created, and he translated it into VR."

"And you think he messed up somehow?"

"No," he said, turning his head so he could look into my eyes. "I think this was deliberate. I think he set up a sort of virtual virus to trap players here."

"For what purpose?"

He shook his head. "I don't know that yet. But I do know that, unlike me, Paul must have had the foresight to program in a back door he could use to access the game, because we changed all the security codes after he left us. He couldn't access it by normal means, which means he must have another way in."

"If he has a way in, can we use it to get out?"

"I don't know. I doubt it, though," he said.

Frustration mingled with panic deep within me, leaving me with a sick feeling in my stomach. "So, what are we going to do?"

His eyes, normally so warm, suddenly went chilly. "We're going to find Paul."

"Find him?" My jaw dropped a little before I realized what it was doing. "You think he's in the game? Right now? Who is he? Where is he?"

"I'm positive he's here, although I don't know who his character is, or where he's hiding," Corbin said, his voice as grim as his eyes.

"And after we find him? What then? How do we make him stop the virus or whatever it is that's keeping us here?"

He slid off the bed, strapping the rapier to his hips. "The only way to stop a virus is to kill it."

"So?" I asked, jumping to my feet to grab my own foil. Even though I knew this was all a virtual world, it made me feel much better to have the cold steel next to me.

He paused in the doorway of the cabin, throwing me a dark look. "We kill Paul, we kill the virus. It's as simple as that."

Simple, my butt!

Chapter 9

I do not think I ought to listen to you.
Yet, mercy should alloy our stern resentment. . . .

—Ibid, Act II

"What's going on?" I asked, bolting up the narrow stairs to the deck as the ship took on the gentle rolling motion that instantly had my stomach protesting.

"We're leaving," Corbin answered, his back to me as he directed his crew. I watched for a moment, envious at the precision with which the six crewmates performed their duties. My crew always had to be nagged into doing anything.

"Leaving? As in, leaving the island? Sailing?"

"Since I didn't write in a teleportation function, yes, leaving in this instance means sailing. We're heading for Mongoose, the island we port at."

"But that means we'll be heading out into the open sea," I said, watching as we approached the silvery black rocks that guarded the harbor like dark, foreboding sentinels. The moon was waxing full, the night skies a dark, velvety indigo sprinkled with glittering stars. I tried reminding myself that none of it was real, that the night sky, beautiful and serene, wasn't really there, but ended up deciding with a mental shrug that so long as I was there, I'd enjoy the beauty of the surroundings. Corbin and Holder had clearly gone to an enormous amount of work creating the visual aspects of the world. Who was I to discount them?

"Aye. Do you have a problem with that?"

"Several, the most pressing of which at the moment is that I get seasick," I told him. He turned to cock a questioning brow at me. "Really seasick. Like ralphing my guts up the entire time."

"Ah." He frowned for a second, then whipped off the navy blue bandana that had been carelessly knotted around his neck. He slapped the pockets on his jerkin a few times, pulling out a small black object, which he held up to show me.

"Is that a pearl?"

"Aye. Black pearl. Very rare. Don't lose it, please."

"Huh?"

Before I could ask what he thought I was going to do with a rare pearl, he tied his bandana around my wrist, tightly, but not tightly enough to hurt or cut off circulation.

"Have you ever heard of seasick bands?"

"Nope, not unless you're talking about musicians on board an ocean liner."

"Not quite. Seasick bands use acupressure to stimulate the Nei-Kuan pressure point on your wrist," he said, slipping the pearl between the bandana and my flesh. "It stops nausea."

"A pearl strapped to my wrist is going to keep me from being seasick?" I asked, more than a little disbelief rife in my voice.

He grinned. "It works, I swear. I was sick as a dog the first few trips I tried until Holder suggested seasick bands. What were your other issues?"

"Well, for one, it's this whole kidnapping thing. You've been reading one too many pirate novels, Corbin. I don't want to be swept away with you to your island paradise. I'm right in the middle of learning how to sail my sloop well, not to mention the wonderful retirement fund I've started for the ladies at Renata's house—honestly, you would not believe the lax sort of record keeping that goes on there, and the wasted profits, oh, God, the wasted profits!—and then there's Bas. I think I have Renata and her ladies close to set, but I've got to get Bas situated so that when we do find a way out of here, he's taken care of. I'm thinking some sort of a trust fund might be in order if I can round up a couple of responsible administrators and a guardian . . ."

Corbin laughed and sat down beside me on an overturned bucket. I had hoisted myself onto the capstan, a large vertical cyndrical winch, and sat with my feet dangling. Despite the situation I found myself in, I was enjoying the soft tropical evening breeze as the ship slid slowly out of the sheltered harbor. "Have you always arranged people's lives like that?"

"Like what?" I asked, bristling a little.

"Like what you're doing—taking over their lives and arranging things for them. You know, organizing them."

"You say organizing like it's a bad thing," I said slowly, frowning down at him. He'd taken off his captain's hat, the moonlight doing wonderful things to the planes of his face that left me wanting to grab his head and kiss the smile right off his lips.

"Of course it's not; not when it's kept in control. But you seem to be bent on organizing everything and everyone within your reach. This is a game, Amy. You're supposed to relax and enjoy yourself."

The urge to kiss him didn't dissipate, as I imagined it

would under such an attack, but it was joined with the mild desire to throttle him.

"I am enjoying myself. So I like organizing things, so what? Everyone benefits, so I don't see where the problem lies."

His hand slid up the bare calf of my leg in an act so startlingly intimate that I was left momentarily speechless. "The problem is that you're supposed to be a pirate—carefree, wild, and heedless, not organizing people's lives and setting up eighteenth-century versions of 401(k) plans."

"Renata and her ladies are going to be rich within a few months, just you wait and see," I predicted. "I have an investment plan going with my daughter's weavery and a tailor shop that should have them off their backs and onto their feet in next to no time."

He laughed again and shook his head, his hand warm on my flesh as he stroked my calf. "You're bringing too much real life to the game, Amy. This is your opportunity to let all those cares and worries go and indulge in your wildest fantasies." He gave me a quick leer. "And I do mean *all* your wildest fantasies."

"You need brain shampoo," I joked, unable to stop myself from reaching out and twining one of his chocolatey brown curls around my finger. "Why do I get the idea that you play all day and never work?"

"All work and no play makes Corbin a very dull boy. As it is, I have the best of both worlds—my work is play. But you . . . you're a different animal altogether. Where's the dashing, wild pirate I know you have inside you, Amy? Where's your sense of adventure? What happened to your inner child?"

"I think she left me a long time ago," I said slowly, mulling over his lightly spoken words. Sitting there on the capstan, Corbin at my side, the wind rustling past us as the ship creaked and muttered a distant song that was starting to seep deep into my bones, I took a good long look at what he was saying and felt a sense of profound sadness when I realized what was lacking in me. "And as for Dread Pirate Amy . . . I don't know that she'll ever exist. I just don't think I'm cut out for the wild, dashing life. I enjoyed beating that merchant in a sword fight, but I just don't think I'm going to be a successful pirate."

"Sure you are," Corbin said, standing up and hauling me to my feet. "You just need a few lessons on how to let go of your . . . er . . . rigidity."

My hackles rose a little at that. "I'm not rigid; I'm organized. There's a difference. In fact, I'm positively flexible, I'm so nonrigid. Flexibly organized, that's me."

"You're not rigid, eh?" he asked. "Prove it."

"What?"

Corbin stood with his feet spread wide, his body swaying with the motion of the ship as we hit open water. I waited for the wave of nausea to hit me, but miraculously, the seasick band seemed to be working.

"I said prove that you're not rigid. Look, even the way you're standing is rigid. Loosen up. Move with the ship; don't fight her roll. Loosen your knees and hips a little, and go with, rather than against, the rhythm of the ship."

I mimicked his pose, adding a hands-on-my-hips touch that I hoped would speak volumes. "See? I'm *so* not rigid."

"You've still to prove it," he said with a grin.

"I don't have to prove anything." I glared at him for a moment or two, then added, "How exactly am I supposed to prove it?"

His grin got bigger. "Kiss me."

My jaw dropped open a little as I gawked at him. "You're out of your mind."

"You like me, don't you?"

"Yes, but—"

"You liked it when we kissed before."

"Yes, but—"

"And you liked the other things, too. I could tell you did."

"That has nothing to do with—"

"You said you wanted to date me."

"That could easily change," I growled, tired of being interrupted.

"Then kiss me. Prove to me that you're not so rigid that you can't let go once in a while."

"We're not alone. There are people around," I hissed, glancing around us. Aft, a couple of men had their backs to us as they coiled ropes, while fore, one of Corbin's crew was taking sounding readings. Below decks Leeward Tom, Barn, and Bas had gone to rustle up some dinner, but they could pop up at any moment.

"So?"

"So, I don't intend on putting on a bawdy show for your men and my cabin boy."

"No sense of adventure," he said sadly, shaking his head. "And here I thought I had a gutsy wench, an audacious, bold woman who sneered at adversity and who would never back down from a challenge when it was presented to her—"

I had a quick look around to make sure no one was looking our way; then I flung myself on him, digging my fingers into his hair as I smashed my mouth against his, my body instinctively rubbing itself against him as I kissed him with everything I had, and boy, all of a sudden did I have a lot.

"Do you always hum when you kiss?" Corbin asked my tongue, which had pretty much gone to his mouth for a sleepover.

"Hmm?"

"You're humming."

I retrieved my tongue and pulled back enough so I could see him without my eyes crossing. "I am?"

"You were."

"Oh. I thought I was just making happy noises."

He pulled me up close to him and brushed little butterfly kisses around the corners of my mouth. "You did it before, too. I don't mind it; it's nice, but I just wondered."

"Have I proven to you the unplumbed depths of my audacity, braveness, and inherent dashing abilities?"

"Not yet. Kiss me some more, and then we'll see."

Normally, I dislike being given orders, but this once I let it go and kissed him until his teeth rattled. I was just getting into it, adding a little hip action against him that had *him* humming, when a soft popping noise, followed by a bemused chuckle, ruined everything.

"Splice the main brace! Looks like things have progressed nicely while I've been away. Quick work, Corb. Are congratulations in order? Am I allowed to kiss the bride? Or perhaps things haven't gotten quite that far. Have I mentioned that I'm an ordained minister in an Internet-based religion? It's legal for me to marry couples in thirty-five states, you know. Including California."

"Ack!" I yelped, jumping back from Corbin, my cheeks firing up with a blush at the thought of someone witnessing us going at it. It was one thing to kiss him in front of a computer character that wouldn't think anything of it, but another thing when there was a real live audience watching.

"Oh, Holder, no, not you," Corbin groaned, rubbing his forehead as if he had a headache.

"Bad timing, eh? My apologies, lass. If *someone* had left me a note telling me not to jump on the ship, I wouldn't have disturbed you two—"

"Do you still have the virtual reality unit on?" I interrupted, feeling my rudeness could be explained away if he could just get us out of there. "Can you log off?"

"It's too late," Corbin said, shaking his head.

"Maybe not. Maybe we can still get out. Maybe there's time," I told him.

He shook his head again. "I know how Paul thinks. The trap would have snapped shut the instant the log-in was complete."

"What trap? What does Paul have to do with anything? What are you guys talking about?"

"Can you leave?" I asked.

Holder looked mildly insulted. "I apologized already—"

"What Amy wants to know is if you can log off. I can tell her the answer, though."

"You two have been dippin' into the rum keg, haven't you?" Holder reached up to his temple. "Since it's obvious three's company here, I'll be on my . . . hmm."

The hope for escape, which had flared for a moment or two, died a sad, lonely death.

"What's going on here, Corb?" Holder asked, his fingers dancing around either side of his head in a fruitless search for the virtual reality glasses.

"You're trapped here the same as we are. I'm almost completely certain that Paul has launched an entrapment module to lock players into the game. And I was about to seduce Amy, which, going by the look she's giving me, is now off," Corbin said.

"I've said I'm sorry about the interruption, but I had no way of knowing. Entrapment mod, eh? Bit beyond my range of expertise, but I suppose it's possible. That does, however, bring one question to mind," Holder said, looking thoughtful.

"How are we going to get out?" I said, nodding.

"What sort of code did he use to trap us, and can we break it?" Corbin suggested.

"Why," Holder said simply. Both Corbin and I stared at him. He made a little grimace. "Why would he want to go to all the time and effort to write a mod like this? There's got to be a purpose behind it, right?"

"I never thought of asking why," I said slowly, glancing at Corbin. He shook his head.

"Neither did I, although it does lead to some interesting speculation," he said thoughtfully.

"Cap'n? We be on the leeward side of the island," Bald Bob called down from the crow's nest. "Be we puttin' in to shore?"

"Aye." Corbin glanced at me, taking one of my hands in his. "I had thought of just whisking you away to my island paradise where I could ply you with fruity tropical drinks and seduce you in my own good time, but somehow, I don't think you'll let me do that."

I gave his fingers a little squeeze before releasing his hand. "You're learning quickly, Corbin. Tempted as I am by the thought of getting to know you better in a tropical paradise, I'd like off, if you don't mind. I've got lots of things to do here, so I think Bas and I had better be on our way. What can I do to help find this Paul person?"

Corbin frowned. "Damn, I wish I hadn't yanked that admin panel out. Now we're going to have to do this the hard way."

"Which is?" I asked.

"Paul'll probably be doing his best to blend in, appearing as much like a computer character as he can. I'd suggest you talk to people, Amy. Talk to as many townspeople as you can. The more he talks, the more likely he will be to slip up."

"That makes sense. I've met a lot of people here, and I

will definitely chat up everyone I can, but surely there're more people in the game than are on this island?"

"There will be in the release version, but for the beta testing, only Turtle's Back and Mongoose are inhabited."

"Corb and I will check everyone on Mongoose," Holder said, his normally jovial face taking on a hard glint.

"Yes, we will. There are fewer people on Turtle, so if you can make a point of talking to them all, we should be able to sniff Paul out."

"There's nothing else we can do to find him?" I asked Corbin, frustrated at the lack of solutions facing us.

"I wish there was, but without that admin panel, we're more or less blind. Talking to everyone is the only way, unless Paul decides to show himself, which is highly unlikely."

"Aye, he's a clever one," Holder added. "I wouldn't be surprised if he turns out to be the person no one notices, the quiet, unassuming one apparently going about his daily business without bothering anyone."

"He well could be," Corbin agreed.

"Luckily, most of the men come to Renata's house," I said thoughtfully. "It shouldn't be too difficult for me to talk to all of them, quiet ones included."

"He might not be a man in the game," Corbin said. My eyebrows did a surprised little swoop upward. "He might decide that hiding out as a woman is safer than being a man. So talk to the women, too."

A little chill went down my back despite the balmy evening breeze. What if Corbin's ex-partner was one of the women in Renata's house?

"All right. I'll drop everything to talk to every single person on Turtle's Back."

"Well . . . it may not be the best idea to drop everything," Corbin said slowly, rubbing his bristly jaw.

"We want to get out of the game," I pointed out.

"Yes, we do, but Paul is clever. Really clever, Amy—I've known him for a long time. If the three of us make it obvious that we're hunting for him, or know that he's behind the entrapment, then he's going to make it harder for us to find him."

"Ahhh," Holder said, enlightenment dawning in his eyes. "I get you. And it wouldn't surprise me to know he had a contingency plan in case he finds out that we know what he's up to."

"Aye, it wouldn't surprise me, either."

I frowned a little at Corbin. "So, you're saying we have to keep playing the game in order to not let on to him that we know he's behind it all?"

"I think it would be best," Corbin said. Holder nodded his agreement. "Paul will know sooner or later that we're savvy to his plans, but I'd prefer it be later than sooner. Besides, he may well have a scenario running."

Holder groaned.

"A scenario?" I asked. "What's that?"

"A series of events that have to happen in order for the storyline to advance. Our game scenarios are all reward-based, which means if you succeed at a task or event, or even level of experience, you are rewarded by some means. The act of you succeeding pushes the scenario along. We're working on tutorial scenarios now, but Paul was hard at work on advanced game-play ones when he left." Corbin looked very serious, driving home just how helpless we were.

"Then we have to do this scenario thing that Paul set up in order to . . . do what?"

"Get to whatever point he has set as the goal of the scenario. And knowing him"—Corbin shot a significant glance at Holder—"I assume that has him triumphing over us in some way. If we haven't found him by that time, I'm almost a hundred percent certain he'll take that opportunity to reveal himself."

I made a face. I didn't like the sound of that. "Man alive. So we go on playing the game and talking to everyone in hopes we find him before that time?"

"Unless someone has a better plan?" He looked at me and Holder. We both shook our heads. "Then that's the game plan. Ha. No pun intended. Are you ready to leave?"

"Oh, yes, please."

Corbin gave his men the order to put in to shore, and without further ado, carried me to shore in the waist-high water so I wouldn't get wet.

I melted a bit at that gesture, I don't mind admitting.

"If you follow that path through the trees, you'll come to the high point of the island," he said after setting me down on a small crescent of white sandy beach enclosed by a thick stand of trees. Although the moonlight was bright, he handed both me and Bas oil lanterns.

"Do you know the path, lad?" he asked Bas.

The boy looked almost cheerful as he considered the dark, uninhabited side of the island. "Aye. I've come this way afore, lookin' for owls."

"Owls?" I couldn't help but ask.

"Aye. They be right bad omens. To see an owl is to see yer own death," he said with a ghoulish glint in his eye.

I looked at Corbin.

"What?" he asked. "I can't help it if the kid has a fascination with death."

"You programmed him! You'd just better program up a child psychologist when we get out of the game," I warned, then waved at where Holder and the rest of Corbin's crew stood clustered at the rail of his ship.

"Don't forget to kiss her!" Holder bellowed, cupping his hands around his mouth.

"Oh, for God's sake . . . *shut up!*" Corbin yelled back.

I giggled. Bas rolled his eyes and stared up the dirt path, Bran the raven squawking as he ducked low beneath a branch.

"I apologize for Holder," Corbin said, looking embarrassed. "If he wasn't my oldest and closest friend, I'd kill him."

I laughed and leaned forward, brushing my lips against his. "I don't remember the last time I saw a man blush by moonlight. It's very romantic. Almost romantic enough to turn my financial analyst's soul to thoughts of a more carnal nature. Thank you, Corbin."

It was his eyebrows' turn to look surprised. "For what? Creating the vehicle that would leave you helpless in a world you want to escape?"

I rubbed the tip of my nose against his. "For making me play. I think you and Tara may be on to something. Let me know if you find your ex-partner."

His jaw went tight. "I will."

"Good."

I started to turn away but stopped when he said, "Oh, Amy?"

He was on me before I could ask what he wanted, his mouth hot and demanding, and I didn't for a moment think of protesting the arrogant gesture; I just melted into him and enjoyed the most blatantly sexual, erotic kiss it had ever been my pleasure to receive. When he was done, I stood breathless, staring in wonder at his lips, my mind stripped completely clean of all thoughts but how I enjoyed the kiss . . . and how much I wanted another one.

"Just a little something to remember me by," he said,

gently turning me toward the path and giving me a swat on the behind.

"Somehow, I don't think remembering him is going to be a problem," I muttered to myself as I watched him wade out to the ship. "No, the problem is what I'm going to do to stop thinking about him long enough to do my job."

Chapter 10

Oh, here is love, and here is truth,
And here is food for joyous laughter. . . .

—Ibid, Act II

I was in the square the following afternoon—trying not to notice how the gleaming blade of a newly crafted sword hanging in the open doorway at the blacksmith's shop looked just like Corbin's eyes when he was kissing me— when an odd figure skulked into view. The man was dressed in a ragged collection of ill-fitting garments: yellow striped knickers, rags strapped to his feet in lieu of shoes, and a long, knee-length red jacket tied around the waist by a dingy white sash. But it was the battered green tricorn hat, the eye patch, and what looked like a poorly stuffed green and blue parrot attached to the shoulder that caused pretty much everyone in the square to stop talking and stare at the bizarre sight.

"What in the Seventh Sea is that, do you suppose?" Sly Jez asked me as the man suddenly adopted a hunched-over stance, skirting the crowd with strange, unintelligible noises. "Is it a leper?"

The man stopped in the shadowed doorway of an empty building and twitched a couple of times.

"I have no idea. Is there an insane asylum around here? He definitely looks unbalanced," I said, unable to take my eyes off the apparition.

"Bedlam, ye mean? Nay, that be on Mongoose Island."

"Hmm." I turned back to the ladies gathered around the well that sat in the center of the square. It was the pirate version of the water cooler, and I found to my delight that almost all the women of the town visited at the well at some time or other during the day.

I had spent the remainder of the night before distracting myself from thoughts of Corbin and his extremely talented lips by coming up with a plan of action for grilling the citizens of Turtle's Back, and had struck what I thought was an excellent idea. Conversation with the ladies of the house had proven that the computer characters, while fully formed in almost all ways and possessed of unique artificial intelligence, had one major fault—they had no past. If I asked one of them what she had been doing a week before, she could tell me in great detail, but when I asked about events in the distant past, all I got was a blank stare and a shrug of indifference.

All I had to do was interview the citizens of the island, gently probing for a past, and eliminate those people who didn't fit the profile of human players.

"That boil remedy is very helpful, I'm sure," I told one of the women who had been telling me about the affliction her husband, one of Bart's crewmen, suffered from. "But how long has your husband been cursed with the boils?"

The woman looked mildly confused. "Eh. Been a long time, now."

"Amy? I think the leper is trying to get your attention."

"Hmm?" I glanced over to where Jez was pointing. The

leper/madman was doing a deranged sort of twitching dance. I'd seen enough mentally disturbed people huddled on the streets to know that he was probably happier on his own, but made a mental note as I turned back to the woman in front of me to locate the head of the island's watch and have the man evaluated for his own safety. "I don't think he wants me, Jez. It's probably Saint Vitus's dance or the bubonic plague or malaria or something like that. I'm sorry to be so nosy, Ruthful, but how long is a long time? Weeks? Months? Years?"

The woman blinked at me, her face devoid of emotion, something else I'd noticed happened to the computer characters when they were faced with something their programming didn't know how to handle.

"Amy, I really think he's trying to get your attention," Jez said, tugging on my sleeve, her face concerned as she watched the madman. He seemed to be struck with some sort of palsy now, his head twitching to the side in a manner that had to leave him with a kink in his neck.

"Ignore him," I told her quietly. "I don't normally approve of pretending the less fortunate aren't there, but there are some times when direct attention only exacerbates the situation. I'll make sure someone takes care of him later."

I turned a bright smile on the woman next to the wife of the boil man, waggling my fingers at an adorable small child resting on her hip. "What a sweet little girl! She looks a lot like my daughter when she was about two. When is your girl's birthday?"

The woman's face went blank. Scraaaaaatch. Another person off my potential villain list.

"Amy?"

"What?"

A shrill whistle pierced the happy chatter of the women at the well. Everyone in the square came to a stop to stare at the lunatic as he stood with his hands on his hips. As I frowned at him, he lifted up the eye patch to glare at me, then beckoned me with an imperious gesture.

The ladies at the well all looked at me. I gave them a tight smile. "Excuse me a moment, please. I'll be right back to talk some more about . . . er . . . your earliest childhood memories."

Seven faces went utterly expressionless. Seven pairs of eyes blinked stupidly. I sighed to myself, crossed them all off my list, and went over to where the deranged man was waiting none too patiently.

"It's about time," he hissed at me in vaguely familiar tones, then said in a loud voice that was probably audible up the hill at Bart's house, "Be ye friend or be ye foe? I'm Mad Jack, I am, and I come from the country of the potato people!"

"Mad Jack?" I asked, squinting at the man.

"Good disguise, eh?" The man lifted the eye patch again, and two blue eyes twinkled their enjoyment at me. "I come bearing messages from . . . well, Corbin's Irish, actually, not Greek, but we won't hold that against him, will we?"

"Holder, what are you doing in those awful clothes? Why are you in disguise? What are you doing here? And what was with the dog and pony show? I thought you were a mentally deficient pirate street person."

"Bart's men are back from their foraging trip. If they caught me, they'd hang me. Hence the necessity of bringing out old Mad Jack, island idiot." He grinned, clearly not too upset at the thought of being within reach of Bart. "As for what I'm doing here, his majesty commanded I bring you a message. Just think of me as the virtual pirate version of instant messaging. I'm duly authorized to hang around and wait for you to write up a reply, even."

"Oooh, a note from Corbin?" I asked, watching avidly as

he dug in the pockets of his jacket. "Did you guys find Paul?"

"Nay, not yet. But we're looking. Ah, here it is." He paused for a moment, giving me a smile filled with all sorts of speculation. "I've known Corbin all my life, you know."

"Have you?" I asked, trying to snatch the piece of folded parchment from his fingers. He held tight.

"Aye. Known him since we were two. We lived next door to each other growing up. He's a nice guy. Solid, dependable, no major bad vices, although he has been known to put ketchup on his scrambled eggs, which we all know is a sin against nature, but other than that, he's primo, grade A marriage material."

"Marriage," I said, startled by the blunt matchmaking. Holder released the parchment, which I noticed had been sealed with a big blob of red wax.

"Did Corb tell you about the in-game marriage feature? We anticipate it will be a big success. It allows players to have access to the items in the spouse's inventory—ship deeds, money, jewels, etcetera. Very handy thing, all things considered, and in no way binding in the real world"—he paused for a quick grin—"unless you want it to be binding, of course."

I smiled, touched by Holder's devotion to his friend and despite the ludicrous nature of the conversation. I wasn't against marriage, but I certainly wasn't going to commit myself to a man I'd known for just a few days . . . or hours, as it was in real time. "Thank you for the sales pitch, but it's not really necessary. For one thing, I already like Corbin, and for another, I don't need his money or his ships or whatever else he may have in his inventory."

"You may change your mind about that once the blockade strikes and there are no supplies coming in or out of Turtle's Back," he answered.

"Blockade? What blockade? What exactly *is* a blockade?"

Holder's grin slid a couple of notches as he glanced over my shoulder. I turned to see what had disturbed his cocky attitude. A group of four men I recognized as Bart's crewmen swaggered into the square, making rude comments about the women gathered at the well, snatching wares off the fruit vendor's cart, and generally behaving in the age-old manner of men.

"Thank you for . . . oh." I turned back to tell Holder how much I appreciated his bringing the note from Corbin, but he had disappeared into the crowd. I couldn't blame him—I knew enough from the limited association I'd had with my new crewmates to know they were a rowdy bunch, and not at all the sort of men I'd like to cross.

I was in the process of carefully breaking the wax seal on the letter from Corbin when a shout had me stuffing the note in a pocket in my striped knickers.

"Ahoy, lass," one of Bart's men shouted as he caught sight of me, waving an ill-gotten, half-eaten apple at me. "The captain sent us to fetch ye back. He's wantin' to have a talk with ye."

"Hoy, guys. Oh. Bart wants to see me right now? Er . . . Ben, isn't it?"

"Bent Ben, aye," the pirate said with a lascivious leer that left me wanting a bath and a strong scrub brush.

"Ask him what's bent," his mate hinted.

"Er . . . thanks; perhaps another time," I said with what I hoped was a smile that was crewmatelike and yet didn't encourage confidences of an intimate nature. "Um . . . I can't help but notice the pockmarks on your face, Ben. Did you have chicken pox as a child?"

Ben just looked at me. I heaved a mental sigh and turned to his two companions. "How about the two of you? Did you have chicken pox when you were little boys? Say, when you were about five or six?"

Two pairs of expressionless eyes gazed at me.

"Right, I think that just about answers that question. I'll go see Bart now."

Life returned to all three men's faces as I spoke. I started up the hill toward the governor's house, pausing briefly when one of the men made a comment about my stripy knickers. Or rather, the contents of the stripy knickers.

"Ham in a cloth sack, my as . . . er . . . bah," I grumbled to myself as I marched along. I waited until I was past the tiny church that sat at the edge of town, then ducked behind the back of the church to the small cemetery to read Corbin's note. He must have had something of importance to say if he went to all the trouble of sending his first mate with it. I perched on the edge of a crumbling headstone, making a quick apology to the stone's owner before opening the parchment and spreading it out.

Dear Amy, the note read, written in a bold hand in indigo ink. I had a brief moment of warm fuzziness over the word *dear,* then decided I had been without a man for way, way too long and I needed to move on before I started indulging in the same sorts of fantasies that had kept me up half the night.

Dear Amy . . .

"Do ye like to come here, too, then? Bran and me, we likes it here." Bas's silhouette blocked the sun, the long black fingers of his shadow spilling across the parchment. The boy had cleaned up remarkably well, considering what there was to work with. He had been scrubbed clean (within an inch of his life, to his way of thinking), his hair had been trimmed, and he'd been given new clothing, faded and worn, but serviceable, and most of all, clean. Even Bran the raven—who had also received a bath to rid him of suspected lice and other parasites—looked less like something out of an opium-muddled Poe poem, and more like a proper bird. "We likes to talk to the dead people. Are ye here talkin' to 'em, too?"

"Eh . . ." I tried to formulate a rule against speaking to dead people, but after a moment of consideration, I decided it was a relatively harmless pastime. "No, I'm not here to talk to dead people. I have a note I want to read."

He nodded. Bran squawked and bobbed his head in a nod, too. "Captain Bart's men be lookin' for ye."

"Thanks, I've already chatted with them."

"Ah," he said, his head tipped to the side as he watched me like I was about to stand up and start tap-dancing. "I polished me hook."

I admired the rusty iron implement that had been crudely attached to a leather strap he wore bound around the remains of his arm, and made another note to myself to have a talk with the blacksmith about crafting the boy something a little more serviceable. "So you did. Um . . . Bas, I don't want to bring up a painful subject, but how exactly did you lose your arm?"

His face went blank. I hadn't really thought he was Paul, but he had remembered his mother's death, so I had to consider him.

"That's okay; don't worry about it. Off you go, then."

"Wot?"

"Go talk to dead people."

"Aye, aye," he said, animation returning to his face as he flashed a smile at me. He and Bran walked off to the other side of the cemetery, pausing to talk to the headstones, looking like nothing so much as a miniature grim reaper and his pet raven.

Dear Amy . . .

"There ye be. Whew! I've just come up from the fishmonger's. 'Tis not a place for anyone with a workin' nose on a day as hot as today," Renata said as she plopped herself down on a headstone a few feet to my left. The tail of some newly deceased fish protruded from the covered basket she set at her feet. "But I got us a nice bit of mackerel for our supper. I do like a taste of mackerel pie now and again."

"Sounds . . . delicious. Did you barter the elderberry wine for the fish, as I suggested?"

"Aye, that I did," she said brightly, looking pleased with herself. "And a right good idea it was. Mr. Thomkins was that pleased to have the wine, and he gave me first choice of fish, somethin' he hasn't done afore."

"Excellent. Since you make that wine at little cost but your time, it makes sense to use it to acquire more valuable commodities. I have some ideas for further cottage industry projects that will provide you with even more creature comforts, but we'll leave that talk for the next budget review."

"Aye," she said, her eyes suddenly not meeting mine. "Are we to be havin' another of them budget reviews soon?"

"I told you—weekly until we get a nice nest egg to pad the lean months, then we'll go to a bimonthly system."

I could have sworn she crossed herself, but the sun was in my eyes, so I couldn't be sure. "I have a nice profit-and-loss graph I want to draw up for you ladies to study at the next meeting," I added.

"What's that ye have yerself there?" she asked quickly.

I looked down at the still-unread parchment on my knees. "It's an IM," I said without batting an eyelash.

"A what now?"

"An instant message, although I suppose the instancy of it could be debated."

"Ah. Is it? Well, then, ye'd best be answerin' it, hadn't ye? If it's instant and all." She heaved herself to her feet, hand on her back as she straightened up. "I'll be on me way home. Will we be seein' ye for dinner, or just supper?"

"Supper only, I think. I'll have lunch with Bart, or do a bit of inventorying at the fruit stall for a few things."

She nodded and scurried off before I could say anything else, which was just fine with me. I took a quick look around to make sure no one else was lurking in the wings, then ran my eyes over the letter quickly.

Dear Amy,

It goes without saying that I hope this note finds you hale and hearty, not to mention deliciously pink and nibbleworthy, especially those delectable breasts of yours, which, I would like to point out with no little complaint, haunted my thoughts all night long. I never should have let you go. Holder lectured me the entire way to Mongoose about the proper way a pirate behaves toward his woman, but despite me pointing out that you weren't, as yet, my woman, he didn't listen to me.

I spent the night dreaming about you. I spent the morning wishing you were here, so I could talk to you. Well, all right, I also spent both the night and the morning fantasizing about what I'd like to do to you at a private little cove I know of, but I'm going to take the high ground here so you don't think I want you just for that lush body that haunts my every waking (and sleeping) thought. No, no, I want you for your mind, too. I like your mind. It's a nice mind. Full of wit and character and interesting thoughts I'd like to get to know more.

I don't suppose you spent the night pining for my strong, manly arms? Sigh. A man can hope. Speaking of me, would you marry me?

Was that a shriek you just uttered? I suspect it was, because although I don't know that witty, interesting mind of yours really well, I'm pretty sure you're even now sitting and shaking your head, cursing me and all men, etc. Before you get your panties in a bunch . . . wait, I need a moment to savor that visual image . . . before you come right out and turn me down, thereby breaking my heart and associated internal organs, I'd like to mention a couple of things that might make you think twice:

1. *A marriage in the game is not a legally binding device anywhere in the real world. It's actually a mechanism by which we allow two characters to pool resources. Nothing more. Well, you could make more of it if you wanted, but I'll leave that totally up to you. Although I reserve the right to dwell with much fondness on thoughts of a wedding night.*

2. *Why do you need pooled resources? If you insist on staying on Turtle's Back, which you give every evidence of doing, you're going to need both money and supplies very soon. The island is about to be blockaded, which means no ships will be allowed in or out of the harbor, and since Bart relies heavily on weekly trips to nearby islands to forage for food and supplies, life is about to become very hard for citizens there. I can't stop the blockade, but if you were my wife, even in name only, you would be able to access the supplies on the blockade ships so that you would suffer no undue hardship.*

3. *Er . . . I guess there is no real third item other than if you married me, we'd be able to continue*

those activities we started on my ship. Yes, we could continue them regardless (and I'd be happy to—just say the word), but Holder is dying to marry someone in the game, and if you don't say yes, I'm afraid I'm going to have to marry a sheep or something just so he'll stop nagging me. So, I guess pity is the third item. Save me from a sheep bride!

Please let me know what you think, and what you're doing, and how you are, and how many times you thought about me resuscitating your breast, and whether or not the other one has forgiven me for not getting around to it. I'll be waiting as patiently as I can for your reply.
Regards,
Corbin

Chapter 11

Go, ye heroes, go to glory,
Though you die in combat gory,
Ye shall live in song and story.

—Ibid, Act II

"Ahoy, lass," Bart said as one of his ruffian pirates opened the door for me to enter the library. Standing around the room were Pangloss and four other men I didn't recognize, but all of them wore the air of men who spent more time at sea than onshore.

"Hoy, Bart," I said politely, giving Pangloss a little wave. "I understand that you wanted to see me?"

"Aye, we're havin' a council of war, and since Pangloss tells me ye be right at home on yer ship, I've decided to temporarily overlook the fact that ye haven't yet fulfilled yer duties to the crew, and include ye in the council of war."

"War?" I wasn't about to touch his reference to my supposed assassination of Corbin. Bart could hold his breath until he was blue—it wasn't going to happen. "What sort of war? The kind with guns and cannons and blood and people dying? That sort of war? Or a virtual pretend war where no one really gets hurt?"

The men all stared at me like I had toadstools sprouting from the top of my head. I sighed and scratched them all off my Potential Paul list. "Right. The bloody kind."

"All war is bloody, lass," Pangloss said grimly, and I knew he was thinking about the brother he'd lost in Corbin's raid on the island. Despite knowing that none of the men who died were real, I was having more and more trouble separating my emotions for the people I met here from the emotions I had for the people I knew in real life. I couldn't help but feel sorry for the survivors and made a mental note to have a talk with Corbin about the hostilities between him and Bart. A game with pirates was one thing, but when they started killing people . . . well, that was something else entirely.

"Aye, and this one will likely be especially bloody," Bart agreed. He hurried through introductions of the four officers, all of whom leered at me in the best pirate style before passing around a bottle of rum. I declined the rum, slumping into the chair Bart offered me and watching as he unrolled a map on the surface of a lovely rosewood desk. "'Tis come to me ears that Black Corbin allied his crew with the Jolie Rouge."

The four officers sucked in startled breaths. I leaned sideways a little and whispered a question to Pangloss.

"They be a powerful crew from the French Indies," he answered softly. "Dangerous, deadly, and 'tis said their captain has made a pact with Beelzebub himself to rule all of the islands in the Seventh Sea."

"Great, just what we need . . . another bloodthirsty, land-hungry pirate," I grumbled.

"It may be just a rumor, since none of Henri Massant's men have been sighted on Mongoose, but knowin' that devil

Corbin"—Bart paused long enough to shoot me a look filled with unspoken criticism, no doubt for the fact that Corbin was still alive; I made a face at him—"I'll not be discountin' it. So we've to prepare for an all-out blockade, mates."

"What about Conard over on Ellipse?" one of the officers asked. "He's an ally, ain't he?"

Bart shook his head. "He's by way of havin' his own hands full with the Spanish attackin' Ellipse. We'll see no help from Conard. We're alone in this, lads. I won't lie to ye and say it hasn't come at a bad time, but we'll pull through it so long as we can hold the harbor."

"We've the new guns," Pangloss said, frowning.

"The thirty-two-pound guns, aye, but they're not in place yet. If the devil attacks us afore the guns are secured, we'll be left to rely on the sixteen-pounders."

The men looked somber. I wanted to ask about the cannons but figured I was there on forbearance and had better keep my mouth shut until I knew what was going on.

Then I'd step in and organize things if their plans weren't feasible.

"There be four guns on the leeward side of the island, just atop Careenin' Cove, in case Black Corbin is up to his old tricks," Bart continued. "We'll divide our forces between that spot and the harbor. I'll command the defensive land force. As for ships . . . Pangloss will be in charge of that. Ye'll be responsible for battlin' the blockade ships as best ye can, and keepin' them from enterin' the harbor."

My eyes widened, but I managed to stop before I squeaked out a startled, "Me?"

Bart pointed to the map with the tip of his dagger. "They'll be likely to bring in their big warships for the blockade—frigates and square riggers. It'll be up to ye to harry them with yer sloops and barques. We're short on men, so ye'll have to do the best ye can, but use yer speed to damage the warships as much as ye can . . . without sinkin', of course."

"Of course," I murmured, part of my mind screaming insanely, the other part feeling a strange excitement at the thought of taking my sleek, pretty sloop into a real battle. Pangloss had told me many a tale of how the small, fast ships could be used to damage the larger, slower, bulkier warships, and despite my protest, I felt pretty confident about my abilities to captain my ship.

What was I thinking? I didn't want war! I wanted Corbin and Bart to work out their issues in a reasonable manner. War, even virtual, was not good. While Bart went over specifics of what he wanted the officers to do, I spent a few moments alternating between panic about what he was asking of me, until recently the landlubberiest of all landlubbers, sharing the growing excitement and grim determination that the men exuded, and listening to the sane voice in my head as it told me the solution to the problem was not force, but an amicable end to hostilities worked out with logic and organization.

"Ye'll be needin' a flag," Bart said to me, interrupting my musings.

"A flag? Oh, a pirate flag? Skull and crossbones?"

"Nay," Bart said with a smile, opening a drawer in the desk and tossing me a yard-long rectangular bit of black cloth. I held it up to admire the image on it: the white silhouette of a man standing on a red heart, which had been stabbed with a knife. The letters BC were written on the handle of the knife. " 'Tis me own design. That's Black Corbin's bleedin' heart I'm standin' on, stabbed with his own knife."

"Eh," I said, folding it up. "Very . . . um . . . vengeful."

"Aye, it is. Ye'll be flyin' me flag so the devils know who ye are as ye blast their ships full of lead."

"Cap'n," Pangloss said, looking at me thoughtfully. "I'm thinkin' there's somethin' we're overlookin' with the lass's ship."

The ship, nothing. They were overlooking the fact that I was the least experienced person in the room. I squished down a sudden spurt of disappointment at the thought that Pangloss might talk Bart out of including me in the attack team.

You're not really a pirate, the sane part of my brain pointed out. *You're a financial analyst who is going to have to have the carpet cleaned in a few short hours (or weeks, depending on your reality) if you don't find the guy responsible for trapping you in the game.*

"What's that, Panny?"

Pangloss took the flag and held it up. "The lass is sailin' one of Corbin's own ships. A distinctive one, what with that garish paint."

I frowned. I thought the glossy maroon trim on the ship was pretty. "The *Saucy Wench* is not garish. She's just colorful," I said with a touch of hauteur.

Pangloss flashed me a grin. "Me apologies, lass. Colorful, aye, that she is." He turned back to Bart, who was lounging on the edge of the desk. "Me point is that Black Corbin's men are sure to recognize her as one of their ships."

"Yeah, but I won her off Corbin," I felt obligated to point out . . . with a smile of warm satisfaction as I remembered my moment of triumph. "Surely they'll know she doesn't belong to Corbin anymore?"

Bart frowned in thought. Pangloss shook his head slowly. "I'm thinkin' they won't. 'Tis not the sort of a thing a man likes bandied about by the swabbies—that he's lost a ship in a duel, and to a woman, yet."

I rolled my eyes and let that statement go without the comment I wanted to make.

"Ye've got a point," Bart said. The officers murmured their agreement. Bart sent me a speculative glance. "We could use the lass's ship to infiltrate the blockade fleet. There's no end of damage she could do then. She might even be able to get to Corbin that way. Killin' two birds with one stone . . . only it won't be a bird's guts which're spilled. Aye, 'tis a good plan, Panny. We'll send the lass in to kill Corbin, and do what she can to destroy blockade ships from within the fleet."

"Yarr!" the officers shouted.

"Oh, Lord," I muttered, wondering how I got myself into these situations. The only thing that kept me from walking out of the room right then and there was the fact that I needed to hear the rest of Bart's plans so I could judge how to deal with the situation.

"Here, ye'd best take this. 'Tis Black Corbin's flag. Ye'll fly that to get into the fleet, then raise me flag." Bart handed me another rectangle of cloth. I opened it up to see the design, looking at him in curiosity.

"There's nothing on it."

"Aye. Corbin's flag is a field of black only," Pangloss said, his face hard. "'Tis a symbol of his black heart."

"Ah. So, exactly what am I supposed to do?"

By the time I staggered down the hill to the town, my brain was spinning with terms like forlorn hope (volunteers who made the first assault on a place of fortification, such as a manned harbor), *masse de décision* (troops or ships kept out of a battle until a decisive moment), and redoubt (someone who is in an independent defensive position . . . in other words, me).

"Man, what a mess. Whom do I think I'm fooling? This whole thing is doomed."

"Hoy, Cap'n," Bas said, suddenly appearing at my side as I walked past the graveyard. "What be doomed, other than me life now that ye're riskin' me early death with those baths?"

"Hoy, Bas. Stop picking your ear with your hook; it's not polite. And I'm not a captain. I'm just a . . . er . . . well, I guess technically I'm nothing, since I'm not even really a member of the crew, but we'll let that go. You can call me Amy."

"Be ye doomed, then, Amy?"

"Me? Probably." I smiled at the hopeful look that flickered across the boy's face, giving in to the urge to rumple his thick black hair. Now that he was cleaned up, deloused, and fed a few days' worth of steady meals, he was starting to look more like a normal kid and less like a small parody of death. Bran the raven squawked and nudged my hand with his heavy beak. I snatched my hand back, thinking he was going to bite me.

"He likes you," Bas said. "Ye don't have to be afraid of him. He don't hurt people he likes."

"Ah?" I eyed the ratty-looking bird, then gave his head a few cautious pets. Even after a couple of baths, the bird was still less than majestic, but he was at least clean. "Nice bird. No biting."

Bas gave me a juvenile eye roll.

"Just ignore me, Bas. I'm a bit wimpy about things today."

"What sort of things?"

We continued past the church toward the town square. "Oh, various and sundry issues. For one, Bart thinks he's sending Corbin a wolf in sheep's clothing, but the truth is I'm no more a wolf than you are."

Bas looked thoughtful. "Wolves eat people. I wonder what it feels like to be eaten."

The memory of Corbin's mouth on my breast bloomed to full-color, surround-sound, feel-vision, delicious life in my mind, making my stomach go all quivery. With much grit and determination, I dragged my attention back to the subject at hand. "The whole thing is ridiculous. It's not like I can actually do anything to make a difference."

The square was bustling with the usual group of women at the well in the center, various children, dogs, and assorted livestock running around, and a few white-haired men who were all that were left to manage the shops after the massacre. I paused at the edge of the square, in the shade of a tailor shop, frowning as I looked around. "Bas, someone mentioned a mine on the island."

"Aye. Emerald mine. 'Tis in the belly of the Turtle."

I glanced behind me at the humpback center of the island, the rounded hemisphere bearing a resemblance to the shell of a turtle, hence the name. "Emeralds, huh? So a lot of the men work there?"

He shook his head. "They're all dead now. Black Corbin killed 'em. Cap'n Bart, he brought in more men, but they're not many, and they're busy in the crew foragin' and keepin' Black Corbin from slittin' our throats while we sleep."

A protest that Corbin would never do anything so nefarious rose on my lips, but I bit it back, instead looking along the arms of the crescent that formed the harbor. On either side, crude wooden structures had been built, upon which even now men swarmed, working to install the new bigger cannons that would be used to protect the town.

I looked back at the square, the pleasant, ordinary scene in front of me contrasting violently with the vision of the cobblestones running red with the blood of the remaining inhabitants of the island.

If what Corbin and Bart said about the blockade was true, then the people of Turtle's Back needed my help.

"I have to write a letter," I said, making a decision. "Who has parchment, do you know?"

Bas's eyes widened in surprise. "Ye be wantin' to write a letter? To a person?"

"Yeah. Yes . . . er . . . aye. I do. An important letter. I don't have any reales, so I need someone who would be willing to barter something for a bit of parchment, a pen, and ink."

Bas continued to look stunned by my request. I gave up hoping for a suggestion from him and scanned the shops around the square, finally settling on the largest merchant shop as being the wealthiest in town, and thus the most likely to have extravagances like parchment and ink.

Two hours later I emerged from a nearby sweltering outbuilding, sucking at a blistering spot on my left palm, my right hand just as sore, but triumphantly clutching a rolled-up scrap of parchment, a cast-off quill, and a minuscule amount of ink in a stopperless bottle.

Bas, who had been napping in the shade of a nearby coconut tree, got up and shambled after me as I headed for Renata's house. "Ye got yer letter, then?"

"I churned enough butter to clog up the arteries of half the town," I said. "And, yes, I got the parchment and ink. Now, for a few quiet moments to write the letter. Oh, are you busy? No? Would you mind staying around the square? I want you to watch for someone."

"Who?" Bas asked, his head to the side as Bran ruffled through his hair. I avoided looking at both of them, knowing the bird had probably found feasts there in the past.

"A friend of mine. He's . . . er . . . he looks like a leper. Or a deranged man. But he's neither; he's perfectly harmless, I assure you . . ." My voice trailed off. Reassurances weren't necessary. The minute the word *leper* left my lips, Bas's eyes lit up.

"If you see him, go up to him quietly, without drawing

any attention to yourself, and tell him I have a message for him to deliver. You got that?"

He nodded. I parked him in the square, gave him an apple I'd confiscated for my lunch, and hurried back to the small room that Renata had let me use.

It took me a few tries, and much of the remaining shaft of the quill, to get a point that would write even remotely legibly, but at last I sat cross-legged on the floor, a board on my lap, the rumpled bit of parchment stretched out on it. I teased my chin with the feather end of the quill as I thought about what I wanted to write.

Dear Corbin,

I've changed my mind about five dozen times in the last few hours about what I wanted to say to you. My first response to your proposal was, as you imagined, to be quite startled. I didn't scream, though, but that's because I figured it would bring everyone in the town on the run, and I'd never get your letter read then. After I was through being startled, I was a bit annoyed. It seemed like you were back to being that blond charmer, interested only in conquests and having women ogle his manly chest. But then I had a chat with Bart, and . . . well, I decided that I wasn't going to say no.

I'm not saying yes, either. I think we need to talk, face-to-face. I've got some concerns that I want to discuss with you, and it's too difficult to do it via not-very-instant messaging. Is it possible for us to get together? I'm free during the evenings. Usually Bas and I hang out around the town, since I don't like for him to be in Renata's when customers start arriving. I can meet you at that little beach on the other side of the island. Don't come in through the harbor—Bart has some new guns, and I get the idea he'd really relish using them on you.

Sincerely,

Amy

PS—I've talked to what seems like half the town so far, and no luck on Paul-hunting. Have you found him yet? I get back spasms if I don't move around, so we need to get out of here soon before my body revolts on me.

I read the letter over, yearning for my handy Wite-Out pen to remove the worst of the inky blotches, splashes, smears, and fingerprints, but in the end, I shrugged and figured Corbin would just have to decipher it as best he could. I used a bit of plain old candle wax to seal the rolled-up parchment, then went in search of Bas, and, I hoped, Holder. I hadn't heard any hue and cry indicating that one of Corbin's men had been caught, so I assumed he was lying low until night, when he could slip out of town.

Night was just falling when we finally found him.

"Psst! Amy!" Holder hissed from an alley Bas and I were passing. A woman and her children walking next to me paused to look down the alley.

"Argh, me beauty, ye're a fine-lookin' wench. Be ye lookin' to play hoist the anchor?" Holder said, doubling over and drooling as he shuffled toward us. The woman hurried her children away quickly. Holder glanced around as he straightened up, grabbing my arm and hauling me into the shadow of the alleyway.

"There you are. We've been searching everywhere for you. I'm glad to see you haven't been caught, although, really, is the drool necessary?"

"Every good lunatic drools," he answered, flashing me a smile. "Hoy, Bas. How's tricks?"

Bas's face fell when he realized that the lunatic was none other than Holder in disguise, a fact I'd kept from him in case he inadvertently let it slip that Corbin's first mate was lurking about town. "Oh, it's ye. Cap'n Amy said ye were a leper. I don't suppose ye are?" he asked hopefully.

"No, sorry, lad, no leprosy, although I get a horrible rash on my belly if I eat nachos. Something in the cheese, I think," he answered, idly scratching the body part in question.

"Can we discuss your rashy stomach another time? You need to get out of town. Bart's men are seriously building up defenses, and it's not safe for you to be here. I have a letter for Corbin." I gave him the rolled-up parchment. He eyed it. "No peeking. It's sealed."

He grinned and saluted me with it. "Aye, aye, m'lady. Corb should be coming back for me just before the moon is high, so he'll have it before the night is over."

"Thanks. Be careful. From what I can tell, feelings are running pretty high over you guys."

A curious look crossed his face, part puzzlement, part interest. "Really? Because of the blockade?"

I gaped at him for a moment or two, making a mental readjustment in my image of him. I hadn't thought he would be so callous as to totally disregard the number of men he and Corbin and the rest of their crew had so coldbloodedly killed, but even knowing they did it in the spirit of the game, I was taken aback enough that I said nothing other than to repeat my warning to be careful leaving the town.

Hours later I was snuggled into my bed, dreaming about skeletons that danced on bleeding hearts. A hand clapped over my mouth was the first indication that all was not right. The second was the (now familiar) black sack that was shoved over my head and torso, confining me into a helpless blob of sleepy woman.

My mouth worked, however. The kidnappers didn't say anything to my scathing estimates of their parentage and ancestry, but I was not in the least bit surprised when, ten minutes later, I was deposited on a hard wooden seat on a rocking platform.

The sacking was unwound from my body and lifted off, the sudden rush of sea air—as well as the man seated across the rowboat from me—confirming my suspicions.

"Hello, luv," Corbin said. "Ready to get married?"

Chapter 12

Here's a first-rate opportunity
To get married with impunity. . . .

—Ibid, Act I

"Dearly beloved—"

"Corbin, you're mad. What on earth were you doing on Turtle's Back?"

"I figured it was safer for you to be with me. Bart is my enemy, after all . . ."

"The key words in that sentence being *your enemy*, not mine. Besides, I have work to do there interviewing everyone. And it's way too dangerous for you to be on Turtle's Back right now. Don't you know that Bart is after your head? He's promised three ships to any man who can bring in proof of your demise. If he'd seen you—"

"—we have gathered here today to witness the virtual bonding of this pirate to this pirate—"

"Sweetheart, it's traditional for the bride to stand next to the groom during a wedding. I'm not sure what the etiquette is about holding a sword to the groom's throat, but I'm going to go out on a limb here and say it's not quite kosher. Especially when it's the groom's own rapier."

I withdrew the sword tip from where I had pressed it against Corbin's neck and handed it back to him. "You weren't listening to me. No one is listening to me. I had to do something dramatic to make you pay attention."

"—within the confines of the game, naturally, although I personally happen to think Corb and Amy are made for each other."

"You may be on to something," Corbin told Holder before grinning at me and holding out his hand. "Shall we, my dear?"

I crossed my arms over my chest and tucked in my hands. "No, we shall not. I told you I wasn't saying I'd marry you. And don't pull that 'I'm safer with you' crap. Bart is no threat to me, and I still have people to talk to on Turtle's Back, so I'm staying there."

"As the midnight blue water of the Seventh Sea flows eternal, so shall the (virtual) love of these two people. Corbin, do ye take this woman to be yers?" Holder, back in his monk garb, was clearly getting way too much into the ceremony that I never agreed to. He looked as happy as a shopaholic on Rodeo Drive.

"I do," Corbin said, still grinning.

"No, he doesn't," I said, adjusting my arm so the pearl Corbin had given me to stop seasickness was hitting the correct pressure point. Amazingly enough, it seemed to keep me from feeling the least bit queasy.

On the main deck a collection of twenty or so men, including Bas, stood in a semicircle around the trio of Corbin, Holder, and me.

"Do ye promise to stoke her guns, and her guns only?"

"I do," Corbin repeated, gently pulling me over until I stood facing him.

I glared. "No one stokes my guns without my permission," I snapped, losing the slim hold I had on my temper.

"I'd never think of stoking without your express consent," Corbin told me.

"Do ye promise to hoist no other mainsails than hers?" Holder asked.

"Oh, for God's sake . . . this wedding is ridiculous! I never said I'd marry you!" I yelled, waving my hands around in frustration. "Why is no one listening to me?"

"I'm listening to ye, Amy," Bas said. Bran squawked his agreement.

"Aye, I do so promise," Corbin told Holder.

"Gah!"

"Amy, do ye take this man to be yers?" Holder turned to me.

I transferred my glare from Corbin to him. "No, I most certainly do not. I would never marry a man who didn't listen to me. Been there, done that, got the alimony, thank you."

"Aw, sweetheart, don't break me heart," Corbin said, grabbing my hands and giving them a gentle squeeze.

"Do you promise to climb no masts other than his?"

"I'm beginning to think you don't have a heart to . . . what?" I looked at Holder, then back to Corbin. "Did he just say what I think he said?"

Corbin smiled a smile that had my legs turning to jelly. His gray eyes were almost luminescent in the glow of the oil lamps and moonlight, and they turned positively quicksilver when he leaned forward and whispered in my ear, "Don't like to be on top? You pick the position, my sweet."

Passion flickered from him to me, firing my blood until an inferno of desire swept through me. I cleared my throat. "I'm not saying no to that. In fact, I'm starting to think that *that* might be a good idea, although I've never done anything like that virtually before. But I'm sorry, Corbin. I want to talk to you first before we discuss terms of a marriage."

"Do ye promise to load his guns with yer finest powder?" Holder asked me.

"You are deranged," I told him. "This game has gone to your head, and frankly, I think you're going to need deep psychological help when we get out, because those innuendoes are just way too over the line."

"I'll take that as an aye, shall I?" Holder beamed at us both.

"No!" I yelled.

"Aye," everyone else on board yelled back.

"Then by the powers vested in me by the CEO of Buckling Swashes, our own Captain Corbin here—"

I sighed and gave up. What did it matter, after all? It was just a pretend marriage in a pretend world. It didn't really mean anything. If it made Corbin happy, then he'd likely be obliged to do what I asked in terms of ceasing the hostilities with Bart.

"—I pronounce ye pirate and pirate, bound together so long as the game runs." Holder paused for a moment. "Or until ye cancel yer account, whichever comes first."

"Yarr!" shouted the crew.

"Ye can kiss yer pirate bride," Holder told Corbin. "Anything else ye want to do is up to ye two."

I tried to thin my lips at Holder, but Corbin claimed every last ounce of my attention when he ran a thumb over my chin, tilting my head back slightly. The warmth and desire in his eyes stripped all thoughts from my mind but how much I liked him, and wanted to be with him . . . and just plain *wanted* him.

"Shall we have a wedding night?" Corbin asked softly.

I stood clinging to him, my head spinning with the kiss he'd just given me, my lips tingling, my body demanding that I fling myself on him right then and there and satisfy all its wants. I started to say no, to explain that I didn't find purely physical relationships at all desirable, that I needed an emotional bond before I could think of enjoying him in all the many and varied ways my mind was exploring, but before I could, Corbin nipped my lower lip.

"Fair warning, Amy—I'm falling in love with you. I know this isn't the best way to say it, or even do it, but I can't help myself. You're all I can think of. You make me ridiculously happy, and I just want to be with you. If you'll have me, I'll do my best to make you as happy as I am." His eyes were bright, and full of so much emotion a lump rose in my throat.

All resistance melted. How could I refuse such an offering of a heart? I couldn't. "Yes, please," I said, then gasped in surprise when he swung me up in his arms in the best romantic pirate hero tradition.

"Rum for everyone!" he called to the crew before carrying me belowdecks, to the captain's quarters.

Their cheers and several suggestions of a ribald nature (which I hoped would go straight over Bas's head) were shut out when Corbin set me on my feet, closing and locking the door behind us.

"What about Bas? I can't just leave him—"

"He'll be fine. Holder will keep an eye on him. He has three kids of his own."

"He does? He's married?"

Corbin nodded. "Since he was eighteen, to his high school sweetheart. Don't let his flirty act mislead you—they're very much in love. Hold just likes women, and comes across as a player, but he isn't really."

"Ah. Good." I looked at the key he set on the desk bolted to the floor. "Are you holding me prisoner?"

His smile was full of promise. "That depends. Do you want to be held prisoner?"

"Hmm." I thought about what I wanted for a moment. Aside from Corbin, which was a given at that point. "I've never been into men acting arrogant and domineering. I've always felt that a relationship, both the physical and emotional aspects of it, requires from both participants consideration, dedication, and an ability to receive pleasure from pleasure given."

Corbin watched me carefully, nodding, his eyes glittering in the soft candlelight. Standing there in his swashbuckler's leather pants, the loosely laced jerkin, the ruffly white shirt beneath it, he looked every inch a true pirate—a dangerous rogue given to heady passions who demanded everything, returning only what he wanted to give. Something incandescent deep inside me burst into being and gave me permission to indulge in my wildest, most secret fantasies.

"Oh, what do I know. Take me, Corbin. Take me now, however you want!" I threw myself on him, giggling when he whooped and scooped me up, depositing me on the big captain's bed in the corner.

"Just so you know," he said, his mouth hovering over mine, "I agree with everything you said about consideration and enjoying giving pleasure. In fact, I plan on being damned close to ecstasy with all the pleasure I will be giving you."

"Oooh," I said, my toes curling in my boots at the look in his eyes. I ran my hands up his arms, braced on either side of me. "How long does it take to sail from Turtle's Back to your island?"

"About four hours," he answered, his head dipping to claim a heated kiss. I squirmed with delight from the intensity of his mouth on mine, his tongue politely asking permission before sweeping alongside mine, curling around it in a way that had me tugging on him, desperate to feel the full length of his body.

He pulled back, gently nipping my lower lip.

"Hey," I protested, disappointed.

He smiled. "You said I could do this however I want."

"So you plan on frustrating me to death?" I asked, propping myself up on one elbow as he stood and peeled off his sword, boots, and jerkin. He stood in the billowing shirt and leather pants. "Oooh. I take it back. This part is nice. Go on, please."

"Er . . ." He hesitated. "Amy . . . I don't want you to be disappointed. You remember the blond version of me? Well, the rest of me doesn't look like him any more than my head does."

I smiled. "Corbin, I want you, not your idea of a woman's fantasy. Now shuck those clothes and start pleasuring me, because I'm about to go up in smoke if you don't."

He hesitated for another second, then pulled his shirt off, quickly undoing the buttons on his pants. I rolled onto my side and smiled again, allowing my eyes to enjoy the view. He wasn't nearly as muscle-bound as the blond version, and he had a cute little smidgen of softness around his belly that melted me, but I had absolutely no complaints.

"I'm sorry, I'm working on that," he said, his hands splaying across his stomach. "Too much time sitting in front of the computer."

"I happen to think you're very sexy, with or without clothes, although right now I admit to having a preference for the without version. I approve of your chest hair, by the way."

"Ah. Good." He brushed a self-conscious hand across his chest.

"You're not too hairy, but you don't look like a plucked chicken, either. And I like your stomach. And your arms, and legs and . . . er . . . everything else. But I do have a question."

He looked down at himself. "Seven inches, I think. I haven't measured lately."

I laughed, giving myself a moment to admire his seven inches, standing proudly at attention. "That wasn't what I meant, although I appreciate the specifics. I wanted to know how you managed to make me look like I really look? I know you must have scanned yourself into the game, but you didn't know me."

"I wondered when you'd ask that," he said with a little smile, moving to the end of the bed. He held out his hand. I rolled onto my back and gave him my foot. He pulled my boot off, his fingers stroking down my ankles and the top of my foot. My leg twitched.

"Ticklish?" he asked.

"Very."

"Ah." He avoided touching the sensitive bottom of my foot, bending over to kiss the inside of my ankle. A little shiver ran through me. "I didn't scan myself into the computer, as a matter of fact. You're telling me what you look like."

He pulled off my second boot, giving that foot a kiss as well. Warmth pooled inside me, spreading slowly along my limbs.

"I am?" My voice was squeaky, but I didn't care. Corbin climbed onto the bed, carefully moving my legs to kneel between my feet, his hands warm on my calves as they swept up toward my knees.

"Yes, you are. Your brain is sending every human player in the game an image of yourself. I'm doing the same. So in effect, you're seeing me as I see myself, and I'm seeing the you that you see."

"Oh, God. I need to lose ten pounds, and my boobs are

too small, and my hips are too big, and we won't go into the cellulite that I just know is growing even as we speak!"

He laughed, then stopped, frowning as he looked down at me.

"What?" I almost shrieked. "You can see the cellulite?"

"No, silly." He flashed me a grin, then got off the bed, squatting next to it as he opened one of the drawers built into the bedstead. "I just thought that since we were doing pirate and the vixen, we might as well do it properly." He held up a handful of navy bandanas. "You did say I could do whatever I wanted?"

"Yeeeees," I said slowly.

"Good." He returned to the foot of the bed, quickly tying a bandana around first my ankle, then the bottom corner of the bed frame. I looked in growing surprise from my bound foot to him as he quickly whipped another bandana around my second foot.

"You're tying me down?"

"Aye." He grinned up at me as he spread my legs, secured the other end of the bandana to the bed, adjusting the knot so it wouldn't press on my foot. I had a brief moment of concern that when my clothes were off, all my secrets would be laid bare in that position, but I decided he'd see it all anyway, so what did it matter?

"That's bondage, isn't it? I've never done bondage," I said, testing the bonds. "Certainly never the first time with a man."

"Neither have I, but somehow, it seems appropriate that we should do something utterly out of character. Is the cloth tied too tightly?"

I wiggled my foot around again. "No. But it's very . . . well, kinky, Corbin."

"Do you want me to stop?" His grin faded. "I won't do it if you don't want me to."

I thought for a moment. I disliked being out of control of any situation, but this was different. This wasn't real, it was just . . . well, basically mind sex. Although Corbin's hands on my naked legs sure felt real. I shivered again. "No, I don't think you should stop. I'd be just as turned on without it, you know, because you're incredibly sexy, but . . . well, I see your point about doing something totally different. It makes us unique, in a way. So it's all right. Just don't get too wild on me, okay?"

His smile returned, this time with extra wickedness as he slid his hands up my thighs. "No promises, my sweet. Now, shall we get down to business?"

Chapter 13

Take heart, fair days will shine;
Take any heart — take mine!

—Ibid, Act I

"Business?" I all but shrieked as Corbin caressed my thighs. "This is business to you? You have no real idea what business is, do you? Business is — oh, my God! That is not business! That's a very sharp knife! This is payback from when I held a knife to your noogies, isn't it?"

Corbin had pulled a dagger from beneath the mattress, the corners of his mouth curving as he bent down over one bound leg. His tongue snaked out and flicked across the crease at the back of my knee. I sat straight up and grabbed his head. "Oh!"

"Oh?"

"Oh! It means . . . oooooh, baby!"

He chuckled and used one hand to free his head from my grasp. "Do I need to tie your hands, too? I thought you'd like them unbound. I know I was looking forward to you touching me. But if you can't control yourself, I'll have to tie them, as well."

I opened my mouth to tell him what he could do with his plans, then thought better of it. We were playing a game. A very sexy, erotic game, but still, it was a game, and I'd come to see the light as far as a little play went. I lay back down. "All right. Hands down. For a while, anyway. But I reserve the right to gasp whenever I feel moved to do so. What are you going to do with that knife? I'm not at all into pain, you know."

"Good. Neither am I." His head dipped again, and he licked the back of my other knee. A tremor of desire shook me at the simple touch. Who knew backs of knees could be so sensitive?

"So then what are you going to do with it?"

His hand slid up my thigh, pushing my skirt up before it, his mouth trailing a line of steamy kisses. He stopped long enough to quickly undo the line of buttons that held the skirt together, tossing it on a nearby chair. "I know it's a traditionally romantic belief that women like to have their underwear ripped off them, but I've always thought it sounded painful. I figured you'd prefer to remove yours in a less brutal manner." He glanced down at the cotton and lace underwear I had fashioned from leftover bits of cloth and dress trimmings. "You don't mind if I slice them off, do you?"

"Actually, I do. This is my only pair, you see. I wash them out every night, and pray they're dry by morning."

He looked up at me. "But you live with a bunch of women. Don't any of them have panties you can borrow?"

"Okay, first of all, borrowed undies? No. Not done. And second, the group of women I live with specialize in activities conducted sans underwear, thus they aren't articles in high demand. Last, but not least, you did your research a bit too well. Most of the women don't even wear underwear, which, I gather from their surprised looks when they saw what I was sewing, is the norm. So, long story short: yes, I mind. Can I just take them off, and you pretend you cut them off me in a manly act of rampant desire?"

"Sweetheart, my manly desire is more than rampant, as you can plainly see," he answered, untying my ankles. I smiled at the rampant parts and quickly stood to shuck my underwear.

"Er . . . I don't have a bad self-image or anything. I mean, men don't barf upon seeing me naked. But I'm not in any way perfect, and I'm afraid that if all you have to go with regarding my appearance is my image of myself, then my flaws are bound to be exaggerated."

Corbin spun the knife upward, impressively snatching it out of midair to point it at me. "Lose them, or I'll cut them off and you'll be spending the rest of your time here going commando."

"Pushy is not sexy," I pointed out.

He looked down at the rampant bits.

"Well, all right, some forms of pushy are, but you know what I mean. And yes, I'm taking them off. But you got to have a disclaimer before you took off your clothes, so I think it's only fair that I get to, as well."

I hurried off with the underwear, my bodice, and my blouse, then stood feeling extremely awkward while his gaze roamed over my (flawed) naked body. "I'm sorry. I told you my breasts were too small, and my grandmother always said I had hips that could bear a dozen children with ease, and I swear the cellulite fairy has been making nightly visits—"

Corbin tossed the knife onto the desk, then scooped me up again and deposited me on the bed with a laugh and a lascivious grin. "We're quite a pair. Here's me with my beer gut and you being silly about absolutely nothing. Your breasts are perfect, pert little morsels just waiting for more resuscitating, and I happen to like your hips. They arouse me like nothing else does."

"You don't have a beer gut," I said, watching as he strapped my feet down again. "You have a tiny little tummy that I like. A lot. Can I lick your belly button?"

He paused in tying down my foot to give me a look that made my insides quiver. "You can lick anything you want. But only after I'm done licking what I want."

"Oooh," I said on a drawn-out breath, the quivering intensifying as he crawled up my body.

"First, I think I need to take care of that poor, abused breast that has been waiting so long for my attention."

"Sounds like a good plan to meeeeee!" The word ended on a shriek as Corbin skipped all forms of breast foreplay and started gently nibbling and sucking on my nipple. My back arched as I grabbed his head, streaks of pleasure so intense it was almost painful zapping outward from where his tongue was now laving my breast. "Oh, dear God, Corbin. How did I survive without this attention?"

He chuckled again, this time against my breastbone as he kissed a hot, wet path over to where my other breast was demanding equal time. "I have no idea how either of us survived. You taste like heaven, sweetheart. Sweet and creamy and so delicious I just want to eat you up." I squirmed against him as he paid his respects to breast number two; then he smiled. A *very* wicked smile. "In fact, I think I will."

"Oh, Lord above," I gasped, my thighs tensing as he suddenly slid down to my spread legs, his hands cupping my hips as he rubbed his cheeks against my inner thighs. "Yes, please. Not that I'm begging or anything, but it's been a really, really long time since I've been with a man, and longer still one that's been willing to indulge me, rather than vice versa. You can start anytime. Are you waiting for me to stop talking before you start? I'll shut up now so you can get to it. Have I mentioned how much I like this? I'm primed and ready, too, in case you were wondering. Corbin? Why are you laughing into my girl parts? Oh, God, I've imagined something horrible about them, haven't I, and now you think that's what I really look like? Don't believe what you see. I'm perfectly normal down there. If the scenery offends you, feel free to close your eyes. I won't mind, really I won't."

Corbin laughed even harder into my privates, making me squirm with embarrassment. What on earth had my mind created to show him? His gray eyes were silver with humor and arousal as they gazed at me over my belly. "I'm not laughing at you, Amy. I'm laughing at the situation. I've wanted you for what seems like so long, I want to make every nanosecond last a year, and you're trying to hurry me along. It makes it difficult to restrain myself from just jumping you and pounding away like a madman."

"Pounding sounds good, too," I said, twisting my hips in an attempt to put his attention where I wanted it. "But afterwards, please. My girl parts want you, Corbin. Badly. As in, right now."

He smiled at the girl parts. "And I want them, too. I look forward to introducing them to my boy parts. But right now, since you are so demanding, my lusty vixen, I will indulge in a light snack just to set the scene for the main course, if you don't mind my mixing metaphors."

My body, strung tighter than a bowstring, positively hummed when his mouth closed on the center of my desire. He nibbled, he licked, he did amazing tongue swirly things, and just when I thought I was going to explode into a thousand incredibly satisfied bits of Amy, he slid first one finger, then a second into me and sent me into orbit.

"You were right," he said into my mouth a few eons later, when I had come back down to earth. His body was hot and hard on mine, and I realized in some dim, distant part of my mind that he had left my feet bound. He kissed me long and hard, and I reveled in our mingled tastes, my body putty in his hands as he positioned himself at the center of my own personal paradise.

"I almost always am," I answered, sucking his lower lip, my hands sliding up his ribs to his shoulders. "About what?"

"You were primed and ready for me. I've never made love to anyone so responsive as you." He nudged himself an inch or so into me, causing me to squirm again in a futile attempt to take all of him.

"I'm very orally inclined, both giving and receiving," I said, half moaning as he slid a little farther into me, my body parting reluctantly for him. He wasn't a massively endowed man, but he seemed positively huge to my previously man-deprived girl parts. "I'd have been happy to show you my own particular talents, but you seem to have caught my impatience."

"Mmm," he murmured into my neck as he nibbled a sweet spot behind my ear.

I dragged my fingernails down his back, causing him to rise up and give me a wild look just before he plunged fully into me.

"Corbin!" I shouted, my hips bucking upward.

"Oh, God, don't move, love. If you move, I'm not going to be able to last. Just lie there and don't move, and I may be able to go longer than another second or two. Don't breathe, either. Breathing is moving, and that's going to be it for me. Just lie there and don't breathe or move or think any sorts of the thoughts I can see in your eyes."

I twisted against him, my fingers digging into the muscles of his butt, trying to pull him in deeper. "I'm still tied down! I want to move against you. I want to wrap my legs around you."

He groaned into my mouth, his hips flexing as he started a stroking rhythm that had me seeing stars. "You moved. You breathed. You spoke. I can't untie you, love. If I do, you'll kill me. I may just survive this if you stay perfectly still and don't do that twisting thing with your hips—"

I twisted my hips again in desperation to have him back where I wanted him, filling me, completing me, taking me to a place I had no idea existed. "Corbin! I want to move my legs!"

He rose up on both hands, giving me the wickedest smile known to man. "I know you do, my sweet Amy, but you aren't going to. I'm going to ride you hard and fast and you can't do anything about it. Dear God, I love this game!"

He lunged forward again, causing my eyes to roll back in my head with the sheer, utter pleasure of it all. My thighs ached with the strain of my attempts to wrap my legs around his hips, but all thoughts beyond the joy he was bringing me were lost as I gave myself up to another wave of ecstasy that was building with each stroke.

"Oh, God, I can't hold out any longer. Are you ready? Please, tell me you're—"

I shouted his name as my body burst into another glorious orgasm, hundreds of little muscles tightening around him, his cry of completion ringing in my ears as he pounded into my body.

My hands slid down the faintly sweat-slicked planes of his back, my body still quivering with a dozen delicious aftershocks of pleasure as I kissed his shoulder, enjoying the slightly salty taste of his skin. Corbin smelled like leather and lemon and man, and he tasted just the same. He lay gasping for breath on me, his body a heavy weight, but not an unpleasant one. Somehow, I had managed to work one foot free. I pulled my knee up around his hip and kissed a path over to his jaw. "That was wonderful, Corbin. I think I can say without any exaggeration that you are the best lover I've ever had, not that I've had many, but still, there have been a couple, and you, hands down, have given me more pleasure than anyone else ever has."

He groaned something into my shoulder and propped himself up enough so he could look down on me. "Why is it I'm thinking I'm about to have a coronary, and you're chatting up a storm? Why aren't you as near death as I am?"

I rubbed my freed knee along his hip, and gave his butt a friendly little squeeze. "Women are capable of having sex and talking at the same time. We're masters of multitasking that way."

He frowned down at me.

"What?" I asked, trying to smooth out his frown with my fingers. "We're not masters of multitasking?"

"You said we were having sex. Is that all this is to you? Just sex? Is all that we are together? Just a way to scratch an itch?"

His eyes were dark with anger. He tried to pull out of me, but I grabbed his hips and held him in place. "I'm sorry, that was unfeeling and rude of me. I don't just have sex, Corbin. I told you that before—I have to have some emotional commitment before I take this step. I like you, Corbin. I like you a lot. I like to talk with you, and be with you, and you make me laugh, which I've always thought is important in a relationship. But if you're asking me if I'm madly in love with you . . . I don't do madly in love. I've never been the fall-in-love-at-first-sight kind of girl."

"I'm in love with you," he said, his eyes watchful.

I kissed the tip of his nose. "I'm not sure that's very wise of you, but I'm flattered nonetheless."

"*Flattered?*" His eyes went blank.

"I'm very fond of you, Corbin," I said, willing him to see the truth in my face. "I wouldn't be here now if I wasn't. But I'm not going to lie to you. I've been in love exactly once in my life, and that lasted a whole year before I realized my husband was more in love with himself than he was with me. It's been so long since I felt that emotion for a man, I'm not sure I know how to do it."

He said nothing but rolled off me, untying my still-bound ankle before turning onto his back, pulling me tight up against his side. I spread my fingers on his chest, looking at the whiteness of them against his tanned skin and the dark curls, torn between the need to ease the pain he obviously felt by me admitting the truth, and a reluctance to delude him.

"I will teach you," he said softly into my hair as I drifted off to sleep, lulled by both the warmth of his body and the rhythmic creaks of the ship as she sailed through the night.

Chapter 14

Away, away! my heart's on fire;
I burn, this base deception to repay.

—Ibid, Act II

"There you are. We have to talk."

"I have better uses for my tongue than mere words," Corbin said, illustrating his point by skirting the portable tub I'd recently been using, and kissing me.

"Yes, you do, but we really have to talk," I said as soon as I regathered my scattered wits. Corbin's kisses had the tendency to leave me utterly bemused, a fact that I simultaneously resented—I hated being out of control—and loved. Who could complain about a man who kissed so well it drove all other thoughts from your mind? I peeled myself off him and grabbed my brown leather bodice. "I have a lot of things to say before Bas and I have to leave."

"Why leave?" Corbin asked. "Everything that is mine is now yours, as well. I have sixteen ships here. If you don't like the *Samurai Squirrel,* we can move to another ship, although none are so comfortable."

"I don't have a problem at all with living on a ship," I

answered, glancing around the cabin. Despite the odd name, the *Squirrel* was a very elegant ship, outfitted with gleaming brass, rosewood, and mother-of-pearl accents. The captain's quarters were particularly luxurious, even running to the large copper tub in which I'd taken a bath.

Corbin looked around the cabin with pride. "Aye, she's a sweet ship." His eyebrows rose as he saw what I'd secured with a rope clip on the lip of the porthole. "Is that what I think it is?"

"It's my underwear. I didn't have time to rinse them out last night, what with all the mad, passionate lovemaking going on."

Corbin was on me in a heartbeat, his hands skimming beneath my skirt, up my thighs. "Oooh. You're going commando."

"I have no choice in the matter. I washed them in the bath with me. Thank you for that, by the way. I appreciate all the men hauling that water in here. Corbin!"

His leer turned up a notch as his hands slid around the curve of my behind, heading for my fun zone. "My pleasure. And I mean that literally, although I would have preferred the ship not having docked right at the moment you were bathing. I wanted to help wash your back. And front. And legs, and breasts, and right here—"

I yipped, melting against him as his fingers found still sensitive flesh. "Corbin, talk! Talk, we must talk! About many things, such as stepping up our investigations regarding Paul."

With a sigh of regret he removed his hands and smoothed down my skirt. "All right, but I think we could make better use of the time. Come on. I want to show you Mongoose Isle, and I need to find out if there's been any progress yet in locating Paul."

"That's well and fine, but I want to talk—"

"You can talk while I'm showing you around," he said, gently pushing me out of the cabin to the main deck. "I've arranged for transportation. I think you're going to like it. Hoy, Holder! Can I have a couple of minutes, mate?"

Holder gave me a knowing grin as he strolled past. I ignored him, walking over to stand at the railing next to Bas. A half hour ago, as I was just stepping into the tub, the ship had ported on Mongoose Isle, a bustling island about three times the size of Turtle's Back.

Mongoose had a proper wharf, not just a rickety wooden dock like Turtle's Back. Warehouses lined the long stretch of docks, with probably a good two dozen ships docked of varying sizes and types. The larger ships, like Corbin's barque, the big, three-masted square riggers, and largest of all, the ship-of-the-line frigates, were too big to dock and were anchored in the deeper water of the large harbor. As Bas and I watched, two of Corbin's crew clambered down a rope ladder to one of two rowboats that were bobbing up and down next to the barque.

"Big island, huh?" I asked Bas as I looked at the town that glistened a rainbow of colors in the bright midday sun. The town itself was much larger than ours, probably taking up five times the space, located on a long spit of land that jabbed out into the gorgeous turquoise water. Even at a distance I could see the busy activity around the wharf, with ships arriving and leaving with regularity. Tree-lined avenues snaked around the town up to low hills blanketed in sugarcane fields. At the tip of the spit, built into the solid rock promontory, a large stone fortress watched over the town with a quiet assurance that no doubt brought much comfort to the residents of the town. Cannons bristled from the high stone walls running a third of the length of the deep channel into the harbor. I doubted whether any hostile ship would be able to make it past that gauntlet and survive. "It's so pretty, too. Just look at those green fields. And the colors! It's like someone took a painter's palette and shook it over the town, coloring all the shops and buildings as brightly as possible. The Crayola people would love it here. This may be only a virtual setting, but this island and Turtle's Back are truly the most beautiful spots I've ever seen. It's so gorgeous, I just want to weep with the pleasure of seeing it."

"I wonder what it would feel like to be shot with a cannon?" Bas asked, looking at the fort. "Do ye think ye'd feel it? Or do ye think ye'd be knocked out and wouldn't know that ye'd been blown apart with a cannonball?"

I patted him on his non-Bran shoulder. "Thank you, Bas."

"Eh?" the boy asked, giving me a curious glance.

"I was waxing poetic, and you brought me back from the edge," I said, ruffling his hair and stroking Bran's feathers before turning at the sound of Corbin's voice. "Come along; we're going sightseeing."

I sat facing Corbin as he and a few crewmates rowed us to the dock, glancing over my shoulder at the ships anchored in the harbor. "Which ones are yours?"

He pointed at two more barques, a square rigger, and farthest away, a frigate. "Those are my warships. The sailing sloops are docked. All but one, and you have her. Her sister ship is at the far end of the dock, there."

Something struck me about his ships. I looked again at the ones he'd pointed out. "You're flying red flags. All red flags, with no design or anything."

"Aye," he said, his face damp with perspiration as he hauled back on the oar.

"I thought you flew black flags?" I hesitated, torn between wanting to tell him about the plans Bart had for him in case it had some importance in finding Paul, and doing what I could to bring about a cessation of hostilities, not enflame them.

"I do, when the ship I'm attacking refuses to yield," he grunted.

"Oh, really?"

"Yes. I always offer quarter—that's the red flag—first. If the ship refuses to yield peaceably, I run up the black flag, indicating there will be no quarter given."

"Quarter being mercy?" I asked, thinking of Bart's crew that Corbin had so ruthlessly wiped out.

"Yes."

"Hmm. So if Bart was going to attack you again—"

"He's always attacking me," Corbin said, waving a dismissive hand.

"He is? Oh." I bit my lip, still hesitant (I hate that). "So you wouldn't be surprised if I told you he has more plans to attack you?"

His grin flashed at me for a moment. "I'd be surprised if he doesn't. Bart was programmed to create conflict in the game with the real players. In other words, his sole purpose is to declare war on me, and anyone else playing the game. You got pulled into his crew, so you're excluded from that particular event, but you don't have to worry on my behalf. Bart is the least of my worries."

Whew. That relieved my mind. If Corbin wasn't concerned, then I could do what I needed to do on my own to settle things between him and Bart—assuming Bart's programming allowed him to be peacable. "Er . . . did you program him so he'll negotiate a peace treaty, too?"

"Yes. Here we go. You ready?" Corbin had arranged for a horse-drawn open carriage to be waiting for us when we reached the shore.

As the horses clip-clopped their way down the cobblestone streets, he pointed out various sights, from the best place to buy rum and cannon shot (both important parts of a ship's stock) to the newly built governor's palace that sat at the base of the spit of land.

"I thought this was your island, but you said someone else is governor?" I asked, a bit confused.

"I helped take the island from the English, right, but I don't run it. Edward Teach is governor here now."

"Edward Teach? Why does his name sound familiar?"

"He was Blackbeard," Corbin said, smiling. "You didn't expect me to create a pirate game and not have Blackbeard in it, did you?"

"How silly of me." I smiled as Corbin hauled me up closer to him, enjoying it so much I missed a few blocks of his narration.

By the time we had seen all there was to see of the town and were headed to a dockside inn for dinner, I felt I'd let him have his way long enough. So long as we were stuck in the game and had to play out the scenario, we needed to talk about the future. The inhabitants of Turtle's Back might not be real in *our* world, but in this world they were, and I was growing extremely fond of many of them.

"Stop looking at me like that," I warned Corbin as he sat down across a rough-planked table.

"Like what?"

"Like you're on a thousand-calorie-a-day diet, and I'm a chocolate éclair. This is a public inn, and we need to talk, so behave yourself."

His smile was so infectious, it was almost impossible to resist returning it. "Well, you *are* filled with creamy good-ness. . . ."

"I want to talk about this blockade," I said, leaning back so a well-endowed barmaid could set down my mug of ale and Corbin's glass of brandy. As I mopped up the splashed ale I gave her a fulminating glare, which was completely wasted because she was too busy trying to get Corbin to look down her cleavage.

He kept his gaze firmly on me.

"You get beaucoup bonus points for that," I told him when the barmaid finally skedaddled.

"Whew. Good. I hoped so, because it was totally going against nature not to look, but I did try. What did you want to say about the blockade? I assume you want to help with it."

"I'm already signed up to do so." I took a sip of my ale. It was the most innocuous of all the beverages in the game, but even so, experience had taught me that it packed enough of a wallop that my brain translated its effect as a form of virtual drunkenness.

Corbin frowned. "What do you mean, you signed up? I'm organizing the blockade—if someone has spoken to you about participating without clearing it through me first—"

"Corbin, I'm not a member of your crew. You said we had to fulfill the scenario, so I have to stick with Bart, regardless of my feelings. Unless you think my switching would have no impact on the game play?"

He thought for a minute, then shook his head. "If Bart approached you to join his crew, then that means the scenario needs a player in that crew. If you left it, the scenario might stall, and we'd never get any farther. Much as I'd like to have you in my crew, it's probably better if you stay a member of Bart's."

I took a deep breath, dreading the moment that had come. "Well, technically I'm not really a member of the crew; I'm sort of probational there. However, Bart has asked me to help protect Turtle's Back from the blockade, and I've agreed to do so."

I leaned back against the wall, waiting for Corbin's reaction to my statement. I had decided that my involvement in the blockade was the best bargaining chip I had to persuade him to talk peaceable negotiations rather than all-out war.

"You're my wife," he said, his frown growing.

"Only in the game."

"We're talking about events in the game," he said, his eyes narrowing. "You can't blockade against your own husband."

"You just said I had to stick with the crew. Could I possibly blockade against my crew without screwing the game plan up?" I asked.

I swear a black cloud started forming over his head. "No. But that doesn't mean I'm going to allow this—"

"Wait before you get all riled up. I didn't think you'd like me on the other side, so luckily, I came up with a solution to the problem."

He waited for the count of five. "What solution?"

"You and Bart get together and hammer out a peace treaty. Or," I said quickly, sensing danger from the way Corbin's eyes lit with menace, "your duly appointed representatives meet and work on a peaceful end to the hostilities between you and Bart. That should be within the bounds of the scenario, and yet would cancel all the war stuff."

"Except the 'war stuff' is what powers the game," Corbin said, a definite note of finality in his voice. "This game is built to generate conflict, Amy. Blockades are a part of that. In this case, I'm going to have to say that this blockade is preordained, and going to have to be carried out in order to further the scenario."

"But you don't know that for certain."

"I think I know the game a bit better than you," he said kind of testily.

"Yes, you do. But—"

"There're no buts, Amy. You don't like the war, and you want to stop it. I understand that. But you need to understand that it's necessary for it to go forward in order to help us end the damn scenario."

Now I was miffed. It's true I wanted the war stopped, but I hated sounding so wimpy. "Fine. So while we spend however long it takes to blockade, how are we going to be finding your ex-partner?"

"I have three men in my crew I use as spies—normally they target Bart's crew—but now I have them feeding me the latest ship sightings and taking note of conversations between pirates. On their own, the computer characters don't chat with one another."

"Whoa!" I thought about the women standing around the well talking and laughing. "I've seen people talking."

"Yes, you have. The minute you come within range, their behavior becomes human. But when no players are around, the computer characters don't interact."

"Ah. Okay." I raised my eyebrows, sidetracked for a moment with the idea that the computer characters could be made to spy on one another. "So your guys can take note of anyone talking, with the idea that someone in that conversation is human?"

"Yes, they can." A look of pride temporarily overrode the irritation in his eyes. "I've got the best AI around powering the characters in this game."

"AI? That's artificial intelligence?"

"Right. Friend of mine works at Caltech developing sophisticated AI models. He stripped down a version for me and gave me the rights to modify it for the pirate world. The result is computer characters that carry sophisticated learning abilities. The more you interact with them, the more real they seem. There's only one area they're limited in—"

"They have no past beyond the game?" I asked.

A tiny little smile flashed across his lips. "You've discovered that, have you? Limitations on data storage make it impossible to give each character a detailed past, so we opted to use the space to increase their ability to learn and develop their own traits."

I looked around the smoky inn. It was typical of what I imagined were the inns of the period and location—a long, low building with tiny glassless shuttered windows, a cross-beam ceiling, the dirt floor littered with debris, bones from chickens stripped of their meat, the tables and chairs scattered around the room in various states of disrepair. The patrons of the inn were just as disreputable as the furniture—pirates of every class skulked around, sang off-key sea shanties, ogled the barmaids (none of whom seemed to mind), laughed, joked, argued, fought, and slept with blatant disregard for the general chaos going on around them.

"Well, I have to say, it was a good choice. Everyone here seems so real. They all have such depth to them, it makes it hard to remember they're not real."

"They are real; at least they are here," Corbin argued.

I smiled. "Yeah, I agree with that. Here, they're real. And that's why if you insist on being pigheaded and stubborn about this blockade thing, I'm going to do my best to help Bart stop you."

"Amy—"

"The scenario, remember? You can't have it both ways, Corbin. Either I have to stick with Bart's crew, or we blow the scenario."

"You're using that as an excuse to try to blackmail me into canceling the blockade," he growled. "You could find a reason to not be a part of the blockade. That would allow it to go forward, but you wouldn't be involved."

"Maybe. But I like the people on Turtle's Back, Corbin. I don't want to see any of them hurt or suffering because no food or supplies can get in because you want to play war.

And if I help Bart, perhaps I can make the blockade end faster. Plus there's the other bonus."

The hard, flat look of anger was back in his eyes. "What bonus?"

"Our marriage, remember?" I set down my mug of ale and leaned across the table to level a glare at him. "You said if we got married I'd have access to your things, and you would get stuff to me through the blockade."

"Yes, but that was before." It wasn't easy to catch the fleeting expressions on his face in the smoky, dark atmosphere of the inn, but I recognized the mulish expression on his face well enough. Lord knows I'd seen a similar expression on Tara's face often enough. Oh, all right, and mine as well.

"Before what?"

"Before I knew I loved you!" he bellowed, slapping his hands down on the table.

Everyone in the room stopped, turning to look at our corner. I smiled weakly and gave a quick wave. "Little argument, nothing serious. Go back to your carousing and wenching and . . . er . . . vomiting."

I looked away from the man ralphing into a slops bucket and gave Corbin my most patient look. "Corbin, I don't want anyone hurt—not you or the people on Turtle's Back; not even Bart."

"No. There's got to be another way."

"Fine. Give me another option."

His jaw tightened.

I put my hand on his, giving it a little squeeze. "I don't think we have any other choice, Corbin."

"Dammit!" He cursed profanely under his breath. I felt for him, I really did, but there just didn't seem to be any other way around it—I was going to have to go to war against him.

"Good-bye, Corbin. I don't want to go, but I don't really have a choice—not if we want to bring an end to this. You'll be hearing from me. I will hold you to your word about supplies for Turtle's Back, by the way." I stood up, gathering my things.

"You're just going to up and leave me?" Corbin stayed seated, as if he didn't take me leaving seriously.

"I'm not leaving you—not really. Bas and I are going home. I'd like to be home before morning since I have a feeling there's going to be a lot to do before the blockade."

He crossed his arms over his chest, the mulish look back. "And just how do you plan on getting there? Whisking on a convenient bit of wind, perhaps?"

"Don't be ridiculous." I lifted my chin, stung by the fact that he didn't seem to understand how badly I was feeling about the whole thing. "I'll find someone to sail us there if you're not inclined to help your own wife."

"*My wife* would not abandon me for another man," Corbin growled, getting to his feet at last.

"Now, that isn't fair at all. Dammit, Corbin, give me an alternative!"

"I've given you one. You won't take it," he said, anger visible in his eyes.

"You're not the only one who has a shred of pride," I pointed out, angry, hurt, and sad all at the same time. "If the game calls for me to be true to my crew, then I'm going to be true. Especially since I think I can help bring about the end of the war."

"You just don't like conflict," he snapped.

"Not when it concerns people I care about, no. I don't suppose there's a mechanism in the game for divorce?" I asked sweetly.

"No."

I smiled. "Then we're still married, husband mine. Good

night. I'll be in contact about the supplies we need on Turtle's Back."

"Amy!"

I turned on my heel and marched out of the inn, hoping against hope that Corbin either would come up with another plan that wouldn't screw us up as far as the scenario went, or would at the very least understand why I had to go to war.

"Good luck findin' yer way to Turtle, lass," Corbin called after me in a voice loud enough to be heard across the entire lower half of the island. "There'll not be a soul here who'll take ye against me wishes. When ye've had enough of yer high-and-mighty act, let me know."

I sighed. Hope is such a fickle thing.

Chapter 15

Ah, leave me not to pine
Alone and desolate. . . .

—Ibid, Act I

"Holder, can you—"

"No."

I gave him a disgusted glare. "You've been talking to Corbin, haven't you?"

The first mate, now clad in tight leather pants, a swishy white shirt, and a red sash tied around his waist, cocked an eyebrow at me briefly before returning his attention to the blond barmaid who stood behind a tall counter polishing a row of metal tankards. "Of course I have. And he told me to tell you no when you asked me to sail you to Turtle's Back, and I, ever the dutiful friend, have just done as I was so ordered. Can you be ready to leave in an hour?"

"Huh?" He grinned at me. I smacked him on the arm and said, "You're going to take me? What was all that no business?"

"Corbin told me to tell you no. I said I would. So I said

no. He didn't actually forbid me to take you home," Holder answered, still grinning. I grinned back.

"I like how you think. Yes, we can be ready to leave in an hour. Er . . . that is, we'll be ready if you tell me where Bas is." I looked around the inn in which I'd finally tracked down Holder. It was located near the governor's mansion, in a much more affluent area of town, and seemed to be patronized by upscale pirates, if there was such a thing. Even so, an inn with bawdy women and drunken men was no place for a child. "You didn't bring him here, did you?"

"Naw, I left him at Wry Wenham's."

I accepted the small glass of ale the buxom barmaid brought and, distracted for a moment by a thought, asked Holder, "I swear I've seen that woman before. Why do all the barmaids here have an overabundance of bosomage?"

He laughed. "Because this game is going to appeal primarily to men, and I like them that way."

"I thought you were happily married," I said, sipping my ale.

"I am. See Saucy Sally there?" He nodded toward the barmaid, who was serving someone at the other end of the counter. She was identical in every way but clothing and hairstyle to the barmaid who'd been ogling Corbin. "That's my wife, Linda."

My eyebrows shot up.

"Or rather, her face and body are my wife's. Linda was one of the models we digitized for the game. She makes a fine barmaid, doesn't she?" He paused to admire the woman as she jiggled her way to the next customer.

"Very fitting. Who or what is Wry Wenham's, and where is it located?"

He smiled indulgently as Saucy Sally slapped the face of a pirate who was apparently getting a bit too fresh. "I had Corb program in that response whenever a man gets too blatant. I don't mind them looking, but no one is going to have her but me."

I opened my mouth to say something about that but changed my mind. "Wry Wenham's?" I prompted, instead.

"Surgeon. His place is two streets down, on the corner. Big bougainvillea bushes outside it."

"A surgeon?" I asked, a little surprised. I had assumed Bas would drift along with whatever morbid whim claimed him. "That doesn't sound too bad. Does his house have a nice view?"

The corner of his mouth twitched. "Not really. He's also the undertaker. The second Bas heard Wenham had in the bodies from a recent shipwreck, he was off like a scalded seal."

I smacked him on the arm. "That is not responsible child care. Now I'm going to have to put up with listening to him yammer on and on and on about drowning victims. I'll get you for this; see if I don't. Which ship will I meet you at?"

He gave me the ship name and directions to find her, and promised to be at the dock in an hour or less.

"One question," I said before leaving him.

"Why am I going against Corbin's wishes?" he asked, taking a long swig of rum.

I nodded.

"Well, I like you, you see. And I think you're good for Corbin. He's worth a small fortune, you know? So lots of gold diggers have him in their sights. They drop into his lap. It's not good for him to just have everything handed to him—but you're not like that. He has to work to win you, and if I can help make things just a teeny bit more difficult for him, then I will."

I smiled, despite myself. "You really are something else. First you go out of your way to throw us together, marrying me to Corbin despite the fact that I didn't want to be married to him, and now you're trying to keep us apart."

His eyebrows bobbled at me. "It's for the best."

"Best for finishing the scenario and finding Paul, or best for Corbin and me?"

"Anything to say it can't be both?"

"Nope." I thought for a moment, unwilling to put into words what I wanted to ask. "Do you think we have a chance?"

"You and Corbin?"

"Yeah."

"Inside the game? Absolutely."

"That's well and fine, but what about outside it? That's what really matters."

The laughing light left his eyes as he gave me a long look. "I'd say that's completely up to you."

Approximately four and a half hours later, Bas and I took a lantern from Holder and marched our way along the leeward-side path up and over the turtle's back, down to the town proper. As I feared, Bas had been full of the (to him) fascinating facets of drowned bodies and had spent the entire trip describing in great detail his time spent with the surgeon/undertaker. I let him go on not only because it was one of his few pleasures, but also because I was currently struggling with a few unwieldy and unwelcome emotions.

I'd only been parted from him for six hours, and already I missed Corbin.

"I am not going to do this," I told myself a short while later as we slipped into Renata's house. I sent Bas off to the small closetlike room Renata had given up to him, and headed toward my own room. Although it was the small hours of the morning, I could hear voices and the sound of a concertina from the main room, while assorted giggles, shouts, and moans from some of the bedrooms told me the ladies were still going strong. "I'm not going to become one of those women who can't exist without a man. They're nice in many aspects, and handy when it comes to dealing with spiders, but I can get along just fine without one in my life permanently."

"Can ye, now?" Renata asked as she emerged from my room just as I was reaching for the half-opened door, causing me to jump in surprise.

"Oh, man, you startled me. Evening, Renata."

"Good evenin' to ye, too," she said, giving me a shrewd look. "Ye're comin' in a wee bit later than normal, eh?"

"Oh. Uh. Yeah. I . . . Bas and I were out sailing, and we didn't get back until late. We ended up on the other side of the island," I said, fingers crossed behind my back even though I wasn't outright lying.

She nodded, but the look she gave me told me I wasn't fooling her. "Ye're a woman with a few brains about ye," she said, surprising me again. Renata wasn't one to heap praise on someone where it wasn't due. "Ye've got yer wits about ye, and ye're not afraid to work. And ye stand up for what ye believe in."

"Thank you," I said, humbled but wondering what brought on the praise. And what had she been doing in my bedroom? I didn't have anything there but a few items of clothing that had been given to me, and the fake leg I'd acquired the first day. Certainly nothing of interest for anyone to snoop around.

Her gimlet glance turned even sharper. "There are times, however, when I think ye've less sense than that tick-riddled harbinger of death that clings to Bas's shoulder. Ye're riskin' losin' the man what is meant for ye over a few scraps of pride. 'Tis folly of the worst sort, lass, but I don't expect ye'll be seein' that until it's too late."

She hobbled past me, leaving me sputtering, "But . . . he . . . we're only . . . I'm not . . . huh?"

"If I was ye, I'd be doin' everythin' I could to join me man."

"Er . . . we're on opposite sides of the blockade. That makes it a bit difficult."

"Does it?" She stopped for a moment at the door to the common room. "Perhaps ye're not tryin' hard enough."

"Not trying hard enough!" I made an impatient gesture. "I like that. Just what am I supposed to be doing that I'm not?"

She made a thoughtful face. "Well, as ye're askin' me advice . . . if we was wearin' each other's shoes, I'd be makin' sure that I talked to Black Corbin as soon as possible. If ye truly want to resolve the blockade, that is."

"Of course I do, and I'd love to talk to him, but there's no time. Bart says the blockade ships will be here tomorrow morn—scratch that, this morning—and short of using Girl Scout semaphore, I don't see how I'm going to be able to talk with him."

"Get him on yer ship, dearie," Renata said, smiling.

"Hmm." I mused that thought over. "That might be possible."

"Aye, 'twould be an unnatural man as could resist a wench as comely as yerself."

"Thank you . . . I think."

Her laughter floated through the door as she closed it behind her, leaving me alone in the hallway. I shook my head before entering my room.

"I don't think it's going to be as easy as she seems to think it is. And why should she care whether or not Corbin and I are on the same side?" I asked the silent room as I entered. Faint moonlight entered through the unshuttered open window, but the room was empty, and it gave me no answer . . . until I started to undress. As I opened the small, battered chest where I kept my clothing, I noticed that someone had been in it. Half tucked down under a pair of striped knickers, as if hurriedly shoved there, was the corner of the letter Corbin had sent me. I sat back on my heels as I considered the fact that it wasn't where I had left it. Just what on earth was Renata doing going through my things and reading Corbin's letter?

I fell asleep with my mind whirling with questions about Renata. Interspersed with them were random memories of my last few hours with Corbin, and the sudden knowledge that what I felt for him was going beyond anything I'd felt for a man before.

My brain amused me with the most erotic dream I'd ever had. In it, Corbin was covering my body in hot kisses that had me squirming with myriad forms of desire and need and want. I begged him to stop the torment and allow me to take my turn romping on his playground, but he wasn't listening to me.

Then I woke up to find out it wasn't a dream.

"What the—" A hand clapped over my mouth before I could scream.

"Shhh! It's just me. Don't yell or you'll wake everyone up."

I glared up at the dark shape that loomed over me. "They'll be awake until it's morning, and what the hell are you doing here?"

"You're my wife. It's traditional to sleep with one's wife. Since you refused my bed, I've come to yours." Corbin slid to the side on the narrow bed, pulling me up tight against him so I could feel how aroused he was. My body hummed a happy little tune of expectation, one I did my best to squelch until I knew exactly what was going on.

"I didn't refuse your bed; you refused to take me home."

"Your home is with me now," he said, his voice tired.

"That wasn't our agreement. Why are you here?"

"I told you—we're married. I want to sleep with you."

I peered up at the dark blob that was his face. "You sailed four hours just so we could sleep together?"

"Yes," he said, rather grumpily to my mind. My anger melted away in a warm rush of a much softer emotion. I slid my hand up his belly, tracing a line over to his ribs. He sucked in his breath.

"Does anyone know you're here?"

"No," he answered, his body tightening as I gently pushed him over onto his back, bending my head to swirl my tongue around his pectoral muscle.

"How did you get here without being seen?" I asked his nipple, giving it a little lick. He twitched beneath me. "Bas and I ran into a half dozen people on the way home."

"I designed the island, remember?"

I smiled at the suddenly rough note in his voice. My dream had given me a clear vision of what I wanted to do, and since Corbin had gone to so much trouble just so we could spend a few hours together, I would be a fool to deny both of us. "Yes, I remember. Ooh, a second nipple."

"There's a hidden cave that reaches a secret tunnel through the emerald mine. I came up through that without anyone knowing I was on the island. Oh, dear God in heaven. Do that again."

I scraped my teeth gently on his nipple at the same time I dragged my fingernails up the inside of his thigh. His hips bucked upwards as he groaned.

"Clever man. I don't suppose you've changed your mind about the blockade?"

"No," he said, stiffening. "Amy, if you think you can change my mind with lovemaking—"

"I don't," I interrupted, kissing my way down his chest

toward his cute little stomach. I swirled my tongue around
his belly button a couple of times. "I just wanted to know
whether I should do the superdeluxe tongue bath, or the
economy version. I guess you're going for economy."

He propped himself up on one elbow to glare at me. I
couldn't see his face in the darkness, but I knew the dis-
gruntled expression that would be there. I grinned at it. "Oh,
all right, superdeluxe it is. But you have to lie there until I'm
through with you."

There was a distinct note of interest in his voice. "What
does the superdeluxe tongue bath entail?"

I bent over his hip and bit it. Not hard enough to hurt, but
with enough force that he sucked in his breath again. "Biting. I'm in the mood to nibble you to death. You up for it?"

He grabbed my hand and brought it around proof that he
was up for it. "What do you think?"

I nipped my way across his stomach, following each love
bite with a little tongue swirling. By the time I worked my
way down to his party zone, inspiration (and a rumble in my
stomach) hit me.

"Don't move," I said, sliding off the bed. I snatched up
my skirt and shirt, ignoring his whispered demands that I return to bed. "I'll be right back. Just stay there."

Miraculously, he was still on the bed when I returned
with my hands full. He'd lit a candle, though, so I could see
the unhappy look on his face.

"Where have you been? What do you have?" he asked.

I smiled and set down the three bowls I was carefully bal-
ancing, quickly removing my clothing before taking one of
the bowls and sitting next to where Corbin lay. "This is
fygey. It's an almond and fig pudding."

"I know what it is. I researched all the food used here,"
he said, frowning as he watched me swirl my finger around
the still warm pudding. "You're going to eat *now*? I have the

commute from hell, Amy. I don't have a lot of time before I have to leave."

I gave him my best leer. "Oh, yes. I'm going to eat now."

Without waiting for him to respond, I tipped the bowl so a bit of the pudding slopped onto his belly. With much gusto, I licked and sucked the pudding up, licking my lips at the taste of Corbin-flavored dessert.

"That was good, but you know, I think we can make it better." His eyes got big as I turned to look at that part of him that was expressing its approval of my change in dining habits.

"Yes, yes, I'm sure we can make it better," he said, grabbing handfuls of bedding as I tipped the bowl again, slathering his penis with the sweet pudding. "Oh my God, Amy. You're not . . . dear Lord!"

His eyes all but rolled back in his head as I licked up the pudding, leaving him hot and hard and clearly wanting more.

As did I. "Hmm. Good start, but a little unsatisfying," I said, licking the last little bit of pudding from him. His chest sheened in the candlelight, his face flushed as he struggled to keep from grabbing me. I smiled. "Such good manners should be rewarded. I have here some treacle tart."

"I love treacle tart," he said, his chest heaving.

"Do you? I've never tried it, but you know, it looks awfully sticky and gooey." I dipped my fingers into the open-faced tart, smearing the thick filling along the length of his shaft. He twitched. "It looks so thick, in fact, that mere licking isn't going to take it off."

"No?" he asked hopefully.

"Nope. This is going to take some serious sucking to get every last morsel of goodness."

"Thank God," he moaned, his head falling back on the pillow as I flicked my tongue across his treacly parts.

"Mmm. Tasty. I think I'm going to enjoy this."

"I know I am," he said, but it was the last coherent thing he said for a while as I consumed the treacle tart in a manner that had both of us keyed up to point where I thought one—or both—of us might explode.

When he warned me that to continue would be folly, I looked sadly at the last bowl. "But I still have the apple cream custard."

"No problem," he said, suddenly lunging up. Before I knew it, he had flipped me onto my back and was nudging my knees apart, the bowl of custard in his hand. "I happen to love apple cream. If you don't mind sharing, that is."

I didn't even hesitate. "It's all yours," I said.

He smiled at the double entendre, but instead of dabbing me with bits of custard, as I expected, he poured the whole thing over me, starting at my crotch and ending at my chest.

"Corbin!" I shouted in surprise. His hand clapped over my mouth.

"Quiet," he warned.

I nodded my head but said when he removed his hand, "Ew! You got it everywhere! Now I'm all sticky."

"Sweetheart, you're going to be a hell of a lot more sticky by the time I'm through with you," he said.

And he was right. By the time he'd licked off the custard bedecking my groin, he'd sent me spinning to heaven twice. My pleasure had pushed him farther than he'd imagined, but neither of us complained when he abandoned the cleanup job to thrust hard into me. The custard acted as a lubricant on my torso, causing our bodies to slide together in the most erotic sensation of flesh rubbing on flesh that I'd ever felt, the feeling of his custard-dampened chest hair brushing against my sensitive breasts almost more than I could stand.

I came again, hard, my legs locked around his hips in my attempt to pull him deeper into me, triggering his own release. I caught his groan in my mouth as he pumped, his hips straining as he poured himself into me.

"I love you, Amy. God help me, I love you," he panted into my ear, following that declaration with a wet kiss.

I kissed his neck, smoothing my hands down his back, wondering if he really meant it, wondering how we were going to resolve the problems facing us, and most of all, wondering why I suddenly didn't give a damn about anything but the man who lay in my arms.

Chapter 16

Oh, better far to live and die
Under the brave black flag I fly. . . .
—Ibid, Act I

"You can't be serious about leaving."

Corbin pulled on his pants and boots, pausing to look around for the black shirt he'd worn in order to avoid being seen. "You can't be serious about staying," he countered, having found the shirt.

I watched him don it, giving myself a moment or two to admire the play of muscles in his shoulders and back as he did so. He might not be a blond bodybuilder, he might not be handsome enough to drop a woman at twenty paces, but he sent my blood boiling every time I saw him. "Me staying does not entail a four-hour sail in the wee small hours of the morning. Aren't you tired?"

"Yes." He stood and looked down at where I lay on the bed, crumpled and exhausted and extremely sated. My limbs felt boneless. "You look like a woman who has been well loved."

I gave him a long, slow smile. "I am a woman who has

been well loved. So well loved that I think you turned my legs to jelly. Corbin . . . gah. I want to beg you not to leave, but I don't want you to stay, either. Bart would gut you the instant he saw you."

"We've been over this twice in the last half hour, sweetheart." He bent to give me another of those kisses that made my toes curl with delight. "The blockade has to go forward. You, however, don't have to be a part of it."

"And for the third time, I'm going to be with my crew, bringing the blockade to a swift and successful end," I pointed out, propping myself up on an elbow. "Corbin, what if you talked to Bart? Would it be possible for him to cancel the whole thing?"

"Not if it's part of the scenario, and I don't see how it can be anything but integral to it. Too much is at stake," he said, giving me another kiss before swinging a leg over the windowsill. "I've got to go, love. The sun will be up in a few hours, and I need to make it to my ship without anyone seeing me."

"Hang on, Corbin—I never got to ask you about how I go about getting supplies through the blockade."

He gave me an unreadable look. "You'll need to go to one of the supply ships and requisition what you need."

"Okay."

"You are aware that you will only be able to get the most basic of supplies? If you think you'll negate the purpose of the blockade, you're in for a disappointment."

"I understand," I said evenly. "I know it bothers you that I'm going to be supplying the people you're trying to starve out, but I'm not going to let you hurt them, Corbin."

He sighed. "I'm not trying to harm the people of Turtle, Amy. As far as the game goes, I'm trying to help them."

I fought an eye roll at that ridiculous statement. Corbin swung his second leg out the window.

"Wait," I said, sliding out of bed despite the fact that I was naked. "What should I do about Renata?"

He paused, cocking an eyebrow at me. "What about her?"

"I told you I thought she'd been reading my letter from you, and she searched my room. And also she . . . well, she feels different from the others, if you know what I mean. She's said some things that, now that I think about it, are kind of odd."

"Hmm." His brows pulled together for a moment. "Renata is the mentor for Turtle's Back. I put one on each island—mentors are put into the program to help the newbies, guiding them to crews, jobs, that sort of thing. Mentors can flip back and forth between colloquial language and modern language, depending on the situation."

"Oh," I said, a tiny bit disappointed. I liked Renata and was very grateful for everything she'd done for me, but the idea that she could be the mysterious Paul who had trapped us here was very tempting.

"However . . ." He frowned again, shaking his head a little. "She shouldn't be inquisitive enough to search your things. That's outside the programming. It's not out of the question that Paul has corrupted her file, however, and is using her character. Keep an eye on her, Amy. Make a note of anything she does or says that doesn't ring true. If the situation warrants it, we'll take a harder look at her."

He jumped out of the window when voices from the square could be heard, giving me a heated look before disappearing into the blackness. My heart twisted at the sight of his shadow blending into those of the trees, the faint remaining moonlight casting an odd silvery tint to everything.

I stayed at the window for a while, resting my cheek against the cool wood of the window frame while I tried to sort out my tangled thoughts. The fact that I *had* tangled thoughts annoyed me—I was a methodical, organized person, and I expected my brain to follow suit. But ever since I'd woken up to find myself in this pirate world, control had slipped from my fingers, and I seemed to be unable to regain it.

"Stop making such a big deal about it, brain," I lectured myself as I got washed up and dressed. "There are just two points that should be concerning you—finding Paul and ending the blockade quickly. Well, all right, there's finding a home for Bas once we do find a way out, so that's three. And I really want to make sure that the retirement fund for Renata's ladies is going to work, not to mention I need to inventory and reorganize Tara's shop so it's more profitable . . . gah. Too many things. All that really matters is getting out of here, and standing around talking to yourself isn't going to help, Amy, so get a move on."

Renata and the ladies never rose before early afternoon, so Bas and I were usually on our own in the mornings. I found him sitting at the scarred table in the common room, morosely eating a bowl of porridge, which was the only thing he knew how to fix.

"Morning, Bas." The raven, who stood perched hopefully on the edge of Bas's earthenware bowl, squawked and flapped his wings at me. "Morning Bran. Bas, don't let him eat off your spoon. You'll get worms or something. Porridge again, eh? Well, we have a big day ahead of us. Let's see if we can't round up something a little more substantial."

By the time I'd cooked up some eggs and fried ham and toasted half a loaf of bread while packing the other half in a basket with cheese, fruit, and some dried meat that looked like desiccated drowning victims' flesh (Bas's opinion) but tasted just like jerky, the sky was beginning to lighten and the square was coming alive.

"Eat up; then I need you to go round up the crew. Have them get the *Wench* ready for sailing."

Bas's eyes lit up as he chewed a huge mouthful of eggs and ham. "We be goin' into the blockade, then?"

"Yup. Just as soon as I get the ship stocked." I pulled a small leather pouch open and dug the eight silver coins from it, holding out my palm so Bas could see. "Look, reales! Bart gave them to me to stock my ship for the blockade."

"Stock it with what?" Bas asked, crumbling up toast and pushing his plate over to where Bran hopped impatiently. The bird had almost as big an appetite as Bas did.

"Shot mostly. Cannonballs and wadding and a couple of kegs of powder. Oh, and Bart said to get some rum, too. I suppose I'd better bring along some ale for those of us who aren't grog drinkers."

Bas's eyes lit up at the mention of cannons, but I left before he could express his hopes concerning cannon fire, with particular regards to its more gruesome aspects.

The square was bustling with people, even at that predawn hour—the women and children holding torches and lanterns and watching with big eyes from the doorways as the men hauled supplies down to the dock to stock the ships being readied for the blockade. I squinted at the harbor but couldn't see anything in the blackness. Even so, I had a feeling Corbin's fleet was out there somewhere. I wondered whether Corbin had gone home to Mongoose first or had just sailed his ship into the blockade line. Regardless, they were coming, and I needed to get ready.

"Ahoy, me hearties," I called out a quarter hour later as I clambered up the wooden plank leading onto my ship. "Pru and Imp, the supplies are on a cart on the dock—please move them onto the ship. Tar, make ready to sail. Bas . . . er . . . do something cabin boyish. I just need to get final orders from Pangloss, and we'll be on our way."

The crew didn't jump to as I had hoped they would, but the twins shambled off with a couple of lanterns to bring the supplies on board, while Tar muttered sourly as he made ready with the lines.

I hurried off to find the first mate. He stood at the far end of the dock, calling orders to the crew preparing his ship. The other officers were doing the same. Supply carts ran back and forth from the town's shops to the ships, casting odd, twisting shadows in the flickering torchlight, turning the normally quiet dock into a madhouse of activity.

I wound my way through the people, carters' donkeys, and barrels of gunpowder.

"Reporting for duty," I said, saluting Pangloss smartly. He nodded to me, signaling he'd be with me in a minute. I used the time to chat up a few carters I hadn't spoken to before, but none of them struck me at all as anything but computer characters.

"Amy, ye look fit and hale today," Pangloss said, waving me over to him. "Are ye ready for the action ye'll see, lass?"

"Absolutely," I said, meeting his questioning gaze. "Any last-minute instructions?"

"None other than we'll want ye to be concentratin' yer efforts on the *Java Guru*."

"I beg your pardon?"

"*Java Guru*. It be the name of Black Corbin's flagship. We didn't know which ship he'd be usin', but there's no mistakin' the *Guru*. She be painted the ungodly colors of red and black." He handed me a spyglass, pointing toward the opening of the harbor. I opened the glass, squinting through it to look out. There wasn't much light at all, but beyond the arms of the harbor, a dark silhouette became visible against the slightly lighter horizon. A flash of light high up on the silhouette gave me a moment's vision of a mast flying a red flag.

"Sounds very distinctive," I said. "So you want me to shoot her up? She looks big."

"Aye, she's a barque."

"Ugh. That could blow me out of the water."

"If ye get broadside to her, aye, she could. But ye won't, now, will ye, lass?" He beetled his eyebrows meaningfully at me.

"I guess not."

"Ye need to be sailin' now, before it gets light enough for them to see that ye're comin' from the island. Hug the shore until ye get to the harbor entrance, then turn leeward and catch up at the tail of the blockade line."

"Don't you think someone will see me?" I asked, hesitant.

"Nay. At the time ye're joinin' up to their rear, I'll be at the head, firin' off a few shots to keep their attention forward. Anyone who notices ye sailin' up behind 'em will see ye flyin' Corbin's flag and think ye're a straggler who just caught up. From there, ye can move up to the heart of the blockade—the flagship."

I handed Pangloss back the glass, worrying my lower lip as I tried to make a decision about what I was going to do. Harming Corbin was out of the question. But if I blithely sailed into the blockade and didn't do anything, it might gack the scenario up. The key, I decided as I made my way back to my ship, was to fire a lot but miss Corbin's ships entirely. Bart would just put down my misses to bad aim, yet I would be doing my part to push the game play forward.

And there was the little matter of running supplies back to the town. I had yet to figure out a way to explain how I was able to bring in supplies, but I was confident I'd think of something when the time came.

"Weigh anchor," I ordered when I returned to my ship, pleased to see that the supplies had been loaded and properly stowed. "We're going to stay close to the shore, so everyone needs to keep an eye out for problems. Once we clear the harbor, we'll join up with the blockade."

Four sets of surprised eyes turned on me.

"We'll be undercover. Like a nautical version of James Bond," I told my men. They didn't even blink, just stared at me with identical blank looks. I sighed to myself and gestured them to their tasks. "Just get us going. We need to be in the blockade before it gets light enough for them to see us clearly. Douse those lanterns. We need to be running silent and dark, like a particularly clever and saucy sort of deadly shark."

I hummed a bit of the *Jaws* theme as my ship slipped away from the noise and mayhem of the dock. I climbed up to my favorite spot—the crow's nest—to watch for trouble as we sailed as close to shore as possible without grounding. Pangloss must have been watching for me, for when we started around the far arm of the harbor and I ordered the ship to turn toward the last silhouette in a long line of ships, Pangloss's ship started firing its guns.

"There's our distraction," I said to Bas, who had joined me in the crow's nest. He had sharp eyes and seemed to see better in the dim light than I did. As we joined the tail of the blockade, I eyed the dark line of ships becoming more and more visible with each minute. "How many ships do you count?"

Bran squawked a protest as Bas scrambled up to the railing and leaned forward out of the crow's nest, as if a few extra inches would help him see better. I grabbed the back of his shirt to make sure he didn't tumble to the deck below, relieved when he hopped back down onto the circular platform with me.

"Eleven."

I sighed. That's the number I'd counted, as well, which meant Bart's crew was outnumbered almost three to one.

"If I really wanted to end the blockade quickly, I could just fill Corbin's ships full of lead, but that would be unforgiveable of me. I'll just give them a harmless show, instead," I said to myself. Bas looked at me in surprise. "Yarr! I mean, I would if we weren't bloodthirsty, gore-lovin' pirates! Kill! Maim! Destroy! And all that jazz."

He smiled in utter delight.

The sky was turning to a slate gray now, indicating the sun's imminent arrival. As my sloop gained speed, it passed the hindmost ship, a blue and white sloop bearing the name *Katrin's Loss*. I watched nervously as we passed, braced and ready to order the ship to turn around if there was any outcry at our sudden arrival, but evidently my saucy ship's distinctive—and well-known—appearance coupled with Corbin's flag was the passport I needed.

"What's goin' to be happenin' now?" Bas asked, scratching his head with the pointy tip of his hook.

"Don't scratch with that thing—you don't know where it's been," I said absently, watching carefully as we sailed past a huge war frigate, the sides of which positively bristled with guns. "What's going to happen now is we're going to mosey up to the flagship all casual-like, and once we get close enough to do some damage, Pangloss and the other officers are going to engage the ships so we can go in with all guns blazing. The first couple of ships should be caught in the cross fire."

"Ah," he said, looking as inscrutable as only an eight-year-old could.

As we passed ship after ship, no one gave us a second look. The foremost blockade warships were dropping anchor in a line-of-ship position that kept their broadsides toward the harbor, so they'd be able to fire on any ship approaching from the island. Pangloss and the others were going to have their work cut out for them—even though I'd been told that cannon fire was remarkably inaccurate at long range, they'd have to get in close enough to have their own guns do good, leaving themselves at risk.

Only three ships separated us from the flagship, which I could now see was painted red and black.

"Corbin has a thing for brightly painted ships, it seems," I said. We were just passing a yellow-and-black sloop—which I was amused to see was named *Bumblebee Tuna*—when all hell broke out.

Bart's officers, who had massed at the entrance of the harbor just out of the range of the blockade guns, suddenly all came to life and started to move toward the line of ships, directly at us.

"Hey!" I shouted, startled as the ships turned broadsides to us. I could hear the shouts of captains ordering their guns loaded as the blockade ships readied themselves for battle. "They're not supposed to be doing that yet! I'm not in position!"

I jumped up and down and waved my hand at the foremost of Bart's ships to try to get the captains' attention, but either they didn't notice me or they didn't care that I was directly in the line of their fire. Their ships started turning so their guns were aimed right at the middle third of the blockade line.

And us.

"Prudence," I yelled down to the deck where my men were gazing with wary eyes at the action, "fire off one of the guns, but not toward any ship. I don't want to hit anyone; I just want to warn Pangloss that I'm not in place yet. Maybe he can't see us."

Bas looked at me like I was deranged.

I shrugged. "It's that, or he's decided to sacrifice us, and much as I love this ship, I have absolutely *no* intention of going down with her."

The midrange boom of my ship's cannon firing echoed off the island in the relatively quiet morning air, the splash of the cannonball as it hit the water almost as loud. I swear nature herself held her breath for a moment to see what the response would be.

We didn't have long to wait. Pangloss's big ship had completed her turn, and from the height of the crow's nest I could see the guns being wheeled out to the portholes. I was between two blockade ships—and dead in the aim of his guns.

"Don't shoot, don't shoot!" I yelled, waving my arms for a moment before scrambling down to the deck. "Let's get the hell out of here," I yelled at my crew. I flung myself at a line that bound one of the sails. "Quickly, we need warp speed. *Right now!*"

A thunderous *boom* blasted through the morning air, a horrible whistling noise accompanying the cannonball as it sailed inches from the bow of my ship. Four other booms sounded as the other officers in Bart's crew opened fire, immediately followed by deep bass responses from the larger blockade ships.

"Should we fire?" Tar asked, frantically lashing down a line.

I looked out at Pangloss's ship and hesitated. Had he just made an honest mistake, or had he, for some reason unbeknownst to me, decided I was the enemy? "No. Let's just get out of the line of fire."

Before we moved twenty feet, Pangloss opened fire on us, seriously opened fire, blasting my beautiful ship with a volley that left the ship—and me—reeling in horror. My crew shouted conflicting orders to each other as they dodged debris from the blasts.

"Stay out of the way," I yelled helplessly, ducking as the top of the mast was blown to smithereens, one of the sails dropping to the deck with a loud, wet slap. "Get down flat on the deck."

"Should we fire?" Tar asked again.

"No time now," I yelled back. "How badly is she damaged?"

"We're takin' in water somethin' terrible, and there's a hole ye could crawl through on the port side. We've lost part of the mast, but she can sail. Just barely," he answered. "If they was to stop now, we could limp back to the island."

"Try to get that sail back up," I told him. "What else can we do to build speed?"

"Lighten the ship," he said before scurrying off to help Impulsive with the line.

"Right, everything heavy overboard," I called out, wrestling with a nearby cask of rum that was used to make grog.

"Not the rum, not the rum!" Prudence yelled, rushing over to wrest the cask out of my arms.

"Too late," I said, my stomach dropping. On Pangloss's ship, the cannons had been reloaded and were being shoved out the portholes. "This doesn't look good."

"Oh, shite," Prudence said, the cask slipping from his fingers as we stood facing the guns.

I knew without anyone telling me that this would be it— the final blow. My sweet sloop wouldn't be able to survive another volley of cannon fire from the larger ship. We were about to sink with her—if we survived the cannonballs.

A flash of yellow at the right caught my eye. The *Bumblebee,* which had dropped anchor, suddenly leaped forward, narrowly missing slamming against us as she put herself between us and Pangloss's ship. Striding along the deck of the ship yelling out orders to fire was a familiar figure.

Corbin wasn't on the flagship, as everyone thought.

Pangloss's ship opened fire, which Corbin returned, but it was clear that the sloop was built for speed and not intended for serious battle. I had a moment of guilt as I realized that this was the ship Corbin must have used to get to Turtle's Back so he could spend the night with me . . . probably he'd sailed around the island, intending to rejoin his fleet, where he would switch over to the flagship. Instead, he was being blasted to bits saving me.

"Turn about," I yelled, flinging myself forward toward the sail.

"Are ye daft?" Tar yelled back. "We're almost clear of the guns."

"I don't care; turn back, turn back! We're not leaving Corbin to get shot up."

Tar looked at me as if I had gone stark, staring insane— which I probably had—but gave the order to turn about. Just as our ship started its turn, a second of Bart's ships joined Pangloss, shooting the crap out of the yellow and black *Bumblebee*. Men bailed out of the ship like fleas jumping off a dog. The two nearest ships in the blockade fleet were turning to help us, the nearest one behind the remains of Corbin's ship. The men who had jumped overboard swam toward them, but as I scanned the water, I didn't seen any sign of the man I wanted most to see.

Until I looked back at the ship. Corbin was wrestling with a gun, trying to do the job of three men and load it himself. The gun bucked as I started to scream out a warning to him, but another blast of cannon fire from Pangloss's ship joined with Corbin's lone gun to drown me out.

Gunpowder was thick in the air, getting in my nose, leaving an acid taste in my mouth, but worst of all, it hung in thick, heavy gray clouds over the decks, obscuring my vision. By the time the gunpowder dispersed enough so we could see, the deck of Corbin's ship was destroyed, half of it gone, the ship slowly sinking into the water. The ship seemed to implode on itself under the cannon fire, but there was enough of it left for me to see that Corbin wasn't still on board.

"Where is he?" I yelled, desperately scanning the wreckage of the ship.

Bas shouted, pointing to the water.

Corbin's body was almost invisible against the dark water, but the shimmer of water on his flesh caught my eye. He was facedown on a chunk of deck, partially draped over a bit of railing. As I watched, the wood started to sink, taking an unconscious—or possibly dead—Corbin with it.

I didn't debate the question of what would happen should one of our virtual selves die while our brains were still hooked up to the game, or whether we even *could* die in the game. All I wanted to do was save Corbin. Without thinking of the wisdom of my actions, I ripped off my boots, snatched up a length of rope, and tossed an end of it to Bas. "Tie it to the railing. If I go down, sail home. Don't try to rescue me."

Bas's eyes were huge, but he nodded, quickly securing one end of the rope. I scrambled up on the railing, took a deep breath, and flung myself into the water.

The shallower waters of the harbor might have been warm, but out in the open sea, the water was cold enough to stun me for a few moments. A floating piece of debris slammed into my head, reminding me that I had a man to save. I trod water trying to see any sign of Corbin, but he had gone down. Without considering the likelihood of my own death, I dived, thanking my stars for the relatively clear water that let me see the sinking body ahead of me. My lungs started to burn as I kicked madly toward Corbin, grabbing him by the shirt to keep him from sinking down to the depths. As I struggled to drag him upward, I wrapped a couple of lengths of rope around him, giving it several sharp tugs that I prayed my crew would interpret as my need for assistance.

Black spots started to dance before my eyes. I looked upward, where I could see the hull of the ship, but it seemed an inordinately long way away. The water didn't seem to be so cold now. In fact, it was rather pleasant, as if it was welcoming me. I drifted toward a deep abyss in the middle of it, clutching Corbin, figuring that if we were together, it might not be so bad. . . .

With a painful jerk, I was slammed up against the side of the ship, my lungs convulsively gasping in both air and water as we broke the surface. Pain blossomed to horrible life all over my body as I collided three more times with the ship while the men hauled us on board.

"We thought we'd lost ye," Prudence said with repulsive good cheer as Corbin and I landed like dead flounders on the deck.

I vomited up a couple of gallons of water, got to my knees, and crawled over to where Corbin lay motionless.

"Anyone know CPR?" I asked, feeling for a pulse.

The men stared at me. I pushed my dripping hair back from my face, pinched Corbin's nose, and blew two breaths into his mouth, watching from the corner of my eye to make sure his chest rose. The men gawked openly as I put my hands over his chest and started pumping quickly, counting to fifteen before I repeated the two breaths.

Around us, the air was filled with the sounds and smells of cannon fire, screams of men as they were injured, and the terrible sound of ships being blown apart, but none of that registered with me. I blew breaths into Corbin's mouth and pumped his chest, my whole world having narrowed down to just one person.

I was aware of blood seeping through his shirt, and dripping off my head, but none of that mattered. The pain that wracked my entire body didn't matter. The fact that my ship was damaged possibly to the point where we might not make it to shore didn't matter. Not even the fact that someone I trusted had turned on me mattered. My whole being, my every breath, every beat of my heart, was focused on willing Corbin to live.

Minutes seemed to turn to hours, and just as I thought my own heart was going to burst, Corbin's body jerked beneath me, his chest rising as he took a horrible long, rasping breath.

He coughed and choked, vomiting up seawater as I turned him on his side, tears of joy blurring my vision so I couldn't see.

"Am . . ." The word cracked as he coughed up more water. He took a long, shuddering breath and tried again, his voice so hoarse it was painful to hear. "Amy?"

"I'm here, my darling," I panted, a painful lump in my throat making it hard for me to speak. "I have you. You're safe now."

"Famous last words," he said, then passed out.

Chapter 17

Revenge is sweet,
And flavours all our dealings!

—Ibid, Act I

"Eh . . . be that Black Corbin?"

"Yes. Will someone get me the ship's first-aid kit? There's blood. I think he's been hurt."

"Oy, Imp, the captain has caught us Black Corbin," Prudence told his brother excitedly.

"What be a first-aid kit?" Impulsive asked me.

I checked to make sure Corbin was still breathing. To be honest, I was a bit relieved he was unconscious—I had other immediate problems to take care of . . . such as the battle raging around us, and the blood seeping through his wet shirt.

"It's a medical kit for emergencies. Please go fetch ours."

The four pairs of legs standing around where I knelt next to Corbin's inert body didn't move.

"Is he dead?" Bas asked, peering with critical interest at Corbin's face.

"No, not yet, but he will be if someone doesn't hop to it and get me the damned first-aid kit!"

"We're not be havin' anythin' like that on board, I'm thinkin'," Pru said slowly. "Captain Bart'll be mighty pleased to know ye've caught Black Corbin."

"Captain Bart isn't going to know anything about this," I said grimly. "I need something to stop this bleeding. Gauze or clean linen or . . . oh, my God." I unlaced Corbin's shirt, ripping the bottom half to peel it back and expose his torso. There were a half dozen small abrasions due no doubt to the flying debris after Pangloss's ship had blasted him, but what had me staring in helpless horror was a large, fist-sized piece of wood that jutted out of Corbin's belly. "This can't be happening. This isn't real. You can't be hurt—none of this is real. Corbin, wake up and tell me you're not really hurt. Corbin? *Corbin!*"

"Er . . . lass, I've no love for Black Corbin, but I'm thinkin' shaking his head like that when his belly's been torn open isn't likely to make him wake up," Tar suggested. "'Tis more likely to be scramblin' his brains."

"Captain Bart will have him dancin' on the jib in no time," Prudence pointed out. "'Twon't make much difference if he's all right in his head or not."

"No one is hanging Corbin, and his brains are just fine because none of this is real," I told them all, releasing Corbin's wet hair to stare at my bloodstained hands. "You don't understand; this is all in our minds."

"It looks like it's in his belly," Bas said, turning his attention to the largest of the wounds. "I knew a man what died after a horse kicked him in the belly. Do ye think a chunk of wood is the same thing as the kick of a horse?"

I pointed my finger at Bas. "Right. That's it. No more comments about Corbin being dead or dying. Got it?" A blast shook the ship. I threw myself against Corbin to protect him from any more flying debris, yelling as I did so, "Tar, get us out of here!"

"Aye, aye, captain," he said, kicking aside a bit of the railing as he limped toward the nearest line. "Where be ye wantin' to go?"

"Anywhere out of the blockade. Go back to the island," I said, biting my lip. Why wasn't Corbin opening his eyes and telling me that this was going to be all right, that it was simply a matter of his mind believing he'd been hurt, but he hadn't really. Why wasn't he yelling at me for being in the blockade, dammit?

"If we go back, they'll likely shoot us again," Tar pointed out.

"Then take us somewhere we can go ashore and get help for Corbin."

"Aye, let's get him to shore. It's been weeks since I've seen a really good hangin'," Prudence said, getting to his feet in order to comply with Tar's order to tack windward.

I glared at the teen. "You are so close to walking the plank, I can't even begin to tell you."

"Me?" Prudence squeaked, his eyes opening wide.

"Yes, you. Oh, I don't have time to explain. Bas, you help Tar and Prudence-the-soon-to-be-planked as best you can. Imp, help me get Corbin belowdecks."

The hellish nightmare of the half hour that followed is thankfully a blur in my mind. Around us, while my beautiful—and now partially blown-to-shreds—ship limped a 180-degree circle to head to the far side of the island, the battle for Turtle's Back raged. I had no time to wonder at Pangloss's attack, nor his deceit in including me on the enemy list. Instead I performed what first aid I could to stop the bleeding and keep Corbin from slipping away from me again.

"It's not real; it's not real" was the mantra that I kept

whispering as I picked out bits of wood and metal from his stomach and chest, leaving the biggest chunk for an expert. I had a nasty feeling that if I pulled it out, I wouldn't be able to stop the bleeding.

Tar managed to find a tiny sheltered cove to run us gently aground.

"Where are we?" I asked him as I came on deck.

"About half a mile beyond the town," Tar told me, pointing to the north. "'Tis the closest I could get us without killin' us on the rocks."

"Good job," I said, snapping out orders to the twins. "We need to make a stretcher to carry Corbin into town. A blanket is going to have to do. One of you take the head, the other the foot. Bas, you run into town as quickly as you can and wake up Renata. Tell her we're bringing . . . er . . . tell her we're bringing a friend who's been gravely wounded, and we'll need a doctor."

Bas cast a longing glance toward the hatch that led belowdecks, but hopped over the side of the ship into the shallow waters quick enough. I watched until he disappeared into the dense growth that surrounded the town, then got my makeshift ambulance team organized.

The trip to Renata's house was slow and awkward. The boys had to stop frequently, and even with Tar and me helping, it seemed to take forever before we stumbled into town. I thought we'd have to snake our way around the back in order to avoid being seen by the townsfolk, but the deep rumble of guns in the distance reminded me that the battle would have everyone's attention. The square was empty of life except for a pair of mangy dogs fighting over the remains of a roast chicken.

Renata was waiting at the door, looking not at all like a woman who'd just been dragged out of bed.

"I'm sorry to wake you up, but I have a friend who needs

help," I said, holding the door open as the panting twins hauled Corbin inside.

"I wasn't asleep. The lads in the harbor have seen to that," she told me, bending over the blanket. She sucked in her breath as she saw who lay there, giving me a long, unreadable glance. I returned it with one that I hoped made it clear that I would brook no betrayal. "Ye've Black Corbin here unless I am mistaken."

"My bedroom is this way," I directed, holding the doors for the boys as they carried Corbin in and laid him down on my bed. I made sure he was comfortable, then turned to where Renata stood in the doorway, Bas trying to see around her. "Yes, it's Corbin. Do you have a problem with that? Because I'm telling you right here and now that if you're not who you appear to be, and you try to do something to harm him, you will know my wrath. I can be very, very mean when something matters to me, and this man matters more than you can possibly imagine."

Renata's lips pursed as she considered me. "I've no problem with Corbin bein' here, although ye should know that Bart's placed the black spot upon him. If ye don't want him dancin' with Jack Ketch, ye'd best be gettin' him out of here right quick."

"Not until he's seen a doctor, and not then if the doctor says he shouldn't be moved," I answered, prepared to fight for my man, ignoring the tiny niggle in the back of my mind that asked just when it was that Corbin had become mine.

"Ah, lass, there be no doctor here. He was killed when that man lyin' yonder murdered Bart's crew."

I pinched the bridge of my nose, trying to forestall both the headache I could feel wanting to blossom to life and the urge to lose my temper. Screaming that Corbin didn't actually kill anyone would do him little good. "Is there someone here who has medical training?"

Renata just looked at me.

"A . . . what do they call them . . . healer?"

"Aye, Sly Jez is by way of bein' a healer," Renata allowed.

"Great." I knelt next to the bed and started to remove Corbin's wet clothing, carefully avoiding the wood jutting out of his stomach. "I'll help however best I can. Tar, you and the boys go take a look at my ship and see how badly she's damaged. I need to know whether or not I can sail her to Mongoose. Oh, and Tar?" I glanced back over my shoulder at where my crew stood huddled together in the corner of the room, clearly uncomfortable at being in such close confines with the infamous Black Corbin. I gave them all a look to let them see the steely resolve that flowed through me. "I will give each of you ten reales for your help in moving Corbin, but if any of you mention this to a single living soul outside of this room, I will hang your guts from the yardarm. With great pleasure, using nothing but a spoon and a dull butter knife. Do you all understand?"

Prudence swallowed hard and nodded. Impulsive just looked scared. Tar had a blank look on his face, but his eyes avoided meeting mine. The three of them left quickly, but doubts about Tar lingered in my mind.

Jez turned out to be a better resource than I'd imagined—she bustled into the room in nothing but an (evidently hastily donned) chemise, a basket on her arm, looking quite proficient until she stopped with a shocked look on her face. "Oh, mercy! That's . . . that's . . ."

"Yes, it's Corbin. He's my hus—er . . . boyfr—uh . . . he's a friend, all right? I'll pay you to take care of this horrible wound he has and keep quiet, but for the love of God, please don't ask questions, and just help him. He's been unconscious for way too long. He might be suffering irreparable brain damage or something."

Jez didn't say anything further, although she did give me an odd look. My confidence in her abilities rose when she quickly examined Corbin, dismissing the lesser wounds to focus on the big one.

"Amy?" Kneeling next to Jez, I spun around so fast I fell back on my butt.

"Corbin? My sweet Corbin. You're awake."

"Yes," he said, a spasm of pain crossing his face as he tried to move. I crawled over to him and put a restraining hand on the upper part of his chest. "Christ, I feel horrible. What happened?"

"You were hit with shrapnel. Don't move. We're taking care of you."

"We?" he asked weakly, lifting his head to look down his body, his eyes widening as he saw the blood and gore. "Christ almighty and all the saints!"

"I'm going to take it out now," Jez said to me softly, laying a couple of clean white cloths next to Corbin's hip, along with a stoppered bottle of what looked to be brandy.

"What did she say?"

I put a hand on Corbin's forehead and gently pushed it back into the pillow, leaning over him so all he could see was my eyes. "Sweetie, I want you to remember something, something very important."

"What's that?" he asked, trying to see around me.

I positioned myself so he couldn't possibly see Jez as she prepared to yank the wood out of his stomach. "This is all in your mind, Corbin. You're not *really* hurt. Nothing has *really* harmed you. Your brain just thinks you've been hurt, so it's manifesting pain and all sorts of other things. All you have to do is be firm with yourself, and make your brain understand that you are just fine and dandy, physically."

"It seems bloody real to me," he growled. "What's that

woman doing down there? She's not going to do what I think she's going to do?"

"She's going to remove the wood, but remember—the wood is just a figment of your imagination as well. Just tell yourself there will be no pain because there is no injury, and you won't be the least bit uncomfortable."

Jez wrapped both hands around the piece of wood and yanked it out with a quick move.

"Amy?" Corbin said, his entire body having stiffened up. I kissed his nose. "My brave little cowpoke. You see, I knew you could get a handle on this mind-over-matter stuff."

Tears collected on the outer corners of his eyes.

"Aaaaaaaaaargh!" he screamed, his back arching off the bed. I grabbed him by the arms and tried to hold him down as Jez muttered an apology before pouring a liberal amount of brandy on the open wound.

"Mind over matter, mind over matter," I yelled at Corbin as he thrashed around on the bed, one long scream of pain ripping from his throat. Jez worked quickly to clean the wound out with alcohol, picking out tiny splinters of wood as I threw myself across Corbin to keep him (relatively) immobile. "You're not really in pain! This doesn't really hurt!"

He took a deep, shuddering breath and bellowed, "Like hell it doesn't hurt! Tell that sadist to stop tearing me open!"

"She's helping you, my sweet darling. She has to get all the bits out of the wound, or it'll get infected."

Corbin opened his mouth to scream again, but an odd look crossed his face instead. "What did you say?" he finally asked.

"I said that Jez has to pick out all the slivers of wood in the wound. She's not trying to hurt you, Corbin; she's helping. She's a healer."

"No, not about that." He frowned, his beautiful silvery eyes dark with pain. "What you said before that."

"Mind over matter?"

"In between. You called me darling. Your sweet darling."

"Oh," I said, for once at a loss for words. I wasn't ready to look at the warm emotions that seemed to be growing inside me for Corbin. I had too many other things to take care of, too much work to be finished. "Did I?"

"Yes, you did." He donned a slightly petulant expression. "Did you mean it?"

I thought about telling him it was just a slip of the tongue, but something held me back. "I don't say anything I don't mean."

"*Darling* is a pretty strong endearment, and *my sweet darling* is just about tantamount to a declaration of love." He took a deep breath, apparently uncaring of the fact that Jez was present, setting up a couple of needles and thread to sew up his wound. "Do you love me?"

I blinked at him a couple of times, taken aback by the bald question, unsure how to answer it without hurting him. "Well?"

"I . . . I don't know," I finally said, unable to think of an answer, but aware that I was telling the truth. "Truly, Corbin, I just don't—"

He laid a finger across my lips, silencing me more effectively when he pulled me down for a kiss. "Don't worry about it, sweetheart. We'll work it out once I'm done being patched up."

I smiled into his mouth, relieved that he hadn't seemed to suffer any brain damage from the injuries or the near drowning. "I told you that if you put your mind to it, you wouldn't feel Jez working on you."

"Oh, I feel it." His hand skimmed up my arm braced next to his head. "It just doesn't matter as much as you."

Corbin yelled a great deal when Jez started to sew him up, but a few kisses soon had him more engrossed in making me burn than in worrying about what she was doing to him. By the time she was done stitching the wound together, had covered it with crushed herbs wrapped inside a cloth bandage, and had forced a fever draught down his throat, Corbin was exhausted.

I was positively limp with fatigue. I thanked Jez for her help, paid her a couple of reales from Corbin's stash of money, and begged her to keep his presence a secret.

She paused in the door and gave me a long look. "I will, but not because ye're payin' me to keep me mouth shut."

I rubbed a weary hand across my forehead. I wanted nothing more than to sleep for a hundred or so years. "Oh? Why, then?"

"Because ye're helpin' us when ye didn't have to, ye talk to me like I'm a real person, not a floozy who doesn't know her arse from her elbow, and most of . . ." She smiled. "Most of all because ye're so in love with that man ye can't see yer nose in front of yer face, and I've ever been one to sigh over a good love story."

I started to protest, but she just laughed and went off to her own room.

"That's a wise woman. You should listen to her," Corbin said, his voice fuzzy and thick from the draught. I suspected Jez had included an opiate in it to make Corbin sleep.

"She certainly is good with a needle," I answered, easing myself down on the bed next to him. His eyes were closed, but one opened up just long enough to give me a sleepy look.

"Corbin, before you fall asleep, we need to talk about what we're going to do. Much as I hate to do it, we're going to have to move you. You're not safe here. I don't trust Tar not to turn you in for a huge reward."

"True, most anyone would," he agreed, his eyelid closing. "You'll have to get Holder. He'll take care of me."

"Dammit, I want to take care of you," I said, fatigue making me irritable.

A lazy smile stole across his lips. "You're falling in love with me, Amy."

"Stop that." I pinched the skin on his arm.

"If you're not already in love with me."

"You're delusional. Maybe you hit your head when Pangloss blasted your ship."

"Once you are, you'll want to spend every waking moment with me."

I shook my head at him. "A mind is such a sad thing to waste. How tragic that yours should be taken from you at such a young age."

He smiled a slow, lazy smile at me. "Soon you'll be so head-over-heels in love with me, you'll fulfill my every whim and fantasy." The words were coming out slower and slower, slurring slightly.

"I thought I already had," I said, unable to keep from leaning forward and pressing a gentle kiss to his lips.

"You have, but if I put my mind to it, I'm sure I can think of more," he answered just before drifting into sleep.

I looked down at the man in my bed and wondered whether everyone else was right, and I was wrong . . . or I was just fooling myself.

Chapter 18

With cat-like tread,
Upon our prey we steal. . . .

—Ibid, Act II

"So, what's the prognosis?"

Tar turned his head and spat before giving me a squinty-eyed look. "She's got a hole the size of a sow in her starboard side, lost the top eight feet of the mast, and there's three feet of water in the bilge."

I looked at my poor shot-up ship, listing heavily to one side so the damage on her right side could be examined. "Hell's bells."

"Aye. 'Tis by the grace of God we made it here without us all bein' sent to Davy Jones, but she'll not be sailin' again without repairs."

I bit back the oath I was dying to yell, instead turning on my heel and heading back to town. Tar and the twins scrambled up the narrow footpath behind me.

"What ye thinkin' to do with Black Corbin?" Tar called out. "There's a handsome price on his head. We'd all be rich if we was to hand him over to Captain Bart."

"I've already told you no, *and* paid you for your silence," I answered, swearing silently to myself. I had to get Corbin out of there, and fast, before Tar had the opportunity to turn traitor and hand him over to Bart. "But don't worry, Corbin will be gone by nightfall."

"Oh, aye?" Tar asked, rubbing the prosthetic metal nose he wore when sailing.

"Yup. He'll be gone as soon as the moon comes up," I lied, just in case the plan my brain was busily hatching went awry, and Tar escaped to rat on Corbin. "Right now, I have more important things to take care of."

"What would that be?" he asked, almost trotting to keep up with me.

"We're going to rejoin the blockade."

"But we don't have no ship," Prudence complained. We crested the hill that led down to the town and harbor. I didn't stop to admire the view.

"No, we don't. So we'll steal one."

"Steal one?" Impulsive asked, his eyes big.

"Sure, why not? We're pirates, right? Stealing is our raison d'être."

All the way down to the harbor I fielded questions— everything from what a "raisen detter" was to what we were going to do in the blockade. There was one question that wasn't asked . . . something that interested me greatly.

By the time we brazenly stole a pretty green sloop from the end of the dock and got her headed toward the blockade, Tar and the boys had stopped peppering me with questions and were instead actually doing their jobs.

I felt so much like a real pirate captain I burst into song.

Prudence gave his brother a quizzical look. "Is the cap'n insultin' us by sayin' we're pirates who don't do anythin'?"

Impulsive frowned. I smiled and ordered someone to stand by with a black flag. As we skirted the edge of the blockade, the noise of guns booming, wood splintering, and men screaming filled the air almost as much as the scent of gunpowder and death.

It was sobering to see firsthand how people died in sea battle, but I didn't let the likelihood that we would again become the target of Pangloss stop me from ordering us right into the thick of the fray, heading straight for the flagship.

Although Corbin's men must have seen me coming from the harbor, the black flag we ran up seemed to act as a passport of sorts. Pangloss and the other officers evidently weren't watching their rears, because they didn't see us until we had sailed quickly past them. I toyed with the idea of shooting Pangloss's ship while we had them broadside to us but opted for a more prudent plan.

"Bring us alongside her, lads," I told my crew, pointing to the flagship. "I need to talk to the officer on board."

Tar gave me a look that didn't take much to read. "They're in battle."

"I know, but only on that side. Not this one. Just bring us in close so I can talk to the people on board."

Tar shook his head and muttered something that I thought it best to pretend not to hear.

"Is Holder aboard ship?" I yelled through cupped hands as we approached the big red and black ship whose starboard guns were in the process of sinking one of Bart's ships. "I'm looking for Holder McReady."

A line of men suddenly appeared on the port side of the ship, directly across from us, all of whom were pointing flintlock muskets and pistols at me.

"Amy?" There was a disturbance in the men and suddenly Holder was at the railing, a bloody rag wrapped around his head, his face shiny and black with gunpowder and sweat. "What in God's name are you doing here? You could have been shot!"

"Grapple them," I told my guys, yelling back at Holder, "I need to talk to you."

"Right now?" he bellowed back. "It may have escaped your notice, but we're a little on the busy side at the moment avenging my best friend's death."

"He's not dead," I yelled, gesturing at one of the twins.

"What?"

Holder's men looked at him as Prudence swung out a grappling hook. Holder snapped an order, and three grappling lines shot out to our ship, snagging us and pulling our ship up close.

"Stay here. I'll be right back," I told my crew before scrambling up a thin rope ladder that had been tossed down. Bas ignored my order and followed me onto the *Java Guru.*

Holder grabbed me before my foot even touched the deck, shaking me as he demanded, "What did you mean he isn't dead? I saw his ship sink."

"So did I. I saved him. He was drowning, but I saved him."

Holder stopped shaking me, staring intently into my eyes. I smiled at him. "He's safe, Holder. He's been injured, but he's safe. At least, for a little while, but I need you to—"

The rest of my words were cut off when my face was squashed into Holder's shoulder, his whoop of triumph leaving me deaf in my left ear for the three hours that followed.

He planted a smacking kiss on my cheek before giving me another bear hug, finally releasing me. "I knew you were the one. I just knew it the minute I saw you. And I told him, too. Bless you, lass. Whatever I have, it's yours. Money, jewels, my prized signed photo of Johnny Depp as Jack Sparrow—nothing is too precious."

I laughed, flinching as the guns belowdecks blasted into life. "This will have to be fast. I need to get Corbin off Turtle's Back, and I can't do it by myself."

Holder didn't wait for explanations. He simply started snapping out orders, and before I knew what had happened, Bas and I were back on board the stolen ship, heading for the far side of the harbor. Holder was at the helm of another sloop, a small, low-slung racing model, which was on its way to the portage where my *Saucy Wench* was lying. I had a pouch full of reales with which I was to buy anything that Corbin needed for the trip, and the assurances of Holder that no one and nothing on this earth would stop him from spiriting Corbin out from under Bart's nose.

It took some time for us to make port, what with having to stay out of range of Pangloss's guns. We had a few sticky moments when we were in firing range, but for whatever reason, we weren't fired upon.

By the time we reached the dock, I was exhausted, both mentally and physically, and wanted nothing more than to go check on Corbin and collapse next to him.

When I saw who was waiting on the docks, however, my exhaustion suddenly disappeared.

"Amy, m'lass . . . surely that isn't yer ship? It looks like one I own, which has apparently gone missin'."

I swung myself over the railing and leaped down to the dock without waiting for the wooden plank to be set into place, stalking over to where Bart stood with two of his pirates. "No, it's not my ship. I stole this one because mine was shot to hell by your first mate, so I guess it's just a bit of poetic justice that it should turn out to be yours."

His eyebrows raised. "My first mate shot ye?"

"Yes, he did. A whole bunch of times. My ship is unsailable."

"Nay, ye're mistaken," he said, shaking his head, a puzzled look on his face.

"It's a little hard mistaking a ship from your own crew when it's blasting you to smithereens," I said grimly. "What made you do it, Bart? Why would you set me up like that? Why did you tell Pangloss to sink my ship?"

"I swear to ye, lass, I gave no such order," he protested, turning to his men. "Ye've not heard me order any action against our own ships, have ye?"

"Nay, never," the men said in unison.

"Look, you can say whatever you like, but I'm the one whose ship is lying on the other side of the island, filled with huge holes."

Bart gave me a sad look. "Ah, lass, the sun has bleached yer brain. Yer ship is right where she should be, in the blockade. Where *ye* should be, as well."

I stared at him, wondering whether some glitch had happened, rendering all the computer characters insane. "What are you talking about? My ship is on the other side of the island, lying on her side because of the damage Pangloss did to her."

"Look for yerself," Bart said, pulling a spyglass from where it was attached to his belt. "Yer ship is to the north of the *Java Guru*. She's been there all day. I thought ye were waitin' until Panny'd stopped engagin' the warships afore ye were goin' to open fire."

I didn't bother arguing further; I just opened the spyglass and scanned the line of ships, waiting for the smoke to clear to identify the *Java Guru* before I turned the glass northward. Two ships were beyond the *Guru*'s bow, on her port side. One, a gray and navy two-masted sloop, was firing on one of Bart's captains. The other . . . smoke drifted across the outline of the ship. As it cleared, the sleek lines of a compact sloop became clear.

A sloop painted a familiar maroon.

"What the . . . that's not my ship," I said, squinting at it through the glass. "My ship is damaged. That can't be her. Oh. It must be the sister ship to mine. I'd forgotten about it."

Bart gave me another pitying look.

"I am not suffering from sunstroke, nor am I insane," I said, turning to my crew. "Tar, tell the captain—our ship was shot up, wasn't she?"

"Aye," he answered, limping his way down the dock toward us. "'Twas Mr. Pangloss who done it, too."

"See?" I crossed my arms over my chest.

Bart rubbed his chin, gazing out at the harbor where the ships were still locked in battle, although judging by the fact that the guns had slowed down, this round of battle was probably coming to an end. "I'm at loss, lass. 'Tis no rightful reason for Panny to fire on ye, but I'm thinkin' there may have been some confusion with the ship I took for yers. She's wearin' yer colors, and is where ye should be, so it's possible that Panny mistook ye for her."

I opened my mouth to protest such a ridiculous notion but decided against continuing to argue. Bart's explanation was possible, although I thought it highly unlikely. More likely, the thought occurred to me, was the theory that Pangloss wasn't who he appeared to be. Could he be the mysterious ex-partner Paul? It would explain why he tried to sink me, given the opportunity.

I rubbed my forehead, confused by the path my thoughts were taking. I had liked Pangloss. Could I be so mistaken about people?

Bart gave me his blessing to use his sloop until mine could be repaired, saying he had to get back to one of the makeshift forts.

"The devil Corbin's been careful to stay out of range of the big guns," he said before he left. "But Panny'll be harryin' the *Java Guru* into range of 'em, then we'll have him."

Evidently he didn't realize Corbin wasn't on the *Guru*. I certainly wasn't about to enlighten him, not while he was all but rubbing his hands at the thought of capturing Corbin.

After a few more words of gloating over his anticipated win, he took his leave. From the corner of my eye I saw Tar sidle toward one of Bart's men.

"Well, thank you for the use of the ship. Buh-bye. Catch you later," I yelled after him, then turned to my crewmate with a saccharine smile. "Tar, did you check the remaining supplies on the ship? No? Be a lamb and do it now, would you?"

Tar clearly wanted to disobey me but didn't want to bring down Bart's wrath by ignoring a direct order. He shot me a look that didn't at all disguise his loathing, and hobbled off to do as he was bid.

"Juuust what I need," I muttered to myself and went off to do my own chores.

By the time I had the ship stocked to go back into battle, the warships' guns had fallen silent. Pangloss had told me that the ships only fought for a few hours before taking a break so that the men could have a rest and the equipment could be repaired and readied for more battle. It seemed an odd way to fight, but who was I to complain? Rather than head back out to battle, I gathered up my crew and hustled them toward Renata's, unwilling to leave them—especially Tar—alone where they might talk.

By the time we got there, Corbin was gone, all signs of his occupancy in the room removed as if by fairies, but on the chest a small folded-up scrap of parchment had been left.

I will never be able to thank you enough for saving my best friend, the note read. *I'm glad you found each other. He needs you.*

I sighed heavily, tucking Holder's note away in my clothes, and forced my thoughts away from where they wanted to sulk over losing Corbin. I had things to do, I told myself sternly. There were Renata and Pangloss to question closely. There were the leading townspeople to approach in order to find out just what supplies I should be trying to get from the blockade ships. I had promised myself to have a really long session organizing and inventorying Tara's weaving shop. As far as I could tell, her looms had been empty for days, which mean that somewhere, a bunch of weavers were lounging around on my daughter's payroll. There was no way I was going to tolerate that abuse. And there was my small crew to take care of, to pay off and swear to secrecy about the day's activities.

I sighed as I counted out reales and left my room, heading for where I had left Tar and the twins in the company of Renata's girls.

I wanted this conflict to end without anyone else being hurt.

I wanted to find Paul, so we could leave the game.

I wanted my brain to stop being confused with unfamiliar emotions.

I wanted Corbin.

Chapter 19

Come, friends, who plough the sea . . .

—Ibid, Act I

Dear Holder,

How's Corbin doing? Does he have a fever? Does the wound look infected? Is he getting enough rest? Make sure he pushes fluids, too. Staying hydrated is an important part of the healing process. Has he said anything about me? Don't let him pick at the bandages. In fact, don't let him do anything. He should just lie around and recuperate.

Best,

Amy

Dear Amy,

Corbin is the same as he was two hours ago when you last asked, which, I should point out, has been three times in the past twelve hours. The answers to your questions are: fine, no, I wouldn't know since I refuse to look at it, yes, yes on the fluids, and you're all he talks about (well, there is some occasional swearing at Bart mixed in there).

I'm fine, too, thank you (not that you asked).

Hugs and kisses,

Holder

Dear Holder,

You refuse to look at Corbin's wound? I specifically told you that you have to keep an eye on it. Corbin is just the type of man to ignore the fact that he needs to rest and not stress his body so it can heal. Please look at it now, and let me know how it seems, especially if it's oozing anything, or if there're reddish streaks around the wound. That means blood poisoning, and Lord knows what we're going to do if that happens. So you see the importance of looking at it. Look now. Then tell me what you see.

Worriedly,

Amy

Dear Amy,

Have you ever seen a freshly sutured wound? Neither have I, and I intend on keeping it that way. I asked Corbin how it felt. His answer was, "Sore." He says there are no reddish blood poisoning streaks. He says he's getting enough rest and liquids and he already has a mother, thank you, and he doesn't need another one.

I'm still fine, not that you've asked (again).

One hug, one friendly kiss,

Holder

Dear Holder,

I have seen a freshly sutured wound, and I don't see

what the big deal about it is. It's not like it's a gaping head wound, for Pete's sake. You didn't tell me if it's oozing. And what did Corbin mean by sore? Normal sore or unnaturally sore, indicating internal bleeding and rampant infection?

Amy

Dear Amy,

Holder has gone to lie down with a cold compress and a bottle of my best brandy, muttering something about never wanting to see a quill and parchment again. Stop worrying about me. I'm fine.

Love you,
Corbin

Corbin! What are you doing up? You're supposed to be resting! You had a fist-sized piece of wood shot into your stomach yesterday—I specifically told Holder he had to make sure you stay in bed, and don't get up and move around. If you stress those stitches, they could pop open. Gah! Go back to bed! No more writing!

A very, very concerned,
Amy

Amy,

I have a blockade to run, love. I'm not stressing the stitches. Stop worrying—you'll give yourself gray hairs. Have I told you how much I love you? It's so much that I'm not even going to point out how ridiculous it is for you to be sitting there imagining me with blood poisoning, torn stitches, and an oozing wound. No, it's so much that I'm just going to imagine you

*taking pity on my poor wounded body, and riding me
like a bucking bronco.*
    Insert leer here.
    Corbin

    *PS—When are you coming to see me? If you need
help getting to the blockade line, let me know. I'll
arrange for you to be picked up.*

Dear adorable, foolish Corbin,
    *I'm not talking to you until you lie back down and
promise not to move.*
    Smooches,
    Amy

    *PS—You're on re: the bucking bronco . . . as soon
as you're well.*

Dear Amy,
    *The bearer of this asks that you please stop view-
ing the sending of these notes as some sort of pirate
instant messaging service, as said bearer is getting
sick and tired of running the half mile to the cove,
sailing to the blockade, delivering the note, and returning only to repeat the process a few minutes
later.*
    You're adorable when you're stubborn.
    Much love and many smutty thoughts,
    Corbin

I looked up from the note to Prudence, who stood before
me with a particularly belligerent expression.

"Cap'n Corbin says ye won't be needin' me to deliver
any more notes," he said, his eyes narrowing at me. "He
says that ye're through behavin' womanish, and ye under-

stand that he's old enough to take care of himself. He says ye won't be embarrassin' him by motherin' him in front of his crew."

I sighed and put down the quill I had picked up the minute I finished Corbin's note. Logically, I knew that he was right—he was able to take care of himself, and not likely to do anything that would hinder his recovery. But emotionally, I couldn't help but worry about him. If only I could see him to make sure he was all right . . .

"Amy? Maggot, he says ye're wanted down at the docks. The ship be ready to sail."

"All right, Bas, thank you. Pru, you go with Bas to the ship. Tell Tar I'll be down in a couple of minutes. And make sure that the supplies I sent down earlier are loaded properly, not just stacked on the deck."

Both boys nodded and hurried off, Pru with a relieved expression, Bas with a hopeful gleam in his eye. No doubt he was hoping for more blood and gore. I had other goals, one of which was managing a few minutes to check on Corbin.

I gathered up my foil and headed down to the harbor, waving when the women gathered at the docks called their hellos. Pangloss was standing at the head of the dock just as he had been the day before—the treacherous wretch. I hadn't had a chance to talk to him about why he'd attacked me the day before, but Bart had sent me a short note the previous night saying that Pangloss had confirmed his guess—the similarly painted ship near Corbin's flagship had been mistaken for mine, and mine for the enemy's ship.

I wasn't entirely buying it.

"Hoy, Pangloss," I said, trying to adopt a nonconfrontational pose. "I understand you're ready for us to sail?"

"Amy!" He spun around, a wide smile on his face that

faded as he saw the grim set to my lips. "Lass, I've been meanin' to see ye so I could apologize in person. Bart says ye're thinkin' I opened fire on ye deliberately."

"Well, the careful positioning of the ship and repeated volleys did sort of give me the impression of deliberateness, but Bart says you didn't actually know that was my ship you were destroying so very efficiently."

"Aye, I thought it was another of Black Corbin's ships. I saw one painted just as yers, close to the flagship, and I figured ye was in position, so it would be safe for me to pick off a few of the sloops at the end of the line. Rumor has it that Corbin himself was on one of the ships that sank."

"Really?" I asked, glancing toward the ship that had been loaned to me. My small crew was busy readying the ship, but that didn't mean Tar hadn't been talking. The only reason I had not asked Holder to keep him in custody was because Corbin was safe—and there was nothing Bart could do to me, not if he wanted me to provide supplies as the blockade tightened.

"Aye, but the devil takes care of his own. Corbin was sighted this morn on the *Java Guru*."

"Probably walking around when he should be resting in bed," I muttered to myself.

"What was that?" Pangloss asked.

"Nothing. I trust there won't be any mistakes in identity today, since I'm sailing one of your captain's ships."

"Aye, there won't be," he said quickly, his blue eyes guileless. "I'm hopin' ye'll forgive me for the mistake yesterday. I'll be happy to send a few of me swabbies to help with yer ship repairs."

"Thank you, I'd appreciate that. There's just my four guys, and I need them to help sail, so my ship is just sitting all crippled."

Pangloss nodded and started to turn away. I grabbed the arm of his shirt to stop him. "There's something I wanted to ask you, if you don't mind."

"Oh, aye? What be that?"

I hesitated, trying to find a way to phrase the question that wouldn't tip him off if he was really Paul. "You've been with Bart for how long?"

"Since I was a wee lad," he answered promptly, turning to bellow out an order about a barrel of gunpowder.

"Ah. Odd; you two look to be about the same age."

He didn't even look at me as he watched his men roll the barrel on board a large ship. "Nay, I was apprenticed to Bart when I was a wee sprog. Use yer deadlights, ye lubbers! Ye damage the mizzenmast gettin' that powder in place, and it'll be the cat for ye!"

"So, what did you do before you were apprenticed to Bart?"

Pangloss shot me a quick look. "What be ye talkin' about? Bloody hell—ye scurvy dogs! Be ye all three sheets in the wind?"

Before I could pump him for more information, Pangloss stormed off to his ship, yelling orders at his crew. I made a mental note to try to pin him down later, and toddled off to my own ship.

Five hours later I stretched and looked in the basket I had used to bring lunch for everyone. "Hey, who ate all the apples?"

Bas burped and looked away. Bran hacked up an apple seed.

"Oh, well, I guess we'll get more when we go back to port. Which I hope is soon. I never imagined a blockade would be boring after yesterday, but this . . . bah."

The blockade ships stretched out in a ragged line across the opening of the harbor. Our ships were staggered inside the harbor, with us slightly to the left of and behind Pangloss. The air was still and silent, the wind almost nonexistent. The guns were quiet, cleaned and prepped, ready to be loaded and fired. Overhead sea birds wheeled and dove, the only movement visible to the eye. I gave the blockade line a desultory look. It hadn't moved; their ships were as anchored as ours.

"'Tis the way of a blockade," Tar said, picking his teeth with the tip of a dagger.

"It wasn't at all like this yesterday," I pointed out. "Yesterday was all about blowing up innocent people's ships, and blood, and drowning, and such."

"Aye, the opening of a blockade can be that way. Then it settles down to this," he said, waving his knife at the ships. "Black Corbin's ships is there makin' sure no one gets in or out."

"I can see why they've dropped anchor—they're in a good position, and they've achieved their goals. But why are we here?" I asked, bored to death. There were a thousand other things I'd rather be doing than spending my day getting sunburned sitting around on the deck of a borrowed sloop.

"We're ensurin' that Black Corbin's men don't take the harbor," Tar said slowly, as if he was explaining it to an idiot. Which, I had to admit, was pretty much me when it came to subjects like the proper etiquette at a blockade.

"How long are we expected to wait here? Do we get to go back when the sun goes down?"

Tar looked at me as if I'd started turning backflips. "If we go back, who'll guard the harbor?"

"Well . . ." I hesitated. "I guess I never really thought about it. I just kind of assumed that everyone ceased the hostilities when it was dark."

Tar muttered to himself and spat over the side of the ship.

I was silent for another half hour, then something struck me. "I didn't bring enough food to last us days. We're going to have to go back so I can get more."

You would have thought sailing back to the dock was a minor thing, but as soon as I had the sails unfurled in preparation for heading for the dock, a small rowboat was launched from Pangloss's ship. The pirate Maggot quickly rowed over to our ship, yelling up a question about what we were doing.

"I need to get food," I yelled down at him.

"Ye what?"

"Food, I need food!"

"Ye're in a blockade, and ye're not fully stocked?" he asked, surprise written all over his face.

"No one told me we'd be out here for days! I'll be back in a little bit, just as soon as I round up enough foodstuffs to keep us from starving for a few days," I told him.

He stared openmouthed at me for a moment until I gave the order to set sail, whereupon he rowed as fast as possible back to Pangloss's ship.

I gave it a little wave as we turned.

On the island, I used the bulk of Holder's money to buy up salt beef and pork, a couple of barrels of ale, one of rum, one of water, dried peas, a form of hardtack that the tradesmen swore would repel weevils and other icky bugs, oatmeal, huge wheels of cheese, and as a special treat, two crates of apples, and one of lemons.

A brief chat with my crew established that Impulsive would be the best person to cook (the others showed a disinterest in proper food preparation that had me envisioning E. coli running amok), so once everything was stowed away, we sailed back out into the harbor and dropped anchor to resume the blockade wait.

And wait we did. I lasted twenty-four hours; then I

couldn't stand it anymore, and sent Prudence off in a row-boat to the nearest blockade ship with a note for Corbin to inquire how he was doing.

He sent back a terse reply saying he was bored out of his head, his wound was much better, and didn't I want to come and play cowgirl with him?

I was tempted; I was very tempted. But daily visits from Pangloss as he made his rounds of all the harbor ships drove home the importance of presenting a unified front to the blockaders.

"Not that Corbin is about to attack with us here," I said aloud the third day of the blockade, glaring at Bran the raven as I paced by him. The bird had apparently decided it was part seagull, and flapped its stubby wings while mimicking a seagull's cry every time a gull soared overhead. "Shut . . . up!"

"Eh?" Prudence asked, looking up from the game of chess he and his twin were playing with crudely carved chess pieces. Tar stood at the bow of the ship, his hands behind his back, staring out at the blockade line.

"Not you; the bird! Bas, can't you tape his little beak together, or something? Two days of him doing his gull impression is starting to wear on my nerves."

Bas looked up from where he was dangling a piece of salted pork over the edge of the ship, hoping, he had confided in me the day before, to catch a man-eating shark. "I couldn't do that! 'Twould be cruel, that would!"

"Not nearly so cruel as having me make him walk the plank," I growled to myself, pacing the length of the ship.

"*Kree, kree, kree,*" called the gulls as they circled the ships hoping for food.

"*Caw, caw, caw,*" answered Bran, hopping around the deck.

Pad, pad, pad went my bare feet as I paced the length of the

ship for the three hundred and twelfth time. "Aaaaaaaaaah!" I
yelled, unable to stand it any longer.

Everyone looked at me.

"Caw, caw, caw."

"Ahhh?" Pru asked me, ignoring Bran as the bird hopped
past him, chasing a low-flying gull.

"Yes, aaaah!"

"Caw, caw, caw!"

"Are ye talkin' to yerself again?" Impulsive asked, giving
me an odd look.

"Maybe. Possibly. Probably. What if I am?" I stopped in
front of him, my hands on my hips.

"Caw, caw!"

"Nothin'. It's just that ye're doin' a lot of that lately."

"Hey," I said, narrowing my eyes. "There's nothing
wrong, nothing at all, with talking to yourself when you've
been trapped on a ship with four people whose idea of personal hygiene is lax, to say the least. In fact, I think it's
pretty much a requirement to keeping your sanity. I'd go so
far as to say it's the only way to stay sane when you're stuck
on a ship in the middle of a harbor doing abso-freaking-
lutely nothing for three endlessly long days just so you can
push the damned game forward, and Bas, so help me God,
if you don't shut that bird up, we're having raven stew for
dinner!"

Complete and utter silence fell on the deck. Four pairs of
eyes—five if you count the bird's—stared at me in mute
surprise.

"All right," I yelled, throwing my hands in the air in a
gesture of defeat. "I admit it; I've snapped. I've had it! I
can't take any more! We're going back to port, and if Pangloss or Bart has a problem with that, they can just stick it
where the yardarm don't shine. And don't tell me yardarms
don't shine, because I don't care! Drop the sails, heave the

anchor, and all that other nautical talk that I am now too insane to remember! We're going back to town."

This time as we made ready to sail, no rowboat zipped out to see what was up. I was a bit disappointed by that, itching as I was for a fight, but we made it back to port without me actually going off the deep end, or strangling Bas's bird.

Fifteen minutes later I gave the men leave, ordered Bas to bathe himself and Bran before he went to bed that night, and commandeered the big wooden bathtub that sat in Renata's common room, hidden by a ratty red silk screen.

It took a while to heat up enough water to fill the tub, but I used the time chatting with the ladies of the house about what had been happening while I was parked in the harbor for three days.

"Food is scarce," Sly Jez said, stirring a smelly pot of fish stew. "We've fish, but all the meat is gone, or been taken for the blockade."

"Aye, and the greens be almost gone, as well," Mags said. She and Red Beth were sewing a dress, sitting next to the open window to catch the last of the daylight.

I frowned as I tested the water in the big copper kettle that hung in the fireplace. "You shouldn't be feeling the effects of the blockade so quickly. Bart knew it was coming— surely he stockpiled as much nonperishable food as he could?"

Mags shrugged. "All I know is there's naught to be had but dried beans and oats. Renata's gone now to try to round up some fruit, but they say there hasn't been a pear or apple seen for days."

"Huh. I'll have to ask Bart what's up. Maybe he has the food stored somewhere safe and he just hasn't released it yet." The water seemed hot enough, so I wrapped a cloth around the handle and dragged the heavy kettle behind the screen to where the tub sat. I'd already added two kettles of lukewarm water, enough to moderate the hotter water.

"We'll starve if somethin's not done about this block-ade," Suky said, coming in from where she had been feeding her baby. "The men, they've got enough food on the ships and up at the forts, but we're left with nothin'."

"Don't worry. I won't let you starve," I said as I hurriedly shucked my clothing. I wasn't a prude, but communal bathing was not my idea of a fun way to spend an evening. I slid into the warm water with a sigh of happiness, letting the tension seep from every pore. Pangloss could yell all he wanted—after three days of blockading, I deserved a little break. I'd let everyone get a good night's rest; then we'd go back out in the morning and resume blockading.

"How do ye plan on doin'—"

The sound of the front door banging open stopped Suky in midquestion and had me wrapping my hands over my breasts. "Eeek! I thought you said you don't have any business now that the men are blockading."

Men's voices rumbled in the outer room. I looked at my clothes piled in the corner, debating leaping out of the tub and trying to get into them before whoever it was came into the room. What kept me in the tub was the fact that the screen, which gave me a modicum of privacy, was neither very large nor particularly opaque.

"—to find Amy. Mr. Pangloss said she sailed back to port. Be she here?"

I recognized the deep voice as belonging to Black Spot Charlie, one of Bart's right-hand men, and a particularly ugly specimen of piratehood.

"Eeek!" I said again, sinking down into the water. "I'm here, but I'm taking a bath so don't—"

The screen was yanked aside, exposing me to the view of three big pirates, all of whom wore grim expressions. My knees stuck out of the water as I clutched them to my chest, a fact the men seemed to totally disregard.

"Captain Amy, I come with a letter from Captain Bart."

I stared dumbly for a moment at the note Charlie held out at me, puzzled by his referring to me as "Captain." An officer in charge of his ship was often called captain but off the ship, no one but the captain of the crew was given that title.

"Um," I said, unwilling to release my death hold on my legs in order to take the note. "Why don't you just read it to me?"

Charlie looked a bit taken aback. "I don't be knowin' much about readin'."

"I can read," Sly Jez said, giving me a sympathetic look as she took the note. "I'll read it for you if you like, Amy."

"Thank you; I'd appreciate that."

Much to my dismay, the three men continued to stand in a semicircle around the tub, all of them watching me somewhat warily.

"*Dearest Amy, I hope this note finds ye well,*" Jez read, frowning over the parchment. "*A matter of some importance has claimed me attention, and I've been forced to leave Turtle's Back for a short time while I attend to it.*"

"That's rather odd, isn't it?" I asked Charlie. "A captain leaving during a blockade?"

He said nothing.

"*Ye can believe me when I tell ye that I've thought long and hard about who to name as me replacement while I'm away. Panny is me first mate, as ye know, but while he's a good mate and the men all like him, he's not got the brains on him to head up the crew. Ye be by way of knowin' that firsthand, what with him shootin' ye by mistake. Ye, however, have the spirit and cunning that a good captain needs.*"

"What?" I yelled, starting to sit upright in the tub, but remembering in time who was watching. I clutched my legs tighter and stared with an open mouth at Jez. She gave me an unreadable look and continued.

"I'm fully confident that ye'll do well by me crew until I can return. I'm leavin' as many men as I can spare for yer defenses, and trust that ye won't let that blackguard Corbin step foot on me precious island."

"He's insane," I gasped, turning my stunned look on the three men standing there. Beyond them, the women stood equally stunned.

"I've never told ye just why it is that I blackspotted Corbin. Most folks hereabouts think it's because of the murder of me crew—but that ain't it. The sad truth is that Black Corbin ruined me life when he took me one true love from me. I swore me vengeance the day he took her, and I'll have it yet, just ye wait and see."

"Corbin *what?*" I asked, but no one answered me. As unbelievable as it was that Bart should leave us helpless (with me in charge), it was utterly inconceivable that Corbin should steal the love of his life, whoever she was. Corbin wasn't the woman-stealing sort.

"I've heard a foul rumor that ye're a bit sweet on that devil's spawn Corbin, but I know it couldn't be anythin' more than the most heinous lie. Even so, I'm beggin' ye, as yer captain and yer friend, not to turn Turtle's Back over to Black Corbin. I love this island with all me heart, and it's breakin' just thinkin' of how he'd destroy it."

I shook my head, unable to say anything.

"There's more," Jez said, squinting to decipher what I could see was cramped, dense writing. *"I've instructed the crew to honor ye as their captain, and to respect yer commands as if they were me own. I've also issued a proclamation naming ye as Governor of Turtle's Back until I return.*

Fair winds to ye, lass. Yours, etcetera, Bartholomew Portuguese, Captain."

Silence filled the room—stunned, disbelieving silence. A silence so thick that not even the noises from the square outside the window could penetrate its denseness.

Charlie cleared his throat, pulling off his dirty bandana before saying, "What be yer orders, Cap'n Amy?"

Chapter 20

We'll be queens, and make decrees—
They may honour them who please.

—Ibid, Act I

My first command as captain and governor was given stark naked from the bathtub.

"My orders are for you guys to get the hell out of the room so I can finish my bath and get dressed," I said, glaring over my knees.

The three men looked surprised for a moment, but duly shuffled out of the room. I waited until Suky and Jez propped the screen up in front of me again, then had the quickest bath in the history of the world, getting dressed in record time.

"Right. Something is clearly going on," I told the men as I entered the front room. "Either Bart is insane, or that note is a forgery, or someone is playing a cruel trick, because I'm the last person on this island who should be given command of both the crew and the inhabitants."

"'Tis no joke," Charlie replied, giving me a long look. "The captain spoke to all of us, tellin' us what he was plannin' to do. I'm not sayin' that all the men are pleased about havin' a female captain, but most of them have seen how ye handled yerself on the first day of the blockade, and they'll be willin' to follow ye. The townsfolk won't be givin' ye any grief, either. They be too worried about their shops and such."

I looked each man in the eye, searching for any signs that they were having me on in the biggest practical joke to hit the Seventh Sea, but they all appeared to be telling the truth.

I sank down into the nearest chair, still too flabbergasted to take it all in. The ladies filed into the room, for once not ogling the men, but watching me with round eyes.

"What be yer next command, then, Cap'n?" Charlie asked.

I started to protest that I wasn't in the least bit interested or experienced enough to be either a captain or a governor, but a sudden mental image rose of me sitting behind Bart's big desk in the governor's house. What was a governor, or a captain for that matter, but someone who knew how to organize and delegate? I knew how to do those things! And I had the financial knowledge to help the people of Turtle's Back. Why should Renata's girls be the only ones who had secure financial futures . . . oh, man, what was I thinking? These people were not real! Then again, who was to say that helping other characters to succeed wasn't part of the scenario?

"Better safe than sorry," I muttered to my knees.

"Cap'n?"

"Sorry, just talking to myself. Let's see . . . I think the first thing I'd like to do is to talk to all of the people who are in charge—the mayor of the town, Pangloss, and whoever is organizing the men on the shore guns."

Charlie nodded. "The mayor be here. Mr. Pangloss be at the blockade, but I'll have a man let him know ye want him.

Cap'n Bart left a note for him, too. As for the shore guns—they don't rightfully have anyone in charge now that the cap'n is gone. I can go out and see if there's any crew mannin' them if ye like."

"Excellent. I'll want to talk to the head gunners, as well. Better have everyone meet me in the governor's house in, oh, say, two hours?"

Charlie nodded again and redonned his bandana. "As ye like. Anythin' more?"

I thought for a moment. "No. I have a message I'll want delivered, but I'll have one of my crew do it."

He started to leave, but I stopped him with one last question. "I find this all so unexpected, Charlie. I can't believe Bart would think anything else is more important than the blockade. Where exactly did he go?"

"Don't know." Charlie shrugged. "He just said he had somethin' important to do, and that ye were goin' to take over as cap'n."

"That's so bizarre," I said slowly, trying to puzzle out what it was Bart was up to. "Did he at least say what it was he had to go do?"

"Nay. Cap'n be tight to the chest with his thoughts," he answered.

The men left after that, leaving me to the barrage of questions the women had for me. I tried to answer them as best I could, but I was just about as clueless as they were when it came to the hows and whys of my sudden—temporary—rise in the world.

"What are ye goin' to do about the blockade?" Red Beth asked.

"Stop it," I said, making a mental list in my head. "That's the first thing. Then I'll—oh, Renata, there you are. You're never going to believe what's happened!"

"Ye've been made governor and captain of Bart's crew,

aye, I know. 'Tis all over the town. Bart had a proclamation posted." Renata handed her shopping basket to Mags and slumped tiredly into a chair opposite me. "'Tis a surprise to everyone that Bart's left the island with Black Corbin just waitin' to pounce."

"Oh. You've heard. Yeah, it shocked me, too, but you know, I think this can be a good thing. I'm not a total stranger to managerial roles, and I do have both the administrative and financial background to take charge of the business aspects of both endeavors. As for the rest—well, it's just a . . ." My lips closed over the word *game*. It wasn't to the people who lived and worked . . . and died . . . here.

"Eh?" Renata asked, giving me a sharp look.

"It's just a matter of asking for help from the people who have the experience I need," I said, coming to a fast decision. I turned to the others in the room. "Ladies, you can all help me, if you would."

"Aye, we'd be happy to," Sly Jez said, sitting up a little straighter.

"Aye," Mags and Red Beth agreed.

"What would ye be likin' us to do?" Suky asked, frowning slightly. "The only thing we know how to do is to please a man. Ye be lookin' for hints about that?"

"No, thank you. But actually, there're lots of other things you can do. Jez, can you please run up to the governor's house and let the staff there know I'll be along shortly? Red Beth, while Charlie is dealing with Bart's crew, would you and Mags round up the leading townspeople—the mayor and anyone else who you think should be in the know about what's happening? And Suky, could you gather my crew? I mean, my former crew—Tar and the twins and Bas. They'll all probably be at the inn. Tell them to meet me up at the governor's house, as well."

The ladies bustled off. I waited until the door closed on their excited chatter before smiling at Renata.

"That were done right handsomely," the old lady said, smiling back, her black eyes shining. "Gettin' the lasses out of the way like that. I'm thinkin' ye'll be just fine as Bart's replacement."

"Good," I said, leaning forward, my arms on my knees. "I'm glad you think so, although I'm perhaps a smidgen less confident than you. Regardless, there are a few things I wanted to talk to you about."

She nodded. "Aye, I thought there might be."

"When did you first meet Bart?" I asked, figuring there was no time like the present to try to ascertain whether she was Corbin's ex-partner.

She blinked a couple of times, clearly not expecting that question.

"I'm just curious," I said, flinching when my explanation sounded lame even to my own ears. "It might help me to know a bit of his history, you see. Er . . . and the history of the island."

She just looked at me, her eyes bright but her expression placid.

"Were you born here? On this island, I mean?"

"Aye," she allowed.

"Ah. Good. So, you must remember what it was like before Bart took over. Who was governor before him?"

"Ye sent me girls away to ask me about the governor afore Bart?" she asked, frowning.

If she was Paul, she probably had figured out what I was doing. If she wasn't . . . well, I couldn't screw this up any more than I already had. "Yes, I want to know. Who was governor before Bart?"

Her eyes never left mine, but she said nothing. I sighed in relief at the blank look on her face, then mentally chastised myself. Renata was my last viable suspect for Paul. Like Pangloss, Renata avoided my questions at first, but both went blank when I pressed hard . . . so if it wasn't either of them, who was it? Everyone else, from Bart on down to Bas, had checked out.

"Never mind, it doesn't matter," I said, smiling to myself as her face came alive again. I questioned her about things her character would know—the price and availability of food—and asked her whether or not she would like to move into the governor's house.

"Nay, lass, 'tis awful kind of ye, but me girls and me are comfortable here. Ye go with me blessin'."

"I don't want to seem ungrateful for all your help and kindness in putting me up when I didn't have anywhere else to go," I said, hesitating.

"'Tis only right ye take over Bart's house while ye be fillin' his shoes," she said. "I know ye won't forget us."

"Absolutely not. In fact, I have high hopes of making life a lot more comfy for all of you."

She looked pleased with that. I chatted with her a bit more, then headed to the governor's house to start putting things into motion.

The town leaders and mayor were the first group of people to answer my summons. They were quickly taken care of, with reassurances given on both sides that the current arrangement of government would continue without significant change (although I reserved the right to make some helpful suggestions about how to streamline the local economy). As they were leaving, Pangloss and Charlie arrived.

"I tried to bring the men from the shore guns," Charlie said as he pulled me aside. "But I couldn't."

"Oh? Why not?"

"There are none," he said, his eyes puzzled. "It seems Bart took the gun crew with him."

I sighed. "Grand. Now we have no protection whatsoever from shore. Well, I'd better make sure that no one attacks us tonight."

"Aye, 'twould likely be a good thing," he agreed.

I took a deep breath and entered the library.

"So, the cap'n's up and left ye in charge," Pangloss said as he spun around to face me, a scowl darkening his face. I walked slowly to Bart's massive desk, reminding myself that Pangloss had every right to be outraged over my new position. As first mate, he should have been the logical choice for captain.

"Yes, he has, and I'm not going to try to begin to explain to you why he made that choice. It seems ludicrous and totally unbelievable to me, but he did, so I'm hoping against hope that you'll find it in your heart to help me. You know more about the sea than anyone I know, and if I'm going to do this captain and governor thing right, I'll need a lot of help."

I could see that he had been working himself up to having a hissy, but I effectively took the wind out of his sails.

"Er . . . aye. 'Tis unbelievable to me, as well. But I've sworn to follow me cap'n's orders, and this be one of 'em, so I'll help ye as best I can."

I smiled and offered him a glass of brandy, grateful the worst was over.

By the time the moon had started its climb in the night sky, Pangloss and I were in agreement that something had to be done.

"I warn you; I plan on stopping the blockade," I told him as he was about to return to his ship.

"Ye'll be turnin' the island over to that devil?" he asked, astounded.

"No. But I will invite Corbin to attend a meeting here tomorrow to discuss a peace treaty between the two crews.

You needn't look at me as if I've gone mad—I know what I'm doing."

"Black Corbin would never agree to a treaty," he said, shaking his head. "Nothin' will do for him but that he rules us."

"Don't worry," I said, giving him a confident smile. "He'll agree to it. I have a secret weapon, you see."

"Oh, aye?" he asked, his head tipped to the side. "What would that be, then?"

"Me," I answered, and gently closed the door on his disbelieving face.

An hour later I lit the lanterns on my borrowed sloop and gave the order for her to sail. The twins and Tar weren't terribly happy at having their shore leave revoked but cheered up to no end when I told them all they had to do was sail me out to Corbin's ship; then they could return to shore and have the rest of the night off.

I was a bit worried that some of the blockade ships might interpret my ship approaching them as an aggressive act, but evidently Corbin had given the word not to open fire willy-nilly, for we sailed past three big warships to the red and black frigate *Java Guru* without being stopped or fired upon.

"Wow, this is a really, really big ship," I said as we sailed alongside her, heading to a spot midway down her length where a group of sailors were waiting with grappling poles and a rope ladder. Due to my concern with Corbin earlier, I hadn't had a really good look at the flagship. I took the opportunity to give her a close examination. She had three masts, a raised quarterdeck (at the rear of the ship), and a forecastle (at the bow). She reeked naval authority and more or less looked exactly how I expected a bad-assed warship to look. "How many guns does she have, Tar?"

"Thirty-eight," he answered. "This be a captured ship from the English navy."

"Really?" I looked up to the railing. A dark-haired figure appeared suddenly, frowning over the edge at me. "Wow. Impressive. Hoy, Corbin! Hoy, Holder!"

"Ahoy, lass. Ye look fetchin' in those knickers. I did well with 'em, didn't I?" Holder called down happily.

"Amy, what the devil are you doing out here at this time of night?" Corbin asked.

"Yes, you did, and thank you," I told Holder before smiling up at Corbin. "I have some things to talk about. Mind helping me on board?"

Bas scrambled up the rope ladder after me. He had made a bit of a fuss when I informed him he had spent long enough in the inn with the other crew, but I turned a deaf ear to his complaints.

Corbin grabbed my hands as I approached the railing, hauling me up and over it and straight into his arms. I'm not a fool; I didn't so much as protest such a domineering action, but I did try to avoid plastering myself on his wound when he locked his arms around me and kissed the very air from my lungs. He might be healing superfast in this reality, but there was no sense in pushing virtual fate.

At the touch of his mouth on mine, my entire body woke up and started making demands.

"Dear God," I murmured when he finally had to stop the kiss so we could breathe.

"No, not quite, although you're free to think I am a god," he said, giving me a roguish smile.

"That was a hell of a kiss," I said softly, licking my lower lip. I swore I could still feel his tongue burning a path over it. "People are watching, though." Just Holder, and he doesn't care. The kiss, by the way, was for being the most delectable, desirable woman in the world," he said, rubbing his thumb over where I had licked.

"I just melt when you say things like that," I said, leaning in for another kiss despite the audience.

"And this is for taking so long to come to me," he said louder, giving me a swat on the behind.

"Hey!" I protested, jumping back and rubbing the abused spot. "You can't smack a captain on the butt. That's illegal or something."

"I'm the captain here," he said, starting to pull me into another embrace.

"You're one of the captains, yes." I backed away, ignoring Holder's smirk as he watched our byplay.

"No, sweetheart, not on my ship. You're the captain when you command your own vessel, but only the captain of a crew can be called captain in other circumstances."

I made a polite bow, sweeping out my hand as I said, "Captain Amy, governor of Turtle's Back, at your service."

"What?"

I thought Corbin's eyebrows were going to shoot off his forehead.

"Bart left. I'm in charge now. My, isn't it late. I'm sooo sleepy. Mind if I spend the night here?" I asked, batting my lashes at him.

Corbin's eyes went molten at my blatant offer, but he managed to restrain himself . . . somewhat to my dismay, although I knew it was smarter to get the talking out of the way before I investigated—in an up-close and personal manner—just how healed he was.

"Come into my quarters," Corbin said, grabbing my wrist and heading for a door under the quarterdeck. "I want to hear everything."

"Me, too," Holder said, following. "This promises to be the most entertaining thing I've heard since Corb tried to explain why he came back to the ship with bits of fig pudding stuck to his chest hair."

My cheeks pinked a little as I remembered that wonderful night. Corbin was evidently remembering it as well, because he shot me a wicked look that had me wondering what sort of desserts a blockade ship routinely stocked.

It took the better part of an hour to explain the recent happenings, hindered as I was by almost constant interruptions in the form of questions from both men. But answer them I did, and eventually they were in possession of as much information as I was.

"But why would he do it?" Holder asked, giving me a critical look. "No offense intended, Amy, but it's not normal for a captain to promote someone over the head of his first mate."

I shrugged. "I have no idea what his reasoning is other than what he said in the letter."

Corbin glanced at it where it lay spread out on his desk, a half frown wrinkling his brow. "Leaving Amy in charge makes perfect sense to me," he said slowly. "She's smart and competent and will do a good job as both captain and governor."

I gave him my very best smile, warmed to the tips of my toes by his support. What a perceptive man he was!

"But what I want to know is what this mysterious mission is that caused him to leave during the blockade."

"No idea," I said, shrugging. "I asked everyone I could think of, but no one had any clue."

"It doesn't make sense any more than his accusation that I stole his woman from him," Corbin said, examining the letter again. He shook his head while reading it, tossing it down disgustedly. "I don't know who he's talking about. I haven't stolen anyone. You're the only woman I've been with in more than a year. He . . . er . . . Bart didn't ever express any affection for you, did he?"

"No, he didn't." I raised my hands and let them fall in a gesture of utter bewilderment. "He's never so much as flirted with me, at least not that I noticed. Holder has been more obvious than Bart. He's ogled me openly, whereas Bart never looked at me twice."

Holder stood up from where he was leaning over Corbin's shoulder rereading the note. "The word you are looking for, dear lady, is appreciate. I appreciate, not ogle! My wife has specifically forbidden me from ogling."

I crossed my arms under my breasts. Holder's gaze immediately shot to where my breasts were smooshed up under the bodice. "Aha! See? You're ogling my boobs right now."

Corbin glanced up at his friend, then over to me, his eyes widening slightly.

"Great, now you both are ogling me." I uncrossed my arms. My cleavage returned to its better-than-normal-but-not-as-nice-as-Jez's state. Holder looked disappointed.

"The fact remains that there is no explanation for Bart's unexpected departure," Corbin said, his gaze still on my chest. I pulled my shoulders back. He smiled.

"I have an idea, but it's a bit of a stretch," Holder said, pouring himself a brandy and taking the comfortable leather seat.

"Make yourself at home, mate," Corbin said dryly, rising from the desk chair and coming to sit next to me on the bed. I leaned into his nonwounded side, enjoying the feeling of his body next to mine. Something about Corbin felt so comfortable, so right, it made me think of coming home after a long, unpleasant trip.

"Thanks, I will. About this idea I have . . . Amy, you said—oh, for God's sake, woman, stop nuzzling him in front of me! You think I want to see that?"

"Sorry," I said, without the least bit of contriteness as I

pulled away from the irresistible lure of Corbin's adorable earlobe.

Holder turned his glare on Corbin. "You think I don't see that you're trying to get your hand under the back of her bodice?"

Corbin stopped trying to do that very thing, looking behind me at where his hand was working its way under the leather and linen. "How could you see that?"

"I couldn't," Holder said, looking abashed for a moment. "But that's what I'd be doing if I was in your place. If you two would try to keep your hands off each other long enough for us to have a rational discussion, I would appreciate it."

"I thought you wanted us together." I said, squirming slightly when Corbin's fingers found a way under the bodice. He caressed a line up my spine that had me suddenly thinking of all the hours that had passed since Corbin and I had had dessert.

"I do, but not when we're trying to have a conversation. Sit still, would you?"

"Get on with it, Holder," Corbin said, clearly thinking thoughts along the same path as mine.

"Fine. Amy, you said that you grilled Bart, and he clearly was a computer player, correct?"

I smiled a slow, seductive smile at Corbin. "Hmm? Grilled might be too harsh a word. I've talked to Bart a lot, and he's always been very piratey and never broken character. Corbin, do you know that you have the most adorable Adam's apple? I love how it bobbles around when I when I touch you right here—"

"No touching!" Holder said, leaping up out of his chair. Before I could protest he yanked me off the bed and shoved me down into the chair, taking the one Corbin had vacated at the desk. "Lord above, you two are insatiable!"

"Yes, we are," Corbin said, smiling back at me, his eyes alight with love and passion and a host of other emotions that made my heart soar. "Make your point, Holder, then get the hell out of my cabin."

"My point, you lust-riddled dolt, is that Bart could well be Paul. And if he is, it's likely we're all in danger right this very moment."

Chapter 21

Go and do your best endeavour,
And before all links we sever,
We will say farewell for-ever.

—Ibid, Act II

I stopped batting my lashes at Corbin to gawk at Holder. Corbin frowned at his friend. "Danger? What sort of danger? We're already trapped here."

"Exactly. Paul has us trapped here, all of us, with no clear way to escape, and no way to find him. And now Bart has done virtually the same thing—he has us trapped, together, stuck in this blockade and unable to find him. Makes sense that this was part of his plan all along. And given that, I'm not expecting him to show up and throw us a party with balloon animals and ice cream."

"Hmm." Corbin stroked his chin, something I noticed he did when thinking hard. "He has a point, love."

"Granted, but I just told you both that I've talked to Bart, and he seems very much a computer character."

Holder waggled a finger at me. "No. You said that you've talked to him a lot, but you didn't grill him. There's a differ-

ence between having casual intercourse with a character"—
he shot Corbin a look—"*social* intercourse with a character,
and trying to determine if they are a player or not."

"But . . . don't you guys know whether you created Bart
or not?"

"Sure we do," Corbin said. "Bart was created to be a
nemesis to players—I told you that. But given Paul's programming abilities, it wouldn't be too much of a stretch to
guess he's taken over the character and is now running it
himself."

"True." I chewed my lower lip while I mentally ran over
all my conversations with Bart. "You're right. I don't think
I ever did really ask him a pointed question. He's always
seemed so perfect for the role, I guess I never questioned
that he could be anything but a computer character."

"The prosecution rests its case," Holder said, leaning
back in the chair.

"Now, wait—just because I didn't ask him about his
childhood doesn't mean he's this Paul guy." I looked from
Holder to Corbin, who was looking thoughtful. "For Pete's
sake, Renata has acted much more suspicious than Bart. In
addition, there must be other people in the game you haven't
tracked down yet to talk to."

Corbin nodded. "We've done about ninety-five percent
of the people on Mongoose, but not all of them. You said
you've done the same?"

"No, I've talked to all forty-seven inhabitants of Turtle's
Back. None of them are anything but what they seem."

"Except Bart," Holder said, a stubborn expression on his
face.

"Possibly Bart. He's in the *possible* category, and I'm
willing to bet that a couple of direct questions would clear
up any doubt."

"Right, but how are you going to ask him questions now?" Holder asked.

I frowned. He had a point.

"Ha, gotcha on that one. Running away is the surest sign of guilt," Holder crowed.

"Not necessarily," Corbin said, rubbing his chin. "He could be exactly what Amy says—a computer character whose actions are driven by the circumstances provided by the player data."

"Really? Did you program computer characters to turn over their crews to players?" I asked, more confused than ever about Bart. Could I have been taken in by him?

"Actually, yes, if the data matched preset criteria, a character might well abdicate in favor of a senior player officer."

"But I'm not an officer," I pointed out.

"Moot point—you're the only player in his crew, so that makes you the senior person. Something you did could well have triggered Bart's AI into making him turn over the crew."

"Or it could be a nefarious plan to trap us," Holder insisted, still looking stubborn.

I rubbed my forehead, my thoughts so muddled I couldn't seem to get them to make sense. "We're back to where we started. It's like we're going in circles. We keep trying to get somewhere but don't actually do anything."

"You're tired," Corbin said, marching over to the door and opening it. He gave his first mate a very pointed look. "You need to go to bed. Everything will be clearer in the morning."

Holder rolled his eyes as he obeyed Corbin's unspoken command, sauntering to the door only to pause. "I'll be the first to admit that a steamy, sweaty night of unbridled sex has many powers, but it won't decide the problem of Paul."

"It's too late to do anything tonight," Corbin said. I agreed.

Holder gave me a quick leer. "I'd wish you a good night, Amy, but I doubt you'll need—"

Corbin pushed him through the door, slamming it behind him. As an afterthought he locked it, tossing the key onto the desk.

I crossed my arms. "Locking me in again?"

"No, sweetheart," he said, his smile so filled with love it made me want to cry. "Locking the rest of the world out."

"Sounds good to me. About this plan for a steamy, sweaty night of unbridled sex . . . I'm afraid there are going to be conditions."

"Oh, really?" Corbin stood on one foot and yanked his boot off. "What sort of conditions? Something exciting? Something naughty? You want to tie me down?"

I was about to tell him that I wanted to see for myself how his wound was doing before I gave the okay to anything so strenuous as a bout of lovemaking, but the image his words presented gave me a couple of moments' pause. "Do you want me to tie you down?"

Corbin looked thoughtful as he pulled off his other boot and started unlacing his leather jerkin. "I'm not sure. I've never been tied down. I generally prefer to be in the driver's seat, but if you really wanted to go Amazon on me, I suppose we could give it a shot."

I smiled as I walked over to the desk. "I have a better idea."

The last thing I saw before I left him was his questioning frown. I hurried up the stairs to the quarterdeck, found Leeward Tom, and gave him my request. He looked startled, but nodded and summoned Barn and a couple of others. While that was being done, I trotted back downstairs, pausing to kiss Corbin quickly as he stood with his hands on his hips in the door to his cabin.

"What do you think you're doing?" he demanded as I headed for the stairs leading belowdecks.

"You'll see. Back in a mo."

It actually took longer than a moment to find something along the lines of what I wanted, but in the end I was happy with the results.

"You want to take a bath? Now?" Corbin asked when I reentered his cabin. Barn gave the big copper and wood tub one last shove so that it sat in the middle of the cabin. Several younger crewmates were hauling in seawater in large leather containers. Others were carefully carrying copper pots with heated water.

"No, you're going to take one," I said, waggling my eyebrows at him as I oversaw the filling of the tub. Five minutes later, the water was at a temperature and level I liked. I thanked the crewmates and shooed them out the door before closing and relocking it. "I know real stitches need to be kept dry, but I doubt if a little water will harm yours. Besides, that wound needs to be kept clean, and what better way to ensure that than to bathe all of you?"

His frown faded. "You're going to bathe me?"

"Oh, yes. Normally I'd pass on this opportunity since most tubs just aren't made for any extracurricular activities, but since this one is amply built, I thought we could give it a whirl." I pulled a palm-sized bottle out of my cleavage. "And to make sure your skin is soft and supple, I'm adding a little lemon oil to the water."

He watched with interest as I poured a dollop of the aromatic oil into the tub. The scent of tangy lemon filled the air of the cabin, making me lick my lips as I knelt next to the tub.

"Stop that," Corbin said, his eyes flashing silver at me as he tore at the leather laces of his jerkin.

"Stop what?" I purred, swishing my hand around in the water to distribute the oil. I bit my lower lip, running my tongue along it with much deliberation.

"That! Stop licking your lips! It's driving me wild. I want to do it."

I stood up and tugged on the laces of my bodice. "That's the idea, handsome." He started toward me. I held up a hand to stop him. "You have to be naked and wet first."

If there was a land-speed record for disrobing, I'm willing to bet Corbin came close to breaking it. One moment he was standing there dressed in his breeches, shirt, and jerkin; the next there was a lemon-scented splash as he flung himself into the tub. "Done. Now, bring those lips here, wench."

"That's Captain Wench to you, me bucko," I said, shucking my striped knickers, underwear, and bodice until I was clad only in my loose linen shirt. I grabbed a sea sponge and a round ball of soap, kneeling next to the tub. Corbin reached for me again, but I put a hand on his damp chest and held him back. "Hang on, let me look at your wound."

"It's almost healed," he told me as I leaned close to his belly to give the injury a long look. "No blood poisoning, as you were predicting. I think the stitches could come out, as a matter of fact."

I gently prodded the area around the stitches. I had to admit, he was right—it was almost healed. Bless the game's accelerated healing. "Yeah, I think you're right about the stitches. I'll take them out now."

He leaned back while I gently snipped the threads with a tiny pocket knife, carefully removing them.

"You're sure this isn't just an excuse to ogle my manly chest?"

"Shh. Delicate work here. Your stomach moves when

you talk, and I don't want to accidently poke you by mistake." He was silent while I picked the last of the threads off, smiling when I folded up the knife and tossed it back onto his desk. "I wish things healed this well and this fast in real life. And for the record, I never predicted blood poisoning. I was just worried about it, but this looks wonderful. It's not giving you any pain or discomfort?"

He wrapped both arms around me and swung me over the edge of the tub. I shrieked as I landed with a splash on his slippery wet thighs. "Would I be able to do that if it was giving me pain?"

"No, I suppose not, although now my shirt is wet," I said, looking down at myself. The thin linen was plastered to my skin, leaving every morsel of me clearly visible.

Corbin slid his hands up my stomach to cup my breasts, his thumbs rubbing gentle circles on my hardening nipples. "I wonder if real pirates did this. The original wet T-shirt contest."

I gasped when he leaned forward and took one of my aching breasts in his mouth, sucking it through the wet material of the shirt. His teeth scraped along my nipple, sending little streaks of molten desire through my veins, leaving me shivering even though my internal temperature seemed to have risen at least a hundred degrees.

"I'm supposed to . . . I'm supposed to . . . oh, my God, Corbin. Do that again!"

He did it again, to my eagerly awaiting second breast, then carefully peeled the wet shirt off me and threw it carelessly toward the bed. I clutched his shoulders as his fingers slid down my spread thighs, the oil in the water adding a friction that made his normally arousing touch something so erotic, I trembled on the verge of an orgasm. "You're supposed to what, sweetheart?"

"I'm supposed to be bathing you," I yelped as his fingers

turned inward, laying open all my secrets, probing, teasing, tormenting me with little touches and circular sweeps of his thumb that just about had me bursting into song.

"You can have your turn with me in just a—" One long finger sank into me, causing muscles I didn't know were there to go wild tightening around him. One last sweep of his thumb was all it took, and I was off flying, my body and mind and soul singing a song of happiness and completion . . . and love. My back arched as I shouted out his name, aware of nothing but how much a part of me he was.

"—minute," he finished. I collapsed on his chest, my heart racing. He chuckled as he nuzzled my neck, nipping at my earlobe. "You're not going to go to sleep on me, are you?"

I pushed myself back, toyed with the idea of giving him an outraged glare at such a ludicrous idea, but decided a wicked smile was much more fun. I smiled. Wickedly. "Mock me, will you, mortal man? Oh, ye of little faith. Prepare to repent such unjust thoughts."

"I warn you, it's going to take some serious work to make me repent," he said, his hands heading for my breasts. The impudent little hussies thrust themselves in his hands for a moment or two, then I slid back along his legs until my chest was resting on his groin.

"I'm not afraid of a little hard work. I think I'll start by kissing your owie and making it better," I said, deliberately moving forward so his penis—standing very much at attention—was caught between my breasts. He sucked in approximately half the roomful of air as I tightened my arms, effectively capturing him in a breasty grip. I flicked my tongue over an area to the left of his wound, not actually touching it, but licking off the lemon oil from the surrounding area.

Corbin's eyes crossed and his head lolled back, his hands

limp on the edge of the tub as I started a little back-and-forth motion that had him sliding along my breastbone. He wasn't the only one who was affected by the erotic silk of the oil and water—the feel of his slick legs against my sensitive breasts was quickly building a familiar pressure deep inside me.

I swirled my tongue around his belly button, noting that he watched hopefully as I nipped my way over to his hip. The water reached just below his belly button, but he shifted so a good portion of his happy seven inches was above water.

I flicked the tip of it with my tongue. His knuckles turned white on the rim of the tub as I got my hands into the action.

His hips bucked as I licked a serpentine path along the length of his arousal, enjoying both the taste and feel of him as I used the oily water to find a rhythm that had him gasping in sheer delight.

"Now!" he demanded as he dragged me up his chest, spreading my legs so my knees were straddling his hips.

I gave a little wiggle. His oil-slicked length slid along all sorts of my newly discovered sensitive nerve endings. "Do you repent?"

"Yes, yes, dear God, yes! I repent! Of everything!"

I smiled as he pulled my hips forward, my body singing a hallelujah chorus as he pushed his way in. His hands slid up my slick back, one hand on the back of my neck, pulling me forward until his mouth possessed mine. He groaned into my mouth as I started moving on him, slowly at first, but soon the feeling of his body sliding along and in and around mine pushed me to a point where I was moving fast and hard on him.

His eyes turned to liquid silver as an orgasm claimed him. I had just enough presence of mind before my own consumed me to kiss him as he shouted out his love. Without thought, I whispered what was in my heart, collapsing on him, leaving us a tangle of lemon-scented, wet body parts, both of us gasping for air, our hearts racing in a similar rhythm.

We didn't wait for anyone to drain and carry out the tub before staggering to bed. As I snuggled into Corbin, my limbs boneless and heavy, I double-checked that our activities hadn't stressed his wound in any way, then kissed his chin and wrapped my arms around him with a happy, tired sigh.

He pulled me even closer, arranged my legs so that one of his was resting between mine, and kissed my ear.

"Amy?"

"Mmm?"

"Do you know what you said? At the end?"

"Mmm-hmm."

Ten seconds passed. "And?"

"Corbin, I'm warm, sleepy, and sated," I said, pressing a kiss against his neck. "Too warm, sleepy, and sated to deal with anything but rest."

He was silent for so long I thought he'd gone to sleep. "You said you loved me."

I bit his shoulder.

"Ow."

I smiled, but he didn't see it.

"Amy?"

"Mmm?"

"You're going to have to face your feelings some time."

"I know."

More silence. His breathing slowed and deepened. I relaxed, my breathing matching his.

"I love you, too, sweetheart," he said, his voice rumbling deep in his chest.

I didn't say anything to that, but I snuggled into him even more, listening with pleasure to the reassuring steady thud of his heart beneath my ear.

Chapter 22

For your foes are fierce and ruthless,
False, unmerciful, and truthless. . . .

—Ibid, Act II

"You, sir, are a poop."

"I may be, but you love me. You, madam, love a poop."

I glared at the man who alternately made my heart soar with joy and left me with an almost overpowering urge to throttle him. "We are not discussing personal things like emotions and who loves whom, although I'd like to point out that you declared your love for me first."

"Keeping score, are you?" he teased.

"No. But it makes me go all warm and fuzzy that I didn't have to pry it out of you. Back to the subject at hand— bringing an end to the blockade and providing supplies to my poor, starving townsfolk."

Corbin leaned back in one of the chairs in Bart's library, steepled his fingers, and tapped his chin with them. "No one in town looked to me to be particularly poor or starving. And I don't deny in the least that I was in love with you before you finally decided to reciprocate. I'm a man. I'm superior that way."

"I didn't decide to reciprocate; it just happened," I said, getting up from the big desk and marching over to stand in front of him. "And superior, my butt."

He leaned sideways to look around at my backside. "Yes, it is, but you're changing the subject."

"I'm not changing the subject; you are! I'm trying to bring an end to these stupid hostilities, and you keep distracting me with talk about our relationship."

His eyebrows rose a hair. "I thought women liked to talk about relationships."

"We do, but not all the time. Now, if you're through discussing whether I may or may not love you—"

"Oh, you love me," he said with a self-satisfied smile. I wanted to kiss it right off his face.

"—then perhaps we can move beyond these transparent attempts to distract me and get to the meat of the problem."

"Your desire to repress your emotions?" he asked.

"Argh!" I yelled, throwing my hands in the air. "I am not repressing anything other than possibly the urge to wrap my hands around your neck and squeeze."

"I'd rather you wrapped your hands around something else and squeezed," he said with a wink. "Ever heard the 'Travelling Riverside Blues'? There's a line in there I think you'll like: 'Squeeze my lemon 'til the juice runs down my leg.'"

"Corbin!" I yelled, frustrated near to the breaking point.

"What?" he asked, an innocent look on his face that didn't fool me in the least. "Don't like the blues?"

"Argh!" I yelled again. "I don't know whether to have you thrown off the island and never see you again, or rip off all your clothing and make wild bunny love to you."

"There's a fine line between love and hate," he said

placidly, then started laughing when I yelled a third time. "All right, sweetheart, I'll stop, but you make it so easy for me."

I glared at him. He held up his hands and promised to be good.

"*That* has never been in question," I said, going back around the desk to reclaim my seat. I picked up the pre-sharpened quill and dipped it in the inkwell, trying to write without leaving huge black blotches and smears. "Now, I'm going to write up a statement that says you relinquish all claims on Turtle's Back, then we can both sign it, and the blockade can end."

"I'm not going to sign any such thing," Corbin said pleasantly.

I looked up from the parchment. "You're not?"

"No."

"But you said you'd stop the blockade."

"I said I'd come here and discuss an end to the blockade, yes. I never agreed to forgo my intentions to take Turtle away from Bart."

"But he's not here. I am," I pointed out.

"Yes, you are now, but what if he was to come back? Would you fight him for control of the island?"

The serious mien of Corbin's face told me he was in deadly earnest about this subject. I decided that the time had come to get a few things straight.

"No, I wouldn't fight him for control. He left me in charge until he returned. It's understood I would hand back the reins at such time as he comes back."

"As I thought." His fingers drummed on the arm of the chair. "And what about the mine?"

"The emerald mine?" I asked, a dull feeling cramping my stomach. I knew that money was the motivation for almost everyone in the game—the acquisition of it and the spend-

ing of it—but I had assumed that Corbin had endless resources as the game's creator, and thus must be above such
mundane things as acquiring wealth.

He nodded.

"Well, I talked to the town leaders about it, and they said
it had been closed down a short while ago."

"And?" he asked, his eyes burning on mine. I frowned,
unsure what the intensity of his gaze meant. "What do you
intend to do about it?"

"The mayor says that the mine brought prosperity to the
island. I thought it would be good if it was reopened. This
island has few natural resources and can't even support the
small population that's here now. It just makes sense to
use—after a detailed environmental impact assessment,
naturally—the resources available. Within reason, of
course. I certainly wouldn't support any practice that provided the wholesale destruction of valuable resources and
commodities."

"You wouldn't?" Corbin asked, a steely note in his voice.
"Valuable resources such as, oh, say, people?"

"Huh?" The quill had dripped a big black inky blotch on
the parchment. I set it down and gave Corbin a puzzled look.
"What are you talking about? What people?"

"Try the sixty-five men that Bart sacrificed to his greed,"
Corbin answered, his words sending a chill down my arms.

"Sixty-five men?"

"Surely you knew about that? Or has his stranglehold on
this island precluded even the mention of the murder of
sixty-five members of his crew?"

The chill swept up my arms to my back, making the skin
on the back of my neck tighten with horror. "What are you
talking about? Bart didn't murder his crew—you did."

It was Corbin's turn to look stunned. "I *what*?"

"Well . . . murder might be a bit harsh since everyone

died in battle, but it was your ships that destroyed them. Pangloss told me all about how you tried to take Turtle's Back and lured Bart's men around to the other side of the island where you had set up a trap."

The look on his face was indescribable, but it made my heart wrench regardless. "You think I killed Bart's crew? You really believe I'm capable of something like that?"

"It's not a matter of capable, Corbin. They're computer people—I knew you knew that, so I figured either you were testing out a function of the game, or you got a little too much into the role of scourge of the Seventh Sea. Are you telling me you didn't kill Bart's crew?"

"No, I did not kill them." His eyes flashed as he jumped out of the chair, pacing the length of the room before turning and marching over to me. He leaned across the desk until his face was an inch from mine. "When Bart discovered that emeralds were the only thing this island produced, he started mining for them without any sort of expert help. And yes, before you ask, we did program in mining experts. They are expensive, though, so a player needs to have a good resource base to use them. But Bart didn't. He sent team after team into the mines, regardless of their safety, all in the name of his desire for wealth. But one day his dreams came crashing down . . . along with the roof of the main shaft in the mine, killing all sixty-five members of his crew that he'd forced to dig emeralds."

"Oh, my God," I said, my stomach twisting in a sick ball. "How could that happen? It's just a game—"

"An extremely complex game with literally hundreds of thousands of variables programmed for almost every eventuality. And since I believed that Bart was a computer player, I didn't think anything of it at the time other than noting that his character chose to ignore a possible option for great wealth. But now I wonder if Paul hadn't taken over

Bart's character right from the start. Disregarding the welfare of others seems very much his modus operandi."

That I could believe.

"There was no battle between us, Amy. No luring, no trap, no honorable death for that matter—just a bunch of innocent people sacrificed to one man's greed."

"But . . . but Pangloss said . . . oh, God, he lied to me? He said he was off foraging for food that day."

Corbin frowned. "The characters can mislead, but only a few can outright lie, and from what I recall of him, he's not one of them. It's possible that Bart lied to him about what happened, hiding the truth behind a story of an attack that killed everyone. That would explain the lack of bodies."

"But . . . people would notice!"

"Perhaps. Perhaps not. If he wanted to remain in charge, Bart may well have covered up the origins of his crew's deaths—the loss of the crew to an attack by a feared pirate would bring the survivors together in a desire for vengeance, rather than setting them at his throat. I didn't say anything about it because I was curious to see how the scenario would play out."

I slumped back in my chair, having some trouble readjusting my mental impression of men I'd trusted. "I suppose it makes sense that Bart would hide it. Especially if he really is Paul, and not a computer player. Although I can't believe that even Paul would be so . . . so . . . heinous as to sacrifice his crew like that."

"Believe it," he said grimly, going over to a leaded window to look out at the sea beyond the edge of the cliff. "You seem to have no trouble believing I was capable of doing the same thing."

I caught a hint of pain in his voice that I knew I couldn't allow to remain. I jumped up and went over to him, wrapping my arms around his stomach. "That was different, Corbin."

He didn't turn around and let me cover his face in kisses, as I had hoped. "Oh, really? How is it different?"

I kissed the back of his neck, instead. "It's like I said— *you* know that these people aren't real, but they don't have the ability to make any such distinction, unless you programmed that into them."

"I didn't," he said, pulling my hands free so he could turn around. "I suppose if I can believe you supported Bart's intolerable cruelties, it's only fair you can think me a mass murderer."

"Waaaait a minute," I said, pulling back. "You thought I supported Bart's cruelties? I didn't know he was doing anything wrong until you just told me."

"You knew I wanted him out of power."

"Yes, but I just figured it was you fulfilling your part in the scenario. All I heard was that you attacked the island willy-nilly and slaughtered almost all the men here. What was I to think but that you were taking the role of pirate to heart?"

He stared at me for a minute, then sighed. "I'm sorry, Amy. It never occurred to me that you wouldn't know what happened. I'm an idiot for not remembering that no one knew the truth."

I took a deep breath. "I'm sorry, too. Even if they were only computer people, I should have known that you wouldn't do something so underhanded."

"Am I forgiven?" He made big gray puppy dog eyes at me. I laughed.

"Yes. Am I?"

"Absolutely. Let's have make-up sex." He kissed my knuckles, then sucked one fingertip into his mouth.

"Man, what you can do with just your tongue," I said,

breathing heavily, praying my knees wouldn't buckle. It took a massive effort, but I managed to pull my hand away from him and calm my suddenly racing heart. "Let's take care of this blockade issue first."

"Party pooper," he said, watching as I (shakily) made my way back to the desk.

"True, but if I wasn't, all we'd do is spend the day in bed having wild jungle sex."

He retook his seat, a slight smile curling his lips. "And what's wrong with that is . . . ?"

I thought. I couldn't come up with anything. "Good point. However, before we indulge ourselves, I'd like to get those blockade ships out of my harbor, and supplies into town. What if we write up a statement whereby you recognize my authority in Turtle's Back and promise not to attack while I or my duly appointed representative is in control?"

"Or you could just give me control of the island, and I'd allow you stay captain of Bart's crew."

I frowned. "*Allow* me to stay captain?"

"I could fight you for control of the island and crew," he said with a smile that I didn't much appreciate.

My eyes narrowed. "Then you'd lose on both accounts. You think I'm some sort of pushover who doesn't know how to defend her island?"

"You've been playing the game for, what, about two and a half hours now?"

"I have been here for almost two weeks," I pointed out, my hackles rising. "I'm not going to let some handsome rogue pirate come along and take my island!"

He burst out laughing, holding up a hand as I started to stand up. "Sweetheart, you really are the cutest thing when you get riled up. Sit down and stop looking like you'd like to shish kebab me on that sword. I'd just have to fight you, then, and I'd probably lose, and I don't think my delicate male ego can stand that."

I gave him a look that let him know I didn't appreciate his toying with me. "So you weren't serious about taking the island away from me?"

"No. You can be governor of all the islands in the Seventh Sea as far as I'm concerned."

I decided it would be magnanimous to forgive him. "Thank you. I happen to think I'm cut out for this governor thing. But captain . . . that's a different matter. How about you take over as captain of Bart's crew? Your men seem to like you, and they certainly respond to your orders better than mine did to mine."

"I suppose I could," he agreed. The next half hour was spent hashing out specific terms of the agreement. He promised to keep sufficient men on Turtle's Back to defend her, to not attack the island while I or my representative was in charge, and to protect us when and if we needed his help against attack from other crews.

"There, I think that's everything taken care of," I said, signing my name below Corbin's. "Perfect! I feel much better knowing there will be no more blockade. Now I can set up some sort of trading program between us and the other islands."

"Sounds like a good idea, but there are still two issues remaining to be dealt with," Corbin said, his eyes twinkling.

I rubbed the feathery edge of the quill against my cheek as I mentally ran over the list of items we'd addressed in the nonaggression pact we'd just signed. "Two issues? What two issues? What to do with Pangloss, you mean?"

"No, he's easily taken care of," Corbin said as he pulled me to my feet. "The two issues are your refusal to accept the fact that you're madly, head-over-heels in love with me, and the make-up sex you promised me once we got the blockade ended."

I thought about refusing him . . . for all of about a second. I'd never been one for much experimentation before I'd met Corbin, but as I sat on the edge of my desk with my legs wrapped around his waist while he pumped hard and fast into me, I decided there was much to be said for having an open mind to new experiences.

The remainder of the day was spent disassembling the blockade, bringing all the ships into the harbor under the terms of our new nonaggression pact. My chat with Pangloss later that evening was less successful.

"Ye sent for me, Amy?" he said as he entered the library. I looked up from the inventory of supplies that Corbin had generously turned over to the town. Pangloss made a face. "Beg pardon, Cap'n Amy."

I smiled. "Amy is fine. We both know I'm a long way from being a real captain. Which is one of the things I wanted to talk to you about—but before we get to that, would you mind answering a couple of questions?"

"If I can," he said, shaking his head when I gestured toward the chair. "I've things to see to in order to protect us from that devil, lass. I'll stand, if ye don't mind."

"Pangloss," I said, sighing, "I've told you three times now that Corbin has signed a statement saying he will not attack the island so long as I'm governor here. You can stop walking around like a dog with its hackles up just because his crew is in our harbor. They're only there long enough to unload supplies—supplies we desperately need—then they'll be gone."

"Aye, but he'll be here still," Pangloss argued, a belligerent set to his face.

"Yes, Corbin will still be here, but that's at my invitation, so you need to just deal with it and move on. Actually, that's one of the things I want to talk to you about—how did you find out about the men in your crew dying?"

He looked at me like I was mad. "When we came home the next day, all the women were weepin', and there was nary a crewmate to be seen."

"Uh-huh. But did anyone tell you about this big battle that Corbin was supposed to have had? I mean, were there any eyewitness reports to it?"

"I don't rightly see where ye're sailin', lass," he answered, a confused expression on his face. "The men are dead."

"That's not what I asked you."

He shook his head. "No, no one saw the battle itself. It was over on the leeward side of the island—how could they? The only ones what saw it died there."

"Don't you think it's the least bit suspicious that this big battle took place on the other side of the island, where no one saw or heard it? Why would Corbin attack there?"

"'Twas so he could set a trap and murder 'em all," he answered, the confusion changing into a familiar stubborn look.

"Or it was a story put out to explain the sudden disappearance of sixty-five men, carefully crafted so as to focus everyone's anger on a scapegoat while the real villain was not held accountable for his actions."

"Ye've lost me, lass," he said, shaking his head.

"What do you know about the mine?" I asked, switching subjects.

"The emerald mine?" he asked.

"Yeah."

"'Tis closed now."

"I know that, but who worked there before it was closed?"

He shrugged. "Townsfolk."

"Not your crew?"

"Nay, why would they?"

I watched him carefully, but there seemed to be no sign he was lying to me. Then again, there was no proof he was telling the truth. Either he was totally ignorant of what Bart had been up to, or he was putting on a hell of an act.

"What's your earliest memory, Pangloss?"

He blinked at me, his face having gone blank.

I sighed, aware of a faint feeling that I was missing something important, but I couldn't for the life of me think of what it was. "Never mind. Go back to what you were doing. We'll talk more about the crew and the future of the island tomorrow."

I had a lonely dinner with just Bas after Corbin sent back a note from his flagship saying he and Holder would be tied up with crew duties until later that night. Bas and I investigated the governor's house, but I decided when I started making a mental list of changes I wanted made in furniture and paint that it was time to get out of there.

"I'm going to go chat with Renata and her ladies," I told Bas. "You want to come with me?"

He pursed his lips. "Wet Willie said I could help him in the kitchen."

"Ah. Are you interested in learning how to cook? That's a very noble profession, and one that I think you could do with just one hand."

Bas shook his head. Bran bobbed his head up and down and squawked at me, just as if he was laughing. "Nay. Willie said I could watch him cut the heads off the chickens for tomorrow's supper. Willie says they run around after their heads is off, spurtin' blood everywhere."

I stared at him in horror. "You are an unnatural child. When I get out of here, I'm definitely going to have Corbin do something about giving you a new interest."

"Eh?" he asked, confused.

"Never mind. Enjoy your headless chickens and blood spurting and God knows what else. I'm going to go talk to civilized people."

Bas trotted off happily enough. I headed down the hill toward the town, carrying a lantern since the moon was hidden behind clouds tonight. A sense of happiness filled me as I made my way through the night. The air was soft and alive with sounds of the distant waves hitting the rocks beyond the harbor, night birds crying high in the sky, and the closer sounds of humans celebrating the arrival of food and drink. Candle- and lamplight flickered in almost every building in the town, spilling out in yellow patches that dappled the cobblestones. Likewise, the ships in the harbor—packed now with Corbin's large warships—were all lit up, the lights from them dancing and bobbing on the waves. Raucous laughter and strains of a concertina came up from the docks, as well as out the doors and windows of the Inn Cognito. I stood for a moment on the fringes of town, drinking it all in, feeling both a kinship with the people of the island and a strong maternal desire to protect them from evil.

"They're all my people now," I said aloud, my voice firm and filled with purpose. "My people and my island, and I'll be damned before I allow anyone to harm either."

"Far be it from me to deny ye any wish," a voice said out of the darkness behind me.

I spun around, my mouth hanging open at the sight of the man who emerged from the shadows, a pistol pointed at my heart.

Chapter 23

With cat-like tread,
Upon our prey we steal. . . .

—Ibid, Act II

"Bart?" I asked, goose bumps marching up my arms at the cold smile he gave me. "Or do you prefer to be called Paul?"

His smile didn't fade one little bit. "Ye may use either, lass."

"I think I'll stick to Bart, if you don't mind. How did you get here?"

"I've me ways. And don't be thinkin' to yell for help," he added as I glanced out of the corner of my eye toward Renata's house. "I've plans for ye yet, but they can be rearranged if I have to kill ye now."

I crossed my arms. "So, what exactly do you want from me?"

"Right now, ye're goin' to come with me. As for later"— his gaze scanned me in a way that left my skin crawling— "well, I'm thinkin' I'd like to know what charms ye have to keep Corbin's interest."

"No," I said, lifting my chin and giving him a lofty look.

"Nay what?"

"No as in no, I'm not going with you now, and no, my charms are not for examination by anyone other than Corbin."

He sighed with faux sadness. "I was hopin' ye'd not come along easily. It's so much more satisfyin' this way. Lads?"

Before I could spin around, my arms were roughly wrenched behind me and bound. I shouted with pain, but my cries were quickly muffled by a bandana being shoved in my mouth. I struggled to free my hands, landing a few good kicks on the unknown assailant behind me before someone cracked me on the head, sending me to my knees with pain and disorientation. I was dimly aware of my feet being bound and of being hoisted up on someone's shoulder, but I must have drifted in and out of consciousness for a while, because the next thing I knew, a cold shock of water hit me.

"Argh!" I spat out a mouthful of water, shaking my head in an attempt to clear both it and the water from my now soaking face. Pain erupted from the back of my head at the movement. I swallowed a couple of times, wondering whether I was going to hang on to my dinner, but after a few seconds the wave of nausea passed and I could take in my surroundings. I was in another ship's cabin, this one done in dark wood, with navy walls. I'd been tossed on the floor, and I struggled to sit up, my arms cramping as I tried to arrange myself as comfortably as possible by leaning up against a sea chest.

"What is it about me that drives everyone to kidnapping?" I asked pettishly. "At least Corbin managed to do it without giving me a concussion or a rotator cuff tear."

Bart, aka Paul the evil ex-partner, was strapping on a brace of pistols and didn't even glance at me. "I trust that ye'll be comfortable here until I return," he said, gathering up some papers that looked like maps.

"I doubt that very much; not until you untie me," I answered crossly, but considering the treatment I'd just survived, I figured I was due a little testiness.

"Ah, lass, would that I could. But I'll be easier in me thoughts knowin' ye're here safely waitin' for me to come back to ye."

I thought about rolling my eyes but vetoed the idea on the grounds it might kill me. "You are so going to get it when Corbin finds you," I said instead.

He just smiled and saluted me with the maps before opening the door to the cabin.

"Hey," I cried, surprised that he was just going to leave me. "You're leaving?"

"Aye. I've some business with allies."

"But—but—aren't you going to tell me why you kidnapped me? Or why you want me? Or what the deal is with trapping us in this game? I think you owe me that, at least!"

He smiled as he looked back at me. "Ye weren't intended to be a part of this, but I must admit, ye've worked quite nicely in me plans."

"What plans?" I asked, hitching myself to one side in an attempt to ease the strain on my left arm. "Why are you doing this? Why are you trying to ruin Corbin?"

He shook his head. "Lass, lass, lass—ye've seen one too many James Bond movies. I'll not be tellin' ye all me plans only to have ye escape and run to Corbin. Just sit yerself there, and I'll be back as soon as I can."

"The least you can do is tell me why," I wailed as he walked toward the door. "What do you expect to achieve by keeping us trapped here?"

"Corbin's destruction, lass. It's a simple matter, truth be told," he said, striding back over to me to check my bonds.

I lunged sideways and tried to bite his leg. He laughed and sidestepped, returning to the door. "First, I destroy the game. Then his company. Finally, the man himself."

"You're insane," I couldn't help but say, wondering whether he could truly do what he planned. "There's no other explanation for leaving me in charge of your crew and the island."

He laughed, a genuinely amused expression on his face. I wished with all my heart he was within biting distance. "Can ye think of a better way to create havoc and general chaos than to put an inexperienced person in charge of things?"

So much for the slick explanation he offered in his letter to me. I bristled at the word *inexperienced* but decided to overlook that slur in an attempt to get one last point cleared before he left. "Why are you using the game to settle what's at heart a personal issue between you and Corbin?"

"Ye're just chock full of questions, aren't ye?" he chuckled, about to leave the room. "Ye remember me flag?"

I started to nod, remembered my head, and instead said, "Yeah. It was a picture of a man standing on a stabbed heart."

"Corbin's heart, stabbed with his own knife," Bart reminded me. "I particularly like the irony of that point, lass. If ye be needin' anythin', yell. I'll tell me mates to keep an ear out for ye."

"Oh, blow it out your blowhole," I muttered to myself as the door was closed, then yelled, "You like the irony of what? Using an actual knife on Corbin? Or is that a metaphor for the game itself?"

Bart didn't return to answer, but I hadn't expected him to, not after that James Bond comment (which made me sigh— I had truly hoped he'd spill everything so I could go running to Corbin with the information). Still, I had gathered up a few nuggets. I cherished those as I tried yelling for help a few times, but although I could hear voices of men outside the cabin, no one came to investigate. So much for them keeping an ear out for me.

"Right, Amy," I said aloud, looking around the cabin for inspiration. "What you need here is an escape plan. Some way to get off the ship before Bart can come back. Hmm. How do people get out of being tied up?"

I struggled with the bonds around my wrists but achieved nothing but sore shoulders and what felt like bloody wrists. I quickly formulated, and rejected, several plans of action, from setting the ship on fire and jumping overboard before I burned to death, to getting gravely ill so Bart would have to send for medical aid. I finally settled on one plan that seemed to have the fewest opportunities for failure.

After ten minutes of me screaming at the top of my head, someone finally came to shut me up.

"We're tired of hearin' ye bellowin'," a big, burly pirate said as he threw the door open. I didn't recognize him as being one of Bart's crew, but I didn't care much at that point.

"It's about time someone came! I've been yelling for you forever!"

The man frowned. I couldn't help noticing that his upper arms—bare since he was wearing a leather jerkin without a shirt—were approximately the size of my thighs. "What be ye wantin'?"

"I have to use the privy."

The man made a face.

"Badly," I said. "There's no toilet facilities in this cabin. And I don't think Bart would appreciate having this lovely Persian rug soiled, so if you don't want me going all over it, you'd better help me up and take me to the nearest privy."

"Ye can piss over the side, like the rest of us," he said, hauling me to my feet.

"Hello, girl here! Can't do that without a siphon or something, and that's just such an icky thought, I don't even know if I can do it then."

"I'll take ye to the head if ye promise to stop yer squawkin'," the pirate said, cutting my feet free. He kept a grip on my bound hands as I stumbled forward, but at least I was spared the indignity of falling. I tried to be not too obvious as I was herded out of the cabin and down the deck toward the bow of the boat. It was a square-rigged three-masted ship, the kind with two gun decks. Groups of men sitting around idle fell silent as my pirate guard hustled me to the bow. I recognized none of them, which made me wonder whether Bart hadn't been keeping a second crew hidden from us.

"Do what ye have to," the guard said, giving me a little shove toward the lee-side head (there was one on either side of the bow—which one you used depended on where the wind was coming from).

I tried to look as dignified as possible, and yet like my bladder was about to burst. "I can't go with you looking."

He growled something and turned his back. I glanced around him. We were the only ones on the bow. Behind me, the blue-black water of the sea lapped at the bow. The head was positioned so that the seawater would wash its grated floor clean, something I tried hard not to think too much about. It would be easy enough for me to jump overboard and swim to shore—the ship was anchored beyond a line of rocks, but not so far that I couldn't swim to the shore—but there was no way I could do it with my hands tied behind my back.

"Um . . . I need to use my hands."

The pirate spun around, giving me a suspicious look. "Why?"

I prodded a small box containing the wide leaves that the

people on this island favored for hygienic purposes. "I would think that's pretty obvious."

He heaved a martyred sigh, roughly grabbing my arm and spinning me around, not even apologizing when he knicked my wrists cutting off the cloth that bound them.

"Hurry up with ye! I've not got all night to stand here waitin' for ye to move yer bowels."

He moved away from me, not quite turning his back on me, but not standing close enough so I could tackle him. Either way was fine with me. I stepped out onto the grating of the head, took a deep breath, and dived over the side.

The shock of hitting the water took my breath for a moment, but even as I heard the guard yell out something, I was finding a comfortable overhead stroke rhythm. A couple splashes followed, and I redoubled my efforts at making the shore before my captors caught up to me. A hand grabbing my ankle disabused me of that hope. I kicked it off and changed my course from the indigo shape of the island that was so temptingly close to the sharp black fingers of rocks that loomed up to my left.

Waves slapped hard against the rocks. I won myself a few precious seconds of time by changing my course so unexpectedly—time I used to try to get enough of an image of the rocks so I wouldn't slam into them.

I did, of course. They were too big and too many, and the current too strong. My leg scraped painfully over an underwater rock, causing me to first yell in pain, then sink when I swallowed a mouthful of seawater. I struggled back to the surface, coughing and sputtering, the experience horribly reminiscent of my rescue of Corbin.

A surge in the current slammed me up against a massive rock that seemed to appear out of nowhere, spinning me around so I was facing the ship. Two men were in the water, about a half dozen feet from me. I yelped from both the pain and the shock of seeing them so close, and dived down, twisting my body so I was swimming in the opposite direction.

I surfaced a little way away, only to be rocketed again up against another rock. My arms and legs stung as salt water washed over the abrasions. I clutched the rock, trying desperately to get my breath, but a huge wave crashed over me then, dragging me down and toward the shore. My back scraped along a sharp outcropping of rock, spinning me around even farther. I fought to break free, so turned around I didn't know which way was toward shore and which away from the rocks.

A shout reached me over the sound of the crashing waves as I surfaced, gasping for air, my body sore and battered. I trod water for a minute, expecting to be grabbed at any moment, but slowly, as my wits returned to me, I realized that I was in some sort of rocky enclave, surrounded by craggy rocks. Above me I could see the cloudy night sky. Below me, the water swirled around my legs via the opening I'd been carried through, bobbing me around the small space made by the rocks. The rocks themselves blocked the sight of anything else—island, ship, or anyone swimming nearby—which meant no one could see me.

More shouting ensued. I shivered and pressed myself up against the smoothest surface of rock I could find, praying all the while that no one else would find that handy little current that brought me there. The quicksilver touch of something against my leg had me adding the possibilities of sharks and barracuda to my list of things to worry about.

The sound of wood splintering on the rocks reached me next, followed by more shouting, but no one suddenly appeared in my little haven. Clearly the men had launched a rowboat in hopes of finding me. I trod water slowly, rubbing my bruised arms, wondering how long it would take before they decided I had drowned.

A long while, as it turned out.

What seemed like an eternity later (but probably was really around fifteen minutes), I crawled out of the surf, tried to get to my feet, staggered back down to my knees, and ended up dragging myself to the far side of a washed-up tree trunk, where I collapsed in a gasping, coughing heap. I rolled onto my back and stared up at the night sky, feeling as if I'd just run (or swum) a marathon.

"I hate this game," I snarled as soon as I had the breath to do anything but pant. "I am so going to get Corbin when I see him. Which should be right this second if he had any idea of how a proper dashing pirate hero acts."

I lifted my head from the bed of seaweed and tree root to glare at the night. No Corbin burst from the surrounding scrub forest to carry me off to a hot bath, warm bed, and lots and lots of antiseptic ointment.

"Dammit," I grumbled, getting slowly to my feet. I had to clutch the tree trunk for a few minutes while my legs decided whether or not they had the strength remaining to carry me, but they came through for me. It took me the better part of an hour to make it back to the town. I had no idea where Bart's ship was anchored, but one of the things I liked about Turtle's Back was that you could climb to the top of the island and look down upon the whole of it.

I stood on the crest and hesitated. I was closer to the windward side of the island and Renata's house, which I could see blazed with warm lights and sounds of people having fun. The governor's house was on the other side of the town and looked uninhabited.

"Amy?"

"Eeeek!" I screamed, jumping a good foot off the ground. "Who's that?"

"'Tis just us," a youthful voice said from behind me. A dark shape emerged from the smooth rock mound and approached me.

"Squawk!" A part of the shape fluttered.

"Bas? What on earth are you doing out here at this time of night?"

"Lookin' for bats. 'Tis said if ye can catch one in yer hands, ye can call up the reaper himself and he'll dance for ye."

"Oh, for Pete's sake . . . come on, it's too late for you to be out summoning death."

"We goin' to Renata's house?" he asked as I headed off in that direction.

"Yes. I'm exhausted and need some medical attention." I stumbled over an unseen rock but managed to keep from falling. "Jez probably has all sorts of antisepticky herbs and such I can use to patch myself up."

I couldn't see his face, but I felt a tentative hand on my arm and was warmed by the thoughtfulness of the boy. "Ye're wet. Ye were swimmin'?"

"No. I've been escaping and almost drowning."

"Oh, aye? Who were ye escapin' from?" There was a cheerful note in his voice that made me smile despite my aches, pains, and general grouchiness. "What was it like? Did ye see yer whole life afore yer eyes? Did the fishes start to nibble ye?"

"Bart, scary, no, and no." A large palm leaf slapped me in the face. I pushed my way forward through the foliage to what I knew was a path leading from a small beach to the town.

The boy chattered all the way down into town, but despite his seemingly endless questions and theories about what it would be like to drown, to be eaten by a school of voracious fish, or to watch death dance, I was grateful for his presence. By the time we made it to Renata's house, he was more or less tugging me along while I stumbled wearily behind.

Light, laughter, and the sound of a fiddle spilled out from the house. I stood in the doorway for a moment, blinking at the scene before me. The outer room, used for general mingling purposes, was packed with men, all of whom had tankards in their hands. A small group was playing cards, others were rolling dice, while in the corner, a couple of men amused themselves with a fiddle and concertina, playing a snappy jig.

"Oh, man, I forgot the guys would make a beeline here from the blockade ships," I said as I pushed my way into the room. A couple of men looked up hopefully at me, but when they got a good look at me, they quickly averted their eyes. "I hope to God that response is due to the fact that I'm the governor of the town, and not because I look so horrible," I murmured to no one in particular.

"Aye, that and the fact that ye're Black Corbin's wife," Bas said.

"You're supposed to keep quiet about that," I reminded him as we went into the common room. One look at the activities there (the room was also filled with men) was enough for me to slap my hand over Bas's eyes. "Oh, Lord. Tell me you didn't see anything."

"Nay," he answered. Bran the raven rubbed his beak on my fingers. I sighed in relief and avoided making eye contact with anyone as I pushed Bas through the room. "Just a bunch of men as naked as the day they was born playin' cards and dicin' like the others was."

I gritted my teeth and shoved him through the doorway to the small back area that sat at the head of the hallway. "Do me a favor and pretend you didn't see anything, okay?"

"Aye, aye. Why was all of those men naked?" Bas asked

as I released him, ruffling his hair in a gesture of affection. Bran bobbed his head and flapped his wings until I gave his head a ruffle, too.

"'Tis something Amy told us," Mags said as she emerged from her room, a man following her who was holding a pair of boots and shirt, clad in the ubiquitous striped knickers. He grinned at us, handed Mags a couple of coins, and went out the back door.

My jaw dropped at such a thought. "*What*? Are you insane? When have I ever told you to fill the living room with naked sailors?"

"Ye told us we had to be efficient in order to make a profit," she said, giving herself a quick look in the cracked mirror that hung next to the door. Mags, thankfully, had thrown on a cotton bathrobe. "Ye said we had to streamline our production, and increase our turnaround time. That's what we're doin'—we strips the men down first, in order to cut down on wasteful time spent takin' off their clothes and such. 'Twas good advice, that. They seems to like it, too. And ye know what they say—a happy Jack is a Jack who'll not linger after his guns has fired."

I stared at her for a second. "I was talking about your production of elderberry wine and the dresses you ladies make! Not . . . er . . . guns firing!"

She shrugged, consulted a ragged scrap of parchment on the desk, and opened the door to the common room. "No matter. Works as well with one as another. Number twenty-three!"

A man sitting in the corner reading a book jumped up and hurried toward Mags, a strip of cloth in his hands. "I'm twenty-three!"

"First room on the left," Mags said, pointing to her bedroom, taking the numbered bit of cloth. She gave me a questioning look. "Ye look all stove in. What happened to ye?"

"Kidnapping, near drowning, almost having a heart attack when Bas appeared out of nowhere," I answered tiredly, limping my way down the hall toward my room. I wanted nothing more than to fall down onto the bed and lie there an eternity or two until Corbin came to carry me home.

"Ah. Ye're bleedin'. Ye want Jez?"

"Yes, please. When she's not busy."

Mags nodded. "I'll tell her."

"Thanks. Is my room still—oh, hoy, Renata." The old woman, coming in the back way, stopped in midstep and stared at me with eyes wide with surprise. She blinked twice. "Renata? Is something wrong?"

"Nay, dearie." She shook her head, her eyes avoiding me. "I wondered when we'd be seein' ye again. Ye're injured?"

"Not too badly, but enough I want to see if Jez has something to keep the cuts from becoming infected." I hesitated, bothered by something in Renata's manner. "If you don't mind, I'll just rest in my old room until Jez has time to look at me."

"Aye, 'tis a good idea, that. Where be yer man this evenin'?"

Red Beth and one of her customers (clad this time) emerged from her room. The man, whom I recognized from Corbin's flagship, kissed her noisily, made a little forelock-tugging gesture at me, and went off with a song on his lips. Red Beth smiled smugly and went to fetch her next customer.

I gave Renata a long look. She wasn't on my list any longer now that Bart had been uncovered, but she was certainly acting in a manner that had my radar pinging. "Corbin is out seeing to the last couple of blockade ships. Why do you ask?"

She shrugged. "I just thought that now that ye've settled the blockade, ye'd have Black Corbin glued to yer side."

"Ah. I thought maybe you had something against him because of his history."

"He be a man. All men are devils at heart," she said placidly. "And I'm right in thinkin' this one has captured yers, aye?"

"My heart? Yes, he has. You were right when you told me I shouldn't let pride stand between Corbin and me." I frowned, remembering something unpleasant. "That was the night you told me to get Corbin on my ship for the blockade . . . the same ship that later got shot to pieces."

"Aye, unfortunate, that."

The hairs on my arms stood on end as I looked at the old lady in front of me, but I told myself I was mad. Paul was Bart—he'd admitted as much. Still, if I'd done as she had suggested . . . "Actually, I think the way things turned out was quite fortunate. If Corbin had been on my ship rather than on his own, he'd never have been able to block the worst of the shots. We were so damaged, we wouldn't have stood another round of fire."

She nodded. "So ye wouldn't. 'Twas lucky he was there to save ye. If ye'll be excusin' me, dearie, I've to run some wine to the mayor's wife. She be sufferin' from the toothache, and me elderberry wine is just the thing to relieve her pain."

I stepped aside so she could pass me, a thousand confusing questions spinning around my mind. I was just about to ask one when a thunderous shout from the next room wiped out all thoughts but one.

"Amy!"

It was Corbin, at last. At *long* last. I didn't wait to caution Bas against following me; I just ran straight for the door that would lead me to the man whom I so desperately wanted.

"Amy, what the devil is going on here? Good God, man,

put some clothes on! You could poke someone's eye out with—*oomph!*"

I hurtled through the door into the living room, flinging myself on Corbin where he stood in the middle of the room, his hands on his hips as he surveyed the naked men around him. We went down in a tangle of legs and arms and his wonderful, adorable face, a face I took every opportunity to kiss.

He stopped trying to speak and kissed me back, which I approved of until I realized two things—we had an audience who were good-naturedly calling their approval, and my collision with the man who had so quickly made himself a part of my life didn't do my injuries any good.

"I think I'm going to faint," I told Corbin as a wave of pain accompanied by inky darkness seemed to suck me in, not wanting to let me go.

"You're what?" he asked, but his voice came from a long way away.

I gave in to the blackness, sure that Corbin would take care of me. Now that we were together, everything was going to be all right.

I really hate it when I'm wrong about things. . . .

Chapter 24

Away, away, away! . . .
To-night the traitor dies!

—Ibid, Act II

"Amy, I forbid you to do that again!"

"Ow! That stings! You're an evil nurse. I was much nicer to you. What's that? And forbid me to do what—be kidnapped, or faint?"

"Both." Corbin held up one of the bottles that Jez had provided him with to take care of my injuries. "It says water hazing."

"Witch hazel," I said, squinting at the tag tied to the neck of the bottle. "That's okay. It shouldn't sting. You may proceed."

He glared at me as he poured a little witch hazel on a clean cloth before dabbing it on the long scratches on my lower calf. I lay on the bed in one of the guest rooms at the governor's house (I couldn't bring myself to sleep in the same bed where Bart had slept), warm and relaxed and as comfortable as one could be when one was stark naked having a miscellaneous collection of cuts, scrapes, scratches, and bruises treated by a man who looked furious enough to bring down the entire house.

"You, woman, are infuriating. What the hell do you think you were doing letting Paul kidnap you?"

"It's not like I had a whole lot of choice in the matter," I answered, feeling the back of my head and wincing when my fingers found a small, painful lump. It didn't hurt unless I pressed on it. "Well, there's one small blessing—at least with being torn up on the rocks the pain from being whacked on the head has faded."

He hitched his glare up a couple of notches and indicated he wanted me to roll over. I turned over to my stomach, sighing with relief as he dabbed the soothing liquid on the burning scratches on the backs of my legs. "You could have yelled for help, or used self-defense moves to disable Paul, or done something to save yourself."

"Save myself?" I asked the pillow, the tight muscles in my back starting to relax now that I was safe. "Where were you, I'd like to know? Why weren't you saving me? Haven't you read pirate books? The pirate always saves his lady love."

"What happened to women not needing a man to save them?" Corbin asked.

"I didn't need you to save me," I said, groaning as his hand brushed my thigh. "If you'll notice, I saved myself just fine. The point is, it would have been nicer if you had rode up on your white horse and saved me so I didn't have to get bashed to a bloody pulp on those rocks."

He dug through the basket of salves and ointments and pulled out a pot of something with a cork lid. He sniffed at it, then dipped his finger into it.

"What's that?" I asked, looking over my shoulder at him.

"Says it's a burn salve. Can't hurt. And I don't have a white horse."

"Nitpicker," I told the pillow, my eyes closing at the pleasure the gentle brush of his fingers on my abused flesh was giving me.

He stopped for a second before getting a roll of gauzy material. Carefully he wrapped it around the worst wounds on my legs, using his knife to cut the ends and tie them in neat knots. "I'm sorry about that, Amy."

"Hmm? Sorry about what?"

"That I wasn't there when you needed me. I should have been guarding you. I should have known that Paul would grab you in an attempt to hurt me."

I rolled over onto my side, tugging him down so he rested on the bed next to me. "Silly man. I don't expect you to be psychic, Corbin. And I was teasing you for the most part— you're absolutely right in that I don't need a man to save me."

"But it would have been nice if I had?" he asked, his eyes dark with emotion.

"Well . . . maybe just a little saving."

His eyes went even darker. "You saved me. You saved my life. I didn't even know you'd been kidnapped."

"And that's why I'm not, at this moment, reading you the riot act," I said, kissing the tip of his nose. "I couldn't have saved you if I hadn't been right there with you, could I? So there's no reason to beat yourself up for not being somewhere when you had no idea I was in danger. Besides, I like you in my debt this way. It means you have to do anything I want you to do."

"It does, does it?" he asked, his hand running up the curve of my hip. "And what is it you want me to do?"

"Make mad, passionate, all-night-long love to me," I answered, sucking his lower lip into my mouth.

"You're hurt," he said before his tongue came visiting

mine. I squirmed against him, my skin suddenly highly sensitized against the rough texture of his clothing.

"Not that hurt," I answered, gasping in air as his mouth moved down my neck, leaving behind a trail of sizzling kisses.

"Mind over matter," he murmured into my breastbone.

"Absolutely," I answered, a thousand and one nerve endings coming to sudden tingling life.

He made slow, sweet love to me, just as I'd asked, his kisses gentle, his touches giving rather than demanding, building the need in me until I was almost frantic. But when he pulled my knee over his hip and slid into me, I sighed with the pleasure of it all, and bit his lip. "I love you, Corbin. More than any other man. I love you so much my heart may just burst."

"I know CPR, too," he said into my mouth, his hips flexing.

"What a romantic answer." I laughed and gave myself up to the moment, pushing aside all the worries and problems that besieged us, and focused on showing the man I loved just how much he meant to me.

I lay awake late into the night, snuggled up to Corbin's side, my hand possessively lying on his chest, right over his heart. His chest rose and fell with slow regularity, his heartbeat a gentle thud beneath my fingertips. Corbin had fallen asleep before I had a chance to discuss the latest developments with him, leaving me with an exhausted body and a brain that wouldn't stop puzzling over things long enough to let me sleep.

What role did Renata have to play in things? It was becoming clearer to me that she wasn't exactly what she seemed. What did Bart have planned for us? How were we going to catch him, and once we did, was Corbin serious about killing him in order to get us out of the game? What was going to happen to the people of Turtle's Back if things went wrong? Who would watch out for Bas?

I finally fell asleep with those thoughts swirling around until they merged into one bright, shining problem that seemed to glow with a blinding intensity that consumed everything in and around me.

Corbin woke me up a short while later with one word that struck fear deep and hard within me.

"The island is on fire," he said, strapping his sword belt to his hips and grabbing his pistols. He'd already pulled his pants and boots on, but before I could pull my thoughts together in my sleep-muddled brain, he was running out of the room, yelling for the few servants who slept in to wake up and help.

"Fire?" I asked, sitting up in bed, sniffing the air. "Are you sure? I don't smell smoke. How do you know there's a—" As I swung my legs over the bed, the window came into my view. Beyond the scraggy line of trees that marked the boundary between the settled part of Turtle's Back and the rest of the island, the sky glowed orangey red.

"Oh, hell," I swore, jumping from bed and grabbing the nearest clothes—my knickers and Corbin's shirt. My arms and legs protested the quick movement, but I ignored the stiffness and hurried into my boots, grabbing my foil out of instinct before I ran from the room. Downstairs, the cook and scullery maid were lighting candles. Bas emerged from a room two doors from mine, rubbing his eyes.

"Bas, I want you to get dressed and go down to Renata's house," I told him. Holder bolted past me from the room he'd confiscated as his own, leaping down the stairs to the main hall.

"What's happenin'?" Bas asked, standing at the top of the stairs.

Corbin was standing just outside the opened double

doors, shouting orders to the remaining servants. Holder joined him for a moment, then took off toward the town, presumably to raise the alarm there.

"Fire," I said succinctly, not waiting to explain further. "Just go to Renata's house and tell the ladies there to get on a ship if the fire reaches the town."

I raced out of the house, following Corbin, intent on helping him fight the fire. Outside, the smoke was thick and heavy as I reached the point where the lawn ended and the scrubby, sparse forest that covered much of Turtle's Back began. The palm trees and surrounding tall grass were fully ablaze, casting grotesque shadows as Corbin and the men danced around it, trying to beat out the burning grass. Billows of black smoke shot up into the night sky, mushrooming as they hit cold air in the upper levels. The heat from the fire at ground level was breathtaking—literally—absorbing the oxygen and leaving everyone breathless and gasping.

"Get in the bucket line," Corbin yelled when he saw me standing, staring helplessly at the burning trees.

I gave the fire a wide swath as I ran painfully around to the back of the house, where I knew the well was located. Bas's black silhouette darted past me as he grabbed a bucket in his good hand.

"Dammit, Bas, I told you to go to Renata's house," I gasped, clutching my ribs where they'd been bruised in my clash with the rocks.

"Do more good here," was all he said.

"Only until I say you have to leave," I warned, rolling up the sleeves to Corbin's shirt as I joined the bucket line. There were about five of us in the line, carrying water from the well around to the edge of the lawn where Corbin, the cook, and a couple of others leaped around the fire, beating the grass with wet curtains and hurling buckets of water on the worst spots.

We hauled bucket after bucket of water down the line. My hands quickly formed blisters from the wet handles; my arms and shoulders ached with the unaccustomed strain. The relief I felt each time I passed on a full bucket fizzled with the sight of the next one approaching. The horror of the situation combined with the repetition of the bucket line soon consumed my brain until all that became my whole world. Ten steps to the left led to my hands and shoulders complaining as a heavy bucketful of water was passed to me, followed by ten steps to the right and the blessed relief of handing it on. We coughed on the acrid smoke that filled the air, turning breathing into a labored chore that left my chest aching. My eyes watered, sending tears down my cheeks, but I couldn't stop long enough to wipe my face.

It seemed like an eternity, but probably a half hour later Corbin called a halt to the bucket line.

"It's no good. It's too far spread," he yelled in between gasps for air. "We'll never get it out."

The scullery maid fell to the ground, overcome by the smoke. Someone pulled her out of the line. My arms were shaking with the strain, my breath raspy and painful, my throat raw. I wheezed as I breathed, my lungs burning as if they were filled with hot embers.

"What now?" I asked, looking at the others in the bucket line. At Corbin's call to halt, the line had collapsed, everyone on the ground panting for air, rubbing aching arms and hands.

"We make a fire break to keep it from going down to the town. We need shovels and axes," he directed one of the male servants. "As many as you can get."

The man nodded and took off at a run around to a small gardening shed. Two others from the bucket line staggered to their feet and followed him.

"Did you guys really write things like axes and shovels

into the game?" I asked Corbin, dragging a half-filled bucket of water over to him.

"Of course. We anticipated towns being fired," he answered, dipping his hands into the water, drinking from his cupped hands. "It was a traditional pirate action upon taking a town, although this . . ."

He looked at flames leaping from tree to tree.

"It's Bart, isn't it?" I asked quietly.

"Possibly. Probably. It's suspicious that the fire should start right behind your house. Sweetheart, I'm afraid you're going to lose it. We can't save it and the town, both."

"That's all right. It's just a house, and it wasn't really mine anyway. The town is what matters."

"I'm glad you feel that way," Corbin said with a hollow smile. "I didn't really like you living in Bart's house. Where the devil is Holder?"

I dipped the hem of Corbin's shirt into the bucket and wiped some of the soot off his sweaty face. "Did you send him to rouse the town?"

"Yes. And to bring back my crew to fight the fire. He should be here by—"

A shout interrupted him. I sighed with relief when I saw Holder lope toward us, but that relief died when Corbin frowned.

"Where the hell is my crew?" he asked me, then yelled that question to Holder.

"Asleep," he answered, grabbing his side, stopping in front of us to double over. "God . . . need . . . start jogging again . . . out of shape . . ."

"Asleep?" Corbin asked, his scowl almost as black as the smoke. "Why didn't you wake them?"

"Couldn't," Holder panted. "Tried. Drugged. All of 'em. All over the floor at the whorehouse. Think it was the rum."

"All of them?" Corbin yelled.

"Yes."

"Renata," I said, remembering my suspicions about her. "It had to be Renata. She drugged them."

"More likely was Bart," Corbin said grimly, grabbing a shovel from one of the men returning with tools. "Amy, you go down to the town and see what you can do about getting us some help. If we want to save the town, we're going to have to have a lot more help.

"I could help dig trenches—" I started to say. Corbin flickered a glance toward my bloody, blistered hands. "Right. I'll go get everyone who's able to wield a shovel or axe. Bas! You come with me. I need your speedy legs."

Corbin held a quick conference with the firebreak workers to explain where he wanted the fire stopped. Bas got to his feet and limped toward me. I plunged both hands into the bucket of water Corbin had abandoned, biting back a scream of anguish at the feel of water on the open wounds, splashing a bit of it on my face.

"You ready?" I asked Bas as he stopped next to me. I frowned at something missing. "Where's Bran?"

"Got him here," he said, pulling open his hand-me-down jacket. "Didn't want him to get burned."

Inside the jacket, tucked into an inner pocket, Bran was snuggled up safe. The bird squawked a couple of times, bobbing his head as he always did in greeting.

"Oh. Good place for him. Come on, we've got people to wake up. I'll take the north side of town, and you can do the—holy crap, what was that?"

We had just reached the gates when a massive blast shook the ground, the sound of it so palpable, it could be felt as well as heard.

Behind me, feet thudded on the grass.

"What the bloody hell—" Holder asked as he, Corbin,

and a handful of other men burst from around the back of the house.

"Earthquake?" I asked, having definitely felt the ground tremble.

"Cannons," Corbin answered, his face grim. He pointed toward the harbor, barely visible through the smoke as a slightly lighter black patch on a field of ebony.

"Cannons? Someone is firing cannons now?"

"Not firing," Corbin yelled, throwing down his shovel as he jumped forward. "Blowing them up. Bart's attacking the town."

Chapter 25

I'm telling a terrible story,
But it doesn't diminish my glory. . . .

— Ibid, Act I

I grabbed Bas by his good arm and followed the men down the hill toward the town, swearing like mad to myself as we stumbled and slipped on rocks. Another blast rocked the island, this time slightly more distant. A huge fireball lit the night sky, illuminating for a few seconds the far arm of the harbor, where one of the makeshift forts was located.

"We're bein' attacked?" Bas asked as we raced down the hill as fast as we could.

"Yes. Those were the big land guns going. Bart must have rigged them to blow up so we couldn't use them to defend ourselves," I answered in between ragged gasps for air.

"Why is Bart attackin' us?" he asked. I glared at him for a moment, annoyed that the little wretch didn't seem to be the least bit winded.

"He's a rotter, that's why. Corbin? What are we going to do about the fire?" I yelled, waving a hand behind us.

He answered something that I didn't hear—he was too

far ahead. But I gathered by the way everyone abandoned the firebreak that the most pressing concern was the attack by water, assuming that was coming next. And it made sense that an attack would follow now that the town's defenses had just been knocked out to almost nothing.

"There are still our ships, though," I argued to myself, pain ripping through my side as my bruised ribs tried to cope with the unexpected activity.

"But no one to sail them," Holder said, slowing down so he could run next to us. "I swear I'm going to gut Paul when I get out of this game. The whole crew is out cold, every last Jack of them."

I stumbled, almost going to my knees, my heart sick with dread. Holder and Bas grabbed me to keep me from falling. "What are we going to do?" I asked Holder, tears burning my already red eyes. "How are we supposed to fight Bart with no crew?"

His jaw tightened as he tugged me forward. "You underestimate Corbin, Amy. You've never seen him in battle, have you?"

"Not really, just a bit before he shot up my ship," I said, miserable, wanting to just curl up in a ball and pretend none of this was happening.

"He's meant to be a pirate, he truly is," Holder said, his hand locked around my wrist, keeping me moving toward the town. We were at the outskirts now, and below us, voices were calling out in horrified confusion, the town already lighting up as people were dragged from sleep by the explosion of the guns. "He's a wild man behind the wheel of a ship. A brilliant tactician, merciless and exacting. Even down a crew, with nothing but a few townspeople to man his ship, he'll take down Paul—or die trying."

"It's the 'die trying' part I object to," I called as Holder released me and ran forward to meet up with Corbin, who was holding court in the middle of town.

Men and women in various states of undress were gathering around him, all of them shouting and calling out for answers to their questions.

"I'll answer your questions later," Corbin yelled. "Right now, we have work to do!"

Most of the people quieted down, circling Corbin as he stood on the lip of the well, looking so heroic that my heart would have burst with love for him if our demise wasn't so likely at any moment.

"Bart is attacking the town. It's clear he'll show no quarter, so if you want to save your families and homes, listen up. We need as many hands as we can get to battle him."

"Why would Bart attack us?" someone called out.

"It's me he wants to destroy—but he'll take this whole island down in order to do it."

"What about the shore guns?" the mayor asked, tugging at a frilly male version of a nightgown. "We were assured those would take care of any attacker."

"Assured by the same man who just blew them up so they couldn't be used against him," Corbin said. "We're going to need to split people into two teams: one to sail with me, one to fight the—"

"Fire!" someone shrieked, piercing the night. Everyone turned to look where the woman pointed up the hill. The fire hadn't been visible from the town before, but now, left to run unchecked, it had swept past the governor's house, flames visibly licking up the sides of the big house. I felt a moment of sadness for the loss of such a nice home, but knew that it was a loss the islanders could well survive—which couldn't be said for their town.

I have to say this for Corbin's friend who designed the AI used in the game—it was nigh on impossible to tell from real people. The townspeople, upon seeing the red glow of fire heading toward them, didn't freeze or ignore it or even get organized—no, they ran around like Bas's headless chickens, screaming, wailing, demanding that Corbin save them, and generally behaving just as a group of real people would have. Luckily, Corbin was well aware of their makeup, and after yelling for attention, he finally fired a shot into the air to get people to stop acting like idiots.

"That's better," he yelled, tucking his pistol back into his sword belt. "If you want to survive this, listen up . . ."

He started detailing a plan whereby half the town would gather up supplies to set firebreaks just beyond the church. The other half—men and women who had even the slightest bit of sailing experience—would go with him to the ships, in order to tackle what was sure to be an attack by water.

I glanced at the people gathered around the square, the lights of the lanterns and candles flickering wildly in the breeze, casting odd shadows on their faces. I didn't see whom I expected to see, and slipped away while Corbin was patiently repeating his instructions.

The scene at Renata's house was like some horrible parody of a slasher movie—only without the blood and gore. Bodies lay everywhere—slumped in chairs, drooped over tables, and lying in heaps on the floor. Next to every man was a wooden or metal tankard, puddles of grog staining the floor. I stopped at the nearest body, lightly touching his neck to make sure he was alive, but was soon reassured that the men were indeed drugged only—in fact, several of them were snoring.

Trying not to step on anyone's arms, legs, or other parts (I've never seen such a variety in "other parts"—clearly Corbin and Holder digitized anatomically correct bodies rather than Ken and Barbie versions), I quickly made my way to the back of the house, where the bedrooms were located, making a mental note to remind Corbin that he'd have to see to his drugged crewmates if the fire reached the town.

"Renata?" I called as I reached the back hall. "Mags? Red Beth? Jez? Suky? Anyone not drugged?"

The only sound that greeted my question was the faint snore of a crewmate slumped up against the sideboard—who, upon closer inspection, turned out to be Pangloss.

"Oh, no, not you, too . . . great," I said, opening the nearest door. It was Jez's room, dark and silent, her slight form on the bed visible in the lantern light. "Everyone's out. Just dandy."

I started to close the door when a sleepy voice spoke from the depths of the room. "Amy?"

"Jez?"

"Aye." There was a scrape of tinder, and a flame burst into life, highlighting Jez's bewildered face as she lit a candle. "Are ye ailin' again?"

"You're not drugged? You didn't drink the grog?"

"Nay, I don't like grog—ye know that. What do ye mean, drugged?"

I explained quickly, getting only a few sentences out before she started pulling on her clothes.

"I thought you were drugged, too, when you didn't answer me, or for that matter, hear the shore guns blowing up."

"I'm dead tired," she said with a wry smile. "We worked hard tonight. 'Twas one customer on top of another. Well, not literally on top, although there were these two who wanted to—"

"Understood, and you really don't have to spill professional secrets," I said quickly, starting out the door. "I'll go check on the others. Maybe they're just tired, too."

We went from room to room, but Jez was the only member of the house who hadn't indulged in the grog. Jez picked up Suky's baby, who'd started fussing, and looked at me with wide, scared eyes. "What are we goin' to do?"

I smiled with more confidence than I felt. "Don't worry, Corbin's taken charge of the defenses. Now let's go out and help get people organized. You take the baby—is there milk to feed her?"

"Aye, we've goat's milk," Jez said, hurrying toward the backyard, where Renata kept a couple of goats and chickens.

"Renata," I said, slapping my forehead. "That was her room that was empty, wasn't it?"

"Aye," Jez called back as she left the house, a bottle and the baby clutched in her hands.

"Come to the square when you're done," I yelled after her, then forced my protesting limbs into a lumbering trot as I ran back to the square.

Just in time to see the ships in the harbor blow up.

"Jesus, Mary, and Joseph," Holder gasped, as I staggered to a stop next to him. The townspeople had just split into two groups, one heading up the hill to tackle the fire, the other starting toward the harbor, Corbin at the lead. Everyone stumbled to a stop at the sight of one of the frigates blowing up, the blast so loud it hurt my ears, followed almost immediately by another ship, a smaller sloop, exploding in a fury of metal and wood.

I ran forward, pushing my way through people until I reached Corbin. He stood with his fists clenched, watching as ship after ship was blown up, the burning remains quickly sinking to the bottom of the deep harbor.

"Corbin?" I slipped my hand into his, wincing slightly when his fingers tightened around my blistered flesh. Around us, everyone was silent in stunned horror, the blasts coming with regularity now as the bigger warships—the frigates—took several explosions before they were utterly destroyed. "What are we going to do?"

The last warship exploded, bits of wood and metal and cloth raining down on the harbor. Corbin watched it impassively, and for a moment, my heart sank with the knowledge that he had given up, that Bart had won.

"I'm going to kill that bastard," he finally said, turning to look at me. His eyes were quicksilver pools of fury so intense it sent shivers of dread down my spine.

"How?" I asked, silently cheering his spirit, but the practical side of me needing to point out the obvious. "The fire is almost on the town. Your crew is out, drugged, and no help. The ships are gone. The townspeople are scared and close to panic. How are we going to stop him?"

"We aren't—I am. This is personal, between Paul and me. You just got in the way of his wrath to me." He started to pull away.

"No, sir," I said, shaking my head, squeezing his hand. "It may have started out like that, but this is *my* town, and *my* island, and *my* people, and I'm just as much a part of it as you. So if you go after Bart, I go after Bart. Only I don't see how we're going to with no ships left but a few dinghies and my borrowed sloop."

Out beyond the crescent arms that guarded the entrance of the harbor, large black shapes moved against the horizon. Bart's ships were coming. Corbin watched impassively for a few moments as the first ship sailed into the harbor, then he pulled me along with him as he started herding the people back toward the square. "Get everyone out of town," he yelled to those people he'd designated as group leaders.

"How?" One of them cried, pointing at the hill where fire had the governor's house fully engulfed. Beyond it a line of fire stretched out, sweeping a path straight for the town. "We can't cross that!"

"The mines," Corbin said, giving me a gentle push forward. "Take them through the mines to Careenin' Cove. I have a ship there—a sloop, but everyone should be able to fit on her. Sweetheart, I know you want revenge just as much as I do, but I need you to do this for me—you have to lead the people to my ship. Get them there safely and set sail for Mongoose. Don't worry about me—I can take care of myself."

There was so much wrong with that ludicrous plan, I didn't even bother to discuss it. "I don't know where the mine is, let alone your secret way through it. You lead the people to the ship—I'll take care of Bart."

The look he shot me was priceless, and I mentally tucked it away in a file to be examined later, when I could appreciate the look of mingled love and exasperation. "Don't even go there."

"I just wanted you to see how it felt," I told him, kissing his sooty nose, but sobering up as our dire situation was made clearer by the sound of the arriving warship opening fire on the town. She was still too far out in the harbor to hit the town, but the sound of her cannons thundering in the night air had a chilling effect. "If you're the only one who knows the way through the mine—"

"I'm not. Holder!"

"Front and center, boss," Holder said, pushing his way forward, saluting smartly. "I heard—you want me to take them through the mine?"

"Aye. Get them to the ship."

"What about the crew and the ladies?" I asked, gesturing toward Renata's house. "They're all asleep. You can't leave them there."

"We'll cart them to the mine, then leave them there until it's over," Holder said quickly, yelling for the carts that had been about to haul supplies to the fire line. "The fire won't go into the tunnels, so they'll be safe there."

Bas stood forlornly at the edge of the crowd. I went to

him, explaining that I wanted him to accompany Holder to the ship, smiling when he frowned at my request.

"Ye be goin' to battle Bart?" he asked. Bran was back on his shoulder, cawing wildly at everyone.

"Yes, but don't even think you're going to come with us."

"I'm yer cabin boy," he said stiffly, and I knew I'd injured his pride.

"You're the best cabin boy ever, but Holder is going to need help with the townsfolk," I said quickly, attempting to smooth his ruffled feathers.

He squinted up at me. "Ye're just sayin' that to get me out of the way."

"No, I'm not. I promise that you can come with me to the very next battle I go to," I said, adding to myself that there was no way I'd risk the life, even the virtual life, of a child if I thought there was a good chance we wouldn't survive the battle.

"Ye promise?"

"Cross my heart," I said, doing just that, then totally embarrassing him by giving him a hug and a kiss on the cheek.

"Women," he said disgustedly, wiping his face with the back of his hand. Bran squawked his agreement but hopped over to me. I kissed his head, too, then sent them both off to Holder.

"That takes care of getting the women and children from town, but how are we going to get Bart so we can beat the tar out of him?" I asked Corbin as he was organizing the remaining people.

He gave me a long look, then suddenly pounced on me, pulling me into a hard, fast kiss. "Have I told you today how much I love you, wife?"

"No, you haven't, husband, but I'll take issue with you over that later. There's a villain to capture, first."

"Aye, and we're going to do that as any true pirate

would," he answered, releasing me as he turned to the remaining people. A handful of men and fewer women stood waiting. "My *Samurai Squirrel* is anchored next to your sloop. We'll use the *Squirrel* to hunt down Bart and bring an end to both him and his vendetta."

I looked from Corbin to the harbor, where the silhouettes of two more big ships were visible as they sailed into the harbor. The first ship—a frigate—was firing again, the shots reaching the docks, tearing them and the sloop to shreds. It would be only a few more minutes before the town itself would come in range of those big guns.

"How are we supposed to fight those ships with just one ship?" I asked, sick at the idea of Bart winning, but unable to see how we stood even a remote chance against him.

Corbin smiled, shocking me. "Sweetheart, you have to have a little faith in me."

"I have oodles of faith in you," I told him, trying to think of a nice way to phrase my thought that retreat may be our best bet. "I am a veritable font of faith in you. But that doesn't negate the fact that one ship, shorthanded at that, against a herd of warships is bound to be doomed."

"Fleet, not herd," he said, giving me a gentle shove forward. "To Randy Daniel's Cove, mates! We've got a ship to sail."

"Randy Daniel's Cove?" I asked as he pushed me along.

"Aye, it's the name of the spot you chose to leave your sloop. Legend says that a pirate named Daniel used to meet his lady friend there, until one day her father discovered her and took her away. His ghost is said to haunt the cove, mourning his lost love."

"Lost love," I gasped, the memory of something Bart said chiming in my mind. "Bart said that you'd stolen his true love. He wasn't talking about a woman—he meant this game."

Corbin's face was thoughtful in the light of the lantern he held. To the south of the town, Holder was leading a trail of people and carts toward the coast, where the entrance to the mine was located. They had to skirt the edges of the fire to get there, but I knew Holder would keep everyone safe. We were headed in the opposite direction, following the path that led to the tiny beach where my ship had been left. Fire had started attacking this side of the island, small patches of grass and dense shrubs burning, but we managed to avoid the worst of it, keeping a quick pace as we went single file through the overgrowth to the cliff path down to the sea.

"That makes sense—Paul always did seem possessive of the game, not wanting to make changes unless I insisted."

"So he set up this whole convoluted plan to trap you to pay you back for . . . for what? You said he left you."

"True, but only after we'd had some pretty serious arguments about the direction the game was taking. He wanted to turn it into a war-focused game, where players could be killed. I wanted it to be a social experience in which war between islands was just one facet—not the sole focus—and people could experience life as pirates. After he refused to take out some mechanisms for completely wiping out towns and entire crews, I fired him."

I blew out a breath, my mind turning over the facts, trying to arrange them in a pattern that made sense. "You fired him, he vowed his revenge and set up this virtual mantrap, and he gets . . . what? He said it would ruin you, but I don't see how."

Corbin pulled me abruptly to the side as I was about to walk right into a burning patch of grass. "Watch where you're walking, love. I suspect his plan is to destroy me in the game, which would disable my access to it. He knows I have just the one character to use—once I'm gone, he can do anything he wants, including corrupting the game data and even wiping the server clean."

"He could kill the game itself?" I asked, pausing for a moment at the edge of the cliff path. Sharply angled, it led down to the tiny beach, little yellow blobs lighting the path as the makeshift crew started their way down it. The sharp tang of the sea stung my eyes, but I gritted my teeth and reminded myself that Corbin was just as tired as I was. I grabbed a root dangling from the edge of the cliff, and jumped the three feet to the path. "Don't you have back-ups?"

"Several, but if he has the ability to kill the game, nothing will stop him from doing so every time I restore a clean version. Getting him out of the game isn't the solution—I need to kill his character so his influences are gone, then I can run diagnostics and see what sorts of things he's modified."

The next few minutes absorbed all of my (breathless) attention as we worked our way down the path, my tired and overworked muscles making the journey much harder than it would have been in normal circumstances.

"What happens to us if we die in the game?" I asked Corbin as we reached the shore, pulling off my boots so I could wade out to his pretty blue and white *Samurai Squirrel.*

"Nothing. Your character is deleted from the game, although the data remains so that you can't resurrect yourself under the same name."

"But what happens to you, the real you? The physical body, I mean."

"Ah. You go to the log-in screen, where you can create a new pirate, or log off."

The warm water stung the scratches on my legs as I held my boots up, wading out to the ship. "Wait a minute—are you saying we could have gotten out of the game by just dying?"

"No. You're taken to the log-in screen—you still have to log off, and you can't do that without using the glasses. Since Paul shut down the access to the glasses—that's why we can't feel them—it means there is no way for us to log off so long as his character is still online and influencing the game."

"Damn," I swore, accepting Corbin's help up onto the ship. There went my plans for an easy way out of the situation.

Corbin took immediate charge of the ship, ordering people to various stations, putting those with knowledge of sailing in the key positions, quickly explaining to the others what they were to do.

"Can you take charge of the people on the sails?" he asked me after moving the couple of women around to the rigging, showing them the correct way to unfurl the sails and raise and lower the boom.

"Sure, although I hate to be responsible for any close-quarter sailing," I answered. "Based on experience, there's no way I'm going to be able to avoid getting us shot to hell."

"You'll be fine. Just get us to the harbor, and I'll do the rest," he said.

"What are you going to do?" I asked as he ordered the anchor lifted and the sails dropped.

"Start loading the guns. I've got twenty-four to load, and it's going to take us a while to get them loaded."

It did. It took until we were at the edge of the harbor before Corbin and the men had those twenty-four guns loaded. It wasn't the number of guns that slowed him down—the process of loading a cannon was an exacting detail, one involving five men. The gun was first primed; then a long "worm" (long stick with scratchy things on the end) was shoved down it and turned a couple of times, scraping out any debris. Following that, a sponge piece (another long stick with a damp sponge on the end) was used to clean it further; then the charge was inserted and rammed down into the breech. Shot was then added, with the cannonballs being rammed tightly against the powder charge. After that, priming powder was poured into the primer vent, and the gun was ready to be aimed and fired.

As we sailed past the inky left arm of the harbor, my breath caught in my throat and stuck there in a painful lump. Corbin was just finishing up the last gun, but as he finished and stretched, everyone on board the ship stood silently as the full extent of our enemy's intentions came into view.

The harbor was filled with ships, big ships, warships . . . and all of them had their guns trained on my sweet little town.

"That's not a fleet," I said softly, blindly grabbing Corbin for some much-needed support. "That's a friggin' armada."

"And we're all that stands between it and destruction," he said softly.

Chapter 26

Let vengeance howl;
The Pirate so decides.

—Ibid, Act II

I turned Corbin so he had to look at me. The stunned faces of everyone on the ship as we slipped silently through the water toward what was sure to be our doom pushed me into action.

"Corbin, my love, my darling, I know that all you want is to get us out of this game. I'm totally with you on that as a goal. By my best estimate, I've been sitting in a chair for three hours, and I am going to have to move soon or my body is going to suffer damage. But even taking all that into consideration, I'm going to have to throw you overboard if you seriously believe we can take on those"—I squinted against the glow of the fire burning behind the town, which effectively cast the warships in the harbor in sharp silhouette—"eight warships with one little undermanned ship."

Corbin brushed his thumb across my cheek in a gesture so sweet it almost brought tears to my eyes. "Sweetheart, remember what I said about having faith in me?"

"Yes, and I do, but this is ridiculous—"

"It would be if we were going to attack those eight ships, but we aren't."

I shook my head, confused. "You said we're going to stop Bart—"

"And so we are. But Bart—Paul—isn't on those ships. He's on a sloop somewhere on the edges of the harbor, well back from the action, but close enough to watch and, more important, direct the attack."

"How do you know that?" I asked, completely at a loss.

He smiled. "That's where the having-faith-in-me part comes in. I know Paul, Amy. I worked with him for two years and, more important, I played the game with him. I've seen him engineer attack after attack on islands, and he's used the same method each time. I see no reason for him to change that now."

"But"—I waved my hand toward the harbor—"where is he?"

"We'll find him. He'll show himself before too long."

I didn't have quite the confidence Corbin had that Bart would act the way he was expected to, but I held my tongue and helped with the sails.

"Light sails only," Corbin ordered. "Rig that steering boom in snug. We don't want to draw too much attention to ourselves until we have Paul in our sights. Amy, get everyone at their stations, ready for hauling off."

"Gotcha," I said, clapping my hands together. "Ladies, let's get the trysail boom on the starboard side, ready for jibbing."

The women, all four of them, looked at me as if I was speaking a foreign language. I felt a moment of pride in how far I'd come from the first time I stepped foot on my sloop, but let that go to explain quickly what was expected of them.

Corbin was in the crow's nest as our ship turned to follow the curved shoreline. I climbed up to join him, every muscle in my body protesting the action. "See him yet?"

"No. But he's out there, hiding in shadows. I can feel him. He's probably waiting for us to get into range, then he'll—"

A flash of orange came from the left, slightly upward of our bow. The noise of guns firing followed almost instantly, but before we could shout a warning to those on deck, cannonballs ripped into the bow. Wood splintered and flew with the velocity of missiles. Men and women alike screamed and ran for cover.

"All hands at their stations," I yelled as Corbin flung himself over the side of the crow's nest, barely touching the rope. He was on the deck and shouting orders to fire before I was halfway down. Another flash and *boom boom boom* ripped through the night, the ship reeling with the blows. The hits were so hard, I lost my grip on the rope ladder and fell to the deck, lying stunned for a few minutes.

I managed to get my brain working again and crawled to my feet just as the ship bucked when Corbin fired off three guns. I felt a moment of satisfaction at hearing the shots connect with a solid form rather than splashing uselessly into the water.

"Drop the sails," Corbin shouted above the sound of cries and orders being yelled by everyone. "Helm hard to port."

I rushed to get the sails lowered so we could maneuver ourselves out of danger, but fell to the ground when our mainmast was struck by a lucky shot, the top part of it crashing down on the deck.

"Port," Corbin yelled, loading one of the guns singlehandedly. "Amy, helm to port."

I dragged myself over to the wheel, jerking hard on it to the left. The ship shuddered and wanted to fight me as she took on bilge, but I tied the wheel and ran to help one of the women pull rigging off another who was unlucky enough to be in the way. We hauled her to safety aft. I ran back to help with the remaining sails, but a horrible grating sound stopped me dead.

"We've rammed her," one of the men yelled. Over the remains of the downed mast I could see that he was absolutely right—we'd run smack dab into another sloop. Dark shadows danced around on her deck, indicating they were as aware of the situation as we were.

"Boarding axes," Corbin yelled. "No quarter, mates. Let's take them down."

"Yarr," I yelled with the others, snatching up one of the short axes that was used on board ship in numerous ways— as a handhold when boarding a ship (or cleaving someone's head) was just one of its many uses. A couple of crewmates threw grappling hooks over the side of the sloop, but that wasn't really necessary—her bow was wedged into the port side of our bow. Corbin leaped onto the railing, throwing himself onto Bart's ship with a cry that would have scared the crap out of me if I'd been a member of Bart's crew.

I scrambled up onto the railing, pausing for a moment to assess the scene. The men from our ship had poured onto Bart's, meeting his crew as they were about to board us. The fighting that followed as the two crews clashed was noisy, chaotic, and bloody—at least, from what I could see it was. One of the women hauled herself onto the railing next to me, her skirt hiked up, an arm-sized piece of wood from the broken mast in her hands. I shoved the boarding axe at her. She protested, but I yelled, "I do better with a sword," as I pulled out my foil and flung myself at the nearest pirate.

He had a flintlock pistol, which he fired in my direction, but his aim was (fortunately) lamentable, and he tossed the pistol down as I rushed him with my sword drawn. For a fraction of a second I truly considered running him through

with it, but in the end I simply whacked him on the head
with the steel hand guard and pushed him over the side of
the ship. Bart had evidently beached his ship in order to hide
in shadows cast by a couple of mangrove trees, so the pirate
wouldn't have far to swim to make it to shore.

"That's one down," I yelled, whipping my sword around
in a dramatic fashion that would have done Zorro proud.
"Right, who wants a piece of this?"

Two men rushed me, both with cutlasses. I did a bit of in-
stantaneous calculating with regards to the strength and general effectiveness of my foil, of my skill using it, and of my
overall health and well-being, and came to a quick decision.
"Cooooooooooorbin," I yelled, running down the deck to
where I could see him madly fighting with another man, the
two pirates in hot pursuit.

One of our guys fell backward in front of us, a short pike
buried in his chest. I stopped, staring down at him, time seem-
ing to halt as he gasped a couple of times, then died right there
in front of me, blood seeping into a pool on the wet deck beneath him. I knew that man—he was one of Bart's crew, *my*
crew, a man who'd been pressed into service, but who had
married one of the widows. His name was Gabriel. He was a
nice guy, relatively gentle and soft-spoken . . . and now he
was dead.

A fury like nothing I've ever felt swept over me, crashing
into me with such force that I literally reeled for a second
before grabbing the pike and jerking it from Gabriel's body
to run screaming at the two men who were pursuing me.
Fear flashed in their eyes as I ran the first one through with
the pike; the second fell a few moments later as my sword
flashed. Blood and seawater were everywhere, the light almost nonexistent as various lamps were knocked down by
the battles, but the screams of the wounded, and the sound
of the wood creaking as the tide rocked the ships together,

all served to combine into a horrible nightmarish scene that I feared would have no end.

I fought like a madwoman, ignoring both physical and emotional pain as I struggled against the almost over-whelming number of crew on Bart's ship. Behind me, the remainder of my crew fought just as hard, but one by one they dropped until there were ten of Bart's crew left, and just two of us. I crouched at the bow, bloody but unbowed, my sword held out before me, while Bart's second crew formed a semicircle around me, laughing and sneering and taunting me.

I was too exhausted to answer, too outnumbered to stand a ghost of a chance at fighting, but I wasn't going to go down without taking a couple of them with me.

"Paul," Corbin yelled, his voice carrying over the groans of the wounded and the wood-on-wood shriek of the ships as they shifted. He ripped open the port hatch. "I know you're down there skulking like the coward you are. Come out here and fight me like a man."

Corbin started down the ladder to the lower deck but fell backward as a shot rang out from below. I screamed and threw myself heedlessly forward as a circle of red appeared on his side.

"Corbin!" The men caught me (but not before I made sure that one of them wouldn't be siring children anytime in the near future), twisting my arms painfully behind me as they hauled me forward to where Corbin was struggling to his knees. Bart leaped out of the hold, standing over Corbin with a pistol in one hand, a sword in the other.

"How very fittin' to have ye grovelin' at me feet," Bart drawled, putting his foot on Corbin's shoulder, knocking him back to the ground. He kicked the sword from his hand, sending it skittering across the wet deck.

"Oh, you are *so* dead," I yelled, struggling to free myself from the pirates who held me captive. "You slimy bastard! Did you have to shoot him there? That was healing so nicely!"

Bart looked over to me, his eyebrows raised. "If ye had done as I asked and killed him when you had the chance, we wouldn't have to be goin' through this now. But ye didn't listen to me, did ye, dearie?"

"Like I would kill the man I lo—" I stopped, something in the back of my head clamoring for attention. "What did you say?"

"Ye heard me well enough," he said, prodding the still downed Corbin with the long, curved blade of a scimitar. "I'll take care of yer business this once, but I'm afraid ye'll not be makin' officer in me crew just yet."

"Dearie," I said, struggling briefly with the two men who held me. They jerked back on my arms in a way that had me seeing stars for a moment. "You called me dearie. But you never call me dearie—only Renata does that."

Corbin groaned and rolled onto his side, pulling his knees up in a protective gesture . . . only I could see the hand underneath his body sliding slowly toward his boot.

"Still haven't figured it out? And I was so sure you did last night when you caught me coming in to dope the grog." Before my stunned eyes Bart's form shimmered and changed into that of a small, elderly woman with shrewd eyes. "I'm disappointed in ye, lass, I truly am. I thought ye were so bright."

My mouth hung open for a moment, I'm not in the least bit proud to admit, but only for a moment. "You're Renata, too? How can you be two people at once?"

Renata changed back into Bart, her smug smile morphing into his. "I confiscated the mentor character when I learned you would be logging on. I had a feeling a hostage might be useful in forcing Corbin's hand."

"How on earth did you learn I was going to log on?"

Bart's smile was so obnoxious, I wanted to slap it off his face. "Do you seriously believe I don't have a program in place to spy on all of Corbin's e-mail? Your daughter sent him an e-mail saying she was giving you a character on her account. I was happy to see that, actually. An adult player worked into my scenario much better than a teenager."

"You . . . you . . ." My brain came up with lots of descriptive words, but I reminded myself that calling a madman a slimewad wasn't the most prudent of ideas.

"Now, now, lass," he said, back to his pirate voice. "Time for talk later. I'll explain everythin' then that ye're a little slow in understandin'."

I raised my chin and gave him a frosty smile. "I might not be the brightest bulb in the pack, but I'm not the one about to fall down those stairs with a stupid look on my face."

Bart narrowed his eyes at me. "What are ye talkin'—aaigh!"

A silver flash shot out and sent Bart reeling backward . . . right into the opened hatch. He fell into it screaming.

I stomped down hard on the bare foot of the pirate nearest me, spinning around to plant a kick in the groin of the man on the other side of me. Corbin, who had leaped up as he threw his knife into Bart's chest, snatched up the scimitar that Bart had dropped and used it to take down the nearest man before waving it at the two men near me.

"You even look at her and you're dead, understand?"

The man I kicked in the happy sacks dropped to his knees clutching himself, moaning loudly. The other one looked like he was about to tackle me, but straightened up slowly as Corbin took a step toward me.

"Come here, love," he said, holding out a hand for me. I didn't have to be asked twice. I threw myself toward him, clinging to him for a moment before I swore and pulled back to look at his side.

"Oh, my God, we have to get you to shore. We have to get a doctor—"

Corbin laughed and rubbed a hand over his face. "Mind over matter, sweetheart, remember? It's not that grievous an injury. All right, ye scurvy lot—on yer bellies, yer hands behind ye."

One or two looked like they thought about trying to fight him, but evidently they had seen him fight earlier—I found out later that he'd taken out eleven men on his own—and opted for the sane route of surrender.

"Shouldn't we check on Bart?" I asked nervously, glancing toward the dark hold.

"Now, why would you want to do that?" Corbin cut a bit of line free, using it to bind the hands of the pirates.

"Well . . . to make sure you got him in the heart. He could be down there loading up more pistols or something, biding his time to blow us to bits. Or he could be escaping."

"He's not escaping. He's dead."

"But how do you know for sure? You were on your side, and although I'm sure your aim is really good, you can't know for a fact that he's dead unless you go down and check."

Corbin laughed again. I put such an unreasonable act down to loss of blood. "Amy, my love, feel your face."

"Oh, Corbin," I said sadly, rushing to his side. "My poor darling. This is some sort of dementia or fever or maybe it's shock from the bullet—"

"Amy," he said again, taking my hand to kiss my knuckles. "Feel your face. Right here."

He pressed my fingertips to my temples. Rather than encountering the side of my head, my fingers touched a long, hard, thin piece of plastic that led to my ear.

"The glasses," I whispered, dropping my sword to use both hands on either side of my head. I felt along my face, tracing the outline of the virtual reality glasses. "I can feel the glasses."

"Aye. That's how I know Paul's character is dead. His control on the game has been lifted."

"We can leave?" I asked, a feeling of joy welling up inside me. "The button right here, on the corner—all I have to do is press that?"

"That's all you have to do to exit the game," he said, smiling at me. "Go ahead, love. I know how badly you want to leave."

Tears blurred my vision as my fingers found the button on the rim of the glasses, but something stopped me from pressing it.

Corbin stood in front of me, love shining in his eyes, bloody, black with soot, sweaty and dirty and covered in grime.

I've never seen any man so handsome. "You're leaving too, right?"

"No," he said, nodding his head toward the town. The fire had reached the outskirts of it, and I knew without a doubt that we would not be able to save it. "There's still Holder and the townspeople to see to. I'll help with them, first, then leave the game and shut down the server so Paul can't do anything until I can run some diagnostics and figure out what he's programmed into it."

I looked from him to the bound bodies of the pirates who lay trussed up before us on the deck. I wanted out of there, but it didn't seem right to leave Corbin with everything.

"Sweetheart, go ahead and leave." Corbin pulled me into a gentle embrace, his eyes as bright as mercury in the lantern light. His thumb brushed over my lower lip. "You know I'll find you as soon as I get things taken care of here. I'm not about to let you go now."

"Good, because if you did, I'd just have to hunt you down and challenge you to another duel," I answered, brushing my lips against his. "I love you, Corbin."

"Sweet words from such a bloodthirsty—and bloody—pirate," he answered, giving me a proper kiss. "But ones I'll hold you to. Go along, now. I'll be with you as soon as I can."

I smiled. "Oh, what's another half hour or so? Let's go find Holder and my people. We have an island to restore, and a new governor's mansion to build. And I'm not about to let just anyone do that! A captain has to have some standards, you know."

He swatted me on my behind as I sashayed past him, but I smiled, happy, relieved, and so madly in love, I couldn't possibly imagine how anything could ruin my happiness.

Sometimes I show a distinct lack of foresight.

Chapter 27

I don't think much of our profession, but, contrasted with respectability, it is comparatively honest.

—Ibid, Act I

"Are you ready?" Corbin asked two days later.

I looked around at the people of the town as they bustled around with the full extent of Corbin's crew and the men from Bart's that we'd rounded up and put to work. Hammers pounded, saws bit into wood, and voices murmured a happy chorus as the rebuilding of the town was well under way.

"I guess. Although now that it's come down to it, I feel almost sad about leaving."

He grinned at me. "And here I thought you'd be so sick of the world that you'd never want to step virtual foot in it again."

I waved at Bas as he trailed behind Sly Jez, carrying a basket for her. Bas grinned back. Bran squawked and flapped his stubby wing at me. Everything was just as it should be. "Well, I'm definitely ready to get back to real life, but I don't want to lose these people forever. You're sure you'll be able to save them?"

"I think so. I hope so. I don't know the full extent of Paul's customized programming, but I'm fairly certain we can remove it without damaging the program data. I'm getting a bit nervous about leaving him running loose out there in the real world, though, so if you're ready, I think it's time to return to reality."

"Okay," I said, putting a hand on my temple. It was a familiar motion—I'd taken to making sure the frames of the VR glasses were still there, but there had been too much to be done to actually press the little button that was now under my fingers. I took a deep breath and had one last look at my town and people. "Ready."

"On three?" Corbin smiled as he reached up for his own glasses. "One, two, thr—"

The world swirled into a black vortex of nothingness for a moment, then slowly a blurry blob of color resolved itself into a familiar-looking logo blinking apparently in midair.

"Welcome to Buckling Swashes. Please log in or create a new pirate to enter the game."

Beyond the logo, the dim outlines of Tara's laptop and my desk resolved themselves to my returning vision.

I was home.

"So? What did you think? You've been playing long enough to have made officer—did you do it?"

My hand shook a little bit as I raised it up to pull off the glasses. My fingers were stiff and sore, as if I'd been gripping the arms of the chair.

"Mom? You okay?" A shadow at the perimeter of my vision moved and turned into the familiar form of my daughter. I was so happy to see her after my prolonged absence that I wanted to jump up and hug her. "You look funny. What's wrong? Don't tell me you didn't like the game!"

"No," I said, my voice a hoarse croak. I cleared my throat and tried again. "I liked it. It's got a lot of . . . promise."

"Really?" she asked, her face suspicious. I gave an experimental stretch, gingerly moving my tight shoulders before I tried to get to my feet. "Well . . . good. So what did you do in game? You spent a long time there. It must have been a couple of weeks or something?"

My knees creaked and popped like an old lady's as I got to my feet, my legs stiff from the hours of incapacitation. "What did I do?" I asked, creaking my way toward the hall and the downstairs bathroom. I paused at the door to give her a wry smile. "Not much. Just took over Bart's crew and governorship of Turtle's Back, helped expose and destroy a villain, fought in a blockade, killed a couple of men, and fell head over heels in love with Black Corbin. I'm going to take a long bath. I'll tell you about it later, after I've had a lengthy soak."

Needless to say, Tara wasn't going to let me get away with an exit line like that. She followed me into the bathroom and sat on the counter while I slipped into the tub with a grateful sigh for indoor plumbing and hot-water tanks.

"Shoo," I said, closing my eyes in ecstasy as the heat sank into my stiff limbs, wishing I'd had the foresight to bring in a bottle of merlot.

"Not until you tell me everything," she said, making herself comfortable on the counter. "And I mean everything!"

In the end, I told her everything . . . well, almost everything. I left out details about the nights spent with Corbin. I had thought about skirting around the whole issue of my feelings for him, worried that she would not react well to the idea of her mother having an interest in anyone but her father, but she surprised me. In fact, she seemed to totally gloss over the point of my romantic feelings, and focused on those she felt were far more important.

"So, if you marry him, does that mean we'll be rich? And

I'll get to try all his cool VR stuff first, before everyone else? I could be like a beta tester! Do I still have to go to school if we're rich?"

I opened my eyes to glare at her. "Whoa, hold on there, missy! First of all, no one said anything about marriage."

"You married him in the game," she pointed out. "You slept with him, didn't you? So that means you have to marry him."

I opened my mouth to tell her that sleeping with someone by no means meant they had to get married, decided that wasn't a message I particularly wanted her to be receiving, and changed my answer. "Yes, I married him in the game, but we haven't talked about what we will be doing in real life. There hasn't been any time to discuss that yet."

"You said you loved him," she said, a familiar stubborn look descending over her face.

"Yes, I did. And I do. But no decisions have been made about how we'll proceed from here."

She frowned, twisting a strand of her hair. "You mean that he may not be in love with you outside of the game?"

Her words hit me with the impact of a Mack truck. Despite the heat of the water, a cold chill swept over me. "No, I—I just meant—sometimes people—you don't think he is that sort of person, do you?"

"I don't know him, Mom," she said with shrug. "I just had a couple of e-mails from him, that's all. You know him better than me."

"I only know him in the game," I said slowly, a wave of doubt crashing down on me. I hated to think about it, I didn't want to think about it, but what if Tara, in her innocence, had inadvertently hit upon a truth? Everything I knew about Corbin was from the dratted game—what if he was a different person outside of it? "Sometimes people use situations like that to role-play."

"Yeah. I like to be a pirate. I get to be all the things I'm not really. It's cool."

I thought about that for a minute. "Corbin likes to role-play. He's a very good pirate."

"Well, that makes sense. He made the game."

"Yes, he did," I said, the words falling from my tongue like little drops of acid. "And I know absolutely nothing about what he's like in real life, outside of his pirate persona. He could be totally different. He could . . . regret some things."

She eyed me as I sat like a frozen block of horror in the tub. "You've got a horrible look on your face, like you're going to be sick. You want me to leave so you can barf?"

"No. Yes. I don't know." I was too miserable to make up my mind. My stomach had balled itself up into a wad of unhappiness and doubt.

"I'll go," she said, hopping down off the counter. She stopped at the door to give me an enigmatic look. "You're always telling me I'm being a drama queen, but you know what? Now you're doing the same thing."

I made an outraged noise. "I am not!"

She nodded her head at me. "Yes, you are, too. I mean, why would he be any different outside the game? You're the same person, right?"

My blood froze.

"Mom?"

"Er . . . I suppose I am the same. Mostly the same. Oh, who am I fooling? I was brave and witty and sexy and all sorts of other things in the game that I'm not in reality." I waved the loofah around in a pathetic gesture. "He's going to take one look at me in real life and know that my brain lied to him about the sort of person I really am."

She rolled her eyes. "Man, and you say I exaggerate."

"This is different," I said, sinking down into the water,

well aware that I was behaving moronically. But I couldn't stop myself. "I have never really met Corbin. So much of an attraction between people is a chemical thing. What if we don't mesh well? What if I'm not exciting enough for him? What if—"

"Sheesh! Get over yourself already! Why don't you just call him and ask if he still loves you and all that stuff?"

"It's not that easy," I said, flicking the water, cold at the thought of what I would do if the real-life Corbin wasn't as madly in love with me as I was with him.

"Doctor Tara's Love Counseling Shop is now closed," she said, leaving the bathroom, her voice drifting into the bathroom as she went upstairs. "Call him up and tell him you want to see him. It's only a little after midnight."

I sank lower into the water and thought about what my smart-alecky—but sometimes wise-beyond-her-years (she got that from my side of the family)—daughter said, and by the time the water had chilled to the point where it matched the coldness inside me, I had come to a decision.

"It's up to the man to call first," I told Tara on the way to bed. She was lying on her stomach on her bed, watching the *Friday Night Late Late Movie*. She made a face at me. "There are some dating rules that are inviolable, and this is one of them. The guy calls first."

"This is 2005, Mom, not 1905," she quipped. "Call him."

I closed the door on her and went to my own room, sitting in bed while the two halves of my psyche battled each other. After a half hour of dashing, daring Amy struggling with worried, confused Amy, I finally gave up and reached for the phone.

Only to realize I didn't have Corbin's phone number.

"Hell," I said, then got out of bed and peeked around Tara's door. She was still up, on her cell phone with one of her equally night-owl girlfriends while she painted her toe-nails a repulsive shade of purple.

" . . . and I said, no way, and Celie said, yes way, totally, and I said—oh, one sec, my mom wants something. What?" She covered the mouthpiece of the phone and narrowed her eyes at me. "You're not going to go all love-struck on me again, are you? 'Cause there is only so much I have to take; then it gets freaky."

I pointed an admonishing finger at her. "Less attitude, please. I wanted to know if you have Corbin's phone number."

She grinned and uncovered the phone. "She's gonna call him. No, not Celie, my mom. Yeah, the computer guy. I don't know, I'll ask. What are you going to say?"

The last was addressed to me. "None of your business. May I please have the number?"

Tara frowned and told her friend to hold on for a moment. She pulled her laptop onto the bed and clicked around on the screen. "His cell phone, you mean?"

"That or his home phone number."

"Meh. I don't know if I have it." She loaded up her e-mail client and flipped through a couple of messages. "Nope. I've got the office number and addy, though, if you want those."

I wrote them down on her notepad, asking as I did, "You don't happen to have his home address?"

She shook her head and picked up her phone. "Nope. You still there? Yeah, I know, but she's old. I mean, she doesn't have a lot of choices, you know?"

I closed the door on Tara's dissection of my love life and returned to my room, curling up in bed with the phone while I debated my choices. Unfortunately, about this Tara was right—I didn't have too many options. A phone call to the offices of Buckling Swashes (which resulted in the expected voice mail—which I didn't leave, chickening out at leaving a personal message that could well be listened to by a secretary or receptionist) and one abortive attempt to get Corbin's unlisted phone number from directory assistance later, and I was defeated. I spent the night restless, held in the grip of one dream of frustration after the other.

"Right, that's it," I told my haggard face in the mirror a few hours later. "This is ridiculous. Time to be proactive, Amy."

Tara was buried under the usual detritus of her bedroom—a miscellany of stuffed animals she refused to part with, pillows of all shapes and sizes, blankets, clothing, and a gypsy shawl she'd found in my closet and claimed as her own—but I pushed them aside to locate her head. Her eyes opened just enough to send me a squinty-eyed glare.

"Do you know if Corbin's office is open on Saturday?"

"Nnnnrf," she answered, closing her eyes firmly and burying her face into the mound of stuffed animals that clustered around her pillow.

"Thanks, you're a big help. I want you up no later than noon, remember. You're not going to spend the whole day sleeping."

"When you marry Corbin and we're rich, I'm *so* never getting up," her voice answered from the mound.

My jaw tightened at her words. "Let's just hope we get the opportunity to have that particular battle," I said under my breath as I snatched up my purse and the paper with Corbin's office address, and paused to have a quick look in the mirror next to the front door. The face that looked back at me looked the same as Amy the pirate—but would Corbin see it the same way?

"Proactive," I told the mirror Amy. She nodded back, adding, "Take charge of every situation, and direct it to the result you want."

"Now if only Corbin will see things the same way . . ."

The drive to his office didn't take too long, it being located in an industrial park that was on the fringes of the local mall. At the rear of the complex of low, two-story buildings a Jolly Roger flag flew in front of a door bedecked with a scowling pirate holding a sign that read, 'WARE, LANDLUB-BERS! THIS BE THE OFFICE OF BUCKLING SWASHES!

Unfortunately, beyond the sign, the windows were dark. I tried the door nonetheless—it was locked.

"Well, hell. Now what?" I asked myself. Curiosity won out, and after a quick look around the deserted section of this part of the industrial park, I stepped over the couple of low shrubs and leaned up against the window, cupping my hands around my eyes so I could see into the darkness. Dimly visible were a couple of desks with the obligatory computers and desk paraphernalia, beyond which was a tall potted palm that seemed to be sporting a number of stuffed, garishly colored parrots. The walls were covered in artwork that I recognized from the game—pictures of ships, one of the inside of Corbin's cabin on the *Squirrel,* and an overhead map of Turtle's Back. To the back of the office was a door with a pair of crossed swords on it. I leaned in even farther, trying to make out the words on the sign that hung above them. . . .

"Hoy, there, lass! Can I be helpin' ye?"

The voice came from behind me, startling me so much I jumped a good foot in the air as I spun around, guilt and embarrassment battling with adrenaline as I stammered out an excuse. "Oh! I'm sorry! I was just looking . . . I was hoping . . . er . . ."

A man swung his leg over a bike, evidently having just ridden to the office, which explained why I hadn't heard him approach. He was a little taller than me, wearing a pair of jeans and a South Park T-shirt, along with a neon pink and lime bike helmet, and impenetrable sunglasses. He paused in the act of pulling the helmet off.

"Amy?"

I stopped stammering, narrowing my eyes as he yanked the helmet from his head. "Yes, I'm Amy."

He grinned and took off his sunglasses, holding out his arms as if he expected me to run into his embrace. I ran my gaze over his long face, took in the tousled black hair, and warm, engaging eyes, happiness filling me as I realized who he was. "Holder!" I shouted, flinging myself at him.

He laughed and hugged me just as hard as I hugged him. "One and the same. And, wow, look at you! Much better in person than in pixel. Corb's one hell of a lucky guy." He looked around me, toward the car, then back to the office. "Where is the boss man? Inside? Were you two playing some sort of voyeuristic game? Do I want to hear the details? Of course I do. Tell me everything."

I stepped back, my happiness at seeing him fading. "I don't know where Corbin is. I haven't seen him since we . . . er . . . returned."

"You haven't? Well, it was probably late," Holder said, slinging a backpack over his shoulder. "Did he say when he'd meet you here?"

"No, you don't understand," I said miserably as I followed Holder to the door. He secured his bike to a rack and pulled out a ring of keys. "I haven't spoken to him, either."

Holder turned around to stare at me. "You what?"

I did that horrible hand-wringing thing that I detest so much (but don't seem to be able to stop myself from doing). "I haven't talked to him. I don't have his phone number."

"You mean he didn't call you?"

I shook my head, the misery inside me blossoming into something so awful, it made me feel cold and physically sick.

Holder shook his head as well. "I don't believe it. Your phone line must have been down or something."

"No, it was fine. I checked every couple of hours. I thought maybe he might not have my number, but I'm listed in the phone book."

Holder's brows pulled together in a frown as we stood there next to the building, the early morning sun starting to warm the air around us, fingers of sunlight snaking around the trees and buildings to touch my chilled body. "That doesn't make sense. Even if he couldn't get your number from the phone book, he's got it on your daughter's account information."

"Well, he didn't call. I'd know if he did. There was no voice mail."

"Something must have come up to keep him from calling until he probably thought you were in bed," Holder insisted, looking puzzled. "That's the only explanation that makes sense to me."

I bit my lip, not wanting to state the obvious, but Holder was Corbin's best friend. If the worst happened, he'd find out. "I thought perhaps he might have decided not to carry our relationship over to the real world—"

Holder interrupted me before I could finish my horrible musings.

"That's the most ridiculous thing I've ever heard. Corb's madly in love with you, as if you don't know," he said, squinting against the sunlight to examine my face. "Whoa. You look like you've had a rough night. You haven't been thinking what I think you're thinking, have you? You have, haven't you? Bleh, women." He took my arms in his hands, then abruptly spun me around and gave me a little push toward my car. "No, I'm not even going to dignify such an outrageous idea with the obvious objections. We'll go see the man himself, and I'll let him explain to you why you're way off base there."

"We're going to see Corbin?" I asked, hesitating before unlocking the car doors. Although that had been my goal all along, I was more and more worried about the reason Corbin hadn't called me. Even Holder was surprised by that. "Maybe you could just give me his number instead and I could call."

He got into the car next to me, gesturing for me to start it. "Stop being such a woman. Take a left out of the parking lot. I'll give you directions as we go."

"I can't help it; I *am* a woman," I snapped, tired of feeling so unsure, tired of the cold, sick feeling inside, and hating the fact that I could doubt someone I loved so deeply.

"Yeah? That doesn't mean you have to act like a wimp. What happened to the fierce, frightening Captain Amy who scared the crap out of everyone whenever she got mad?"

"That Amy doesn't really exist—" I started to say.

"Bullshit!" I opened my mouth to protest, but Holder gave me a look that left me speechless. "Just what do you think you were doing in the game, Amy? Pretending to be someone you aren't? Buckling Swashes doesn't work that way. People who play someone totally against their character drop out after a day or two. It's just too much work to be someone you're really not. The game taps into your inner dreams and desires; it doesn't manifest ones at odds with who you really are. So don't give me any more of that crap about the pirate Amy not being the real you, because I know better. Now, are you going to continue to whine and snivel, or are you going to find out what is keeping Corbin from lavishing his attention on you?"

A thousand protests came to my lips, a thousand objections to what Holder was saying, and a couple of pithy (and obscene) suggestions about what he could do with his advice, but all that evaporated as I thought over what he said.

Dammit, he was right. There was nothing I had done as a pirate that I wouldn't do in real life . . . with the exception of running a couple of men through with a sword. Metaphysically speaking, though, all I had been doing was protecting the one I loved, and that I would do in a heartbeat. But it all boiled down to one thing—I was the same person no matter if I was in a virtual environment or a real one. And if I was the same, then Corbin . . .

"Call him," I said as I gunned the engine. "Tell him we're on the way over to see him, and he'd bloody well better have a damned good excuse for making me spend the night worrying!"

Holder grinned as he pulled out his cell phone. "God help him if he doesn't. Glad to see the real you back, Amy."

Determination and reckless abandon filled me as I yanked the steering wheel, slamming my foot on the gas petal. Holder laughed as I said grimly, "He's going to need all the divine intervention he can get if I find out he's been yanking my chain!"

"I don't doubt that he'll live in mortal fear of your can of whoop ass, but I'm equally sure it won't be necessary. He's got it bad for you. Nothing short of global meltdown would keep him from you."

I just wished I was as confident as Holder. I had a horrible feeling in the pit of my stomach that something was seriously, horribly wrong.

Chapter 28

A rollicking band of pirates we,
Who, tired of tossing on the sea,
Are trying their hand at a burglaree,
With weapons grim and gory.

—Ibid, Act II

"I want a new stomach," I said twenty minutes later as we stood outside the warm cream-colored brick house that sat on a bluff overlooking the turbulent, rocky northern California shore.

"It looks okay to me," Holder said, giving my stomach a quick glance as he banged for a third time on the door. "You women are always obsessed with your weight. My wife has a few extra pounds, and I love it. Wouldn't have her any other way. A man likes to have a woman with something to her, not one of those walking skeletons you see modeling clothes on the E! channel."

"Boy, we need to bottle that attitude and sell it to every man in America," I said, still worried but able to give Holder a little friendly punch in the arm to show him I appreciated the comment. "I was referring to the fact that my stomach is apparently psychic. Is the door locked?"

"Yeah, but"—Holder pulled out his big key ring again, poked through the keys until he found one he liked, then held it up with a triumphant grin—"I have a set of his keys. And don't let your stomach dictate to you. He may not have answered the phone because he was in the shower, or taking a crap, or any number of other perfectly legitimate, non-stomach-worrying reasons."

I let that go as I looked around the foyer of Corbin's house. I don't know what I had expected—computer-game machines at every table?—but the bright, modern, minimalist furniture, vaulted ceiling, and floor-to-ceiling windows along the ocean side of the house didn't at all fit my idea of the house of a computer-game guru.

Until I turned around and saw the wall behind me covered in a variety of mounted swords. "Now, that's Corbin."

"Nice to see you smiling again," Holder said before marching to the foot of a curved oak staircase. "Corb? You awake? I've got Amy here, and if you're not down in exactly ten seconds to molest her as is her due, I get to keep her."

I whapped him on the arm but held my breath, listening for any sounds of someone in the house. Despite his protests, I had seen a faint line of worry on Holder's face when Corbin didn't answer either his home phone or his cell phone on the drive to his house. Now here we were on the spot, and all I could hear was a whole lot of nothing.

"Maybe he's got his headphones on," Holder suggested, starting down the hall past the staircase. "His computer room is back here. We'll sneak up on him and give him a heart attack, okay?"

I followed, my spirits spiraling downward with every step. Holder pushed open the door at the rear of the house, leading into what once must have been an atrium, but which

was now a UV-filtered glass room full of computer equipment. A long table along the windows was filled with three
different computers and related peripherals, while on the
opposite side of the room, a large glass-fronted metal case
squatted, a plasma screen monitor perched on top.

The room was Corbin-less.

"Hmm," Holder said, his brow wrinkled with puzzlement. "I was sure he'd be here. Maybe he's in the shower,
like I said. Or he could be asleep after pulling an all-nighter.
I'll run upstairs and check."

"Why does he have so many computers?" I asked, moving over to the nearest one, jogging the mouse so the screen
blanker turned itself off.

"That one is his personal computer. It's tied into the
server and the Internet. He manages the game from it. The
other two computers are secure—the one farthest away runs
Linux, for programming. And that middle one is devoted to
rendering graphics, not that he does much of that. The server
is behind you, in the air-conditioned rack. Be right back. If
he's asleep, I'll let you come up and dump a bucket of cold
water on him."

I sat down in Corbin's chair and looked at the computer
screen, convinced from the empty silence of the house that
Corbin wasn't at home. Maybe he had gone to find me? I
clicked to minimize a document full of technical computer
info, and blinked at the sight of the Buckling Swashes client.
It was the same as the VR model that had seemed to float on
air, only this one was shown on the flat plasma computer
monitor.

A little smile formed at the sight of the town square on
Turtle's Back. A line of icons to the left showed thumbnails
of other spots in the game—a couple of ships, key shops
and inns, and maps of three islands. I clicked on Corbin's
Samurai Squirrel and noticed that even without the captain

present, his crew was busily maintaining the ship—swabbing down the deck, mending rope and sails, even doing a bit of carpentry.

"What an amazing world you've created, PC Monroe. Now, where the hell are you so we can share *this* world?"

I looked around the room but found no answers. There were no big "I've gone to find Amy" notes pinned up anywhere, no clues to tell me what he was up to and why he hadn't called me. Like the rest of the house, this room was silent, nothing but the swish of the air-conditioning, a faint hum from the computer's fan, and the soft, muted flutterings as the hard drive fired up to carry out some task.

The thump of Holder's footsteps as he came back downstairs broke my angsty thoughts. "All right. Now I'm worried. His bed hasn't been slept in. His bathroom is spotless, which means he hasn't used it since the housekeeper cleaned up yesterday afternoon." Holder stopped in the middle of the room and pinched his lower lip while he thought a moment before grabbing the phone on the table next to me. "I'm calling the police."

My eyes widened, the sick feeling inside me morphing into something much, much worse. "Police? You think something's seriously wrong? Like he might have been robbed or attacked?"

"No. But I don't like this. The security system was off when we came in, the lights were all on, and nothing is out of place. If he was robbed, there is a good fifty grand worth of computer equipment in this room alone. Something is going on, and I don't like it. What's my emergency? Oh, sorry, police. I need the police, please. I've got a missing person to report. A missing millionaire person. Yeah, I can hold." Holder covered the mouth of the phone and asked, "Is there anything on the computer there that says where he went?"

"No," I said, scooting slightly to the side so he could see the monitor. I clicked around to show him the open programs. "There's just the game client, some sort of financial program, what looks like a user database, and a document full of computerese."

Holder peered at the screen. "That's the game control, not just a client. And yes, that's the user database—looks like he was pulling up your daughter's info. Probably was looking for your phone number. That looks like his bank client. No idea what he was doing with that, unless it was to check and make sure he has enough bucks to keep you happy. That file isn't computerese; it's codese—part of the security protocol code used in the game. No doubt he was locking down the game so Paul couldn't hack his way into it again. Hello? Yes, I want to report a missing person."

Holder turned away while he gave the pertinent info about Corbin. Something about the computer bothered me, but I couldn't figure out what it was. I saved the document with the computer code, then closed it, looking at the icons on the desktop, wondering what it was that was making me uneasy. I closed the user database, glancing over to the computer's front. The little green hard drive light was blinking away madly. I clicked on the game client and brought it to the fore.

"Is it okay if I close the game control?" I asked Holder.

"Yeah, sure. The server has the same control panel running," he answered quickly before explaining to the police dispatcher for the third time his relationship to Corbin, and why he felt the disappearance should be taken seriously.

I closed the client, frowning at the computer unit. The green hard drive light was still flickering, indicating the hard drive was running. "That leaves you," I said softly as I maximized the financial program's screen. It wasn't one I used, but it was simple enough for me to do a little snooping into Corbin's financial state. Bank accounts, investments, tax information—it was all there.

That's when I noticed what the program was doing. Before my astonished eyes, one of Corbin's accounts suddenly generated a transfer and zeroed itself out.

"Holder?" I said, clicking back to the account tracking page, pulling up a history. Goose bumps crawled up my spine as I did some mental addition of the amounts that were involved in the last few transactions. "Holder, can you come here?"

"Busy with the cops," he muttered. "Fools don't seem to understand how unlike Corb this is."

"I seriously think you need to see this," I said, investigating the transactions with a few clicks of the mouse. "You said that Corbin is a millionaire."

"Yeah, but he puts most of it back into the company."

"Well, according to this, he has approximately one hundred and eighty-two thousand dollars to his name," I said, clicking on the sum function. "But another one million, four hundred thousand has been transferred away in the last couple of hours."

"What?" Holder yelled, leaning over me to look at the screen. "Holy shit! What's going on?"

The hard drive ran again. I clicked back to the account screen just in time to see another account transfer trigger. "Someone is moving Corbin's money. See?" I pointed to the transaction list. "Those are the accounts the money is being sent to."

We looked at each other and said the same word at the same time. "Paul."

"He's stealing Corbin's money," I said.

"Trying to ruin him any way he can." Holder nodded. "Can you stop him?"

"I'll try."

"Officer, I think I know where he is," Holder said, turning away from me. I tried to cancel the transaction in progress, but the program wouldn't allow me to. I would have closed it to stop it, but the program was tapped into Corbin's bank, and there was no way I could shut down the bank's servers.

"I can't shut him out. He's using Corbin's password to access the accounts, so the bank's software thinks it's really Corbin."

Holder swore.

"What's Paul's address?" I asked as he argued with the police. He continued his attempt to convince them of the gravity of the situation while scribbling an address on a sticky notepad. I snatched the top page off it and headed for the front door.

"Fine, we'll just see you in court when his mangled body is found because you wouldn't do anything for forty-eight hours!" Holder snarled into the phone, slamming it down to run after me. "Wait, Amy, you can't go there alone. You need backup."

"No, this is what I need," I said, snatching a heavy scimitar off the wall. The blade gleamed wickedly in the sunlight pouring in through the glass panels on either side of the front door. "But you're welcome to come, too."

Holder sighed as he took a matching scimitar, hurrying after me as I leaped down the stairs to the path that led to the detached garage. "A sword, Amy? Those who live by the sword die by the sword, remember. This is real life, honey. If you shove a sword into someone here, you're going to go to jail."

"Yeah, well, after the last few virtual weeks spent with a sword strapped to my hip, I just feel a lot more comfy with one at hand," I answered, tossing the scimitar onto the backseat of my car before scooting behind the wheel. "Jump in if you're coming; otherwise, watch your toes."

Holder leaped into the car as I started it, grousing as he strapped himself in that I was just like Corbin, determined to be the hero at every opportunity.

"I'd settle for just *having* the hero," I muttered and tried to push down my fears for Corbin so I could concentrate on driving safely.

It turned out that Paul lived a good hour's drive away, at the foothills of a nearby mountain range, in a suburb of yet another high-tech town. The ride there was ample time for me to envision all sorts of horrible scenarios involving Corbin, visions of him lying dead or near fatally wounded while the evil Paul danced around him waving his bank account statements filling my brain with morbid frequency. Holder tried alternately to reach Paul (he just got voice mail) and to reason with the police, but they were sticking to their policy of investigating disappearances only after a certain length of time had passed.

"They say the only way they will send someone out to Paul's house is if we have actual proof of a crime. Speculation isn't enough. Damn, what happened to the police state where you used to be able to send cops out to check up on someone without having anything more than a gut feeling?"

"Someone is going to have more than a feeling in his gut if I find he's harmed Corbin," I muttered. The rest of the ride was in silence, Holder confining himself to consulting the GPS unit on his Palm Pilot and giving me occasional directions.

"Game plan?" Holder asked, breaking the quiet as he directed me down a street. "His house should be the third one on the left."

"The game plan is we go in, rescue Corbin, and call the police to haul Paul's ass to jail." I pulled into the driveway of a typical sixties housing tract rambler, staring at the blank windows for a moment as if they'd give me a clue to Corbin's well-being.

"So in other words, no game plan."

"Just that big ole can of whoop ass you mentioned earlier," I answered, snatching the scimitar off the backseat. "Ready?"

He twirled his scimitar and saluted me with it. "Aye, aye, Captain. Lead on."

"You know, I find it refreshing that you don't want to take charge and try to protect me or any of that sexist crap," I said as we marched up to the front door.

"I've been married far too long to have any false impressions as to the supposed frailty of females," he answered with a slight smile. "My wife has a black belt. She can kick my ass all the way to Cleveland and back."

"I like her already. Damn. Door's locked."

"You didn't even knock," he said, a slightly shocked look on his face.

"You don't knock on the door of a kidnapper's house," I argued as I followed stepping-stones around to a wooden fence that surrounded the backyard. "Haven't you ever watched *Cops*?"

"Wife won't let me. She says it instills too many bad ideas of male dominance in my mind. Um. Amy, just playing devil's advocate here. What if Corbin isn't here? What if Paul isn't the one moving Corbin's money around?"

I opened the gate to the backyard, pausing to say over my shoulder, "Then I will apologize profusely to Paul and probably get charged with breaking and entering, which I won't fight. But I don't think that's likely."

"Nor do I, but I just felt like someone had to be the voice of reason here."

"Shhhh. Eek!" A fat spaniel waddled out of a small doghouse on the edge of a cement patio, wagging its stubby tail like mad at me. I squatted down to give it a couple of quick pats, figuring it wouldn't hurt to make friends with an animal that might send up an alarm, not that the old dog seemed to be the least bit inclined to bark. Holder paused to pat as well, then we ducked down under a couple of windows to sidle up to a set of French doors. I took a quick peek in the doors, then slid a cautious hand to try the handle, breathing a sigh of relief when the doors opened with a soft click. We found ourselves in a formal dining area.

"What now?" Holder whispered as we skirted the dining table.

I held up my hand to stop him, holding my breath to listen. The house seemed to be quiet, but it felt different from Corbin's house. This house was not empty. I tiptoed to the opening to the hall, peeking quickly around it, then gesturing with the scimi for Holder to follow. The doors nearest me on either side of the hall were shut, but at the far end, one was tantalizingly half-open. I walked as silently as I could on the wood floor, taking a good, firm grip of my scimitar as I gently eased the door open.

The room had clearly been intended to be a master bedroom, but like Corbin's atrium, this one was filled with computer equipment, the table directly across from the door holding an impressive array of computers. An empty computer chair sat pushed aside. On one of the computer monitors, a familiar financial screen was blinking slowly.

"Gotcha," I said softly as I stepped into the room.

"Mmarfm?"

I spun around at the muffled voice, gasping at the sight of the bloodied man who lay bound and gagged, propped up against a metal filing cabinet. I ran to squat next to him, tossing down my sword in order to run my hands over him in an attempt to assess how badly he was injured. Holder was right behind me, doing a protective sweep with his scimi.

"Corbin! Don't move, my darling. We'll have you out of here in a second."

"Oh, I wouldn't count on that," a familiar voice drawled from the doorway. I glanced over my shoulder to see a man who bore a faint resemblance to Bart leaning against the door frame. In his hand he held a gun. "You see, this time, I *will* win. And that means bye-bye Corbin."

Chapter 29

Away to the cheating world go you,
Where pirates all are well-to-do;
But I'll be true to the song I sing,
And live and die a Pirate King.

—Ibid, Act I

I am the first person to admit that there are times when my common sense takes a leap out the nearest window. This was one of those times. Rather than be concerned with the fact that Paul, a man who had absolutely no qualms about kidnapping, embezzling, and attacking people, stood before me handling a very deadly looking gun, I was furious over the fact that he had hurt Corbin.

"Just what the hell have you done to him?" I demanded to know, getting to my feet so I could stand in front of Paul, my hands on my hips, my jaw set in an aggressive manner. I prayed that Holder would realize that I was blocking Paul's vision, and get Corbin's hands untied. "What did you do, you bastard? Sneak up behind him like the dog you are and attack him when he was at his computer?"

Paul's eyes lit with a fury that had me rethinking the

wisdom of taunting a man with a gun, but I stuck to it, wanting to keep all of his attention focused on me rather than what Holder was doing. "Still the brash, foolish little spitfire, I see," Paul drawled in a fashion that left my palm itching to slap the smug look right off his face. "We'll see how feisty you are after I've put a few holes in Corbin. As for your guess, it's not quite accurate. I didn't have to sneak up behind Corbin to crack him on the head. I arrived in his house a short while before he logged out of the game. If you two had stayed there a few minutes longer while I reinstalled my modifications, I wouldn't have had to take such drastic actions, but I believe this will work out well after all."

I deliberately closed my mind to the faint rustling noises behind me that indicated that Holder was removing Corbin's bonds. It was vital that I keep Paul's attention on me, keep him talking, until we could overpower him and beat the crap out of him. Or call the police, whichever came first (and I knew which one I wanted to come first). "So, this whole thing, your big elaborate plan with Bart and Renata—it was all about stealing Corbin's money, not getting revenge by messing up his game?"

Paul laughed, an evil, nasty laugh like villains in the movies indulge in shortly before they order someone into a tankful of hungry sharks. "Don't be stupid, Amy. Hasn't dear Corbin told you how many years of my blood I've put into this game? Didn't he tell you that I was the one who suggested bringing a simple Java script into virtual reality? Did he leave out the fact that I redefined VR in order to make it possible so that anyone running a home computer could access it? Did he neglect to tell you how many years of my life I spent making this dream, my dream, a reality, only to have it stolen from me by a man who saw only what he wanted to see? If no one told you this, then let me be the first—Corbin Monroe owes me. I'm not *stealing* anything. He owes me for all of his success. I'm only taking what is mine!"

He was yelling by the time he ended, making me take a step back despite my need to block his view of Corbin. A low grunt behind me, and a beloved voice put that need to an end, however.

"You were paid for your work on the VR environment, Paul. You seem to have conveniently forgotten that fact, as well as a few others including the very generous settlement that was made when you agreed to license the VR environment to us for the next ten years. You have been paid. We owe you nothing."

I turned slightly to give Corbin a quick assessing glance, my mind taking a moment to adjust to the familiar image of the face that I had only before seen digitalized. He looked almost exactly the same as the Corbin I knew and loved— his face was a bit more gaunt, his jaw and chin covered in dark stubble, but his eyes were the same. Warm and bright despite his injuries, his gray-eyed gaze held mine for a moment before he moved to stand next to me. Blood streaked down his face from a stiff, matted section on the side of his head, but other than that, he seemed to be fine. Certainly the hand that took mine was strong and reassuring, his thumb stroking over the back of my hand in a manner that all but had me melting. He was Corbin, my Corbin, just the same as he had been as a pirate, and I wanted nothing more than to throw myself on him and cover his dear, adorable face with kisses.

"What do you think you're going to do, Paul?" Holder asked, moving to my other side, neatly tossing a bit of cord that had been used to bind Corbin into a waiting trash can. "There are three of us and only one of you. You're outnumbered, mate."

"Oh, but this evens things up a bit, wouldn't you say?" Paul answered, gesturing toward him with the gun. "As for what I'm going to do . . . I believe there will be a tragic three-way murder-suicide. Dear Corbin here is going to be distraught to the point of insanity when he finds out his lover here preferred Holder to him, and shoots both of them before blowing his own head off. I as mediator will have sadly failed in my attempt to reason with him, but I will serve as a sad witness to the tragedy that I could not stop."

A chill ran down my spine at the sadistic light of enjoyment that glowed in his eyes. My fingers tightened around Corbin's. He gave them an answering squeeze of reassurance. Just being in physical contact gave me a confidence that had been lacking the last few minutes.

"Sounds like something out of a movie of the week, but we'll let that go. There is a major flaw in your reasoning, however," I said.

"Oh?" Paul tipped his head to the side in a parody of curiosity. "And that would be what, Amy?"

"This is the first time I've ever met Corbin," I said with a smile. "How on earth can we possibly be lovers if we've never met? Surely even the most gullible of police aren't going to buy a story about a jealously raging Corbin when I am, in reality, a total stranger."

Paul laughed again, and careful to keep the gun trained on all of us, sidestepped to the nearest computer. A couple of taps on the keyboard, and a video came up on the computer screen, showing a couple sitting naked on a bed.

"I know what it is. I researched all the food used here," the man said, frowning at the woman as she held a bowl in front of her. "You're going to eat *now*? I have the commute from hell, Amy. I don't have a lot of time before I have to leave."

The woman gave him a look that would have melted iron. "Oh, yes. I'm going to eat now."

I gasped, not just at recognizing myself and Corbin on the computer screen, but at the horrible, skin-crawling knowledge that Paul had somehow used the program to watch us while we were making love. "You bastard! Stop it!" I yelled, moving forward to stop the computer. Corbin grabbed my arm and pulled me back as Paul leveled the gun at me.

"What's wrong, dearie? Object to me making your little cyber-sex games with Corbin public? I'm afraid there's no way to help that. It's the proof I need to convince the police that not only did you have an intimate relationship with him, but also of his murderous intentions toward me."

I looked at Corbin. "I want that hard drive reformatted the second the police grab Paul."

"If not before," Corbin agreed, his eyes twinkling at me.

"Are you doing what I think you're doing?" Holder asked, trying to look around me at the screen. "Is that a fruit cobbler of some sort?"

"Holder!"

"Sorry," he said, giving me an apologetic look. "My bad."

"Extremely!" I agreed, glaring.

"If you three are finished, I'd like to get to the fun part where I kill you all," Paul said, glancing at his watch. "I still have to transfer the funds from the Cayman Islands to my Swiss accounts, so if you don't mind—"

"Now you're the one being stupid," Corbin told him. "You're not killing any of us."

"Oh, really?" Paul asked, looking amused. He pointed the gun at Corbin's chest. "You seem to forget that I have the gun."

"Yes, and I have this," Corbin answered, pulling my

scimitar out from where he had been holding it tight against his leg.

"Me, too," Holder said, showing his. "Two against one, Paul."

"Indeed," Paul said, smiling. "Two swords against my Glock; how very frightening. Is anyone else here reliving that tragic moment on the sloop? It's a remarkably similar situation, except, of course, that injuries here are not so easily ignored. That being so, I suppose I should follow the script and do something like this."

He fired the gun at Corbin. I screamed and threw myself forward toward him, but Corbin yanked me backward, sending me crashing into the computer chair behind us as he lunged to the side. I was so involved with disentangling myself from the chair that I didn't see what he was doing, but I heard Paul's scream of rage and fury and smiled grimly to myself as I kicked the chair away from me. Corbin had skewered Paul's right arm to the wall behind him, the gun dropped helplessly on the floor. Holder kicked it aside as he held the tip of his curved scimitar to Paul's throat.

"Ha!" I yelled, getting to my feet to stalk forward. Blood was pouring out of Paul's arm, but with Holder keeping the tip of his sword to Paul's jugular, he clearly didn't wish to tempt fate by trying to remove the sword in his arm. I got as close as I could and waved my hand toward Corbin. "We beat you again, you bastard! You missed him!"

"Er . . . sweetheart?" Corbin asked, slowly turning from where he had been facing Paul. His left hand was clutching his side . . . his blood-soaked side. "He didn't actually miss me, I'm afraid."

"Noooooooo," I wailed, rushing to him, trying to pry off his hand to see his wound. "Goddamn it! It's in the same spot where he shot you the last time! It's never going to heal at this rate!"

Corbin started laughing, causing me to read him a little lecture about laughing while he was gushing blood from a gunshot wound, but I had to stop in order to call the paramedics and the police.

"Are you going to tell me it's all mind over matter?" he asked ten minutes later as the paramedics loaded him into the aid unit. I didn't release the hand I was holding, walking alongside him as he was carted out of the house. Behind us, police were hauling a bandaged Paul out to another ambulance. I ignored the obscenities he was screaming at us to focus on the only thing that mattered.

"Absolutely. You can do anything. You're Black Corbin," I said, allowing my love for him to fill my eyes.

"Excuse me, ma'am, but are you family?" one of the paramedics asked as I was about to climb into the back of the aid unit with Corbin. "I'm afraid only a family member is allowed to come with us."

I opened my mouth to tell her what she could do with that ridiculous rule, but Corbin spoke before I could. "Yes, she's family." His eyes held mine for a minute, a wicked glint visible even through the pain dulling them. "She's my wife."

"I'm going to hold you to that, you know," I whispered as I knelt beside him, brushing my lips over his in a quick kiss.

"Good. I was a bit worried that you wouldn't like me in real life. I'm not nearly as exciting or dashing or any of those things that Black Corbin is," he said, looking so endearingly unsure of himself that I ignored the paramedic attaching sensors to him to kiss him again.

"I love you, Corbin. I loved you in the game, and I love you out of it. It took a little bit for me to realize it, but now I know that I fell in love with your mind, not your body, and the real you, the you I love is the same no matter where it is. So stop worrying. You're exactly the same person here that you were there—the perfect man for me, despite your penchant for getting yourself shot by ruthless programmers."

He laughed, winced at the pain it caused, and pulled me down for another kiss. "And I knew you were the perfect woman for me the minute you beat me in that sword fight. If getting shot for you is what it takes to prove that I'd give my life for you, then so be it."

"Don't be so melodramatic, Corbin. I have many, many plans for you, and you'll need to stay hale and hearty to satisfy them." I was talking a lot more brave than I felt. Outside I joked lightly with Corbin all during the trip to the hospital, but on the inside, I was weeping, shrieking, and swearing eternal revenge on Paul if he had seriously harmed Corbin.

Luckily, I didn't need to risk my own safety or sanity to seek revenge on Paul—the bullet that struck Corbin missed vital organs and exited without doing any major damage.

"Thank God," Holder said as I burst into happy tears when the doctor came out of the emergency room to announce that Corbin was as fine as anyone could be who'd just been kidnapped, given a mild concussion, and shot in the side. "Now maybe you'll stop making a list of all the things you're going to do to Paul. I was getting worried when you started in with medieval tortures. It's not easy to find an ironworker to melt lead for a really quality drawing and quartering anymore."

"Can I take him home now?" I asked the doctor, focused on the only thing that mattered.

"Let's give him an hour or two to make sure his vitals are stable, then, yes, he can go home."

Home meant one thing to me—my home, something Corbin found out that afternoon when I pulled up outside my cute-but-uninspired little yellow and white house rather than his sprawling stuccoed beauty.

"You know, I have five bedrooms," he said shortly thereafter, leaning forward slightly so I could stuff yet another pillow behind him. "More than enough room for everyone."

"Wow. Do you have an indoor swimming pool? I've always wanted to have an indoor swimming pool," Tara said from the doorway, where she'd been banished for getting in my way and bothering Corbin when he should be resting.

I eyed the mound of pillows propping him up and decided he could use another one.

"As a matter of fact, I do have an indoor lap pool."

"Woohoo!" Tara did a little dance of victory in the doorway. "And I get to beta test everyone from now on, right? I'm a really good beta tester. I take all sorts of notes and stuff."

"You'll be my number one beta tester," Corbin agreed, his lips quirking as I approached him with another pillow. "Amy, any more and I'll be leaning forward."

"My friends are so going to die when they hear about you," Tara said, doing another little dance. "When are you and Mom getting married?"

Corbin's eyebrows rose as he looked from my daughter to me. "Who said anything about marriage?"

"That's it; no more Florence Nightingale," I said, slapping the pillow over his face and holding it there. "Tara, close the door after you. I have a few things to say to your stepfather-to-be, and I don't want you picking up any of the bad language I'm about to use."

Tara looked worried for a moment, then grinned as Corbin, rather than fighting me, made shooing motions with his hands. "We're gonna be rich! And I'll have PC Monroe for a stepdad! I'm going to tell *everyone* I know!"

I waited until the door was closed before pulling the pillow off his face.

"Just so you know, I'm not actually related by birth to her. She was left by a pack of wolves."

One side of his mouth twitched.

"Now, on to more important things. *Who* said anything about marriage?" I asked, my eyes narrowed.

He raised a hand. "I did?"

"That is correct. I will allow you to live."

"Good, because there's something I need to tell you."

I smoothed a strand of hair off his forehead. I'd managed to clean most of the blood off of him, but he had been given strict instructions neither to get his six stitches wet, nor to do anything strenuous that might open the gunshot wound. "What's that?"

"You don't look like you did in the game."

My hand froze in the middle of stroking his hair. "I don't?"

His eyes glinted like mercury in the sunlight. "No. You look better. Your brain lied to me about just how beautiful you really are."

I smiled, warmed to my toes by the love that shown in those bright eyes.

"But that is just icing on the cake so far as I'm concerned. What you said in the ambulance was absolutely right—it's the inner you that I fell in love with, the you that shines through everything else. I love you, Amy Stewart. Marry me again?"

I pretended to think about it. "Will you share what you have with me?"

His eyes widened a little in surprise. "Of course. Holder turned over Paul's notebook with his bank account numbers and passwords, and the police assure me it shouldn't be any problem recovering the money he stole from me."

"Silly man." I kissed the end of his nose. "I don't mean worldly goods. Despite the avaricious nature of my daugh-

ter, I don't care anything about your fortune. I meant important things, like time. You're not going to turn into one of
those workaholic people who are never around and never
have time for their families, are you?"

"You mean someone who spends her free time doing
other people's work? That sort of person?"

I punched him gently on the shoulder. "I've changed. I
know now what's really important in life."

He laughed and tugged me down so I rested on his chest,
careful to avoid his injured side. "Sweetheart, you haven't
changed one bit; you've just adapted a little. You're going to
manage me just as you've managed everything else in your
life, but I'm not going to complain. So long as I'm on the receiving end of your attention, I'm happy."

His lips were as sweet as they were in the game—
sweeter, because I realized just how much my brain hadn't
included in our intimate activities. I flicked my tongue
across his lower lip and said, "Well, at least we know that
this is going to be better than virtual reality."

"Better?" He pushed me back a little and looked slightly
insulted. "Madam, are ye implyin' that I wasn't man enough
to satisfy yer lustful needs?"

"Of course not! I just meant that sex in reality has to be
better than mind sex—"

"That's a challenge if I've ever heard one," he interrupted, pulling me back so my mouth was on his. His hand
slid up my waist to cup my breast. "Prepare to make good
your slur, wench."

"Corbin," I said in between kisses that were growing
more and more heated. My body started to tingle in a familiar fashion. "Remember what the doctor said. No strenuous
activity."

His fingers slid down my hip, pulling up my skirt and

tugging my leg so my knees were on either side of his hips. "That's why I'm going to let you do all the work."

"But . . . your stitches," I said, the pressure inside me demanding a release, but worry about his health taking precedence. I pushed down the blanket to look at the small bandage on his side. "Doesn't it hurt?"

"A little, but there are other parts of me that hurt much worse, and since you've devoted yourself heart and soul to taking care of me, I think you should start with the biggest ache."

I wiggled a little, his "biggest ache" apparent under the thin blanket that covered him. "Well . . . there is a little matter of a promise that you've yet to keep."

He frowned. "A promise? Other than marriage?"

I climbed off him to lock the bedroom door, returning to pull off my blouse and skirt before leaning over to kiss the wits right out of him. "A promise inherent in the game."

His fingers were busy removing my bra and stroking the flesh he uncovered in the process, but he stopped long enough to raise both his eyebrows.

"The title of the game, my darling." I smiled into the kiss I pressed to his welcoming lips. "I fully expect you to buckle my swash, baby."

Blow me down if he didn't!

AUTHOR'S NOTE

Those of you who are pirate fans are probably shaking your heads and saying, "Whoa, you took some serious poetic license here, babe." I'm not going to deny in the least that I did, overall, play fast and loose with certain aspects of pirate history, just as I played equally fast and loose with the world of virtual reality.

I did try to have as many elements of both topics as factual and accurate as possible, and still keep this an entertaining work of fiction. I feel obliged nonetheless to point out that there is not, to my knowledge, a VR game in existence such as Buckling Swashes.

There is, however, an Internet massive multiplayer online role-playing game (MMORPG) called Puzzle Pirates (www.puzzlepirates.com), which has provided me with countless hours of pleasure, along with the desire to write a book about pirates, albeit virtual ones. Daniel James, the CEO and brainy guy behind PP, has been of much help to me in talking about the mechanics of running such a popular game, and tolerated countless questions and naggings, for all of which I'm truly grateful.

Yarr!

Katie MacAlister